In the Cold
of the World,
a White-hot Battle Flares . . .

PETER MacKENZIE: The captain of the *Seawolf* had earned his reputation under fire. Now everything he had was at stake in a tactically murderous situation beneath the shifting arctic ice . . .

JUSTINE SEGURRA: MacKenzie's CIA wife had been a jungle guerrilla fighter. Chosen for her mission by the Navy and the CIA, she parachuted onto the polar icecap—and into a death trap . . .

VASSILY KALIK: The Soviet captain's mind was as sharp as a blade on a cold morning, especially for battle under the ice. Once he began his duel of wits with the American captain of the *Seawolf*, he would never turn back—for in the politics of the Kremlin, victory was his only hope . . .

DR. KARL LIGICHEV: The white-haired Soviet Nobel laureate invented an underwater propulsion system based on a superconductive compound called irinium. Obsessed with proving its worth, he plunged the *Red Dawn* into disaster . . .

IGOR GALININ: The captain of the *Red Dawn* believed that life was war. Trapped under the ice, his battle with Ligichev would end with life or death for everyone on the *Red Dawn* . . .

RAISE THE RED DAWN

Books by Bart Davis

Takeover
Blind Prophet
Conspiracy of Eagles
Full Fathom Five
Raise the Red Dawn*

*Published by POCKET BOOKS

RAISE THE RED DAWN

RAISE THE RED DAWN

BART DAVIS

POCKET STAR BOOKS

New York London Toronto Sydney Tokyo Singapore

Excerpts from "The Love Song of J. Alfred Prufrock" in *Collected Poems 1909–1962* by T. S. Eliot, copyright 1936 by Harcourt Brace Jovanovich, Inc., copyright © 1964, 1963 by T. S. Eliot, reprinted by permission of the publisher.

An *Original* Publication of POCKET BOOKS

A Pocket Star Book published by
POCKET BOOKS, a division of Simon & Schuster
1230 Avenue of the Americas, New York, NY 10020

ISBN: 0-671-69663-7

First Pocket Books printing May 1991

10 9 8 7 6 5 4 3 2 1

POCKET STAR BOOKS and colophon are trademarks of Simon & Schuster.

Printed in the U.S.A.

ACKNOWLEDGMENTS

I am deeply indebted to Rear Admiral J. Weldon Koenig (ret.) of the United States Navy for his contribution to the writing not only of this book but of its precursor, *Full Fathom Five*. He is a true gentleman whose knowledge and skill have always been the basis for Peter MacKenzie's. I am also deeply grateful to my editor, Paul McCarthy, whose wisdom, humor, and guidance provided a fixed star every time I sat down to write. I know that all things are possible because of the unfailing love and support of my wife, Sharon. And I wish to thank Robert Gottlieb of the William Morris Agency, who is, quite simply, the gold standard of agents and friends.

For Jordan and Allie,
the lights of my life

Chapter
One

In winter the Kola Peninsula is a land of frozen granite mountains and snow-covered glacial valleys. Fifty years ago Allied merchant ships fought Nazi U-boats and numbing arctic cold crossing the North Sea to reach the port of Murmansk on Kola's northern coast carrying supplies to the Soviet army resisting Adolf Hitler. They were cheered when they limped into the harbor, battle-scarred and weary, lighter only for the dead they had left in the slate gray waves along the way.

Captain Vassily Kalik stood in the control center of the Soviet Northern Fleet's main submarine base at Kola Bay, only miles from his boyhood harbor, remembering the cheers. He and the other boys out gathering wood for fuel would race back from the pine forests to help their mothers and the old scarf-draped babushkas pass cargo hand over hand in a line that stretched all the way from the ship to a waiting convoy of trucks. Kalik fancied that the bright new rifles and the stubby green grenades the ships brought would find their way to his father's regiment fighting outside Leningrad. State atheism aside, Kalik was a religious boy who believed in fate and the power of God. He thought about signing his name to a weapon, as one might a letter, hoping that would somehow help it find its way into his father's hands. He didn't, and his father never came home. More than once over the years, as the boy grew into a man, he wondered if there could have been a connection.

The fleet main submarine base was built right into the icy mountains surrounding Kola Bay. Engineers had carved out the interiors of the granite monoliths, and the resulting network of watery chambers housed both submarines and the equivalent of a small city to service them. The subs entered and left through tunnels cut into the base of the mountains. The command staff observed their comings and goings from a cantilevered control center jutting out of the sheer cliff face overhead. The panoramic view from the center stretched from the outdoor pens to the misty horizon where the steel blue Barents Sea met the pale northern sky. Beyond that lay the polar ice cap, easily accessible to the ballistic missile and attack submarines that left Kola Bay regularly to lurk beneath it.

Kalik picked up a pair of binoculars and scanned the concrete pens below. Dark green water lapped at a hump-backed Delta IV. A fat, stubby Typhoon with its 25 meter beam was being serviced at one of the dockside stations and he counted a Victor III and two Alfas floating in parallel pens. Beyond these his own ship waited, the sleek *Akula* with the distinctive T type sonar pod mounted on top of her rear fin. *Akula* was the newest Soviet attack sub, and her speed and quieting were justifiably giving the Americans a fit. *Akula.* In English the name meant "shark." Kalik smiled. That she was. That she was.

"Comrade Captain? Senior Lieutenant Volkov radios that preparations for sailing are almost complete."

Kalik located the source of the voice in the busy room, a young radio operator sitting before an instrument console. "Tell him I'm on my way." The operator spun his chair back around to his console to comply, but Kalik had an after-thought. "What about *Red Dawn?*" he asked.

"They are holding, Comrade Captain. At least half an hour."

Kalik took up the glasses again and swung his gaze past

Akula to the reason he and his sub were in Kola Bay. He saw what the American satellites would see, looking down as they assuredly were: just an aging, nondescript Tango class diesel submarine commissioned over twenty years earlier. No glamour, no fancy electronics masts, nothing to suggest that her familiar lines harbored anything unusual. But appearances were deceiving. Kalik was sure that right now *Red Dawn* was inarguably the most important submarine in the world.

A knot of technicians wearing thick yellow parkas stood by *Red Dawn*'s aft hatch arguing or conferring—it was often hard to tell the difference—with the rest of the scientific team as they had done ad infinitum during the months of preparation, refit, and preliminary testing. As usual, the elderly Nobel laureate, Dr. Karl Ligichev, was at the center of the knot. Ligichev was chief scientist at the Kronsky Naval Institute and solely in charge of this project. Even from this distance, Kalik could spot the mane of white hair that Ligichev combed straight back from his widow's peak like some manic conductor. Next to him was his daughter, Dr. Ivanna Ligichova, whose bold mane of jet black hair was as thick and straight as her father's. But the similarity between the two of them ended there. Ligichev was a myopic, scholarly type. Ivanna had a confident carriage and the fiery eyes of a racehorse. The father was almost painfully thin. Youthful Ivanna had the figure of an athlete, with breasts that rose like arrows against her coveralls. Physical differences aside, however, word was that although she was barely into her twenties she was almost as brilliant as Ligichev, and he was rarely without her. Scoffing at ancient custom, he had chosen to take her with him on what was, in a fundamental way, *Red Dawn*'s maiden voyage.

Kalik left the control room and took a high-speed elevator down to sea level. He stepped out into a concrete arena bustling with pedestrian traffic passing through to office buildings, dormitories, factories, and docks. On the pier the smell of the sea mixed with gas and oil fumes and the sounds of men hard at work welding and hammering metal. Stepping over tangles of cables on the grimy floor Kalik flipped his I.D. at the guard, settled into an electric cart, and barked a quick *"Akula"* to the uniformed driver.

Kalik clenched his thick blue coat tighter around himself and held his cap down over his steel gray hair as they sped along the docks. He blew out a frosty breath. Goddamn January. Another new year he'd start out freezing. This far north the cold reached in and crept up your clothes. True, it was a damn sight colder where they were going, but having reached his fifties, Kalik was too much the fatalist to worry about the future. Now there was only the pleasure of *Akula*'s sleek black hull looming ahead and the fish-briney smell of the harbor water filling his nose, which, like his own *petite madeleine*, always prompted memories of the shores of his youth.

Ahead, the conference on *Red Dawn*'s deck broke up and the figures disappeared below. Good. Enough talk. Either it would work or it would not.

Kalik was pleased by the expectant air of preparedness about *Akula* as he dropped through the hatch and moved about. Sailors worked attentively at their stations under what had come to be known as Kalik's Maxim: check it, recheck it, and then check the son of a bitch twice more. In the galley, cooks wrestled heavy milk tins into storage. In the weapons area, the torpedomen made sure their potentially violent charges were nestled in for the ride.

He stepped into the control room where his senior officer, Viktor Volkov, was hunched over the navigation officer's console.

"Hello, Viktor. Things looks good."

"Comrade Captain. Glad to have you on board," the senior lieutenant said warmly. "We are almost ready to sail."

"I got your message. Very good." He was pleased to add, "As always."

Volkov accepted the compliment with a quick nod of his head, but Kalik knew it was appreciated.

"By the way," Volkov announced, "Cook promises to make blinis as soon as we're under way."

"Tell Cook for blinis I will promote him to admiral . . . or marry him, whichever he wishes."

Volkov laughed. The hardest thing about being in command was leadership—and the hardest thing about leadership was learning it. He had learned a lot serving under Kalik for the past two years. The captain was a proud man, scrupulously fair, and his mind was as sharp as a blade on a cold morning when it came to battle tactics at sea, especially under the ice. Kalik took immense pride in *Akula*, the first Soviet submarine to reduce the long-standing noise vulnerability. More than once Volkov had watched Kalik spend hours cagily stalking an unsuspecting American sub, waiting for the perfect moment to attack. Then he would give them the peacetime equivalent of a torpedo launch—a nasty raking with active sonar pings at max power. For Kalik, Volkov knew, sneaking up on the Americans' most advanced Los Angeles class subs was, basically, thumbing his nose at the competition.

For his part, Kalik watched Volkov with the crew and found his senior lieutenant's calm professionalism a balm. Volkov was flexible in his management, a sensible way to deal with men working in cramped confines for months undersea, yet he had sufficient force of personality—a thing that could not be taught—to maintain order and discipline, especially among the junior officers. Someday he'd be a fine captain.

"Comrade Captain, it's *Red Dawn*," announced the radio officer. "Preparations are complete. She is ready to get under way on your signal."

"Signal *Red Dawn*: Proceed as previously directed."

"Maneuvering watch is stationed," Volkov reported. "The ship is ready to get under way and prepared for dive except for the deck."

"Very well." Kalik hit the intercom. "Engine Room, this is the captain. Stand by to answer maneuvering orders."

"We are ready to answer all bells, Comrade Captain."

Kalik nodded. "Radio Officer. To *Red Dawn*: Proceed to Point Alpha. We'll keep her forward of us all the way. To

Base Command: *Red Dawn* and *Akula* under way as directed." That completed, he ordered, "Take in all lines."

The diving alarm sounded throughout the ship. The crew took their stations, and the mooring lines were coiled below decks.

"All lines on deck, Comrade Captain."

"Very well. Engine Room, answer bells. All engines slow astern."

Slowly *Akula* backed out of her slot. Deftly Kalik swung her about and headed into the channel.

"*Red Dawn* diving," reported Sonar.

"Excellent." Kalik was happy. He felt the power of the ship in his loins as if it were an extension of himself. No woman had ever made him feel so good. "Navigation, depth."

"One hundred fifty meters and increasing, Comrade Captain. We're out of the channel. Open water ahead. Depth two hundred meters."

"Very well. Prepare to submerge."

"Topside clear and rigged for dive," Volkov reported.

"Submerge the ship," Kalik ordered. The diving bell sounded throughout *Akula*. "Take her down to sixty meters and steer course zero zero zero due north."

Akula slid beneath the cold waters of the Barents Sea.

"Engine Room, all ahead two-thirds. Viktor, take control. Stay close to *Red Dawn*. Remember, she doesn't have our muscle."

"We'll keep as close as if she were our little sister out on a first date." Volkov said reassuringly.

Kalik smiled. He said, "Notify me when we reach the ice pack," and left for his cabin.

Red Dawn

Chief Scientist Ligichev pushed his plate aside and peered at *Red Dawn*'s captain, who was glowering at him across the table in the officers' mess. "Please, won't you tell me what the problem is, Comrade Captain?"

Captain Igor Galinin did not answer, but his gaze took in Ligichev's daughter, Ivanna, sitting calmly next to her father.

"Ah, I see," Ligichev said softly.

"Perhaps you do," said Galinin, stroking his black beard, "but then again, perhaps you do not."

"Why don't you enlighten us?" Ivanna suggested coldly.

"There, you see?" Galinin said. "Such attitude. Am I master of this ship or am I not?"

"Actually," Ivanna said, meeting his gaze, "you aren't. My father is. And if you doubt it, feel free to call Admiral Nicolai Korodin, deputy minister of defense and commander in chief of the navy, who authorized all of us to be here."

"One moment, daughter," Ligichev said, seeing Galinin's color rising. They all had to work together, and squabbles would be unproductive. "Please, Comrade Captain, you were saying . . . ?"

"I was asking how I can govern my ship when my own engine room is off limits to me and my chief engineer!" Galinin exclaimed, exasperated. "I am not privy to our sailing orders, and worse, this . . . female seems intent on doing everything she can to rub me the wrong way."

"Rubbing you *any* way is the furthest thing from my mind, Comrade. Believe me."

"Again she taunts me!"

"Ivanna, you must stop," said Ligichev softly.

"Then I demand he treat me as an equal. I will not be dismissed."

"Listen to reason," Galinin stormed, "The men are not used to having a woman on board. You must not continue to flaunt yourself."

"For God's sake, I was exercising."

"Must you do so in such provocative garb? And when I order you to return to your cabin to change, what do you do? Such profanity!"

Ligichev sighed. "I should have seen this coming. A ship can have only one master—"

"My point exactly," said Galinin.

"But that master must remember he is part of a team and that the team has a momentous responsibility to test equipment that has taken years and many millions of rubles to build. A team, I might add, to which my daughter has made invaluable contributions."

"I accept that," Galinin said, cooling. "But a crew must have discipline. I cannot have the men's minds taken off their work."

"Ivanna, you can see that, can't you?" Ligichev's tone was light, but there was no mistaking the steel underneath.

Ivanna bristled, but acquiesced. "All right, Father. I will try to be more respectful of the captain's needs."

Galinin had always thought a stiff breeze could knock Ligichev over, but he regarded him with new respect. If the man could control a daughter like this . . . He said, "I am sorry if I have not given Comrade Ligichova the respect due her position in the *scientific* community." There, thought Galinin, make something out of that, bitch.

But Ivanna nodded peaceably enough.

"Good," pronounced Ligichev. "Then if you will come with us, Captain, we'll tend to matters that should have been taken care of at the outset."

The engineering section took up almost half of the sub. Set into the steel wall by the bulkhead door was a newly installed electronic keypad.

"Captain, the combination is three, six, two, two. We three are now the only ones who know it." Ligichev moved in front of Galinin and pressed it in.

"Of course, it will never pass my lips," said Galinin, his tone indicating he was finally getting proper respect.

"Of course," Ivanna repeated.

Electronic bolts slid back, and Ligichev spun the locking wheel. Bending low, they stepped across the bulkhead.

"Good day, Comrade Ligichev. Comrade Captain," said Ligichev's chief technician as they entered the compartment, which was bathed in a soft blue light. The other coveralled technicians looked up from their work.

"And to you, Comrade Chief Technician," echoed Ligichev. "Perhaps you would permit us a brief inspection tour?"

"Naturally. Excuse me. Many things to tend to."

"We will try not to get in your way." Ligichev beckoned for Galinin to follow.

Galinin could find his way around a sub's engine room blindfolded, but as his vision adjusted to the odd lighting he could see very little resembling anything he had seen before.

The common misconception about diesel subs was that diesel engines drove them. They didn't. Diesel engines were used to generate electricity to charge the ship's storage batteries. The batteries powered electric motors that spun the propellers. It was a simple system, extremely quiet and almost without flaw. A diesel sub could go for days without recharging if she stayed in one place and did little, as silent and undetectable as a hole in the ocean. But a diesel sub operating at the limit of her speed for defensive or offensive reasons would exhaust her batteries within hours. Running the engines to recharge was very noisy, which meant the sub could be easily detected and therefore destroyed. Worse, diesel engines used up oxygen. To replenish its air the sub had to surface or send up a snorkel. Either method made the ship an easy target.

"Please be careful, Captain. The equipment is very delicate," said Ivanna. "I will be happy to explain it."

Galinin stared. A hexagonal metal tube, roughly two feet in diameter and perhaps fifteen feet long, stretched in an arc from the deck under them to the rear bulkhead beside the main drive shaft. Enclosing the tube was a secondary metal housing and a series of gleaming, compact motors, all strangely surrounded by what looked like refrigeration coils.

"What is this?" Galinin asked, too curious to dissemble.

"A prototype of the first water jet drive capable of

propelling a submarine," Ligichev said proudly. "The result of years of intensive research and the reason we are all here."

"That kind of a system isn't new," said Galinin, a little deflated. "We've experimented with spit-drives for years. They're a conjurer's trick, without real use. I've even seen experimental systems demonstrated. They were big and inefficient."

"Not anymore," countered Ivanna. "Father?"

"The systems you've seen, Captain, would take up every inch of space on this submarine," Ligichev agreed, "but our unit is one-third the size of a standard nuclear reactor and twice as powerful."

Galinin's tone changed. "How is it possible?"

Ivanna pointed. "The motors and the superconductor are revolutionary in design. They are the reason for the refrigeration coils."

"Wait a minute," Galinin said. "No simple refrigerator can bring superconductors down to the temperatures you'd need. Even the newest materials won't work above the temperature of liquid nitrogen."

"You're correct, of course," said Ivanna. "But that was the previous barrier for superconductors. What makes our system feasible is a material my father invented. It's called irinium after my mother, Irina, who died when I was a child."

The look of genuine affection Ivanna gave her father made Ligichev's stock with Galinin rise again. One of the prices he paid for his submarine service was divorce, and he rarely saw his children. A look like that would have meant a great deal to him.

Ligichev took up the explanation. "Up till now, to get superconductivity, which is the loss of all electrical resistance in a material, you needed temperatures close to absolute zero, minus 459.4 degrees Fahrenheit. Even *high*-temperature superconductors needed to be cooled to the temperature of liquid nitrogen." Ligichev's eyes were bright. "My irinium loses its resistance at a real temperature of thirty-two degrees Fahrenheit, or zero degrees Centigrade, the freezing point of water. That's hundreds of degrees warmer than any other superconductor known to man. For practical purposes it's almost room temperature! Irinium virtually eliminates heavy windings and steel magnets so our motors are one-quarter the size and weight but ten times the strength of conventional ones."

Galinin looked over the coils, musing out loud. "Subs could be ultra-quiet, half their present size, and still be able to carry more weapons than even *Akula* does now. I am sorry, Comrades, I didn't understand *Red Dawn*'s importance. I am proud to be part of this historic mission. You can count on my complete cooperation."

"Thank you, Comrade Captain. Remember, your presence here shows the confidence Naval Command has in your abilities."

Galinin swelled visibly. "May I ask one more question?"

"Of course."

"Why test under the ice cap? These waters are the most treacherous in the world."

"Simple," said Ivanna. "Heat."

"Under certain conditions," Ligichev explained, "the interaction of irinium and seawater produces intense heat. It's possibly an electrical phenomenon. We aren't certain. All things considered, cold waters were thought to be best suited."

The intercom sounded overhead. "Comrade Captain?"

Galinin flicked the switch. "This is the captain."

"We are at Point Alpha. Radio message from *Akula*. Captain Kalik asks confirmation of our readiness to go under the ice."

"I'm coming up," Galinin responded. "Comrades, we'll be at the test site in less than six hours."

"Very good, Comrade Captain. Ivanna and I will spend the time making final adjustments."

As soon as Galinin left the engine room, Ivanna gave a snort of disgust. "I can't say I agree with trusting that big ape. He's the kind who either bites at your back or fawns at your feet."

"I don't want any more fights," said Ligichev. "It's easier to trust him."

"But you didn't trust him all the way," Ivanna observed slyly.

"No, I didn't, did I?" Ligichev smiled, "Well, prudence, daughter, in all things. Now let's get to work. There is much to be done and six hours is not so long a time to do it in."

Chapter Two

The USS *Seawolf* sliced through the frigid waters of the Arctic sea several hundred feet underneath the North Polar ice pack in the kind of warmth and comfort that would have seemed starkly inconceivable to earlier polar explorers. In the control room, Captain Peter MacKenzie accepted a plastic cup containing a single sip of champagne from his grinning exec, Tom Lasovic, and joined the others in *Seawolf*'s conn by raising it in a toast.

"Happy New Year, Tom. And to everybody," MacKenzie said.

His toast was greeted by affectionate calls of "Happy New Year, Skipper," from those in the conn. The affection the men had for MacKenzie was heartfelt. Many had sailed with him on his prior command, the USS *Aspen,* during its battle with the rogue submarine, *Kirov.*

"And a happy New Year to *Seawolf.* After all, it's her first," young Lieutenant Ed Randall, the blond crew-cut diving officer, said proudly.

"The first of many, Mr. Randall," declared MacKenzie.

"Here, here," echoed the men around him.

Trial runs were complete, and they were on their first operational mission since *Seawolf*'s commissioning just months earlier. MacKenzie was pleased with the way the crew had come together. Under-the-icepack maneuvers were difficult even for experienced submariners, but his officers, under big Tom Lasovic, and the veteran seamen in the crew had molded even the inexperienced men into a tight working unit.

After his command experience on *Aspen,* the widely respected Mr. Lasovic could have had his own command. But the black Annapolis graduate had preferred XO on the state-of-the-art *Seawolf* to command of a lesser ship. MacKenzie was delighted. There was no finer executive officer in the fleet. And in all the world he had no better or more dedicated friend.

"Well, that's enough reg breaking for one holiday," Lasovic said mildly, tossing his cup into a plastic bag the steward held out. "That's it, gentlemen. Party's over." The crew followed suit.

MacKenzie looked around the conn proudly. "She's a helluva boat, Tom, isn't she? The first of her kind and tops in every way. You can feel it."

"Sure can, Mac. That's why I figured, the new year . . . well, she deserved champagne."

"I agree. All in the best interests of morale. Makes everybody feel a little easier being down here."

"Down here," echoed Lasovic. "I swear, Mac. I know it isn't any colder inside *Seawolf* than it would be in the Caribbean, but my skin has goose bumps half the time."

"It's hard to forget a million tons of ice overhead," MacKenzie agreed, shifting his attention to the closed circuit television screen that gave them a clear view of the ice sheet over them. Icy stalactites jutted down like angry spears. Huge keels extended as deep as a thousand feet. Most startling on the screen were the occasional polynyas, originally a Russian word, areas of thin ice that let just enough of the pole's dim light shine through to look like streaks of jagged lightning across a dusky sky.

MacKenzie ran a hand over the planes of his sharp, rugged Scottish features and felt the deep lines that wind, weather, and responsibility had put there. Tom was right.

Seawolf deserved champagne. He watched the ice for a while, running through a mental roll call of his ship's special abilities.

She could cruise at more than a thousand feet below the surface at speeds up to thirty-five knots, with a maximum diving depth of over two thousand feet. She carried an arsenal nearly twice the size of the Los Angeles class SSN's, including the newest acoustical homing torpedoes, which could track and attack enemy subs or surface ships. From almost a hundred feet down *Seawolf* could launch a mix of nuclear-tipped and conventional missiles or rapid-salvo-fire torpedoes through the eight large-bore tubes—the L.A. class had only four—in her state-of-the-art torpedo room, the biggest ever built to outgun the big Russian boats with their six tubes.

Seawolf's advanced BSY-2 combat system integrated acoustic and fire control systems and tracked more targets than ever before at greater range. In fact, measuring 353 feet from stem to stern with a 40-foot beam, she was the biggest, fastest, deepest-diving nuclear attack sub in the navy fleet. Her high-tensile steel hull was built to withstand pressures of over a thousand pounds per square inch, and not even six-foot-thick polar ice posed a problem for *Seawolf.* Her low, streamlined sail had been hardened to absorb the shock of breaking through the ice, and her bow planes were retractable to permit fast under-the-ice navigation and maneuverability. Finally, her multiblade controllable pitch propeller was encased in a precisely engineered "shroud" to make her even quieter during attack.

Ultimately, *Seawolf*'s under-ice capabilities might be her most important attributes. Soviet ballistic missile subs lurking under the 5.4-million-square-mile Arctic Ocean and polar ice pack had made the Arctic the new battleground of undersea war. In wartime, Soviet subs could deploy from the Kola base and hide beneath the ice pack's vast, complex regions before cruising American attack subs could attack to bottle them up. This would give the Soviets a distinct tactical advantage. They could lie in wait under the ice, silently listening for the attack sub's approach, ready to fire as it sailed into their trap. Locating Soviet subs under the ice pack had therefore become the top priority for both the Navy Department and the Defense Advanced Research Projects Agency, known by its acronym, DARPA. This cruise was going to be the major test of *Seawolf*'s capabilities.

MacKenzie's thoughts were interrupted by the crackle of the intercom.

"Conn . . . Sonar. We've got a contact, Skipper. And problems."

"On my way. Tom, take the conn."

"Okay, Skipper." Lasovic stepped onto the slightly raised periscope platform. "This is the XO. I have the conn."

In the sonar room, Sonarman First Class "Bear" Bendel was hunched over his instrument table with his headset clamped over his ears and a faraway look in his eyes. He was concentrating deeply, his auditory senses extended for miles around *Seawolf* by the "passive" sonar listening devices that studded her hull all along its length.

Sonar was an acronym for *so*und *na*vigation *r*anging. Passive sonar "listened" and collected sound with ultra-sensitive electronic "ears." Active sonar was the familiar pinging probe, which originated on the sub and was used to navigate or to locate, or range, a target. Active sonar was more accurate and, all things considered, would be the preferred choice in locating an enemy or in close battle quarters. But active sonar was a double-edged sword because nothing else revealed one's own position quite like that burst of sound. The sub commander who used active sonar to range a target found quickly enough that the target had also ranged him. Classic high-speed, end-around World War II maneuvers were obsolete. In the nineties, you could be destroyed by wire-guided torpedoes or "smart" missiles launched from miles away. Only the silent survived.

Standing behind Bendel was his division officer, Lieutenant Jim Kurstan, a tall man with the youthful, unlined face of a choirboy. It masked a dedicated veteran officer who encouraged his men and let nothing slip by him. Bendel was a former college linebacker with hands like ham hocks, but he had a feel for sound that was a thing of beauty. Kurstan and Bendel were an exceptional team. Both had served with MacKenzie on *Aspen*.

"What have you got, Jim?" MacKenzie asked.

"Bear's pretty sure, Skipper," said Kurstan. "A Soviet sub."

"What type?"

"Can't tell yet." Kurstan pointed to the wildly wavering lines on the oscilloscope-type gauge in front of them. *"Seawolf's* got range to her ears we didn't dream of a few years ago, but all this ambient noise is making it hard as hell to correlate signatures. Sounds like a cocktail shaker with a bunch of ice cubes in it."

"Can you get a fix on course and speed?"

"Not yet." Bendel slipped off his headphones, frustrated. "Give me a nice open ocean with a zillion fish anytime, Skipper. With all this ice shifting and cracking . . . it's like trying to pick out one particular car horn during rush hour in Tokyo."

"During an earthquake," added the division officer darkly.

"God, I hate the ice pack." Bendel's big hands made delicate adjustments on the dials.

"You have my sympathy," said MacKenzie. "But stay on top of it, Bear. This is what we're here for."

"Aye, sir." Bendel put back his headphones. "This guy makes less noise than a flashlight, but he's there all right. Just lemme get one solid contact for signature verification."

MacKenzie grew thoughtful. "Maybe I can make things a little easier for you."

"All help gratefully appreciated, Skipper," Kurstan said seriously.

MacKenzie reentered the control room. "Tom, Sonar thinks we have company. I'm going to hug the ice for a while and see if we can tag him. I have the conn. Rig for ultra-quiet."

"Ultra-quiet, aye."

MacKenzie hit the 1MC channel to broadcast through the ship. "This is the captain speaking. Sonar believes it has picked up an unknown ship in the area. In order to facilitate identification, we are going to shut down as many systems as we can, come up under the ice cap, and let it hold us in place. You'll feel a bit of a thump, but if you've ever played bumper cars it shouldn't be too much worse. This is not a drill. Let's look sharp. Commencing maneuver now. Maneuvering, make minimum turns."

"Make minimum turns. Maneuvering, aye."

MacKenzie studied the closed circuit TV picture of the ice sheet overhead as it undulated past like the hills of some vast inverted prairie. Glistening ice keels jutted down to a thousand feet in depth. Ice stalactites looked like rows of barbed spikes. They were still learning their way around in this hostile environment, one the Soviets were so familiar with, and every canyon entered might be a valley of death that could trap a sub. But if you trod carefully there were also things that you could use to your advantage. Up ahead Mac saw a spot that suited his purpose, a broad plane of thick ice surrounded by keels jutting down at least a hundred feet. They would make a perfect curtain around *Seawolf*.

It was a delicate maneuver because the ship would still be moving forward even as she rose. Timing was critical, but if they slid in nice and tight *Seawolf* would be almost impossible to spot.

"All stop. Mr. Randall, start pumping to give us positive buoyancy. Take us up easy. Zero bubble."

"Start pumping for positive buoyancy, zero bubble, aye."

"Chief, watch the fore and aft trim."

MacKenzie watched the ice sheet grow closer. "Slower. Slower. Steady now. Right ten degrees rudder. Give me a sounding, Mr. Santiago."

Quartermaster Joe Santiago, tanned and sun-lined from spending every waking moment of his recent shore leave playing golf, peered at his upward-looking sonar Fathometer closely. Santiago's love of the game was legendary. "Two hundred feet to contact, Skipper. Deep ice keels ten degrees off the starboard bow."

"Keep the distance coming. Helm, rudder amidships. All back one-third."

"Rudder amidships. All back one-third, aye."

Santiago's eyes were fixed on his gauges. "Rising. One hundred seventy-five . . . one hundred fifty . . . one hundred twenty-five——"

A sudden screeching groan sent shivers up Mac's spine like nails on a blackboard. Just forward and slightly below him he saw tension bunching Randall's shoulders and, in front of Randall, the helmsman and planesman who steered the ship in tandem under the diving officer's direction. "Steady," MacKenzie soothed. "We're just rubbing up against some ice."

"Seventy-five . . . seventy . . ."

The distance to the ice was measured from the bottom of *Seawolf*'s keel. Only ten feet remained. "Maneuvering, all stop." MacKenzie grabbed the steel railing around the periscopes. "Hold on, everybody. Here we go."

Santiago looked up. "Contact."

Seawolf settled up against the ice with a heavy thump and some rough, grinding noise. She rocked for a few seconds, then held steady. MacKenzie looked at the TV screen. They were wedged in neatly, screened on both sides by hanging ice.

"Maneuvering, conn . . . Quiet as a church mouse. Spin the main engines only as necessary. Sonar, conn. How is that?"

"Sonar, aye. All ears are out. Much better. Thanks, Skipper."

"My pleasure. Let's see if the navy got its money's worth with all that new equipment. Keep me posted."

So much of a submariner's life was waiting, MacKenzie thought. Sonar would keep the area under surveillance, listening for any noise that meant the Soviet sub was nearby. And if their unseen rival got a little too bold or careless he would never know that his signature—the distinctive sound his propellers, engines, and operating equipment made underwater—had been logged and reported to Naval Operations, where computers would remember it always. Then other attack subs who came across its path could instantly identify it, or the navy's Sound Surveillance Systems (SOSUS) planted underwater across the Greenland-Iceland –United Kingdom (GIUK) Gap and the Bering Strait would be able to recognize and track the sub should it try to reach southern waters to attack vulnerable tankers and merchant ships.

MacKenzie visualized both subs floating in the cold silent world under the ice.

"You're it," he whispered, and settled in to wait.

Akula

Kalik was hunched over beside his sonar operator with a grim expression on his face as they studied the scope.

"Where the hell did he go?" Kalik wondered aloud.

"He was there. I'm certain of it, Comrade Captain."

Kalik nodded. "Yes. I think so, too. Could you get a fix on him?"

"It was too quick. He is very quiet."

"Keep listening." Kalik hit the intercom. "Engine Room. All engines slow ahead, make turns for five knots. Keep her very quiet, Vladimir."

"Like a drifting feather, Comrade Captain."

Kalik grinned and stepped back into the control room. Volkov looked up from studying the charts. "Americans?"

"I think so. How do you feel about playing the decoy, Viktor?"

"I would much rather sneak up and rake them with our sonar if I have the choice."

"Me, too. But I want them as far away from *Red Dawn* as possible. Maybe we can get them to give chase, eh?" Kalik grew pensive, considering options. "We caught only a trace of him. Too little to get a signature. And there's more noise out there than an Arab bazaar."

Volkov watched Kalik weigh things in his mind like a calculator.

"But they are working under the same handicaps, eh?" The captain went on. "So it's likely they only caught a ghost of us, too. I'll bet they're still looking, Viktor. That's why he disappeared off the scope so suddenly. He went silent. Maybe he even stopped. Yes, I like that. Stop and hover under the ice and let us make the first noise." Kalik laughed. "Well, he's going to get his wish."

"What do you have in mind, Comrade Captain?" asked Volkov, intrigued.

"All in due time, Viktor." Kalik smiled. "Navigator, how far to the marginal ice zone?"

"Two hundred fifty kilometers, Comrade Captain."

"We could make it there in less than twelve hours. Hmm . . . A day to draw him off and get back here. Sonar, are there any other contacts in the area?"

"None, Comrade Captain."

"Very well. Radio Officer, signal *Red Dawn* to remain in the testing area, but inform them that the test is to be postponed one day. We are breaking off and will rendezvous back here at . . ."

"Fourteen hundred hours tomorrow," supplied the navigator.

Surprised, Volkov leaned close to Kalik and spoke so that only he could hear. "But Comrade Captain, aren't we under strict orders not to leave *Red Dawn?*"

Kalik frowned. "Viktor, our responsibility is to protect *Red Dawn* and the security of the test site. I can do both by drawing the American sub away. I'm certain Naval Command would agree it is the better strategy."

"You are in command, of course," Volkov agreed, "but I just thought—"

"Besides, that could be a Los Angeles class sub out there. Even better, maybe the famed new *Seawolf* herself. In our last briefing, Command said the Americans would be conducting under-ice maneuvers." Kalik smiled wolfishly. "How can I pass up a chance to lead them around by the nose?"

Volkov shrugged. One couldn't argue past a certain point. He'd raised the issue; that was enough. Privately he wondered if Kalik's desire to demonstrate his superiority over the Americans was clouding his judgment.

"Navigator. Once again, return time?"

"Fourteen hundred hours tomorrow, Comrade Captain."

"Lay down the course. Radio Officer, inform *Red Dawn*. And now, Viktor, for our little surprise." Kalik opened the intercom. "Torpedo Room, this is the captain. What is the status of our forward tubes?"

"All loaded and ready, Comrade Captain."

"Fine. Now remove the torpedo from tube one and flood the chamber with air. Build up as much pressure in the tube as possible. Be ready to fire on my signal."

The voice over the intercom was plainly caught off guard. "Be ready to fire . . . air? Comrade Captain, do I hear you correctly?"

"You do." Kalik cut the connection. "Viktor, do you see it yet?"

Volkov scratched his head. "Frankly, Comrade Captain . . ."

"Here is my thinking." Kalik ticked off points like a teacher. "I must lure the American captain out of the testing area before we can let *Red Dawn* proceed. But I don't want him to get close enough to *Akula* to gain her signature or learn her secrets, any more than he would want me to learn his. So I must be a decoy he would follow, but not the *Akula*."

The intercom saved Volkov from having to admit he was lost.

"Comrade Captain? This is the torpedo room. We are ready to fire . . . er, air, on your signal."

"Excellent." Kalik looked to his navigator.

"Course two seven zero will bring us to the nearest marginal ice field, Comrade Captain."

Kalik nodded. "Lay it down. Michman, transfer ballast from the starboard tank to the port side. Be prepared to transfer it back quickly."

Michman Rostov, a professional seaman roughly equivalent in rank to a chief petty officer, looked surprised. "But that will roll the ship over almost to forty-five degrees, Comrade Captain. Is that what you want?"

Kalik's voice was hard-edged. "Viktor, make a note to have the crew's ears checked. Yes, Michman, you heard the order correctly. Now comply."

Trim pumps began pumping water from one side of the ship to the other. It created an imbalance, and *Akula* slowly rolled over. Kalik clung to the periscope housing. "Hold her there, Michman," he ordered.

Hanging on right beside him, Volkov suddenly grinned. "Of course, if we put the torpedo tube near the top of the ship and blow air, we will sound just like a missile sub readying our tubes for a launch. Brilliant, Comrade Captain. It will fool them."

"I hope so," Kalik said with the craftiness of a hunter who has heard the brush rustle. "Torpedo Room, fire tube one," he ordered.

Seawolf

MacKenzie heard Bear's excited voice crackle over the intercom. "Conn, Sonar. Contact, Skipper. We're picking up a big blast of air. Bubbles rising. Unless my ears deceive me, sir, they're blowing a missile tube. Might be running a launch. We've got us a Boomer. A Typhoon, maybe. I can't tell yet."

"Can you give me range, course, and speed?"

"Estimated range five miles. . . . Wait . . . she's turning, turning. . . . Estimated new course two seven zero, speed ten knots."

"Maintain contact," MacKenzie ordered.

"It's fading. God, she's quiet. Turn count decreasing. . . . Damn, we lost her, sir."

MacKenzie lost no time. "Take her down, Mr. Randall. Make your depth five zero zero feet. Ten degrees down bubble as soon as we clear the ice."

"Five zero zero feet, aye. Flooding ballast now."

Seawolf shuddered. The helmsman looked up from his gauges. "Captain, Diving Officer, we are breaking clear of the ice. Ready to answer bells."

"Helm, steer course two seven zero. All ahead two-thirds."

"All ahead two-thirds, aye."

"Passing three zero zero feet, ten degrees down bubble," Randall reported.

"Pump ballast to sea. Zero bubble," MacKenzie responded.

Seawolf leveled off. "At ordered depth, sir," Randall called out. "Five zero zero feet."

MacKenzie leaned back and ran a hand over his chin thoughtfully.

"Mac?" Lasovic inquired. "What's bothering you?"

"I don't know for sure. We pick up a contact. Then we lose him. Then we pick him up again and he blows a missile tube, then turns and runs." MacKenzie shook his head. "Maybe it's nothing, but . . . Navigation, let's make the R-and-D boys happy and give the SALDIRI program a dry run."

"We can access, Skipper. Coordinates?"

"Sonar, Conn. What did you make that best range to contact?"

"Five miles."

"Jim, use Sonar's contact area as the radius. Run it up on the screen."

Santiago flipped the switches on the new satellite look down infrared imaging instrumentation. He was locking into the new joint French-American Topex-Poseidon orbiting radar satellite, which was ordinarily used to track ocean currents for navigational purposes and to have its infrared scanners isolate a complete picture of the desired area of the polar ice cap as seen from above. Since as much as two percent of the ice cap was open water even in the coldest months, the SALDIRI program was meant to provide the captain of a ballistic missile submarine with the location of the nearest open water launch window—or to give an attack sub captain the locations an SSBN might head for.

"Coming on screen now, Skipper," Santiago reported.

MacKenzie looked over. A circle-type polar projection representing the area around the Soviet contact had replaced the TV picture of the ice overhead.

"Infrared imaging proceeding," said Santiago.

The image on the screen rolled, then refocused into bright blotches of color as the orbiting scanners plotted temperatures over the surface of the ice pack. As expected, almost all of the area was dark blue—thick ice, the coldest areas. Toward the edge there were small areas of green—thin ice, with slightly higher temperatures because the water underneath bled some fragile warmth. Open water, which had the highest temperatures, would be red. There was no green or red near the contact's last position.

"No polynyas or open water anywhere near him," MacKenzie said thoughtfully. "In fact, it's all thick ice. Ten to fifteen feet. Too tough to break through. So it wasn't an actual launch. And if it was a training simulation, why turn and run?"

"Because they heard us?" offered Lasovic.

"We were dead silent when we heard that launch, Tom. If he heard us at all it had to be before it. Hmm . . . Mr. Randall?"

"Sir?"

"Your opinion. What do you think all this means?"

Randall was not unused to the captain's snap quizzes, as he thought of them. There was no one in the fleet he respected or admired more than the steel-nerved MacKenzie. He firmly believed that the captain's personal courage in piloting the DSRV *Mystic* through the Cayman Trench and his able battle tactics during the engagement with *Kirov* had saved the lives of *Aspen*'s officers and crew.

"He knew we were listening, sir," Randall surmised. "He wanted us to hear the launch."

"I'm beginning to think so, too," MacKenzie agreed. "First he offers us a tempting target, an unknown ballistic missile sub operating in our area. Of course we'd pull off to try for a signature and check out his systems. Gentlemen, do you get the feeling we're being decoyed for some reason?"

"It's starting to look possible," Lasovic conceded.

"I feel like I'm in a chess game," said Santiago, "and I'm two moves behind. A decoy? Why pull us off at all? He doesn't have any idea of our mission."

"Which means it isn't our mission that he's interested in," said MacKenzie firmly. "It's his. Joe, project his track. At his present course and last speed, where will he end up in, say, twelve hours?"

Santiago leaned over his charts for a few seconds, then looked up. "In twelve hours, he'll be in the marginal ice zone."

MacKenzie smiled. The marginal ice zone was at the outer edge of the polar ice cap and had a special set of conditions that gave ulcers to sub captains. The interaction of the ice edge with the oceanic waves caused so much grinding and splashing that the zone was filled with enough ambient noise to render sonar practically useless. Worse, water temperature and salinity gradients caused major distortions of the sound velocity field. All in all, it was a perfect place in which to lose a pursuer, and they all knew it.

Lasovic's face held genuine admiration. "He runs, we follow. Then he disappears and comes back here. This is a smart son of a bitch."

"I'm forced to agree," said MacKenzie. "Joe, let's run a search track, as if we're hot to pick up his trail. Establish a pattern. Stay on course two seven zero and let him catch a glimpse of us at a stop point—say, fifty miles, then again at a hundred miles. But instead of staying with him from there we'll double back here and hug the ice again. Wait for him to come back."

"Right, sir."

MacKenzie eased back on his heels. "I wonder what the hell he's up to. In any event, you're right, Tom. He's a smart one."

"Maybe. But I think you nailed him. Nice pickup, Skipper," Lasovic said happily, his tone indicating who he thought the smarter son of a bitch really was.

Red Dawn

Ligichev stood in the captain's mess looking at the order sent from Kalik on the *Akula* and shook his head. "Ridiculous," he said flatly. "I cannot imagine delaying the test one full day."

"It is out of our hands," said Galinin. "An American submarine is in the area. Kalik needs time to draw it away."

"Fine. While he is doing that, we will proceed."

"Naval Command says the *Akula* must be on station nearby during the test run. If anything were to go wrong—"

"Nothing will go wrong," Ivanna said. "And if it did, what help would *Akula* be? This is the worst kind of paranoia, the need for military power when there is no threat."

"I am not unsympathetic, but I have my orders. We will delay."

"More obstructionism." Ivanna stood firm. "We will not."

Galinin's face clouded over. Ligichev saw the storm coming and stepped in. "All right, Comrade Captain. We will do as you say. Ivanna, come."

"But . . ."

Galinin was gracious. "Thank you, Comrade Ligichev. *You* at least are a reasonable man." With that, he left the room.

"Why do you let him push us around?" Ivanna asked, exasperated, when he had gone.

Ligichev sighed. "Two rules have always served me well, daughter. First, never ask for permission if you can't afford to hear a no. Second, never fight when you are going to do what you intend to do anyway."

"Ah."

Ligichev sighed. "I suppose it's asking too much for you to learn these rules, too. You will always be a fighter. Just like your mother. That's where you get it, I suppose. God, we had some rows," he said, remembering the past fondly. "One time she found out that I was entitled to shop at a Party store but didn't because I didn't want to have more than our neighbors. The stores they could shop in had nothing but old bread and near rotten meat. She hit me. Actually knocked me down, and I fell in the snow. Naturally, I saw it her way. When we got to the shop she bought everything in sight and shared it with half the apartment building. Quite a woman."

Ivanna laughed. "Then we'll test as planned?"

"As soon as we're ready. I haven't worked for ten years to be told to wait like some schoolboy. Now come. Any more of this coffee and I'll need new insides."

Ivanna followed him down the cramped corridors. Crewmen still stared, regarding her as an oddity, a woman on board a submarine. She ignored them. "Father," she began hesitantly, "you're sure you're not worried?"

"We will exercise proper scientific caution."

"I'm still not happy with the temperature gradients."

"I've been thinking about that. What if we . . ." He began to outline the workings to her. She was soon nodding, amazed as always at the leaps his mind could make.

They entered the engineering section lost in discussion.

Back in the control room, Galinin spoke to his chief electrician. "Comrade, there is a small detail you will tend to."

After a few moments, the electrician's brow furrowed, "But why would you want to bypass the—"

"It is enough that I want to, Comrade Electrician. Go and do it."

"Of course, Comrade Captain, I didn't mean to—"

"Then proceed."

Galinin returned to running his sub, pleased by his foresight. Fools didn't become captains, he thought to himself, and scientists who played tactical games with a sub commander would find themselves outflanked.

Once, long before, during Galinin's first year in the Naval Academy, an upperclassman named Rislin had taken a dislike to the gangly new boy from the provinces with his rough manners and uncultured way of speaking. Not Russian enough, Rislin used to taunt him. Farm boy. Galinin's fists clenched when he remembered the unceasing torment Rislin had heaped upon him. But he had been determined to stay in the academy, determined to survive. The taunting went far beyond the usual new-student baiting, but he bore it.

The height of Rislin's torture came with a plan to humiliate Galinin past the point of endurance. Rislin even convinced some of his friends to help. They would kidnap Galinin from the academy, strip him naked, and leave him in a sack on the doorstep of a degenerate bar on the waterfront where it was rumored that men slept with men. The likelihood of Galinin's escaping without being the victim of homosexual rape was slim. Word of the plan reached Galinin through one upperclassman who, while he could not actively oppose Rislin, refused to accept such cruelty without at least some attempt at intervention.

The upperclassmen gathered as planned, but Rislin never came. They found him the next morning in his room. Someone had driven a sharp stake through a chair and suspended Rislin over it by tying his hands to a ceiling rafter. Only by holding himself up could he escape being impaled on the stake. Sometime in the night his arms must have tired. . . .

The episode, with its nasty psychosexual overtones, was

hushed up. No charges were ever filed, but later one of Galinin's instructors was to write of him, "He has an almost uncanny ability to anticipate aggression, which his intuition tells him will come, and strike first. He is an attacker *by nature.*"

Galinin put it more simply. Life was war. Get them first.

Chapter Three

MacKenzie was conferring with Tom Lasovic when Santiago looked up from his console. "We're one hundred miles along course track two seven zero, Captain." *Seawolf* had arrived at the second of Mac's prescribed bait points, halfway to the marginal ice zone.

MacKenzie nodded. "Time to let our friend know we're still here. Sonar, Conn. Active sweep. Let him hear us, Mr. Kurstan."

"Sonar, aye. Active sweep."

"Mr. Santiago, plot a course and speed back to our original position. After the sweep we're turning back."

"Aye, Skipper."

Tom Lasovic had a look of grudging admiration on his face. "Gotta hand it to them, Mac. They're quiet as hell. I'd estimate they about halved the distance we can hear them from. Got it down to five miles or so. Less in this noise."

MacKenzie nodded. "Sonar, any idea what we're chasing yet?"

"No, sir. Sorry."

"Try for a partial on the signature. Be helpful to know what type of Boomer we're dealing with."

"Yes, sir."

31

MacKenzie turned back to Lasovic. "This is how the *Augusta's* captain must have felt."

"Wasn't she the sub that collided with the Soviets off Gibraltar?"

"That's the one. I talked to her captain a while after. Said he never heard them. Not a sound."

"Still," said Lasovic fondly, "I'd bet *Seawolf's* ears over any sub's in either fleet, all this noise notwithstanding."

"In this bullfight, Mr. Lasovic," Randall joked lightly, "they don't give you the ears."

"No," Lasovic said, smiling, "just the horns."

MacKenzie cast his thoughts out, his telepathic sonar searching for their unseen and as yet unidentified opponent lurking somewhere in the icy waters. No, it wasn't a bullfight. It was a man fight . . . and those were always deadlier.

Akula

"Control Room, Sonar. Contact, Comrade Captain. We are picking up an active sonar search. The American is still following on course two seven zero, ten kilometers astern."

Kalik slapped a stanchion happily. "He's still taking the bait." In another few hours the ambient sound would increase to where it would mask them completely. Then Kalik would turn back. "Keep coming, my friend. Engine Room, full ahead." He let the burst of speed continue for ten seconds, then ordered, "Engine Room, all engines slow ahead."

Volkov smiled. "We are like Hänsel and Gretel laying down a path of crumbs."

"One he continues to follow," Kalik agreed, knowing *Akula's* brief burst of speed would surely be heard by the sub trailing them. "Steady on course two seven zero."

Lay down a few more crumbs, Kalik mused, then be gone.

"Sonar, Conn. Contact, Skipper. Got him again. Turn count increasing. The engines kicked in hard. Decreasing . . . decreasing . . . lost him. He sure is quiet. Sorry."

"Not to worry, Sonar. We're not hanging around. Mr. Randall, make your depth seven zero zero feet. Slowly."

"Depth seven zero zero feet, aye. Three degrees down bubble."

"Conn, Sonar. Thermocline at seven five zero feet."

"Mr. Randall, take her down to seven five zero. We'll hug that gradient."

Sound, like light, changed direction when it passed through media of different densities. A stick inserted into a glass of water looked bent because the light waves were refracted; sound waves acted the same way. Riding a thermal, the ridge where two currents of two different temperatures met, made sound bend away. The Gulf Stream was a good example. A sub captain saw it as a river in the ocean in which he could hide his sub undetected.

Seawolf slid downward in the icy waters. There were places where the ice actually rose from the bottom in addition to hanging down from the top, a situation that could trap the unwary commander, but the charts showed there was plenty of depth in this area even so far into winter.

"At ordered depth, sir."

"Very well. Now give me a nice slow one-hundred-eighty-degree turn to new course zero nine zero. Keep her quiet. I don't want our friend to hear us slipping away. Right five degrees rudder, steady course zero nine zero."

"Commencing slow turn to new course zero nine zero," echoed Randall. "Helm, right five degrees rudder, steer course zero nine zero."

"All ahead one-third," MacKenzie ordered.

"All ahead one-third, aye."

"Sonar, Conn. Any sign of our contact?"

"None, Skipper."

"Steady zero nine zero," Randall announced.

"Very well. Hold her steady, Mr. Randall." MacKenzie pulled at his collar, feeling the need for a shower and some sleep. "Tom, take the conn. I'll be in my cabin."

"Yes, sir. . . . This is the XO. I have the conn."

Walking aft as *Seawolf* sped back to its original position, MacKenzie enjoyed the thought of his unseen opponent sailing blithely for the marginal zone, assuming they were trailing right behind. But they weren't. Instead, *Seawolf* would be lying silently in wait for the Soviet captain to return and expose what he'd worked so hard to conceal.

"Home free, all," MacKenzie whispered to no one but himself.

Red Dawn

Ligichev entered the control room. Galinin was making notes in the ship's log. "Comrade Captain? Excuse me."

"Yes?"

"Is there any word from *Akula?*"

"None yet, Comrade Ligichev. It is unlikely that we will hear before morning."

"But that's twelve hours."

"Be certain I will inform you at once."

Ligichev started to argue but thought better of it. Remember your own maxim, he decided. Instead he said, "Thank you, Comrade Captain," and left the control room.

He trudged back to the engine room. The cook was clanging around in the galley, and some off-duty sailors were in the crew's mess playing cards and eating what smelled like some pretty fair borscht. An overhead speaker spewed tinny classical music. Ligichev smiled amiably, "Good evening, Comrades."

Unsure, the crewmen stumbled to attention, ill at ease. They were peasant boys, mostly from the far-flung provinces. More than likely few spoke Russian as their native language. It was another of the inequities that was bringing the "classless" society to its knees. The majority of officers were native Russians while the crews were conscripted from the hundred other nationalities in the Soviet Union. "Comrade Chief Scientist," one mumbled in greeting, uncertain how to respond.

"Relax," counseled Ligichev. "I don't bite. Truth be told, I'm not even in the navy. And my politics?" He winked. "Disastrous."

Smiles threatened to break out.

"Worse, I have even been to America."

Now, that was impressive. "What was it like?" asked one sailor, who took the liberty of gesturing invitingly to the central bowl of borscht. "Comrade?"

Ligichev sat. "Thank you. Delighted."

They were a physically fit group, young, with broad faces, all dressed in their wool blues. Ligichev had been in their tiny berthing areas, as cramped as everywhere else on the ship. Comfort wasn't a major concern of Soviet naval designers.

"You were saying, Comrade Chief Scientist . . . about the West?"

Ligichev took a mouthful of borscht and tried to sum it up. "For all its material wealth, it is still a new place, a country finding itself. And I came to understand something in the weeks I was there. All our lives we've been taught to hate and fear Americans . . . but the truth is there is no such thing as an American. Everybody there is from somewhere else. Transplanted Poles, Germans and Britains, Africans and Asians, Buddhists and Jews, even Russians. They're not remotely identical. Actually, it's an altogether impossible mix."

"Just like the Soviet Union," someone observed dryly.

Ligichev nodded. "But here is the difference. They are unified not by the Red Army but by belief. That's the secret. America is not a nationality; it is a system of beliefs. All anyone has to do to be an American is to believe in their basic ideas."

"Like?"

"Oh, that anything is possible with enough ingenuity. That individuals have inalienable rights. That real grass is better than AstroTurf, although there are many who feel . . ." Ligichev looked up. He had lost them. He smiled kindly and ate some more.

One crewman spoke up, albeit hesitantly, a big man with the tattoo of a snake wrapped around a dagger on his thick forearm. "Comrade Chief Scientist, of course we have wondered—not that we are worried in any way, but most of us have wives and children—if it is permissible to ask what we are doing in such an old ship in such difficult waters."

"What is your name?"

Instantly the man feared he had overstepped some boundary. "Seaman Fyodor Vaslayavich Boslik, Comrade," he said fearfully. "But please, I didn't mean—"

"Relax, Seaman Boslik. I am no Zampol political officer. It's just easier to talk to a man whose name I know. Well, I can't tell you much, of course, but suffice to say we are making history. After today, Comrades, everyone will remember the *Red Dawn.*"

"That is good."

"Yes," Ligichev agreed, "I think it's very good. As does the captain and my daughter and the Naval High Command. If all of us do our jobs, I think we can expect quite a few medals to be passed out when this trip is over. So rest assured."

"In all my years at sea," said the burly Boslik, "no one has ever spoken to us about such things." The others nodded in agreement.

Ligichev laughed. "Read *Pravda,* eh. Things are changing."

"So we hear. You can depend on us, Comrade Chief Scientist."

"Thanks for the borscht."

"Where were you?" Ivanna asked as Ligichev entered the engine room, locking the hatch behind him.

"Talking to some of the crew."

"And?"

"I tell you, Ivanna, we are going to have to work hard at unlearning the servility seventy years of communism has bred into decent people."

"Not news."

Ligichev sighed. "But it is, Ivanna. It means it's even more important that irinium work. When the walls around our country are finally gone and we stand in front of the world having to explain our . . . our sleep of this last century, I want to show we achieved something more than"—he spat out the word—*"slogans.* We have to face the West and show we did more than just trample people into the ground. Yes, we made mistakes, but in the end, look, we did achieve some fine things. We can join you as equals."

Ivanna smiled. "I love your passion. Well, things are changing, Father, but till they do it's the old joke for a while longer—we pretend to work, they pretend to pay us. Now calm yourself. Even you don't hold the entire Soviet self-image on your shoulders."

Ligichev stripped off his jacket and went to work. There were final connections to be made and a last set of computer runs to be checked. At last they stood there, both looking like expectant parents.

"Are we going to wait?" asked Ivanna.

"No," her father said flatly. He turned to the technicians. "Everyone. Get to your stations."

Ivanna grabbed her clipboard and stationed herself at the control console. "Running preliminary checklist. I can't wait to see Galinin's face."

"Pay attention to your work," said Ligichev. "Temperature?"

"Irinium at required temperature, zero degrees centigrade."

"Scoop?"

"Operational," the senior technician called out.

The cadence continued over the constant whine of the electrical motors driving the main shaft. Tension mounted. Ligichev felt this was a *global* moment, like Sputnik's first orbit or the first time the Americans' *Nautilus* crossed the

North Pole under the ice. Folded in his pocket was the note he would hand Galinin for transmission to Naval Command. "System operational." That was all. "System operational." It wasn't necessary to be long-winded. This was history.

Ivanna met his gaze with a nod. "All systems operational."

"Shut down," Ligichev ordered, and his hand slapped the cutoff switch. Suddenly the motor whine they had lived with for so many days died. The propellers stopped their ceaseless spinning. He could feel the sub lose its momentum, slowing.

Ivanna hit another row of switches and fail-safe motors sprang into life. "Scoop operational, pressure building."

"Activate," Ligichev ordered, bright-eyed. Ivanna flipped the final row of switches on the console.

Power flowed into the irinium plates. Tiny but powerful motors sprang into life. A series of electromagnetic pushes and pulls flashed on and off moving water through the tube in a steady, powerful stream.

"Speed," Ligichev demanded.

"Two, no . . . three knots," the technician read happily from his gauges. "Five knots!"

"It's working!" shouted Ligichev. In his excitement he danced around the engine room. Ivanna and the technicians shouted and clapped one another on the back and ran their hands over the drive tube as if it were spewing gold out the other end and not just a pressure jet of water.

In the control room the helmsman took his hands off the steering yoke and looked back at Galinin. "Comrade Captain? Our speed is decreasing. I'm losing feel in the ship. I don't understand . . ."

Galinin turned furiously. He understood. He slammed his fist into the intercom. "Engine Room, I'm losing power. What is going on in there? Comrade Ligichev? Comrade! What are you doing in there?"

He was stopped by a whoop of delight emanating from the

speaker. It sounded for all the world like a wild party in the engine room.

"It works, Comrade Captain. Isn't it fantastic? Isn't it wonderful?"

Galinin's face was suffused with anger. "How dare you disobey my orders? Your drive is fouling the operation of my ship. Turn it off and wait for proper orders to be given. If you comply at once I will overlook this transgression. If not, I will put a stop to it myself."

"Captain, you can't mean it. The system is working! Ten years of effort. God, what a moment."

"I order you to turn it off."

"Never," cried a female voice. "Turn off your obstructionist attitude."

Someone snickered in the control room, and Galinin's face grew beet red. Ivanna's impudence was the last straw. "Comrade Electrician, you installed the override?"

Any trace of a smile vanished from the electrician's face. "Yes, Comrade Captain. As you ordered."

"Then engage it."

"I cannot speak for—"

"Engage it, damn you!"

The electrician flipped the switch.

Two hundred feet aft, the water jet died. Ligichev stopped, his face turning white. "What . . . ?" A strange crackling sound filled the room, along with the smell of ozone.

A technician was pointing to the gauges, ashen-faced. "Comrade Ligichev, there's no system power. No electricity. He's somehow cut the batteries out of the loop. We never prepared for this. The temperature will be critical in a matter of minutes."

Ivanna's gauges told the same story. "Father, the magnetic field is dead. The irinium is coming in direct contact with the seawater. We're getting a very strong heat buildup."

Ligichev could feel it. The temperature was rising rapidly, the drive tube already hot to the touch. The crackling was louder, too. "Quickly, close the outer doors," he ordered the technicians. "If the tube ruptures it's going to flood the ship."

"But there's no power."

"Do it manually, damn it, but do it. Ivanna, help them. Quickly!" He grabbed the intercom. "Comrade Captain, please, I beg you. The ship is in danger. Without electricity the magnetic field is gone. The irinium is in direct contact with seawater. Heat is building up as well as a strong electrical pulse. I must have the magnetic field back in place."

Galinin's voice was defiant. "I'm sorry. I cannot permit my authority to be superseded. You should have thought of these things before you disobeyed direct orders."

"You stupid fool, can't you see what you're doing?" Ligichev shouted.

Galinin's voice was cold. "Yes. I have restored order. I am on my way aft to complete the task."

Ligichev could hear that Galinin was almost obscenely happy with his oafishness. He dropped the intercom, and it swung against the bulkhead with a crack. He yanked his collar open. Ivanna's clothing was already soaking wet. Sweat coursed down her face. The atmosphere in the room was stifling.

"Father, what do we do? The heat is rising too fast . . ."

Ligichev was thinking hard. "We have to channel it out. If it hits the asymptotic curve . . . I've got to clear my head. No time to be angry. Come on, old man. Think."

A technician reached out to touch a switch but yanked his hand back, stung by a hot spark. "Comrade Ligichev, the electrical pulse is building. Fires will start soon in the mains."

"Father?"

"Yes, yes. All right." Ligichev grabbed his head. "We are in the middle of the largest pool of cold water in the world. We ought to be able to take advantage of that." He called a technician over. "Can you reopen the access vent physically and block off the output valve? Then create a backflow into the main ballast tank?"

"Yes, I think I can," said the technician, nodding slowly. "But what will that accomplish?"

Ligichev put a hand on the outer bulkhead. "The main ballast tanks are right over here adjoining the tube. We'll channel the heat to the tanks. Then we jettison the water to dump the heat. Then we refill, reheat, and dump again. Keep pumping the hot water out to sea."

"A heat exchanger! Yes, it might work."

"Get to it." The technician slipped under the drive tube, careful not to touch its scalding walls. Ligichev peered through the steamy air. "Ivanna?"

"I'm here, Father."

"Isolate the secondaries. If there's a pulse coming, we're going to need working circuits when it's over." She grabbed a set of tools, dropped behind the command console, and began to work furiously.

Ligichev cursed Galinin for the tenth time in as many minutes and bent down to do what he could to save the ship. By his calculations they had less than twenty minutes to live. An electrical pulse was building that would explode out from the contaminated irinium and fuse every electronic circuit on board. At that point the ship would be inoperable.

But while Ligichev worked, the scientific part of his mind could not avoid the conscious realization that all their effort might be just a study in redundancy.

Within minutes of the electrical pulse that was going to kill the ship, an inexorable heat flash was going to incinerate every person on board.

Chapter
Four

Seawolf

MacKenzie's cabin was a six-by-eight cubicle with more apparatus built into its walls than the old Volkswagen camper he had driven across-country when he was in college. It was also the only one that had its own head. When Mac woke from his short nap, he slid his trim frame off the bunk and splashed some cold water from the sink into his face.

The forty-three-year-old man who stared back from the mirror looked older to him than he had just a few short years ago. He ran a hand through his thick black hair, surprised that he didn't see more gray. In many ways he was a different man from the one who had commanded the *Aspen*. He was wiser, more mature, more . . . married. He grinned ruefully. When you were married to a woman who could toss several heavily armed men out a second-story window should she choose to, marriage was never dull. He just wished they could have more time together. Time was their great enemy. Justine's work and his long cruises often put their marriage on a catch-as-catch-can basis. And when they were together, there seemed to be more than enough chores to keep them too busy to relax. Funny, he thought, he'd come all this way thinking he'd made it to a different kind of life only to discover he had the same kind of problems as any yuppie accountant. Fate, he decided, liked irony.

He and Justine had talked about his taking a desk assignment someday, but not now. Now there was *Seawolf.* The most powerful sub in the fleet was under his command. This was where he was born to be.

MacKenzie ran a towel over his hard, athletic body, savoring how good he felt. It went deeper than just the physical. He had a feeling of personal power that had grown with his age and accomplishments. He felt fuller, more of a man in the best sense of what it meant to be one, and he had to admit that his relationship to Justine let him discover new lands within himself, a new domain of loving and being loved in return.

He finished dressing and sat at his desk to get some paperwork out of the way. He'd been at it for less than ten minutes when the intercom buzzed. It was Tom Lasovic. "Contact, Skipper. Our boy could be back."

The timing took MacKenzie by surprise. He pushed the papers aside and leaned back in his chair. "What's he doing here so soon, Tom? Still got a few hours by my watch."

"Don't rightly know, sir. But Sonar says it's got something."

"Hold on. I'll be right there."

MacKenzie closed up his desk and trotted down to Sonar. If the Russian had returned to the area, either he had turned back the same time as *Seawolf* did or his return speed was far greater. The latter possibility was ominous. If they hadn't heard the Russian till now, he was too damn quiet for anybody's good.

"What's up, Jim?" Mac demanded as soon as he entered Sonar.

"I'd like to know myself, sir," the tall lieutenant said sincerely. "I've never—repeat, never—heard anything like this. Mr. Lasovic thinks it could be our earlier contact returning, but I don't think so. For one thing, she's a lot noisier. Listen for yourself, Skipper."

MacKenzie pulled on a set of earphones. Like most captains, he was familiar enough with sonar to identify basic patterns, but this was out of his league and he said so. "Bear, I'll take your best guess. Don't be shy, now."

Bear Bendel's eyes were hazy, his senses extended far out into the freezing waters. "It's not the same contact, Skipper. I'm gonna go pretty far out on a limb, sir, but I don't think it's even a nuclear boat. You don't hear many diesels nowadays, but that's what I think we've got."

Lasovic wasn't the only one who looked surprised. "What's a diesel boat doing way out here?"

"Do the signatures correlate?" MacKenzie asked.

"Computers are working on it, sir. Should be just a few seconds more . . . there." Bear pointed to the screen with some pride.

"Well done, Bear," MacKenzie acknowledged. "A Soviet Tango class diesel sub. Definitely a new player, not our Boomer from before. Do you think he knows we're here?"

"It's unlikely a Tango's old sonars could have picked us up the way we snuck back here, Skipper."

"I wonder if this sub is why our other friend didn't want us around," MacKenzie mused.

"What's he protecting?" asked Lasovic. "Tangos are over twenty years old. Nothing to interest us."

"That's not all, sir," Bendel continued. "For a while I got a pretty good fix on him—that's why I was sort of sure—but all of a sudden I lost contact completely, like the engines were shut down. Now she's drifting and I'm getting pump noises like I never heard before, and, well, I'll put it on the speaker."

A cacophony of noise filled the room. There were the usual shrieks and groans of the ice pack, but under that they heard bass thuds that sounded like hammer blows, and the steady whooshing of pumps running at top speed. Abruptly, new sounds emerged.

"That's his propellers turning, Skipper," Bendel said excitedly, "He's back on batteries. Speed five knots . . . surging . . . Wait, his turn count's decreasing. Course one nine five. Sir, I think he's in some kind of trouble."

"Don't lose him, Bear. I'll be in the conn. Tom, let's get in closer."

Red Dawn

Galinin roared up the main corridor like a storm. A steady vibration had returned, which meant the engines were back on. Damn that Ligichev, endangering his submarine. He reached the engine room bulkhead and pounded on the door angrily.

"Ligichev, open up at once. The ship is in danger. I have to restore control—" He was gratified to see the wheel turn and the door begin to swing open, but instead of men, hot fetid air burst out and sent him staggering backwards. "For Christ's sake, what is going on in there?" Galinin demanded.

Ligichev stumbled out of the engine room looking as if he'd been in a steam bath. He leaned against the bulkhead for support, drawing in cooler air in great heaving gulps. "Please, help Ivanna . . . still inside."

Galinin shouldered his way into the engine room. He could barely breathe, the air was so foul and musty. He saw a shadowy form in the mists—a technician still gamely working at his console. "Out, now," Galinin yelled. The man wasted no time in complying.

"Comrade Captain . . ." It was the chief technician, almost overcome by the heat.

"Can you get the motors running?" Galinin demanded. "We are drifting."

"I can try . . . if the exhaust fans clear the room."

Galinin spotted Ivanna lying on the floor. He bent down and carried the limp form out of the impossible room and laid her down next to her father.

The hot, wet air was spreading quickly through the ship, giving it a stale, swampy feel. "Comrade Ligichev," Galinin demanded, "you must tell me what has happened."

Ligichev nodded weakly. "Help me up. We have to get to the control room. Dump as much ballast as you can. Heat transfer . . ."

Galinin got Ligichev to a standing position and supported him as they ran for the control room, Ligichev explaining as best he could. "So you see, we have to dump the hot water, bleed off as much heat as we can. Do you have secondary circuit protection? The electrical pulse is only minutes away."

"It will blow every circuit. Can't you stop it?"

"You caused the feedback when you cut the power. The only way to stop it is to dump the irinium overboard, and to do that you would have to lose the entire engine room. The plates are built right into the drive, and that's welded to the ship."

They entered the control room. Galinin was still a competent sub commander and his ship was in danger. His commands were quick and precise. "Blow main ballast. I want those pumps working at top speed. Michman, keep the ship in trim. Add ballast to secondary tanks. Maintain our depth. All engines slow ahead."

Hot water was blown from the main ballast tanks with a loud whoosh.

"Keep it going," urged Ligichev. "We need a constant flow."

Galinin barked the orders. "Flood main ballast tanks. Get those pumps going. Balance her by putting water in the secondaries. Damn it, watch our depth. Keep us in trim!"

The temperature in the control room was nearing the hundred-degree mark. Uniforms were plastered to sweating backs. Gauges had to be wiped clear of condensation every few seconds. Galinin was deeply worried about his electronics. They were easily fouled by this much moisture.

"Radio Officer, send a distress signal."

"I am trying to send it, Comrade Captain."

"Main ballast filled, Comrade Captain."

"Blow main ballast." Galinin looked at the temperature gauge again. One hundred ten. "Goddamn oven," he swore, tearing open his shirt.

Again the loud whooshing. "Main ballast blown, Comrade Captain."

"Shut down your electronics," advised Ligichev. "Quickly."

"As soon as I can. Communications, radio *Akula* that—"

It happened all at once. The Michman reached for the ballast lever but pulled back in pain when a hot spark burned his hand. Suddenly electrical discharges were leaping from console to console. Sailors fell back, shouting in fear. The smell of burning flesh was added to the noxious atmosphere. Saint Elmo's fiery balls of electrical energy danced in the air and over instruments that were suddenly too hot to handle.

"What is going on?" roared Galinin.

"It's the discharge! I told you. Shut down at once," Ligichev yelled.

It was too late. Circuits shorted and burned. Acrid clouds of smoke rose from melting insulation. System after system failed. Burned men fell back from their fiery consoles.

"Damage reports. Answer me, damn it! Damage reports!"

Men tried to come to order, coughing, having to force noxious air into seared lungs. They held on to their burned limbs and pressed sodden cloths to bleeding foreheads. "Comrade Captain, communications are out."

"Helm refuses to answer."

"Planes are locked, Comrade Captain."

The litany continued. "Comrade Captain, speed is down to one knot."

"Sonar is out."

The lights dimmed. There was barely enough power in the batteries to keep the fans running. Galinin pounded a railing in frustration. "We're drifting. The ship is almost dead. I must have power to steer us. Your system . . . ?"

Ligichev shook his head tightly. "Ruined."

Whatever Galinin's next comment was going to be, it was ut off by the frightened voice of the helmsman whose eyes were glued to the closed circuit television giving the forward view of the icy sea in front of them. "Comrade Captain, look! The ice!"

Galinin rushed forward. Heavy interference almost obscured the screen, but there was no mistaking the huge undersea ice keel that lay right across *Red Dawn*'s path.

"Mother of God," Galinin swore, "it must go down five hundred feet. Helm, steer to course!"

"I cannot steer the ship," said the sailor, eyes wide.

"We're going to die!" yelled another crewman, panicking like a trapped animal. Galinin grabbed him. "Steady! We are going to live. Hold on. Do you hear me? Hold on!" The crewman's panic subsided. Others helped him wrap his shirt around a metal railing and lock his arms around it. Galinin gave them a firm nod of approval.

The ice keel in the TV picture was larger now, shining blue-green in the water. All eyes were glued to it. Galinin grabbed the microphone and spoke over the all-ship channel.

"This is the captain. We are going to hit an ice keel. I repeat, an impact is unavoidable. *Red Dawn* will survive the crash. Believe me, we will survive the crash. Then we will effect repairs. *Akula* will return soon and they will help us. Hold on, everyone. Wherever you are, hold on!"

There was a terrible screech and then a crash that tossed the ship about as if a giant hand had seized it and smashed it into a wall. Galinin was thrown to the deck and scalded by steam that burst from a ruptured fitting. Pipes burst, spraying water all over the control room. Men were thrown into the sharp edges of steel consoles. Bodies were crushed by instrument tables torn from their moorings and sent careening across the room. Ligichev went down under a crush of falling bodies, his face pressed into the rising pool of water beneath him. He grabbed a railing to get out from under the bodies and out of the water that threatened to drown him. He felt hands reach for him and pull him out, and he sprawled painfully on the periscope deck, gasping for air.

The deck was listing at a difficult angle, aft high in the air and rolled partly to the port side, but the worst of the shocks was over. *Red Dawn*'s hull held. Galinin plunged his burned hand into the water for the smallest relief and yelled into the spray. "Close off those valves. Rostov! Don't just stand there. Get to it. You want to drown?" Even Ligichev lent his hands to the task. Slowly they secured the burned and flooded control room.

"Pumps," directed Galinin. "Start pumping the water out manually."

"Father!" It was Ivanna. She made her way into the control room. Ligichev almost cried with joy as she came into his sodden arms. "You're all right?" he asked, checking her wet face.

"Just bruised. You?"

Ligichev started to speak but instead shook his head and hugged her. He had been about to say "I'll live." But that was still far from certain.

"Father, what are they doing?"

Ligichev turned. It was a strange scene in the twilight. Dripping wet, hair and clothing plastered to their bodies, the bedraggled crewmen had picked themselves up and were staring at the television screen powered by the emergency batteries, the only oracle left to them. What they saw had stopped them dead in their tracks, a single question on every face. Galinin was the first to give it voice: "Comrade Ligichev, look at the screen. Am I seeing . . . ?"

Ligichev saw and was transfixed, too. He made his way through the men gathered in front of the screen, staring in awe. "Yes," he answered. "Yes, but how . . . ?"

The picture on the screen was a shifting blue-green translucent haze. The television cameras were looking *through* a crystalline curtain of ice that surrounded the entire ship. With all the momentum of a ten-thousand-ton projectile, *Red Dawn* had not only hit the ice keel—*but had buried itself deep within it.*

"Like a fly trapped in amber," Galinin said softly.

"The hot ballast!" Ligichev seized on the thought. "Of course. When we hit the ice keel we were enclosed in an envelope of scalding water from the ballast we were dumping. It melted the ice around us. I think it probably made the impact bearable, Captain. Without it, we might have been crushed."

"But the ice, it will refreeze, yes?"

Ligichev nodded. "It is doing so now. Look. See the shifting? It is also saving our lives. Feel it?"

Galinin could. "Cooler. The temperature is falling. But . . ."

"But we are trapped," Ligichev said in a measured tone, "trapped in solid ice without the power to break free."

Galinin waved his red and blistered hand. "We must have electricity. The emergency batteries won't last long. And without heat, trapped in this ice . . ."

Ligichev understood. "And air."

"Yes, air."

They stood amid the wreckage of what had once been a functioning submarine control room. Their eyes met in unspoken agreement. Cooperation was essential. Hostilities had to be put aside. It didn't matter now who was responsible for the predicament or why. All that mattered was using their knowledge and skill to survive.

But they knew. They saw it in each other's faces: their chances weren't good, not good at all.

Seawolf

The scene on *Seawolf* almost duplicated the one in *Red Dawn's* control room. MacKenzie, Lasovic, and every other officer and crewman who could look up from his work had his eyes glued to the closed circuit TV screen. The Soviet submarine was embedded in the ice keel as if driven in like a dagger.

"I've never seen anything like that," MacKenzie said, staring raptly. The water was crystal clear under the ice. Nothing obstructed the view *Seawolf's* lights gave them. "They're in solid ice. Just stuck there. How could that have happened?"

Randall described it best. "It looks like they just . . . melted right in."

"Conn, Sonar. We did pick up a brief distress signal before their radio cut out and the crash broke their masts.

Very low power. The ice overhead is twenty feet thick there, Skipper. Add that to the thickness of the keel. We don't think anyone else could have heard them."

"Do we answer them, Mac?" Lasovic asked.

"I don't know yet. Sonar, what about the other contact?"

"Nothing on the scope, Skipper."

MacKenzie shook his head mutely, still staring at the screen. "Could anyone be alive in there?"

"We are getting sound. Repair work, maybe. No pumps or motors."

"Engine room failure," Lasovic guessed. "They're going to freeze pretty damn soon unless they get some power. And how the hell do you raise a snorkel for air through thirty feet of ice?"

"I want to talk this over before we go any further," said MacKenzie. "Mr. Randall, you have the conn. Hold her steady. Mr. Lasovic, Mr. Santiago, Mr. Kurstan, conference in the wardroom, five minutes."

The uniformed steward poured hot coffee for the men who sat around the Formica table in the wardroom. MacKenzie wrapped his hands around the steaming mug and sat back against the cushioned bench seat.

"One of my old teachers used to call this a 'situation.' Well, we've got us a situation, gentlemen. Let's start with what we know. There's a crippled Russian sub stuck up to her props in an ice keel the size of Rhode Island. It appears to be unable to extricate itself. Now, I expect the contact we made earlier to return to the area in the mistaken belief that it has decoyed us away, but unless it gets awfully lucky or that sub repairs its communications gear soon, it doesn't stand a chance of finding it. I will also go so far as to tell you it's my hunch that the Boomer's attempt to pull us out of the area is in some way connected to the sub now trapped in the ice. Beyond that, I'm open to all comments and observations."

"First, Skipper, this sub's got a name. It's the *Red Dawn*," Kurstan said. "The distress signal carried it. Visual observation confirms it is a Tango class diesel. Book says she's ninety-two meters long, has a submerged displacement of thirty-nine hundred metric tons, carries torpedoes and maybe antisub missiles. The initial operational capability for the class was 1973. They built them for about five years."

"What I'd like to know is what a Boomer is doing escorting an old diesel boat around here," interjected Lasovic. "If anything, the diesel should have tried to decoy us away from the Boomer, right?"

"Which leads me to believe that *Red Dawn* is the more important ship," said MacKenzie. "Mr. Kurstan, you have *Red Dawn*'s last half an hour or so on tape?"

"We logged the entire contact, Skipper."

"Good. Encode it in a high-speed pulse for transmission to Norfolk. Let's see what they make of it."

"Aye, sir," said Kurstan, "but I'd like to echo the point Mr. Lasovic made earlier. Unless the Boomer was real close, I don't think it or anyone else could have heard the distress signal. *Seawolf* couldn't transmit through twenty feet of ice at full power. They were fading fast and barely had time for a single transmission."

"They're in trouble. I agree. Do we have any way of estimating their air supply?" MacKenzie asked.

Lasovic shrugged. "No way to be certain, Skipper. I'd have made sure I was full up before I went under the ice cap in a diesel. They could have at least two or three days, but like I say, no way to know for sure. One thing's certain, though. Heat's potentially a bigger problem for them. They can't run the diesels to recharge the batteries without the snorkel for air. It's a catch-22. If there's any juice in the batteries they'll have to bleed it off. It's gonna get cold mighty fast in that ice."

"Is there any way to ascertain the scope of any injuries to her crew?" MacKenzie asked.

"None, Mac," said Lasovic. "The distress signal didn't elaborate."

"Then for the moment," MacKenzie summed up, "we assume roughly forty-eight hours before their situation is critical."

Santiago frowned. "Lot of assumptions, Skipper."

"I know, but informing Norfolk has top priority right now. Till that's been done I don't want either our presence or our position revealed."

The others nodded. MacKenzie drained the last of his coffee. "Tom, prepare to launch the new underwater locators. Use the transmit-only-when-activated type. The Boomer's not going to be able to find *Red Dawn* unless it transmits. I want the locators to sound loud and clear when we want to find this keel again."

"Right away, Skipper."

"All right. Thank you all. Back to your stations."

Most of the faces in the conn were still turned up to the screen. MacKenzie found the sight equally compelling. This was something no one had ever seen before, something no one had ever even predicted could happen to a submarine. The image was startling. *Red Dawn* was embedded in ice so thick and massive she looked like a toy sub in a cube of Lucite. As a professional sailor and as a man, MacKenzie felt a deep concern for and kinship with the crew on board the crippled sub. The awful cold would be creeping in by now, and their helplessness at being unable to free themselves from their icy prison was surely growing. But in this situation there were other considerations. What had *Red Dawn* been up to? What had caused her predicament? And what made her so valuable that a ballistic missile sub, itself an immensely valuable asset, risked showing itself to protect her? Something still bothered him about that, a gnawing doubt that refused to go away. He put it aside for now.

"I have the conn, Mr. Randall. Return to your station."

"Aye, sir." He hesitated for a moment. "Skipper, can they see us?"

MacKenzie looked at the image on the screen. "I wouldn't think so. Too much ice around their scopes. And without power, they have no sonar."

"It's eerie, you know? I wonder what it feels like in there."

"Let's hope we get to ask them." MacKenzie hit the intercom. "Torpedo Room, Conn. Is Mr. Lasovic there?"

The intercom crackled. "Here, Skipper. Locators ready for launch."

"Fire Control, lock in coordinates on that ice keel."

"Conn, Fire Control. Coordinates locked in and transferred to launchers."

"Launch locators."

Rapid deployment sound system sonobuoys could be put into place temporarily by airdrop, usually from P-3C Orion antisubmarine aircraft or, as now, by a submarine launch. RDSS buoys had an operational life of at least ninety days and could broadcast data in short, high-speed bursts on predetermined frequencies to avoid revealing their positions. The underwater locators worked in a similiar manner for use under the ice.

"Locators launched," Lasovic's voice confirmed.

Released from *Seawolf,* the locators sped for the surface and embedded themselves in the base of the ice keel. There they would wait until Mac triggered them. Without them, finding this same spot would be tricky and perhaps impossible because of the ever-changing nature of the ice floe.

"Take her down, Mr. Randall. Eight zero zero feet. Nice and quiet."

MacKenzie caught a last glimpse of *Red Dawn* encased in her icy prison before the ice keel fell away like a high-speed elevator and *Seawolf* dropped into the icy depths.

Chapter Five

Akula

Captain Kalik should have felt pleased with himself. The American sub was lost in the marginal ice zone, and *Akula* had made it back to the testing area with time to spare, but their repeated failure to raise *Red Dawn* had turned mild concern into full-scale alarm.

"I am sorry, Comrade Captain," said the radio officer. "We cannot raise them."

"Keep trying. Sonar, anything?"

"No, Comrade Captain. No contacts. The area is clear."

"Viktor, I am at a loss. Suggestions?"

Volkov responded slowly. "Perhaps we should go active. Make a complete search pattern."

"I don't know. All this ice hanging about . . . Some of these keels go down a thousand feet. Galinin may not be brilliant, but he's competent enough to hold a sub in position. Where the hell is he?"

"I have checked with Naval Command, as you wished, Comrade Captain." advised the radio officer. "They report no communication from *Red Dawn*. They want to know if there is a problem."

"Radio all is well. I don't want Kola sending the fleet out yet." Kalik turned back to his XO. "So he's either in trouble or hiding," he reasoned.

"Why hide?" said Volkov. "The area scans clear. But even assuming he is hiding, surely he would have heard our signal and replied by now."

"Then he is in trouble," Kalik decided. "Maybe they tried the drive and there was an accident."

"Your orders said specifically to postpone the test."

"And if we had only Galinin to contend with, I'd feel fairly sure he had obeyed them. But Ligichev? You ever meet a genius with the slightest respect for authority? No. Ligichev could have ignored my orders. So could his daughter." He hit the railing in frustration. "Where are they?"

Volkov saw self-recrimination in Kalik's rage. Pride was a dangerous quality in any man, but it could be fatal to a submarine commander. Kalik had left *Red Dawn* against orders, and now the sub was lost. That would mean some pretty fancy explaining if it wasn't found soon. Volkov was not optimistic. "The waters here are five kilometers deep. The ice above is ten meters thick. There's a forest of keels the size of ocean liners. How do you intend to find *Red Dawn?*"

"God only knows," Kalik said grimly. "And you'd better hope He decides to help us, Viktor, because we're going to need it. Commence search pattern."

Seawolf

"Conn, Radio. Captain, message for COMSUBLANT coded and ready to transmit, sir."

"Very well, Radio," MacKenzie said. "Mr. Randall, make your depth one zero zero feet. Prepare to surface. Get those radio antennas up as soon as we clear the ice."

"Aye, sir."

MacKenzie had put more than fifty miles between

Seawolf and *Red Dawn* before he felt comfortable with the noise he was about to make. "Sonar, I need some thin ice."

"Can do, Skipper. Upward-looking Fathometer engaged."

"Call it out."

"Aye, sir."

"Mr. Santiago, keep me informed of distance to surface."

MacKenzie swiveled the video screen toward him for a better view. *Seawolf*'s sail was ice-hardened, so up to six feet of ice wouldn't pose a problem, but from the looks of the ice pack's undersurface in this area, thin ice might not be so easy to find.

"Thick ice, ten feet. Thick ice, ten feet. Eight feet. Eight feet. Thick ice, nine feet . . ."

For several miles the ice was just too thick to break through. Then MacKenzie saw the lightninglike pattern up ahead that meant polynyas. "Right ten degrees rudder. Steer course zero five zero. All ahead slow. Call it out, Sonar."

"Thick ice, twelve feet. Ice, ten feet. Clearing . . . ice, six feet. Thin ice, Skipper, four feet. Four feet, three feet, three feet . . ."

"All stop." MacKenzie took the mike and opened the 1MC channel to broadcast ship-wide. "This is the captain. We are about to surface the ship through the ice in order to facilitate radio communications. There's going to be a bit of a bump, so hold on. Captain out."

"Thin ice, three feet. Five feet. Three feet."

The thinness of the ice sheet was holding. "Prepare to surface the ship through ice, Mr. Randall."

"Prepare to surface the ship through ice, aye."

"Mr. Santiago?"

"Aye, sir. Depth to surface, one hundred feet. Ninety feet. Eighty-five feet . . ."

"Ice five feet. Seven feet. Ten feet. Ten feet . . ."

MacKenzie peered closely at the screen. The ice was thickening again. And up ahead, something else . . . hard to make out.

"Ice ten feet. Ice twelve feet . . . Wait, a pressure ridge, Captain! Thick ice! Thick ice. Twenty feet!"

"Depth to surface seventy feet."

Measured from the keel, they were only yards from the ice cap surface. "Mr. Randall, flood main ballast. Emergency deep. Take her down without any bubble to one zero zero feet."

It was too late. With a grinding crash *Seawolf* rammed hard into ice more than twenty feet thick. It was no contest. Barely cracking it, *Seawolf* was tossed about from the shock of the harsh impact. Men lost their footing and sprawled on the deck. The hull groaned and shuddered.

"Damage Control. Report," MacKenzie barked as the ship steadied.

Suddenly a pressure fitting burst, spraying water all over. Tom Lasovic grabbed a wrench. A thick-armed CPO named Kelly left his board to lend a hand. Together they stopped the flow.

"Back at your board, Chief. Check the electronics," MacKenzie ordered. "Clear that water."

"Depth one zero zero feet, Skipper."

"Hold her steady, Mr. Randall."

One by one the section chiefs reported little or no damage. Order returned.

MacKenzie was angry. No way that pressure ridge should have been there. He sighed internally. That was one of the things he was learning about this region. Nothing worked the way it was supposed to. "We're going to try it again," he announced. "Stations, everyone. Take her up slowly, Mr. Randall. Sonar."

"Sonar, aye. Ice six feet. Six feet. Thin ice, three feet."

The thinness of the ice sheet was holding again. "Prepare to surface the ship through ice, Mr. Randall."

"Prepare to surface the ship through ice, aye."

"Mr. Santiago."

"Depth to surface one hundred feet. Ninety feet. Eighty feet."

"Ice three feet. Four feet. Four feet. Five feet . . ."

MacKenzie cursed. The ice was thickening again.

"Ice eight feet, eight feet . . ."

"Seventy-five feet. Seventy feet . . ." There was a sudden

crashing lurch. Santiago looked up. "We are in place under the ice."

"Ice overhead is ten feet thick, Captain," Sonar reported.

MacKenzie considered. Ten feet? Well, maybe it was time to see what *Seawolf's* new ice-hardened sail could take. "Surface the ship, Mr. Randall."

"Surface the ship, aye."

With a groan, *Seawolf* pressed against the ice umbrella overhead.

"Ice is holding . . . holding—"

Seawolf strained against the ice sheet. Shocks vibrated through MacKenzie's spine like a car crash. The hull groaning increased. MacKenzie could feel the ship trying to rise against the ten-foot slabs of ice that held her back. "Blow main ballast, Mr. Randall. She'll hold. Take her through it, son."

"Blowing ballast . . . rising . . . It's giving, Skipper!"

With a final push *Seawolf* broke through the ice cap into the glistening white world of the North Pole. Her sail split the ice like a mighty dark sword, pushing it up and aside so that thick slabs rolled off her deck and crashed back onto the ice cap. Gray-metal waves chopped at *Seawolf's* hull.

MacKenzie scanned the ice cap around them through the periscope. Endless white land, vast white sky. In the warmth and silence of *Seawolf's* inner confines, he felt dwarfed by the enormity of the frozen waste. "Raise the radio antenna," he ordered.

"Antenna extended."

"Transmit."

A petty officer raised the UHF antenna and relayed a transmit signal to the radio room, which sent out the signal on the UHF satellite band.

MacKenzie settled in to wait for the reply. Their window into this barren upper world would remain open for only a while. Soon enough the inexorable pressure of millions of tons of shifting ice would begin forcing it closed. *Seawolf's* hull couldn't withstand that pressure for long.

"Message sent and acknowledged, Skipper. Channel open for reply."

"Let me know as soon as it comes in. Tom, send a lookout onto the sail to watch the ice buildup around the hull. Stand ready to take us down."

MacKenzie thought about the Soviet sub trapped in the ice. The Boomer's captain was surely back in the area now, searching for it. With the flick of a switch Mac knew he could turn on the locators and alert each to the other quickly enough. How many lives was he risking by choosing as he had? What were the Russians doing out here in these cold, silent waters that was so important?

MacKenzie hoped Norfolk had some answers.

Chapter Six

Chief of Naval Operations Admiral Benton Garver was wakened out of a sound sleep by the ringing of the phone in his comfortable bedroom at Tingey House in the Washington Navy Yard. He grabbed the receiver off the night table, coming awake fast, wanting to be ready if the news was really bad.

"Garver here."

It was his chief aide. "They've found *Red Dawn,* sir. Crash briefing in an hour. Code Zephyr Alpha."

He rubbed his jowly bulldog face to stir the blood. "Right. I'll be there."

Twenty minutes later a fully uniformed Garver kissed his sleeping wife good-bye and slipped out of the bedroom. He wanted a cup of coffee desperately, but it would have to wait till he got to the Pentagon. Garver shoved his beefy arms into the sleeves of his overcoat, rammed his cap down over his head, and grabbed his briefcase from the shelf beside the door. He stepped out into the freezing cold with a muttered curse.

His shoes crunched in the icy driveway as he walked to his waiting car. A smoky trail of exhaust spiraled up in the frigid air. Being CNO was the cap on a long and distinguished career, but nobody was going to convince him it wasn't a damn sight easier to get up facing the tropical sunshine of his former posting at Guantánamo Bay than to deal with this bullshit weather.

The Washington sky was just beginning to lighten, and Garver could see the Pentagon's gray bulk a few miles away as his car crossed the highway from Virginia to Washington. In a short while tens of thousands of clerks, typists, enlisted men and women, and officers from the five branches of the service—all the way up to the secretary of defense himself —would be streaming into the largest office building in the world. In fact, pedestrian traffic was so congested during the morning and afternoon rush hours that concrete ramps rather than stairs handled the tremendous traffic between floors.

Garver had a few minutes to collect his thoughts. So somebody had located the *Red Dawn*. Well, it was about time. They'd been looking for that damn sub for over a year, ever since the first reports came in to Central Intelligence. Speculation was rampant. It had a radical new weapon system, some said. It had an ultra-quiet propulsion system. It could fucking fly. Garver snorted. A million theories and no one knew shit.

And that made him angry.

Even after all this time he was still surprised by the infighting among agencies. There was conflict instead of cooperation, turf wars, appropriations battles—it made him sick. But that was the system and strangely enough, it managed to work more often than it didn't. He smiled, thinking about all the people who would be galvanized into action by the find. Things this morning would be interesting as hell. And the navy was in the catbird seat. If *Red Dawn* really had been located, then they were going to be managing things and Central Intelligence would have to like it or lump it.

Garver got out at the closest entrance and walked up to his office. He put his briefcase down beside his desk and hung his coat in the closet. Garver blessed his predecessors. The room had rich, conservative furnishings in nautical taste. The other offices in the building were endless variations on Institutional Modern—Formica tables, stainless-steel coffee urns, gray metal desks with bulky Selectric typewriters, fireproof file cabinets, and bulletin boards on green walls announcing blood drives, dances, due dates, and banking hours.

This early the CNO office was deserted but for Garver's red-haired aide, Captain Ferris. "Meeting's in ten minutes, sir. I have your papers."

"Very good, Frank," Garver said, leafing through them. Times, places, codes, and there was the transmission from *Seawolf,* signed Captain Peter MacKenzie. Garver grinned. Figured it would be MacKenzie. That son of a bitch had a knack for being in the right place at the right time. "Where's the meeting, Frank?"

"SECDEF's office, sir."

That raised Garver's thick eyebrows. *Red Dawn* had sure garnered the "A" treatment. He motioned to Ferris to go. "Let's not keep him waiting."

An armed marine was always posted in the corridor outside the office of the secretary of defense when the SECDEF was in attendance. Garver went in wishing he could light the first of his many daily cigars. Customs changed too damn often, he thought sadly. Years ago the air would have been thick with sharp, aromatic smoke. Now it was as clean as a baby's nursery. Shit.

Garver was the last to arrive. Secretary of Defense Paul Channing was already seated at the head of the mahogany conference table. Admiral Merton, the chairman of the Joint Chiefs was seated on his right, Bob Manson, the national security adviser on his left; white-haired Senator Halstead from the Senate Intelligence Committee next, and then a dark, well-groomed, middle-aged man in a gray business suit whom Garver didn't recognize but who seemed to be the focus of those present.

"Come on in, Ben," said Channing. "We're just about ready to start."

"Morning, sir. Admiral. Gentlemen," Garver said, taking his seat. "Hell of a morning, eh?"

"Freeze your balls off out there," Manson agreed.

"I used to walk five miles to school in weather like this," declared Senator Halstead. "Used to say it was colder than a witch's left tit. Damned if I ever knew why the right one was warmer." He glanced at his watch. "Paul, if we're all on board . . ."

Channing put his hands on the table. "Everyone's here. Let's get down to business. Gentlemen, this is Arthur Winestock of the Central Intelligence Agency. We've got something of a situation up at the North Pole, and Mr. Winestock has taken a major interest in it. Let me bring you up to speed, and then he can take over.

"For over a year our intelligence services have been tracking the progress of a Soviet scientific team headed by Dr. Karl Ligichev, Nobel Prize winner and chief physicist at the Kronsky Naval Institute. Now this is for your ears only. We are running a source close to the project, one of Ligichev's people. A year ago we got word from our source that Ligichev and his team made a breakthrough and were moving on to the prototype stage."

"What are they supposed to have accomplished?" asked Halstead.

"They've put together the first water jet drive capable of propelling a full-size ship," said Channing, "and installed it in a test ship, a diesel boat named the *Red Dawn*."

Admiral Merton had reservations. "Well, that's impressive, sure. I mean it'll give our ASW boys a real headache, but Japan is testing the same kind of system next year, and we could probably field one ourselves in two to three. Less if we run a crash program. If that's all *Red Dawn*'s got, frankly, I don't see what all the fuss is about."

"You're quite correct, Admiral. The propulsion system is secondary. The fuss is about something entirely different."

Winestock spoke for the first time. "We're after a part of the system. A new material that makes it work. If I may, Mr. Secretary?"

"Be my guest."

Winestock leveled his gunsight gaze at Merton. "Intelligence reports that Ligichev has invented a new compound he calls irinium. It's a perfect superconductor at thirty-two degrees Fahrenheit, several hundred degrees warmer than any other superconductor known to the West at present. We have nothing like it, no idea how to make it, no guess as to what it's composed of. But if you know anything about electronics, it just about as important as the invention of the transistor, the integrated circuit, and the microchip all rolled up together."

"We have more high-tech parks in my state than a dog has fleas," said Senator Halstead, "so I know a little something about superconductors. Christ, a material like that'd make for a revolution in almost every technical field—electronics, computers, telecommunications. Big Cray computers that have to be water cooled would be half the size and able to sort sound like the ASW boys never dreamed of."

"Dream's the right word," Winestock continued. "I'm not usually given to hyperbole, but the implications for our country, maybe even for the entire globe, are staggering. With this stuff you could build power plants a thousand miles from population centers and send the electricity back in superconducting wires without *any* loss of power. Giant arrays of solar panels on the equator could light the West Coast. You could put nuclear plants in the middle of the desert. And get this. Once the power is generated, superconducting rings could hold it indefinitely without any loss, ready for peak demand."

Winestock looked at the men around the table, reading their excitement. But he wasn't finished yet. "It gets even wilder. Miniature superconductor motors could power everything from refrigerators to toothbrushes, and they'd be a tenth the weight. Cars using light, ultra-efficient superconductor motors could be battery-powered, virtually eliminating the need for fossil fuels. Anyone seen the smog in L.A. lately? There'd be no pollution this way. Senator, how'd you like to take that news back to your constituency?"

"Don't joke. They'd nominate me for president on the spot. But why can't your source smuggle some of this stuff out or at least deliver the formula?"

"We've tried," Winestock admitted. "And failed. First, there's only a small quantity of irinium and it's guarded like the crown jewels. Second, this source absolutely cannot be compromised in any way. You're going to have to take my word for that."

"So this *Red Dawn* situation must have been the answer to your prayers," said Halstead.

"Let's just say a few hours ago I got religion again." Winestock grew sober. "Look, I'm all for being friendly as hell with the new Soviet Union, but irinium would give them strategic advantage in a dozen vitally important fields. I don't want *anybody* to have that. Bob?"

"No. There's agreement on that." Bob Manson, the president's national security adviser, unfolded his hands and leaned forward. "Let me come at it from another angle. Times are changing fast. We have to grapple with what the mission of the U.S. military may ultimately be. Sooner than anyone expects we could be pulling back from force readiness in most areas. Christ, our budget constraints will probably push disarmament faster than peace with the Russians will."

"Look at it this way," continued Manson. "In the not so distant future we stand to limit or lose two-thirds of the strategic triad when land-based missiles get treatied away and Stealth bombers get scrapped cause they cost too damn much. Then where will power lie? The answer is obvious— in the oceans. Sea-based forces, SLBMs and cruise missiles are undetectable, survivable, to some extent recallable, and for the most part quite cost-effective. Same thing holds true for the Soviets. In the end, submarine technology may be the key to national security."

"You know," said Halstead, "it's hard to be a hawk when the Warsaw Pact is breaking down before our eyes."

"Precisely why the Soviet military won't reduce their own armed forces," Manning responded. "For the conceivable future, they will remain the most formidable land force in the world. The KGB is more active than ever. So the president has authorized this mission as priority one. We have to have irinium to stay on a level playing field with the Russians."

"What's the Soviet response to all this?" asked Garver.

"So far, quiet," Winestock said. "According to the captain who found *Red Dawn*, the ballistic missile sub that was escorting her may not even know the real situation. That gives us a head start. And we'd better grab it, because the minute the Russians find out what's going on up there you better believe they're gonna send every sub they have under the ice."

Channing turned to Merton. "I know it's short notice, but considering what we stand to gain . . . Can do, Charlie?"

"Just a damn minute here, Paul," Admiral Merton said testily. He gestured to Winestock. "I don't mind telling you I am more than a little pissed off. At the DDI's request we've been looking for *Red Dawn* for almost a year now. We've chased everything from trash barges to goddamn dolphins. We've used an amazing amount of time and manpower searching the seas, and not once, not for one single solitary moment has the navy been taken into your confidence till now. How the hell do we know this isn't some Russian ruse to kick our butts up under the ice one more time?"

"There's the evidence of MacKenzie's tape," Winestock said calmly. "And we even think we have an explanation for what happened up there."

Merton was unmollified. "Which is?"

"Our source informed us there's a problem with heat buildup when irinium comes into direct contact with seawater. Our analysts constructed a scenario using this to explain *Red Dawn*'s penetration into the ice keel and her subsequent silence. See for yourself." He passed copies of a dark, bound document marked Top Secret to Merton and then to the others.

Merton put down the report. "So we've got a Russian sub stuck up to its ass in the North Polar ice cap with some stuff inside that we'd love to get our hands on. We appreciate the briefing a year late so that we could be completely without resources in the area. What do you expect us to do?"

"Simple," said Winestock. "Raise the *Red Dawn* and deliver us a sample of irinium. According to the experts, a pound will do quite nicely. And, yes, photographs of the propulsion system would be a pleasant bonus."

"Is that all? Ben, call Superman and see if he's busy, huh?"

"Easy, Charlie. We know we're asking a lot," soothed Channing. "You'll have every resource, believe me."

"At least it's *Seawolf* we've got up there. How good is your Captain MacKenzie?" asked Manson, the national security adviser.

"MacKenzie is the one bright spot in a tactically murderous situation," Merton said. "You remember the *Kirov* incident?"

"The stolen Russian sub? Sure. That was MacKenzie?"

"One and the same," Garver said. "He's the best we have. He's had combat experience and he's DSRV-qualified. And I'll tell you right now we're going to be needing a DSRV up there. Probably one of those new robot subs we built for salvage work, too."

Halstead looked up. "DSRV?"

"Deep submergence rescue vehicle," Garver explained. "We'll probably need it to evacuate *Red Dawn* and then maybe for some of the close-in work, too."

"I repeat," Channing said, "use whatever you need. Get it up there."

"We know Captain MacKenzie," said Winestock. "He's a superior field commander. In fact, this is remarkably good fortune for reasons I'll explain in a minute."

"What's our position legally?" asked Manson. "Do we have a right to salvage?"

"No, not actually," Winestock admitted. "The lawyers say government vessels are not subject to right-of-salvage. Remember when they discovered the *Bismarck* a few years back? Couldn't touch her. It's still up to the Germans. The *Titanic* was a merchant ship. That made her fair game."

"So even if we raise the sub we'll have to give it back?" asked Halstead.

Winestock's tone was cordial, like a snake before a bite. "Of course. And recognizing the new relationship between the two countries our hope is that your rescue attempt will succeed so *Red Dawn* and her surviving crew can be returned to our Russian friends"—Winestock's face lost its amiability and the man's steel core showed through—"minus one pound of irinium."

"I want one thing clear," Merton stated flatly. "If we go for *Red Dawn* this will be a navy operation. I don't know if we can do it or not, but one thing I won't stand for is a bunch of amateurs waving security directives at us while we're trying not to freeze our asses off or drown or whatever else there is to run into up there."

"We want liaison," insisted Winestock. "We have an interest."

"You have bullshit!" Merton exploded. "What the hell do you know about raising a downed sub?"

"Regardless, I want someone up there trained in intelligence matters running that part of the show," Winestock demanded.

Merton was ready to erupt again, but the CIA man held up his hand in a conciliatory gesture. "I think I have someone. A specialist, one you've both worked with before. Believe me, it all fits together quite nicely."

"Who's your man?"

"You're behind the times. It's a feminist world. If it's acceptable to you, we'd like to use Justine Segurra."

"MacKenzie's wife?" Garver exclaimed.

"That's right," responded Winestock. "She's one of us and we thought, well, given her relationship, she'd be acceptable to you."

"If I remember the *Kirov* situation correctly, the woman's a guerrilla fighter," said Merton.

"Among other things," Garver interjected. "Like having been, of all things, a concert pianist."

"It's a long way from the jungle to the Arctic, Mr. Winestock," said Senator Halstead.

"True, but Ms. Segurra moved out of Operations and into

Policy when she married Captain MacKenzie. She's been at Langley for over a year. She's got the rank and broad experience. What do you say, Admiral?"

The choice was a curve ball, but it seemed to sit well with Merton. "Do we agree the salvage is a navy operation?"

Winestock nodded. "Agreed."

Merton thought it over. "Ben?"

Garver's response was immediate. "Sir, I was at their wedding. I know Justine well and I trust her completely. She's a fighter, she has a working knowledge of subs, and she isn't going to get caught up in bureaucratic bullshit."

Merton nodded. "I accept the olive branch," he said to Winestock.

"Good," pronounced the secretary of defense. "It's settled, then."

Garver had heard enough. Compromises were the order of the day. Winestock had his agent in place, but it was a navy operation—the only way to guarantee professional management. Privately, Garver wondered if Merton was hoping that bedroom politics and Justine's being a navy wife would outweigh her Agency loyalty. He smiled. Clearly Merton didn't know Justine Segurra very well. But it wasn't his concern anymore. The objective was clear and urgent. MacKenzie's report said *Red Dawn* could be critically short of air and power. They had to get moving.

"Excuse me, sir," Garver addressed Merton directly. "I could probably be more useful getting things going . . ."

"Go ahead, Ben. I'll be there shortly."

"Gentlemen." Garver saluted and left the room. He was sure Merton would keep pressing till he got something for being kept in the dark. A couple of IOUs. Additional appropriations. Well, that was how the system worked.

He was already planning details of the operation as he walked back to his office. It was going to be terribly difficult. Under most circumstances raising a submarine was next to impossible, but at the North Pole in the dead of winter? He shuddered. Besides, the book on how to get a sub out of solid ice hadn't been written yet.

"Sure, raise the *Red Dawn*. Just like that," he snapped his fingers, muttering as he walked. A thought hit him. "You know, I should've asked Winestock. Maybe the goddamn CIA's *got* Superman's number."

Chapter
Seven

Akula

Kalik's eyes were bleary from staring at the screens hour after hour searching for *Red Dawn*. Sonar was picking up nothing. Radio had drawn a blank. Kalik had tried every search pattern, every trick in the book, to find the missing sub, even active sonar. If the Americans hadn't been out of the area it would have given away *Akula*'s presence a dozen times over. The sonar did no good. In the end he had to admit to himself that the search was futile.

Kalik had never composed a communication to Naval Command with less relish than the one he sent informing them *Red Dawn* was missing. He continued the search while waiting for their response. Command would surely demand an explanation as to why he had disobeyed orders and left *Red Dawn*. The only way to forestall that inquiry was to find the sub. He was having difficulty facing the fact that he could tell them nothing. He had no ideas. Had the sub sunk? How could he know? There was a mile of ocean under them, and *Red Dawn's* crush depth was only a fraction of that. It was maddening to think they might never find out what had happened. Sure, there was still a chance *Red Dawn* was disabled somewhere, maybe even caught in an ice cavern unable to surface or withdraw. Under those circumstances it could be rescued. But none of that explained the ship's total silence. And it had a limited air supply that was dwindling every second. Maddening.

The navigator, under instructions to find a place to surface, suddenly called out, "Comrade Captain, open water ahead. Two hundred meters."

Kalik glanced at the screen and saw it. "Right ten degrees rudder," he ordered. Well, it was time to pay the piper. "Engine Room. All stop. Prepare to surface. Radio Officer, raise the masts as soon as we clear the ice."

Akula broke through the surface into cold Arctic waves. Kalik scanned the area through the periscope. Jagged hills of sullen white ice surrounded the tiny patch of open water. The sky overhead was overcast, as gray as the freezing water.

As soon as the mast was up, the radio officer turned to Kalik, "Comrade Captain, incoming message."

Kalik had known there would be one. He accepted the paper and read the message carefully.

Volkov moved to his captain's side. The news wouldn't be good. No one gave you medals for losing submarines. "Vassily? What do they say?"

"The tone is as cold as the ice around us, Viktor. The gist of it is that other ships have been dispatched but none are close enough to be of any immediate help in the search, so the responsibility for *Red Dawn* is ours. Given estimates of her air supply, we have two days to find her. Then the other ships will be here and we are to return home. To face a court-martial, I imagine."

"Two days. What can we do?"

Kalik saw his senior lieutenant's crestfallen expression and clapped him on the back. "Relax, my friend. A world can be won in two days. We don't have to slink home just yet. And besides," he added, "there's only one head to chop. Mine."

"That's not a comfort."

"Let's have some coffee. We will talk. Maybe we can see together what I cannot see alone."

Seawolf

MacKenzie leaned quietly against the sonar console. Lieutenant Kurstan put the sound over the loudspeaker. The active sonar pings *Seawolf*'s sensors were picking up were as regular as clockwork.

"He's back, Skipper," said Kurstan. "And running a search pattern. He's looking for something. Not being very quiet about it, either."

"He figures he lost us. My bet is he's looking for *Red Dawn.*"

"Could be, sir. He's in the shallow zone. Course one eight zero. He speeds up to twenty knots, stops, searches, then runs fast again to a new sector."

"Can we correlate the signature yet?"

Kurstan shook his head. "Still no luck, Skipper. That's the quietest damn Russian sub we ever laid ears on. The computers are working overtime on this one. We've got a few more bytes, but it still doesn't add up. As soon as it does . . ."

MacKenzie smiled dryly. "I know. You'll call me."

"You'll be the first, sir."

Akula

Two hours had passed and they were no closer to an answer.

"'I have measured out my life with coffee spoons,'" Kalik observed, tapping one against the table as the steward removed the latest round of empty mugs. "That's T. S. Eliot. Did you know that, Viktor?"

"No." Volkov was tired and frustrated. "No, I did not. A writer?"

"A poet. A great poet. American. You like poetry?"

"Only if it rhymes. The rest confuses me. As do Americans."

"Understanding Americans is quite simple if you remember one thing, Viktor: they truly believe God loves them."

"Does he?"

"There are times," Kalik said with a sigh, "when I believe he does."

"Well, you fooled the Americans before easily enough."

"I . . ." Kalik stopped. "You know, Viktor. We've gone at this thing from every angle except one."

"Which is?"

"Maybe I *didn't* fool the American captain." Kalik hit his head with his hand angrily. "I'm getting old, Viktor. So set in my ways. It is like the fable of Comrade Elephant and the new dress."

"There are facets of your education that astound me, Vassily. Enlighten me, please."

Kalik leaned back. "Comrade Elephant goes into a store—a Party store naturally—and tries on a new hat. It is horrible. It makes her look like—well, like an elephant. But the clerk flatters her and tells her she looks beautiful, so Comrade Elephant buys it. As soon as she goes out on the street, several passersby laugh and point. Adoration, thinks Comrade Elephant. Others shake their heads and frown. Envy, thinks Comrade Elephant. Viktor, too often we see and hear what we want to. In all this time we have never considered that maybe I am Comrade Elephant and perhaps the clever American captain was not fooled at all."

"But he followed us. We heard him."

"Yes, we did. We heard him at regular intervals, just as we were supposed to. Fifty miles, a hundred miles. But did we ever hear him again? Christ, I am a stupid man only now beginning to see the light."

"You think he broke off? And did what?"

"He came right back here. He guessed we were decoying him away, and he doubled back."

"Then he got back here before we did," said Volkov, seeing the logic. "And if he did . . ."

"He knows we're here. And he might also know what happened to *Red Dawn*. Christ, he's been listening to our search."

Volkov shrugged. "We can't ask him where *Red Dawn* is."

Kalik shook his head excitedly. "Of course not, but this presents a whole different problem, one with a potential solution, for a change. We aren't looking for *Red Dawn*. We're looking for the American sub that will lead us to *Red Dawn*."

"I don't know, Vassily. So many if's . . ."

"Too many," Kalik agreed, "but what is the alternative? Scour the ocean floor for wreckage to send home? Come, Viktor. Now we have something to look for." He rose quickly to his feet, suddenly back in control. "And if our very clever American captain makes just one little mistake, we will be back in the game."

Seawolf

The communications officer looked up as the hot printer began to chatter, discharging the reply from Naval Command in its original coded form. He pressed a button, electronically rerouting the message through the cipher machine and the secondary printer and handed it to MacKenzie, who read it quickly.

"Take a look, Tom." MacKenzie handed it to his XO.

TOP SECRET
FR: COMSUBLANT
TO: USS *SEAWOLF*

1. U.S. INTENTION TO RAISE THE *RED DAWN*.
2. *SEAWOLF* TO REMAIN ON STATION AS COMMAND POST.
3. OPERATION MANAGER ARRIVING EN ROUTE. C-130, GEORGIA ONE.
4. BRIEFING FOR MACKENZIE, ETC., UPON ARRIVAL.
5. RESCUE TEAM FOLLOWS.
6. WELL DONE, *SEAWOLF*. GOOD LUCK.

(S) GARVER, ADM, CNO.

"Raise the *Red Dawn*. Wow." Lasovic whistled. "Command's got some pretty big ideas. Think it can be done?"

"It won't be easy, but if Garver is in on this, it's bound to be creative." MacKenzie chuckled. "We'll know more when their man gets here."

"He'd better be quick if they expect to get the crew out alive. You figure that's what this is all about?"

"I doubt it," said MacKenzie, suddenly reflective. *"Red Dawn* wasn't out here on any regular cruise. Look at the way the Boomer is behaving. I'm not impugning our concern for life, but everything about this sub is unusual. I think this is more than just a simple rescue mission."

"Where does that leave us?"

"On alert. For now let's get ready to receive our guest."

Polar Ice Cap

Pilot Mick Halperin fought to stay on course in the high Arctic winds that were buffeting his aircraft. He had only one passenger, a special delivery he'd picked up in Fairbanks, who was now staring out the cockpit window with a disturbed expression that Mick didn't have to be a mentalist to read.

Ten thousand feet below the warm interior of the C-130 military transport was the ice cap's compassionless frozen wasteland. Wind-driven snow obscured everything but the highest, sharpest pressure ridges. Temperature on the surface was minus ten degrees. Mick fought a sharp gust and fed power to the engines, raising the noise level in the cabin considerably.

Mick had invited his passenger to come forward and sit in the copilot's seat when his copilot went back to get the drop load ready. He'd been told nothing about his passenger or the reason for the priority flight up here. He had simply been rerouted from his regular duties and ordered to make a nonstop pickup and an even faster hop to the pole. It was unusual, but Mick had been ferrying for a long time and didn't ask about things that didn't concern him. That included his passengers' missions and the deeply tanned skin visible under this one's heavy down parka, which spoke of recent habitation in far warmer climes. Flying, that's what he knew. There wasn't a square inch of the desolate ice cap that he hadn't landed on or flown over.

"It looks awfully cold down there." His passenger sighed.

"You got that right." Mick smiled. "First time up here?"

"Does it show?"

"Well, you got what we taxi jocks call the how-can look."

"How can?"

"How can there be so much goddamn ice in one fucking place?"

The passenger had a good laugh, full and hearty, and it warmed the cabin. She extended her hand. "Justine Segurra."

Mick took it. A strong hand, firm. Not masculine, but confident. "Mick Halperin. Pleased to meet you."

"It can't be as bad down there as it looks. Can it?"

Mick mimicked a real estate salesman. "Well, you got your long periods of total darkness, dense fog, storms, and freezing temperatures. On the bright side, you got no neighbors and you'll never run out of ice. By the way, if they didn't tell you, permanent addresses are in short supply 'cause all that ice is moving due to the wind and the undersea currents."

"But you can get one helluva house for the money, huh?"

It was Mick's turn to laugh. "Make sure you check the insulation."

The copilot poked his head into the cabin. "Mick. Ten minutes to the drop point." He leaned close to Justine. "We've got your gear loaded and your chute packed. Ready when you are, ma'am."

"On my way. Appreciate the lift, Captain."

"Mick, okay?"

"Thanks, Mick."

"Any time. Safe landing. Oh, one sec. Forgot to give you this. Came by special pouch. Eyes only."

Justine slipped the envelope inside her nylon parka. "Thanks again."

The copilot took his seat, and Justine moved to the back of the plane. There the jumpmaster had lashed the tarpaulin-covered crates together with heavy netting. He pointed. "These go first. You jump on the second pass. Use the beeper when you hit. It'll lead you right to them."

"Gotcha."

"You ready for this, ma'am?"

"Honestly? No."

The jumpmaster grinned. "That's the spirit."

Justine's white nylon parka and trousers were cinched at ankles and wrists and worn over a special body suit and insulated undergarments. Her goggles were darkened to prevent snow blindness. The heavy parka fit snugly into a jumpsuit. The jumpmaster helped her into the parachute harness and attached it to the jump line.

A buzzer sounded and an overhead lamp flashed yellow. "Get the hatch open," he ordered. His men slid the door back, and a bitter, howling wind filled the cabin. The jumpmaster patted her on the back. "Show time."

Justine nodded in spite of genuine fear. She was fighting for control, and it was a point of pride to her not to show it. The men respected her silence. Nobody jumped into that mess below without fear. The really brave ones just shut up about it.

The buzzer sounded again, and this time the light flashed green. The men shoved the crates out the hatch. The parachute billowed open.

"Okay, ma'am. We're coming around fast."

Justine muttered a truly heartfelt prayer, and when the buzzer sounded again she took a last look out the hatch into the face of heaven, yanked her face shield into place, and stepped out into space. There was nothing left to do but fall. The crates, distant by now, tumbled below her in what seemed like slow motion in the screaming wind. Then the jump line jerked her chute open and she dropped in a long, fast swing to the ice cap below.

"Sonar, Conn. Is the captain there?" It was Lasovic.

MacKenzie leaned over and hit the intercom. "Here, Tom. What's up?"

"Message from Captain Halperin, pilot of a C-130 just about right over us. The party we're expecting just left the plane. Wants us to know the wind is a real mother out there. Visibility's way down cause of the snow. Tough for our pickup."

MacKenzie thought for a moment. The ice pressure around *Seawolf* was tolerable but increasing. It would help if they could speed things up a bit. "Break out the cold-weather gear and take a shore party to meet him. I want to be out of here within the hour, Tom."

"Okay, Skipper."

He wondered who they were sending. Poor bastard. MacKenzie himself had no qualms about spending months hundreds of feet underwater or diving over a mile deep in a tiny DSRV, but jumping out of an airplane several thousand feet up onto the polar ice cap—Jesus, *that* took balls.

Lasovic stuck his head into the sonar room. "We've got a fix on the homing signal. I'm heading out."

"Good hunting. Keep us informed by radio."

A few minutes later Joe Santiago called in to say the snowstorm was worsening. Visibility was way down and the light was going fast.

MacKenzie hit the intercom again. "Chief, cut in communications to the bridge and get me a cold suit. I'm going up top."

Ten degrees below zero, MacKenzie mused. Bring in your brass monkeys.

Polar Ice Cap

The ground came up faster than Justine expected, and the impact took her breath away. She slid on the ice and fell trying to get her footing. The wind took up the billowing chute. She found the breakaway catch and released it. Visibility was poor because of the swirling snow, but locating the crates proved easy with the beeper. They had landed only a few hundred feet away.

Looking around, she found it hard to imagine a more desolate place. The endless white plain was broken only by low, sharp, lunarlike crests. She shivered. Life itself was unwelcome here. The cold wasn't just some minor annoyance. It tore at you, slapping you hard across the face. Drops of moisture froze on her cheeks like a collection of tiny diamonds.

Justine had grown up in the jungles and high plateaus of Central America. Life there was rich, fecund. This was an alien place, a canvas that had no color. It lacked brush strokes and form and substance. Where were the blues and greens? What about animal noises and the rich smell of dark earth and the insect hordes that burrowed incessantly within it? She fervently hoped Mac's sub was close by. Freezing to death in this white haze was a distinct possibility.

She had nothing to worry about. The homing device lit up and beeped contentedly the moment she turned it on. The sub was indeed near, over in that direction, beyond a group of low ice hills. She could remain here and wait for a party to be sent out to her. "The hell with it," she muttered. "After that jump, I need a bathroom too badly to wait."

She trudged to the crates, feeling the crunch of the snow under her feet. Snowshoes and ski poles and a backpack were neatly tucked between the crates. Two small tubes, each containing a weather balloon complete with transmitter, were taped beneath the tarp. She fished one out and hit the trigger on the gas cartridge. A silver foil balloon attached to a wire line fixed to the crates inflated and shot up into the sky. She hoped it would be visible from a distance. She slipped the other tube into the backpack, struggled into it, and slipped on the snowshoes.

The arctic clothing was a miracle of lightweight protection. With the hood up, the face shield in place, and the goggles down over her eyes she could withstand the cold. She tested the snowshoes and found walking in them fairly easy. The hills beckoned; the warmth of the sub was just beyond them. She figured by now Mac had sent men to get her, probably led by Tom Lasovic. Should she wait or head off? She shivered. It was an easy decision.

The wind was rising and it was getting hard to see. She moved out into the rising snow to meet them.

Red Dawn

Wet and hot. That's how the interior of the sub still felt. Ligichev had figured the temperature curve. It didn't look promising. At the rate the ice was bleeding heat out of the ship, they had a day till the temperature dropped back into a comfortable range and then plunged into deadly cold. For now, since they were unable to vent the ship, moisture dripped from glass gauge covers. A slime of oily water lay on the steel deck, making it treacherous to walk on. Men wrung out their shirts and hung them over hot pipes, and tendrils of steam rose from the sodden cloth.

In the control room, Galinin pulled out from under the main console and shook his head tiredly. They had been at it for twelve hours but were no closer to restoring communications. Air supplies were also perilously low. But how the hell did you send up a snorkel through solid ice? Galinin smiled humorlessly. Freeze to death or die of asphyxiation. Talk about a rock and a hard place.

Ligichev entered the control room. "I need to talk to you."

Galinin nodded. Emergency lighting cast a dim glow in the corridor. He followed the scientist to the mess where the steward, clad only in an undershirt and trousers, handed him a cup of hot coffee. Galinin raised an eyebrow in query when he felt the heat.

The man understood. "Candles, Comrade Captain."

Ligichev sat down heavily in the booth. A red-brown scab had formed over his right eye, and he looked pale. "Comrade Captain, we must accept the fact that we are alone and unable to communicate with *Akula* or any other ship. Under the present conditions we have less than two days to live. Thus, desperate measures are called for."

Galinin took a sip and felt the warmth spill down his parched throat. "I'll try anything with the slightest chance of success."

"Good. First, we must have air. Without that precious commodity all our efforts will come to naught. I have done some thinking. There may be a way."

"How?"

"Tell me. Can a torpedo tube be opened at both ends?"

"Sure, if you care to flood the torpedo room and sink the sub." Galinin looked as if he were talking to an idiot child. "Open the tube to the sea, of all the . . ." He stopped, his expression suddenly changing. "Christ, but you wouldn't, would you? There's no water out there. I mean, none that would flood in."

"That's what I suddenly realized," agreed Ligichev. "The tube is blocked by ice. We are in a completely new situation, one that calls for new thinking. If we opened both ends of the tube, the ice would be accessible to us and we could tunnel our way into the very keel that holds us."

"Assume it could be done. What then?"

"Your men tell me the torpedoes themselves are wire-guided. Do I understand that correctly—an actual wire trails from the sub to the torpedo as it travels through the water?"

Galinin nodded. "We can maneuver the torpedo from the control room till its sensors pick up the target. Then it homes in and destroys it."

"Could something be attached to this wire? It would have to be quite a ways behind the torpedo."

Galinin inclined his head thoughtfully. "Something like a small, temporary snorkel? Yes. Yes, I think it could. By God, I see what you have in mind."

Ligichev continued. "If we tunnel through the ice till there's only a foot or so left why couldn't we fire a torpedo right through it out into open sea with the snorkel towed behind? Then we could direct it up at the ice cover, blow a hole in it, and the snorkel will float naturally to the surface. I first thought of tunneling straight up to the surface, but we have no idea how far down we are or how thick the ice is overhead, and a vertical shaft of any length seems impractical at best. It's shorter to the outer edge of the ice keel."

"I've never heard of anyone trying anything like it, but then again, no one's ever been in this situation before. It just might work," said Galinin, enthusiasm growing. "My hat's off to you, Comrade. We'll have to improvise the entire mechanism, and the torpedo will have to pack a big punch to break through so much ice, but it might just be possible."

Ligichev shrugged tiredly. "Unfortunately, a whole host of things might prevent it from working. A charge sufficient to blow a hole in the ice might also destroy the snorkel or, worse, split the very ice keel we are embedded in and send us all to the bottom of the ocean. But we have to try something."

"How are you coming with the engines?"

"We're working on them. Ivanna is trying to salvage enough parts from both machines to get one going. If she does, it could provide power to the batteries for heating."

Galinin's hopes were evident. "Heat *and* air. We'll get out of this ice castle yet. Comrade Chief Scientist, you have made me a happy man."

"If it works," cautioned Ligichev. "I wouldn't count on things too quickly."

"Come now," the captain said happily. "Don't be such a pessimist."

Ligichev's smile was as dry as the tabletop between them

was wet. "On the contrary, Comrade Captain. A pessimist thinks ill because he does not see the world as it is," he said. "I'm an optimist. I know how bad things really are. Get your men and we'll begin."

Polar Ice Cap

Justine tried to ignore the panic rising within her, but she finally had to admit she was lost. The shrieking, howling wind was driving a blizzard that obscured the land and the sky and made everything look alike. The homing device had to be malfunctioning, because it glowed in every direction. She shouted into the wind, but the sound was swallowed up in the noisy gusts.

She kept walking. Her tracks were obliterated almost as soon as her snowshoes left the ground, so she had no way to trace her path back to the crates and wait for rescue. She cursed the Arctic. In the jungle at least you could climb a tree and look around to find out where you were. Here there was nothing. No landmarks, no way to judge distance. Just an endless swirling snowstorm and cold white ice.

She felt the first touch of cold bite at her extremities. It startled her, like the first time she was in the woods at night far from the light of her rebel group's campfires. That was when she had understood what night was, how black it could be. She was only now beginning to understand the cold here. It could kill you.

She walked on. She was getting tired. God, the wind was incessant. She stopped. Just wandering around in circles was going to exhaust her. Where were the hills she had spotted from the crates? She saw a dark shape briefly at the periphery of her vision. It was barely visible through the storm; then it was gone, obscured by the snow. It had to be the sub. She tried not to run from relief. To run was to stumble. Go slowly. She felt the ground sloping upward under her feet. There, ahead, she could make out something.

She climbed the ridge. These had to be the hills she had seen before. The sub would be just beyond them. But then she looked down and saw something on the ground that clutched her heart with hands colder than the air around her.

With a sinking feeling, Justine realized she was not alone.

Seawolf

MacKenzie was standing in the sail and the storm was all around him. He pulled the hood of his fur-lined parka tighter around his head and lifted the binoculars to his eyes again.

"Skipper?" Tom Lasovic's voice came through the headset. "We found the crates, but there's no sign of our pickup. Snow's wiping everything out."

MacKenzie scanned the ice but saw nothing. "He's supposed to have a homing device."

"Sure, but it won't be the first thing not to work the way it's supposed to up here," came Lasovic's voice. "Can you see anything?"

"Nothing, Tom. Get back here. We'll have to organize a quadrant search."

"Okay, coming in."

MacKenzie was worried. The pressure of the packed ice around *Seawolf* was steadily increasing. Large chunks were already stacked up against the sail. They couldn't stay here much longer without risking being frozen in. MacKenzie pursed his lips grimly, well aware that submerging would be tantamount to passing a death sentence on the pickup. He could never survive out here without *Seawolf*'s refuge.

He spoke into his throat mike. "Mr. Randall, you are relieved of your station. Assemble a second party and mount a search. Guy yourselves to the ship. If I want you back, it's going to be in a hurry."

"Aye, Skipper. On my way."

MacKenzie wiped the snow from his goggles and looked over the side. More ice. And the driven snow was like mortar between the bricks. Whoever Garver sent better get here soon. Very soon.

Polar Ice Cap

Justine heard it before she saw it. Suddenly there was a roar like nothing she had ever heard before and it sent primordial chills up her spine. She bolted, running back down the ridge before conscious reason could stop her. It was the wrong move. She tripped and sprawled forward, losing one of her ski poles. As she twisted around to recover it, a massive shape reared up behind her, snarling and growling. The terror of it paralyzed her. Transfixed, she watched it rise higher and higher till it reached fully fourteen feet and the sheer monstrosity of it froze her to that spot like a pin through an insect on a specimen board.

The polar bear stood fully erect on its hind legs. Its slavering mouth was drawn back to reveal sharp yellow teeth. It threw its head back into the wind and roared again, the king of its domain. It wove back and forth, the claws of its powerful forelegs slicing the air. A thousand pounds of white fury moved a step closer to her with muzzle wide open and teeth ready to rend and suddenly it dropped toward her like an avalanche.

Justine was close enough to see the stiff bristles on its paws. Panic had frozen her brain, but she was fighting for her life and her combat-trained reflexes took over instinctively. As the polar bear attacked she thrust her remaining ski pole with all her strength at the bear's mighty chest. She had time only to feel the point bite home as a miasma of hot breath and the fetid smell of rotten fish engulfed her. Then she was rolling aside, plunging the rest of the way down the hill, landing in a heap. She struggled to right herself as the bear howled more in surprise and irritation than in pain, and stumbled into a run.

The bear went down on all fours shaking its massive body from side to side, trying to dislodge the ski pole sticking out of its bleeding chest. Angry red eyes sought the source of its torment. With a mighty shake of its torso the bear dislodged the pole and roared angry defiance to the wind. It fixed its eyes on its prey, but this time it was warier. The prey had sharp teeth of its own. It rumbled forward, picking up speed. The red eyes seemed to glow.

Justine ran, not even pausing to wipe the snow off her goggles or risk a look back. She climbed slipping and sliding up a hill, plunged over the top, and skidded down the other side without concern for anything but escaping the monster behind her. She felt the vibrations from its weight on the ice through the soles of her feet, felt it pounding after her, taking the hillock with huge strides. The hardest thing she had ever done was to stop and force herself to search through her backpack till she found it. Food. Wrapped in foil bags. She spread it over the snow, hoping the bear would stop to eat it.

Then she ran for her life.

Seawolf

"Skipper!" It was Tom Lasovic's voice. "Maybe something. Closer to you than to us. Two hundred yards off the starboard bow. I can't be sure with all this snow. Can you verify?"

MacKenzie swung the binoculars around quickly. It was difficult to see, but someone was coming fast over the hills between him and the ship. As MacKenzie watched, the man slid over a summit and down the next slope. His legs were pumping and his arms flailing to keep his balance. He fell, only to rise again and continue running. What was driving him?

"I've got him, Tom. Head to him. Mr. Randall, you, too.

Converge on that spot. One five zero yards—zero five zero north of *Seawolf*. Looks like he's in trouble."

"Aye, Skipper."

"Chief, bring me a sidearm and some men. On the double. Meet me at the forward hatch."

"Right, sir. Coming up."

MacKenzie clambered down the sail ladder to the deck. He didn't need the binoculars to see that the man was running at full speed, and what MacKenzie saw charging after him removed all doubt as to why. The polar bear was a good distance behind but closing quickly. Lasovic was too far away to help. So was Randall. He'd have to leave the ship himself. He spoke through his headset. "Mr. Santiago, you have the conn. Watch the ice and get the hell out of here fast if you have to."

"Aye, Skipper."

The hatch was flung open and two crewmen scampered out. The chief of the boat himself followed, a grizzled old seaman everyone called Casey. He pressed a .45 into MacKenzie's gloved hand. MacKenzie didn't have to explain anything. A roar reached them and all eyes turned instantly to the spectacle of the man running for his life from the huge white bear.

"Check your clips and move out," MacKenzie ordered, and they hit the ice running.

Justine surmounted the crest of the last hill and saw the sub, but it was too late. She heard a thundering tread and then the bear hit her from behind and sent her sprawling with one swipe of its huge paw. The impact tore the breath from her and ripped the backpack open. It cushioned her from the sharp claws and prevented the blow from slicing her open like a ripe fruit.

She tumbled down the slope and lay dazed at the bottom, flat on her back amid the things spilled from the pack. She couldn't move, but it didn't matter now. Things were warmer. Farther away. The noise of the wind wasn't so loud, and the snow was a pleasant blanket slowly covering her. Long ago her father had had a blue satin down comforter on his bed. She and her brothers had often snuggled under it before the revolution forced them all to become soldiers. The snow was like that now. She heard voices calling to her from a distance, like the voices in dreams. She tried to force her arms and legs to move. They wouldn't.

The bear stood on its hind legs and roared its conquest. The crimson stain on its chest was larger now. Drops of blood fell onto the snow and froze into tiny rubies. Its prey was helpless before it. The huge jaws opened.

Justine closed her eyes.

The first shots hurt the bear less than a swarm of angry bees, but they distracted it. It looked around angrily. Men were approaching. It roared fiercely and slashed at the air. MacKenzie put his sights on the bear and pulled the trigger again. The .45 bucked in his hand, and he saw his bullet hit home. But the monster just shrugged it off and stood there weaving angrily over the fallen body as it studied the new threats arrayed against it.

"Circle it," MacKenzie yelled. "Watch those claws."

One of the crewmen charged in bravely, weapon firing, hoping to get the man out while the bear was distracted by the others.

"Wait," warned MacKenzie. "Not yet. Stay back."

The warning came too late. The bear's paws flashed out and knocked the man off his feet. Its claws sliced through the parka. Massive jaws clamped down on the crewman's leg and he screamed in pain. Casey ran in to drag his fallen mate away, but the bear dropped to all fours and bowled him over. Casey was trapped under the bear. With a last-ditch effort he managed to lever the muzzle of his gun under the big torso and pull the trigger.

The explosion was deafening. The bear shrieked in agony and rolled off, eyes glowing madly with rage and pain. A black powder burn scarred the white fur alongside the red. Mac and the others pulled Casey and the crewman away as the bear rolled on the ground rubbing the burn in the snow to ease the pain.

MacKenzie shoved his gun into a pocket and raced to the fallen pickup. The chest rose and fell weakly but there seemed to be life in the body. The contents of his pack were strewn about the ice. MacKenzie made no effort to collect the things. He got his arms under the limp body. The bear's claws had torn long gashes in the nylon parka. MacKenzie stood up, surprised at the lack of weight.

"Skipper, watch out!"

Taking his eyes off the bear had been a serious mistake, and MacKenzie barely had time to regret it as the animal, sensing the theft of his prey, turned and blasted into him like a freight train. He'd never felt such raw power. He went down hard, and the man was flung from his arms. The bear slashed at him, and MacKenzie felt his parka being sliced open. Frigid wind seared his chest. The smell of fish made him gag. He got his hands under the bear's muzzle and pushed with all his strength to keep those deadly teeth away from his face.

The bear bit and slashed. MacKenzie was thrown from side to side wrestling with the animal to keep it from him. He needed a weapon, any weapon. He couldn't find his gun. He heard weapons firing, even felt the impact of the slugs through the bear's body, but nothing short of a cannon was going to kill this creature. The bear shook off the slugs with a toss of his massive head and bit for his exposed neck. MacKenzie fought with all his strength. He felt the teeth right through the parka. His hand searched in the snow for anything to use against this monster. He felt the objects that had spilled from the pack. He heard his men shouting.

His fingers closed on the tube containing the weather balloon. There was a red haze in front of his eyes. He tried to concentrate. The bear was no weaker, and MacKenzie was fading fast, but suddenly the tube clarified itself like a TV picture suddenly tuned in. With his last ounce of fading strength MacKenzie shoved it in between the bear's drooling jaws and pressed the trigger.

Deep in the bear's throat the balloon inflated with a rush of gas. It rolled off MacKenzie tearing at the offending object but could do nothing to dislodge it. It rammed its muzzle into the ground. It rolled onto its back. It roared with what was now a sickly wheeze and rambled off. The balloon would dislodge in time. MacKenzie managed to raise himself. He knew he was bleeding. He felt warm, sticky fluid coursing down inside his clothing. He crawled over to the fallen pickup and pushed the face mask aside to check his pulse. Let him live, he prayed. Don't let all this be for nothing.

Nothing could have been more of a shock than the face that stared up at him. "Justine? My God, how—"

He rubbed her leaden limbs and covered her face with his, breathing warm air to keep her skin from freezing. "On the double. Over here," he shouted.

"We're here, Skipper." It was Tom Lasovic beside him.

"Tom, it's Justine. Help her. And remember the ice." He was mumbling and he knew it. "Pressure. Gotta watch the ship."

"It's okay, Mac. We'll get it."

MacKenzie felt himself lifted and carried forward. Justine was carried, too. Good. Tom would be in charge. He could sleep soon. He had a sudden thought that his wife would tell him how stupid it was to go up against a polar bear with a handgun and a weather balloon. She was probably right.

"She'll be okay, Mac. Don't worry. Her pulse is strong."

MacKenzie heard the steel clang of *Seawolf*'s deck under their feet. Lasovic grabbed MacKenzie's headset from where he'd left it. "This is the XO. Prepare to take her down. Secure all hatches. Dive, dive!"

From far away MacKenzie heard the dive Klaxons blaring. He made a mental note to kill the dumb bastard who'd sent his wife up here. Then they lowered him into *Seawolf* and he surrendered to the darkness that rose up and engulfed him.

Chapter Eight

MacKenzie woke up thinking he'd had a bad dream about Justine being attacked by polar bears. Then he saw the dressing on his forearm and felt a pain that ran from his wrist to his elbow. Memory came flooding back as sharp as one of Justine's karate kicks.

He rolled out of his bunk—and almost broke a leg, because he wasn't in his own cabin but Tom Lasovic's, and in the top bunk at that. He landed on wobbly knees. There. Okay. He needn't have worried. Justine was sleeping peacefully on the lower bunk.

"Honey?"

He knew better than to startle her awake, although she was less likely to attack him now, after two years of marriage. She was beautiful in repose, her raven black hair thick and lustrous and her skin so clear it was almost translucent. She was classically beautiful with aristocratic Spanish features and a fine figure that had called to him from the very first. She was tough and smart, and he hadn't believed in love at first sight till he met her. Two years of marriage hadn't changed that. What had changed was that she was softer now than when they had first met. A lot of the pain of her childhood had been put to rest. She had lost one brother but found another. They had a home now, children someday. But reflexes died hard. He called to her softly.

"Justine?"

She mumbled something, coming up fast through the stages of sleep. She woke fast, as always. Her eyes opened and he saw old familiar fears rise in them for a moment—that the Somocistas were attacking, that she and her brothers would have to make another border crossing, that it was time to douse the fires and fight—but the fears faded, quicker now than ever before. She saw him.

"Mac? Oh, thank God. Are you all right? That bear . . . I thought I was going to die."

"You're not the only one." He reached out and she came into his arms. "Christ, I'm glad to see you."

"Where are we?"

MacKenzie pointed to the pictures of Tom Lasovic's family on the dresser. "We're on *Seawolf,* in Tom's quarters. Christ, Justine, I didn't have any idea you were the one they sent."

She chuckled. "In that case, aren't you glad you gave it your best effort? Actually, it was Ben Garver who sent me. You can blame his sense of humor. He figured it would be a surprise."

"It sure was," he said sincerely.

He felt her relax. She had that capacity. When the fighting was over she could leave it behind as if it had never happened. All on or all off. That was Justine. He told her about Tom Lasovic's spotting her, the fight with the bear, and the lucky use of the weather balloon.

"The last thing I remember," she said, "was getting hit from behind. Animal rights aside, I hope that damn bear has a helluva time digesting the balloon."

"Better it than you. Or me," MacKenzie said with feeling. "So tell me. How come they sent you?"

"I was a bureaucratic compromise. *Red Dawn*'s a navy mission, but the Agency has the highest stake. I guess both sides figured I'd take their interests to heart." She looked around. "So this is *Seawolf,* eh? The other woman I've been hearing about for the past two years."

94

"She's an amazing ship, Justine. I can't wait to show her to you."

"Won't she be jealous? After all, it's kind of like having two wives."

"Don't laugh. Your being here is an entirely new situation, one I'm sure is unique in navy annals."

"I don't think so. I remember reading where British navy captains got to take their wives along on long trips like to Tahiti and the New World."

"You figure the North Pole qualifies?"

Justine grinned. "Sure do."

MacKenzie picked up the intercom. "Conn, this is the captain. Where's Mr. Lasovic?"

"Right here, Skipper," came the familiar voice. "Glad you're up. No one wanted to call the honeymoon suite before now."

Mac sighed. It was only the first of many barbs to come. "Belay that. Give me a status report."

"We're cruising at three zero zero feet, on track around *Red Dawn*'s position. Our Russian friend's gone quiet. He may have left."

"I doubt it."

"In any event, we're listening for him."

"How's the crew?"

"Casey has a few scratches. Seaman Mitchel will be in bed for about a week, but he'll keep the leg. Other than that, all okay."

"See that both are written up for commendations. Send them my personal thanks. I'll be by later."

"Skipper, the medic would like to know how Justine's back is. He did his best with the wounds. All things considered, he says, she was lucky. They aren't that deep."

Justine heard. She tensed her muscles experimentally, then flashed Mac a thumbs up.

"No problem. All right. Briefing in the wardroom in half an hour. You and all the division heads. Mr. Randall, too."

"Right, Skipper. Half an hour."

MacKenzie put the intercom back and sat down on the bunk next to his wife. "You're okay?"

She smiled. "Now I am. By the way, Ben Garver did send his best."

"Where'd you see him?"

"At the Pentagon briefing where this operation was worked out. He and Admiral Merton are taking personal charge of things, and the secretary of defense got his brief straight from the president who, I understand, said something like 'It figures' when he heard it was you who found *Red Dawn*. He also wanted to know if you were still hell at tug-of-war. You copy that?"

MacKenzie grinned. "Something from when we talked that time at the White House about using the DSRV to reach *Aspen*. It's just his way of saying hi. But tell me, what's going on? What's so important about *Red Dawn?*"

"Mac, why don't we save the briefing for later? I haven't seen you in three months."

"But we ought to—"

"Later. Come to bed."

"You're not serious," MacKenzie said.

"Try me."

"Justine, you're wounded, this is a navy submarine, and there are a hundred and twelve men under my command right outside that door."

"You figure they're listening?"

"No. Of course not, but, Justine, dignity demands . . . Hey, put that back on, will you?"

She tossed her shirt past him. Her proud breasts pointed upward and when she stretched he saw her chest muscles shudder in that funny way that always made it hard for him to think. There was a familiar tightening in his chest. "You're not listening to me."

She ran a hand through her thick hair, loosening it till it fell in waves across her bare shoulders. She slid her briefs off. "C'mon," she whispered mischievously, "We've never done it on a submarine."

"This isn't the Love Boat, Justine. It's a military warship on a mission vital to . . . *mmmpf.*"

She pulled him to her and covered his mouth with hers.

Her fingers found his chest hair and wound into it. Her breath was coming hotter against his face. She raised his hands to her breasts and held them there.

MacKenzie felt forces take over in him that had nothing to do with military matters, except for conquest in a far more basic sense. He lowered his hands to her firm body. She arched back and he felt her move, and suddenly his sweats were pooled around his ankles. He stepped out of them.

When they came together it was an act of passion and of love. She surrounded him; he was a steel core inside her. She wrapped her legs around his back, locking him into her, and they found a rhythm, rocking back and forth on the narrow bunk. She threw her arms around his neck and sank her teeth into his shoulder. He grabbed her face and locked his mouth over hers stifling their moans.

They made love like a married couple, not so acrobatic, more knowing and intimate with the remembrance of every special spot and the precise way to stoke it into flame. There was comfort in each fold of skin, the familiarity of all those hidden places previously discovered. Finally there was a moment when they reached the point of no return together and fell over the edge into a deep place where there was only one person. Justine cried out and jammed her face into the crook between his shoulder and neck, and he buried his face in her sweet-smelling hair to stop his own voice as muscles locked . . . and then sweet eruptions took them and they slid down the long slide together. Then his lips nuzzled her neck and her hands traced the hard muscles of his back and they lay together and it was over.

They assembled in the wardroom for the briefing. Tom Lasovic, Ed Randall, Jim Kurstan, Joe Santiago, and Fire Control Officer Sam Talmadge. They slid into the booth around the captain's table, and the stewards served coffee and plates of sweet rolls.

MacKenzie made the introductions. "Gentlemen, this is Miss Justine Segurra, a senior staff member of the Central

Intelligence Agency. I'm sure the scuttlebutt has already reached you, but for those it hasn't, I have the good fortune to be married to her."

Justine was met with a chorus of pleased-to-meet-you's and a few nice-to-see-you-again's from the men she had known when she was a passenger on the *Aspen*.

"Good to see so many familiar faces." She smiled warmly and put a hand on Tom Lasovic's broad shoulder. "Tom, I guess I'm still counting on you to carry me back to the ship, eh? And you, too, Mr. Randall."

"A pleasure, ma'am," Randall responded. "Lot less water this time."

"At least the wet kind." Justine laughed. "I remember. Mac, can I start?"

"It's your show."

Justine took a sip of coffee and looked to the assembled officers. "First, a real pat on the back to all of you from Navy Command for finding *Red Dawn*. Well done."

There were murmured okays and back slaps.

"Not a lot's been broadcast about it, but I can tell you that this particular Soviet sub is one of the highest priorities for the intelligence community."

"What makes her so valuable?" asked Tom Lasovic.

"Simply put, *Red Dawn's* propulsion system is powered by a new substance called irinium, which we very much want a sample of. I'll go into detail later, but for now let's just say either we get some of this stuff or we risk running second to the Russians in about half a dozen critically important technological areas. We're barely keeping abreast of the Japanese now. I don't think anyone here wants to see us running a poor third in what promises to be a very competitive world in the not so distant future. Also, there are serious national security issues. There isn't a man here who doesn't understand the threat of a far quieter Soviet submarine fleet."

There were hard looks of assent to that. Justine continued. "We intend to free *Red Dawn* from the ice she's trapped in and tow her to open water. After that's accomplished a special team will board her and remove what we need. Then she'll be returned to the Russians. We assume there are people still alive in there, so speed is of the essence. Here is our plan.

"In about three hours, a specially equipped Lockheed C-Five Galaxy will make a landing on the ice above *Red Dawn's* position. Navy SEALs are standing by to off-load a temporary base to operate from. They'll blow a hole in the ice and use special equipment to lower and operate one of the National Oceanic and Atmospheric Administration's TV-equipped unmanned robot subs, the *Argo,* to give us a more accurate picture of *Red Dawn's* situation.

"Concurrently, the DSRV *Avalon* is being ferried piggyback on the Los Angeles class submarine, *Phoenix.* Assuming we can free the *Red Dawn's* escape trunk, we'll use *Avalon* to get her people out. Then—and I'm sorry to spring this one on you, Mac—you're going to pilot *Avalon* and use her robot arm to plant the shape charges that will blow *Red Dawn* free of the ice. We're under the gun on time for this one if we expect to rescue anybody alive from in there. Mac, I know that thoughtful look. . . ."

"I'd like Luke Johnson if it's at all possible. He's the best with that arm. Can you get him for me?" asked MacKenzie.

"Already anticipated and in the works," Justine said. "Finally, assuming we can blow her out of the ice, we'll attach a cable from *Phoenix* to *Red Dawn* and pull her the hell out of here with *Seawolf* riding shotgun. That's about it. It may seem like a lot, but we all have great faith in *Seawolf* and her crew. Any questions?"

"What are the Russians up to?" asked Lasovic.

"They were surprisingly very quiet. Then suddenly, about twelve hours ago, an Alfa, a Victor III, and a Sierra left Kola Bay in a hurry, and several subs on patrol in the North Atlantic suddenly changed course and headed here. Since then the level of activity of the entire Soviet navy has been heightened."

"They know *Red Dawn* is missing," surmised MacKenzie.

Justine nodded. "Right. But they don't know where it is, and it'll take their ships at least forty-eight hours to get here. So if we block the Boomer you reported and stay within our time frame we should be able to get out of here before the Russians arrive."

The conversation was interrupted by the voice of the radio officer over the intercom: "Captain, we're receiving a signal from a C-Five overhead looking for landing coordinates. Do we supply?"

MacKenzie turned to Justine. "Your team is ahead of schedule."

"It's going to be a hell of a trick, landing a C-Five in that weather overhead," Santiago said warily.

"I wish we could wait for better conditions," Justine responded, "but we can't. The pilot's under strict orders. The plane is expendable, and he's to bring it in even if he's got to make a landing on his belly."

"Justine, if I trigger the locators, the Boomer will know we're here. It will also give him *Red Dawn's* position."

Justine looked thoughtful. "The first can't be helped. Any way around the second?"

MacKenzie hit the intercom. "Radio, tell the C-Five we're working on it and to stay close. Captain out." He turned back to his officers. "You heard the situation. If we trigger the locators, we give away *Red Dawn's* position. This is the time in the movies where the captain says 'I'm open to all suggestions' and some bright officer gives him one. Okay. I'm open to all suggestions."

"Skipper?" It was Randall, looking a little hesitant. "Maybe I've got one."

"Go ahead, Mr. Randall. Make my day."

"Make him not see the forest for the trees, sir. If you know what I mean."

"Come again?"

"What I mean is, we could plant lots of locators, all preset to different wavelengths, every mile or so over a wide area and fire them all at once. Only we and the C-Five will know the right one. Even if the Russian sub hears the signals, it won't know which is the real marker for *Red Dawn's* position."

MacKenzie smiled the way a teacher does when a good

student lives up to expectations. "Mr. Randall, you are a comfort to me. Mr. Talmadge, set the locators."

"Aye, sir."

"Mr. Santiago, plot us a course and speed. Justine, I'll call you as soon as they're down on the ice."

"Fine. Thank you, Captain. Gentlemen."

MacKenzie stood up. "That's it. We have our mission. Return to your stations and let's bring that plane down."

Red Dawn

Galinin stood next to Ligichev in the engine room. Ivanna was making final adjustments on the remaining diesel engine. She had cannibalized the others for parts to make this one work, and if it did there would be enough power to restore something of a working order to the sub. If not, well, the temperature was already dropping out of the comfort zone, and men who just a few hours before had been sweating were now looking for additional layers of clothing to ward off the chill.

"As soon as we start this we're going to increase oxygen consumption at a great rate," said Galinin.

"It can't be helped," Ligichev said. "We're caught in a vicious cycle. We need power to create heat, and oxygen to create power. To get either, we must get both. Fail to get one or the other . . ." He shrugged. Why state the obvious?

Ivanna wiped her greasy hands on a towel. "I'm ready. Cross your fingers." She went to the control panel and flipped a series of switches. She put her hand on the red start lever and rotated it. The starter turned lazily with a hesitant *whir-whir.* The engine shuddered, coughed once, and fell silent.

"Again," Galinin commanded.

Ivanna rotated the lever again. This time it cranked with more authority, and after a few fits and starts the diesel roared into life. There were cheers from everyone in the room. Galinin pounded a big fist on the engine. Ivanna patted the gray metal housing affectionately . . . and the engine shut down from excessive exhaust pressure.

"Damn," Ivanna cursed. "I forgot the exhaust path would be frozen, too."

"But at least we know it will run if we get enough air and establish a clear exhaust path," said Ligichev. "Any success with the radio, Comrade Captain?"

"None. Even if every circuit weren't fused, the ice prevents the masts from being raised anyway. I'm sorry. We are incommunicado for the near future. But if the snorkel trick your father is preparing works, we'll have enough air to breathe and operate the engine."

"Good work, Ivanna," Ligichev said.

"Yes. Very," conceded Galinin.

"Let's see how things are coming in the torpedo room," said Ligichev.

"If you need me I'll be in the control room." Galinin left them with a pat on the back, a remarkable show of support as far as Ligichev was concerned.

"Father?"

Ivanna's voice was timorous, a quality he was unused to. He wondered why. "Yes?"

"In the torpedo room . . . well, there's something . . . someone . . ."

"Couldn't get through the tube hatch? No? What, then?" Ivanna seemed at a loss for words. Ligichev figured that this must be an unusual technical problem. "No matter." He patted her arm. "We'll see to it when we get there."

The torpedo room had been hard hit by the crash. Weapons weighing several thousand pounds had broken loose from their moorings. One had crushed a young crewman to death. Pipe fittings and electrical conduits had been torn loose. Two of the loading mechanisms were useless, bent grotesquely out of shape.

Chief Engineer Lieutenant Petrov, a young man with a thick mustache and the dark good looks of the southern provinces, was working on restoring some control over the firing mechanism in the event full power was ever restored. Ligichev judged him to be about his daughter's age. Along with his nice looks he had a fine air of intelligence about him.

"How is it going, Comrade Lieutenant?" Ligichev asked. "Any progress?"

"Some," the young man acknowledged proudly. "I'm following your daughter's advice and salvaging what I can from the other tubes to make this one functional." He looked at Ivanna. "She was a big help to me."

It was the way the boy said it that made Ligichev's fatherly radar go off. And the look. It was the one that had made fathers since time immemorial reach for the nearest shotgun. "Ivanna, do you know this boy . . . young man?"

"We have been working together since the crash. And while you were with the captain . . . I thought we should have things commencing on both fronts," she said lamely. "So when Pytor asked me for help—"

Ligichev raised an eyebrow. "Pytor?"

The man snapped to attention. "I beg your pardon, Comrade Chief Scientist. Lieutenant Pytor Ivanovich Petrov."

"You understand what we intend to do, Comrade Lieutenant Petrov?"

"Ivanna . . . I mean, Comrade Ligachova explained it to me. I've been working on the board in preparation for your arrival. I think I've also worked out the valve arrangement you want. Look here. See?"

"Hmm. Very interesting. Yes, that might work. You won't need that circuit?"

"It's tied into sonar. No sonar . . ." He shrugged. "And this way we don't have to cut through the hatch cover."

"Yes," said Ligichev. "Very good. We'll do it your way, Comrade Lieutenant." Ligichev began to take off his coat. "Now if you'll open the inner and outer doors, please. I want to have a look."

Ivanna took his arm. "Father, please, I don't think you should be the one to go out there. After all, I mean . . ."

"Well, then, who is going to go?" Ligichev stopped, struck. He'd always wondered when this time would come. He was being superseded. His male ego reared its head for a moment. He'd always known that sooner or later a man would arrive who could turn Ivanna's head. Of late he had begun to despair that any would. He decided he shouldn't be too surprised to discover it happening so suddenly, or that it had happened here and now. In light of the urgency of their situation and the real possibility that the ship would turn out to be a coffin, basic and ever-optimistic biology was making a final stab at things. Well, people fell in love for worse reasons and with less hope for the future.

Ivanna said it delicately enough. "Well, Pytor could go, couldn't he?"

"I will be happy to volunteer, Comrade Chief Scientist."

Ligichev put his coat back on and smiled affably. "Thank you, Comrade Lieutenant. I'm grateful for the help." The old order changeth. One had to accept it graciously.

Ivanna smiled and relaxed. It was done. The seal of approval had been given. "We'll need a harness of some kind. Can we use this line?"

"Good idea." Pytor tied it around his waist. He hit a switch on the board, and a small hydraulic motor whined, opening the outer hatch. After checking the pressure in the tube and breaking the normal interlock, he swung the inner hatch out. "Ivanna, you understand if the ice seal ruptures the pressure may be too great to close the inner hatch. Cut me loose and close the outer hatch or the ship will flood. All right?"

"All right, Pytor." Ivanna nodded bravely.

Ligichev had to stop himself from singing the national anthem. Well, all things considered, it was a brave speech, valiantly delivered. So instead of amusing himself at the boy's expense he simply said, "Well, then, let's try not to muck it up, shall we? My calculations say you must leave eighteen inches of ice at the end of the tunnel you'll carve. That's sufficient to retain the seal and not too thick for the torpedo to break through." He handed Pytor a drill and an ice pick from the ship's stores. "Okay, my boy. In you go."

The torpedo tube was only slightly more than two feet in diameter, so Pytor lay on his stomach and slithered forward. Ivanna fed the power cord for the drill in after him. They would be using precious battery power, but that couldn't be helped.

There was a slight blue glow that grew brighter as Pytor made his way forward. A solid sheet of ice covered the far end of the tube. He chipped at it with the ice pick. The drill was faster. It bit in easily and he began to carve out a tunnel a bit bigger than the diameter of the tube itself, enough to sit in cross legged to make working easier.

"How far does the ice extend?" shouted Ligichev over the drill noise.

"About twenty feet," Pytor called back. He finished drilling a section, took up the ice pick, and pried out the ice. It was like slicing a pie; after the first piece the rest came free with less effort. His legs were soon covered with icy debris. He pushed the shards behind him, already feeling the cold creeping into his calves. Ivanna swept the ice out onto the torpedo room floor.

When the tunnel was long enough to allow Pytor to leave the torpedo tube, he moved out into the ice keel itself. It was the eeriest feeling of his life to crawl out into the heart of the ice surrounding them. A light blue glow was everywhere, filtering down through the ice above. Pytor sat there suspended in a faerie world of glistening ice, a mile of crystal-clear ocean beneath him and an undulating under-icecap surface covered with stalagmites and ridges overhead. He was actually *in* the ocean and could see beyond his own crystal chamber to other keels nearby, some descending far deeper than the one *Red Dawn* was trapped in. Behind him the sub was suspended as if in midair, tilted at a slight upward angle like some perfect model on an admiral's desk. He had never before seen anything like it. No one had.

His senses were astounded. He was underwater without scuba tanks, in an ice cave without arctic gear. He was an interloper in a pristine world. The warm air from the torpedo room circulated in. He had once seen pictures of girls skiing in bathing suits at some mountain resort. It seemed that way to him now, the contrasts were so striking.

The drill continued to bite into the ice without meeting resistance. The ice pick did the rest. The chamber was bigger now, at least ten feet long. Behind him he could hear Ivanna steadily clearing the ice from the tube.

A fish swam by. It startled him. Again, perspective was confused. He was on the inside of a vast fishbowl, looking out. Farther away, seals swam with simple, graceful motions. Fish drifted by. Tiny square ice scales under the ice cap looked like shingles on a roof. In his warm, transparent chamber, he felt as if he were at the center of a stream of life. Below him, the ocean depths descended into darkness. What primordial creatures lived there? Above, he watched a walrus do rollovers, lazily flipping its powerful tail.

His work was forgotten for the moment, and it was only Ivanna's sudden presence beside him that interrupted his reverie.

"My God," she said. "It's beautiful." There was awe in her voice. "How could anyone even imagine it?"

"No one could," said Pytor, putting down his tools, reveling in the sight of it and of her, suspended together like leaves in the wind. His hand found hers. There was an answering pressure, an intertwining.

"We have to—" he began, but she stopped him with her soft hand. Her lips sought his.

"Shh, my lieutenant," she said quietly. "I know." There was the quiet rustle of garments parting, a demand that life assert itself even in the face of death. Her soft voice said in his ear, "No one has ever had such a wedding chamber."

Suspended between the ice cap and the ocean in a crystal cave, they came together.

* * *

Ligichev heard the noises and gently closed the inner hatch. Things would have to wait awhile. Maybe they would be saved, but if not, at least he could allow them this final gift.

He sat down with his back to the hatch to guard it and passed the time thinking about his wife, Irina.

Chapter Nine

Akula

Kalik had been pacing the control room liked a caged tiger for the better part of an hour. Volkov wondered whether the strain was getting to him. There was no sign of the American sub, and countless traverses of the area had failed to locate *Red Dawn*. The time remaining to him was more than half over, and half the northern submarine fleet was on its way to take over the search. Maybe that made the admirals rest easy, but it only increased the pressure on him. It wasn't going to help one bit if someone other than Kalik found *Red Dawn*.

Volkov had no trouble imagining the dour faces of the Politburo when this issue was considered. Kalik had put himself and Volkov at risk when he left *Red Dawn* to lure the Americans away—and he had lost. The only way to salvage their careers was to find *Red Dawn*.

A call from Sonar broke the tension.

"Comrade Captain, we are receiving signals on several wavelengths. American locators. Ten . . . no, at least twenty different locations."

Kalik felt relief flood his entire body. Anything was better than the endless silence. A signal meant his adversary was still there, and that meant *Red Dawn* could not be far away.

"Track and plot every one," Kalik ordered. He marched

into the sonar room. The points glowed on the screen like a fistful of sparks.

"What are they doing?" asked Volkov.

"Hiding the real signal in a pack of false ones," Kalik said with calm assurance. "Look at all those tracks. He's interested in only one. The others are just camouflage. He'd like us to spend days checking them out."

"So how do we find the right one?"

"I don't know yet. There is nothing to differentiate any one signal from all the others. You were right, Viktor. He is very smart. Too smart to be caught with his pants down. So we have to concentrate on what he is not too smart to conceal."

"Which is?" Volkov wondered.

Volkov had seen Kalik do this before, explore several logic chains at once, picking and choosing from a host of facts with an intuition that made sudden leaps from the known to the unknown and back again. To Volkov, who never thought of himself as other than ordinary, it was a humbling sight.

Kalik was testing his thoughts out loud. "You mark a spot when you want to find it again or when you want others to find it. Either he's returning to *Red Dawn* or someone else is."

"Another sub?"

"Maybe. But in that case he could send the coordinates by radio and meet there."

"A landing party? Comrade Captain, could the Americans be sending a search-and-rescue team here?"

"Excellent, Viktor. That would make sense," Kalik said. "So now answer the final question: how would you get them here?"

"By plane, of course. If there's one up there . . ."

"We prove our hypothesis," finished Volkov. "Come, we must be quick." They strode into the control room. Kalik wasted no time. "Comrade Navigator, how thick is the ice above us?"

"We are in a field of thick ice, Comrade Captain. Three meters minimum."

"*Akula* can handle it," Kalik decided. "Prepare to surface."

"Comrade Captain? Three meters—"

"Take her up. I want some speed. Blow main ballast."

"Blowing main ballast."

Akula rose toward the surface like a shot. Kalik grabbed the intercom and opened the all-ship channel. "Attention all crew. We are about to surface through some very thick ice in roughly . . ."

"Ten seconds to impact," called the navigator.

"Ten seconds. The shock will be quite severe. Prepare yourselves and remain calm. Captain out."

Lockheed C-5 Galaxy

Pilot Jack Holloway scanned the surface of the ice cap below ruefully. The light was bad, and the ground was covered by a winter storm. He decided someone on board the submarine had to have a sense of humor—he had to be kidding expecting them to land down there. His copilot, Lieutenant Frank Washington, put it more succinctly.

"No fucking way. I mean it, Jack."

Holloway shrugged. "We've got a delivery to make. Who do you want me to complain to?"

"Call Operations."

"Frank."

"I mean it. Hey, show me a runway and I'll fly this thing through hoops to get to it, but there's no concrete down there. There's nothing but ice. We're not equipped for this."

"We got our snow gear on. Besides, you heard the man. The plane's expendable. Get the SEALs and their equipment down—that's the mission pure and simple. Charlie, are you picking up the homing signal?"

"I've got two dozen signals on as many wavelengths, but we've been cued into the right one," said Charlie Woodson, the navigator.

Holloway picked up the radio. "Georgia Leader, this is Georgia One. We have a lock on your position. We're gonna take a pass or two down low to survey the scene, then bring her in. Roger?"

"Georgia One, this is Georgia leader. Get close, but don't fall in, fellas. Roger."

"See? Wha'd I tell you? Fucking wise guys," Washington said darkly.

Holloway banked gently, losing altitude. The Galaxy was the largest cargo plane in the world, over 250 feet long with a 220-foot wingspan. The cockpit stood three stories off the ground and the tail over six. The Galaxy had seats for seventy-five troops in its upper deck and enough space in its cavernous hold for two tanks or three helicopters. In fact, the Wright brothers could have flown their first trip *inside* a C-5 Galaxy.

They descended into the rough weather. "Release flares," ordered Holloway.

"Flares away." They drifted down with an orange light. "Maybe . . . there," said Washington. "See that broad plain? On your right. Looks pretty flat."

"I see it. That's a go, buddy." Holloway brought the big craft around and reached for the intercom. "Attention, loadmasters. We are beginning our final approach. Watch your cargo. It's going to be a bumpy landing."

The intercom crackled back. "This is Winestski. We got eyes, Cap. And that's got to be one of the world's great understatements."

Holloway grinned. "Without doubt, Sergeant."

Red Dawn

The small group gathered in the torpedo room, Ligichev, Galinin, and Ivanna watching Pytor display the final preparations for the snorkel launch.

Galinin peered down the torpedo tube. "You've cleared it?"

Pytor nodded. "There is less than eighteen inches of ice at the end. The torpedo will break out without any problem."

"In all this I think there's something I forgot," Ligichev said suddenly. "Won't hitting the ice seal ignite the torpedo? The ice is as hard as a sub's hull."

"It's already taken care of, Comrade Chief Scientist," Petrov explained. "We can set minimum rotations for the motor so the torpedo will be armed only at a certain depth. The warhead will not arm itself till that point has been reached. That way it can never turn back on us armed." He held out a snorkel, just a larger version of the ones carried by skin divers everywhere. It was enclosed in a flotation housing and attached to a long length of hard vinyl tubing. "The snorkel has been fixed five hundred feet behind the torpedo on the wire guide. That's far enough away so the explosion won't damage it. The trajectory is a programmed sine curve, like a roller-coaster ride. The exhaust tube and the snorkel line will be coiled in the torpedo tube. The torpedo will travel down to a depth of a hundred meters with the snorkel trailing behind it, then arc upward and head for the surface, bringing the snorkel directly under it. The snorkel will be right under the area of impact and will hopefully float up through the hole created by the explosion. We have the intake tube rigged to the fan room to pump the air in and blow it throughout the ship. We are loading the torpedo now."

"How long to finalize all this, Comrade Lieutenant?" asked Galinin.

"We're ready to fire on your order, Comrade Captain. This snorkel is one of several in storage we would use for dewatering in an emergency."

Galinin shook his head. "No sonar. We can't even use the scopes. We're firing blind. We could hit an ice keel or the line might get wrapped around something out there. It's going to take a lot of luck."

"The alternative is to have someone swim it out, Comrade Captain," said Ligichev, "and I can't imagine any volunteers."

"No, of course not," Galinin said. "Well, I suppose we'll know soon enough whether it will work. All right, Comrade Lieutenant. Open the outer door. Flood the tube and the tunnel from the torpedo tank."

Petrov hit a switch and the door motor whined. "Outer door open. Flooding tube and tunnel, Comrade Captain. . . . Ready to launch tube one."

"Fire tube one manually with minimum air pressure."

"Firing tube one."

Seawolf

"The C-Five is coming in for a landing, Skipper. Final approach."

"Keep them on your scope, Sonar." MacKenzie pictured the huge aircraft coming in overhead. He had a lot of respect for pilots. Imagine spending half your life up in the air depending on the vagaries of the atmosphere and jet engines to keep you aloft. He just couldn't see it . . .

His thoughts were interrupted by Jim Kurstan's voice crackling out of the speaker in alarm. "Emergency! Emergency! Captain, high-cycle motor noise. Incoming torpedo. Repeat, incoming torpedo. Range four hundred fifty yards and closing."

MacKenzie reacted without conscious thought. "Helm, right full rudder. Ahead flank. Attack Center, launch decoys in a full pattern. Emergency deep. Emergency deep!" He hit the alarm handle and the alarm blared stridently throughout the ship. "Main battle stations. This is the captain speaking. We are under attack. This is no drill."

"Torpedo four hundred yards and closing."

"Sonar, where did that thing come from?"

"Captain, it was launched from *Red Dawn!*"

Pumps whined as *Seawolf* took in water by the ton. The helmsman shoved his yoke forward hard, without regard for anyone who might be caught unaware. The down angle increased radically and men clung to whatever they could. *Seawolf* dived as fast as she could, propelled by her engines increasing to maximum speed.

"Torpedo three hundred fifty yards and closing."

"Conn, Attack Center. Decoys launched in full pattern, Captain."

"Give me a sounding, Mr. Santiago. Sonar, where is that torpedo?" MacKenzie demanded.

"Three hundred yards and closing."

"One mile of depth, Skipper. No obstructions. Plenty of room."

MacKenzie held on. They weren't out of the woods yet. It was still a race. Could *Seawolf* outdistance its pursuer?

"Maneuvering. Cavitate. Depth, Mr. Randall."

"Six hundred. Six hundred twenty-five. Six hundred fifty . . ."

"Conn, Sonar. We have a decoy match!"

The explosion could not have been more than a hundred feet from *Seawolf*'s hull and it rolled the sub like a giant fist. The shock wave burst pipes, and a vicious cloud of steam shot across the conn. A crewman screamed and clutched his face. Tom Lasovic jumped over the guardrail and yanked him out of the way. MacKenzie wanted to race over, but the safety of the ship came first. She was still diving fast. Too fast.

"Maneuvering, all back emergency! Mr. Randall, five seconds on blow the forward group. Chief, full rise on all planes." The angle began decreasing. "All right. Vent the forward group. All stop." MacKenzie waited, feeling the ship respond. Then: "All ahead one-third. Make your depth one thousand feet. Sonar, sweep the area."

"Conn, Sonar. All clear, Skipper. No noise at all."

MacKenzie started to ease up. Goddammit! He suppressed a primitive and quite visceral urge to point *Seawolf* at the ice keel and blow *Red Dawn* out of existence. The rules of engagement would have permitted it, too, if they had deliberately taken a shot at *Seawolf*.

But they weren't out of trouble yet. Lasovic was pointing at the TV screen worriedly. "Skipper, look!"

"I see it. What the hell is that?"

"Conn, Sonar. There's a keel from the ice cap coming straight at us. It must have been blasted loose by the explosion. It's big, Skipper. Almost as big as the one *Red Dawn's* in."

MacKenzie's mind ran options like a battlefield computer. The keel was too big to race around. The suction alone might sweep them into the powerful currents. There was no time for second guesses. The huge ice keel was coming toward them too fast.

MacKenzie stood his ground. "Snap shot tubes one and two. Torpedo Room, open outer doors on tubes one and two. Fire Control, compute a basic straight-running shot. Firing point procedures. Sonar, give them the inputs. Lock on to the ice keel. That's our target."

"Course, Skipper?" Randall sounded shaky.

"Remain on this course, Mr. Randall," he said sharply. "Hold her steady." The ice keel was closer now, almost filling the screen.

"Captain, ship ready, solution ready, torpedo room ready."

"Conn, Sonar. Target bearing one one five degrees, range one thousand yards."

Tom Lasovic stood calmly by MacKenzie's side. "It's going to throw off big chunks if we don't blow this thing into ice cubes. Could hole us pretty easily."

"My thinking, too. But if we miss it and hit the ice cap, we might shake *Red Dawn* right off her perch. Gotta be right on the money. Sonar, range."

"Six hundred yards and closing."

MacKenzie waited.

"Five hundred yards and closing."

MacKenzie watched the ice keel. It looked like a dagger coming at them.

"Mac?" Tom Lasovic pointed to the screen. The huge ice mass filled it.

"Not yet . . ." MacKenzie said softly.

"Four hundred yards and closing."

MacKenzie commanded, "Fire Control, match sonar bearings and shoot tubes one and two."

"Set. Stand by. Fire! Unit one away. Set. Stand by. Fire! Unit two away."

"Right full rudder. All ahead flank." MacKenzie saw the wake from the speeding torpedoes on the screen as *Seawolf* pulled away. Two plumes of white water speared toward the ice keel. It looked good. . . .

"Skipper, both units running hot, straight, and normal. . . . Torpedoes and contact bearings are merging. Explosions!"

Blazing light filled the television screen, and they felt the force of the explosions as *Seawolf* rocked in the wake. Light debris rained down on the hull. When the screen cleared, the ice keel was gone.

Shouts of victory filled the conn. "Way to go, Skipper!" and "We got it!"

"Nice shooting, Mac," Lasovic said happily.

"Good work, everybody," MacKenzie said. "Mr. Santiago, take us back to *Red Dawn*. Mr. Randall, make your depth one zero zero feet."

"Aye, Skipper." And he added, "Nice work, sir."

"Conn, Radio. Skipper, there's something wrong up top. We're getting a transmission from the C-Five. They're in trouble, sir!"

Akula

"We have them!" Kalik pounced on it. "Do you hear me, Viktor? We have them. We are all out in the open now." Kalik stood behind his sonar operator and gazed raptly over his shoulder at the screen. "Someone fired on the American sub. Did you see how he ran? I think the torpedo came from *Red Dawn*. We have no other ships in the area, and the American wouldn't fire on one of his own subs." He put a hand on the sonar operator's shoulder. "You have the coordinates for the origin of the torpedo track?"

"I do, Comrade Captain. And I think we have enough for a signature on the American sub."

"Excellent." Kalik opened the intercom. "Comrade Navigator, match sonar's coordinates and lay in a course. All ahead two-thirds. Bring us in at a depth of seven hundred meters. Let the depth cloak us. I want to be unnoticed."

Kalik thought he understood what had happened. Sonar told the tale. For some as yet unknown reason *Red Dawn* had taken a shot at his adversary, but the American captain had deflected it by launching a decoy. That in itself was quite interesting. It was good to see how someone reacted to danger—especially if you might have to shoot at him one day. The American dived to starboard and sent up a screen of decoys. A reflex. Basic. Those habits were the hardest to break. You did them without thinking. So if one day they had to fight and he could force the captain to react . . .

"We have the signature. We're trying to correlate it now, Comrade Captain."

"Keep at it."

The American sub could not conceal its identity any longer after running at top speed from *Red Dawn*'s torpedo and shooting the ice keel that had almost crushed it. Kalik was sure it was an ice keel. Sonar couldn't have been mistaken about the size. And nothing else could be so large, unless a chunk of the ice cap itself had been knocked loose by the torpedo. Remarkable. With a thousand tons of ice coming straight at him the American captain had just stood his ground and blasted it to hell with a pair of torpedoes. What nerve. What confidence and poise under pressure.

"Comrade Captain, our computers indicate the American ship is not a Los Angeles class as we first thought. It is larger and faster than a Los Angeles. We have a signature match and preliminary findings indicate—"

"Seawolf!" Kalik pounced on the thought. "The Americans' newest. One of a kind. Make sure the engagement tapes are sent to Naval Command. A very good job, Comrades."

"Thank you, Comrade Captain."

"Viktor, it seems we have two prizes—*Red Dawn* and the Americans' vaunted *Seawolf*." That would explain much, Kalik mused. Only their very best would captain her.

"I'll be happy to compose the message to Naval Command," said Volkov, relieved. "It should postpone our courts-martial."

Kalik laughed. "At least for now. One never knows."

Volkov smiled at the candid admission. "One never used to know. Maybe it's changing. At least they've eliminated that infuriating Zampol on board. No more second-guessing all the time, eh?"

"True enough. It used to make me furious having to check every promotion with some ideological fanatic," admitted Kalik. "But as much as things change, Viktor, I fear they remain the same."

"The cat's out of the bag, as they say. I don't see how it can be put back in," Volkov said.

Kalik's response was cut off. Michman Rostov poked his head into the sonar room in an obviously highly agitated state, "Comrade Captain, you'll want to see this. It's unbelievable. On the control room screen, quickly."

They followed him in. The crew was huddled tightly around *Akula*'s TV monitor, but parted for Kalik and Volkov.

"Now, what is all this about—" Kalik began, but he stopped dead in his tracks when he saw the screen. "That's *Red Dawn*. But . . . is it possible? It's embedded in solid ice! I must be dreaming."

"Then we all are," said Volkov, wide-eyed. "Vassily, how could this have happened?"

Kalik shook his head. "I don't know. Sonar, do we have a contact on the Americans?"

"We've lost them, Comrade Captain. They must have gone silent."

"Helm, steer a circle around the ice keel at a depth of thirty meters. Rostov, use the videotape machine to make a record of *Red Dawn*'s situation for transmission to Naval Command with the engagement tapes. All ahead two-thirds. I want to be out of the immediate area in ten minutes."

The burly Rostov took a video cassette out of a locker and inserted it into the heavy steel machine under the second periscope. As *Akula* circled the ice keel a green light showed it was recording.

"It's . . . unbelievable," breathed Kalik. All eyes were glued to the monitor as they completed the circuit. As an afterthought, Kalik added, "Rostov, make a copy of that tape for me. I'll want to study it later."

Volkov was still staring at the image of *Red Dawn* in the ice keel, unable to take his eyes off the screen. "Sonar, what's going on in there?"

"We hear noises, Comrade Senior Lieutenant. They could be trying to make repairs. How many alive is impossible to tell."

"Keep listening. Alert us to any change."

Rostov announced, "All finished, Comrade Captain. I'll prepare the pickup balloon."

"Fine. Viktor, take us down to eight hundred meters. I wouldn't think *Seawolf* can follow below six hundred. I want a chance to think this over without disturbance. Rostov, bring the other tape to my cabin."

Volkov moved to comply. Kalik came up beside him. "We have to establish communication with *Red Dawn*. Any ideas?"

"Vassily, I need time to think. It's too much to take in all at once."

Kalik noticed that the sight of *Red Dawn*'s entombment had unnerved Volkov so much that twice he had called him by his first name in front of the crew. Kalik decided not to mention it. The lapse would bother his meticulous senior lieutenant for days.

"Do that, Viktor. But first have Navigation find us some open water and send for a jet pickup. There are going to be a lot of very surprised faces in the Kremlin tonight."

Lockheed C-5 Galaxy

The roar of the engines was a constant whine. Jack Holloway and Copilot Frank Washington leaned over their steering yokes peering into the dim light and swirling snow below them.

"Steady . . . steady now . . ." Holloway brought the big plane in. Twice before, they'd had to pull up when the storm sent sudden severe gusts across the plane's bow. They were lucky the new computers sounded an alarm. Wind shear like that could pull them right down into the ice cap—and nobody survived a crash landing in this terrain.

"Georgia Leader, this is Georgia One. We're attempting another pass over the landing site. The storm is worsening. Visibility is way down."

"Roger, Georgia One. We're down here watching. Good luck."

Holloway looked over to his copilot who, for all his complaining, was steady as a rock. "What do you think, Frank?"

"The light up here isn't going to change. The wind can only get worse. If we go, it's now or never."

Holloway looked back at his navigator, Charlie Woodson. "Charlie?"

"You're covered, Cap. Final approach. Vector Blue."

Holloway picked up the radio mike. "Loadmasters, prepare for landing. Charlie, altitude, every fifty feet. Call it out."

"Yes, sir. Steady on course zero nine zero."

Holloway banked the plane into line. "Zero nine zero, roger."

"You're in the glide path, cap," Woodson called out. "Begin your descent now. Altitude, one thousand feet. Nine hundred fifty. Nine hundred . . ."

Strong winds buffeted the plane. Holloway concentrated. There was nothing in his mind except getting his airplane down in one piece.

"Lower landing gear."

The navigator called out their descent. "Eight hundred.

Seven hundred fifty. Seven hundred. Glide slope . . . glide slope."

Holloway pulled his nose up and stopped thinking about his passengers. You couldn't worry about the lives in your charge; it just made you nervous. He couldn't afford that. Lower . . . Hold her on line. Skids were going to be a bitch when they hit, but they had twice the usual landing length and the special studded tires. They would stop in time.

"Landing gear down and locked. Steady on glide path." Washington's voice was reassuringly calm.

The SEALs in back were going to think they'd been thrown into a giant washing machine and left to tumble. "This is the pilot. We are making our final descent. Check your harnesses," he radioed back.

"Four hundred. Three hundred fifty. Two-fifty . . ."

Holloway could see the ice cap below, long and wide and flat. They could do it. The Galaxy had a strong back, and the load she was carrying wouldn't overtax her. Easy now . . . Wind tore at the plane. Holloway cut his airspeed and brought them lower.

"Two hundred. One-fifty. One hundred . . ."

"Georgia Leader, this is Georgia One. Coming in for a landing."

"Roger, Georgia One. Georgia Leader standing by."

It was all in the handling. Find a good spot to set her down and the rest would be easy. Hit the braking jets hard. The wings would hold. Taxi in the rest of the way. He hit the landing alarm and it blared throughout the ship.

"Hold on, everybody."

"Fifty feet. Forty. Thirty. Twenty . . ."

Holloway knew it was wrong from the first second the wheels hit. He felt the big plane slide out from under his control in a wide fishtail. The studded wheels weren't holding.

They bumped and roared over the ice at eighty knots an hour and almost took off again. Holloway fought the flaps and brought the plane down, feeding power to the braking jets. He felt a sudden tug and their speed dropped ten knots.

"Parachute open," Washington called. Holloway could hear the worry in his voice as they slid over the ice cap out of control. Traction. He needed traction. The wheels weren't holding. Snow and ice hit the windshield like bullets. Vision was down to nothing. He peered into the violent storm, looking for the flats he'd seen from the air, desperately trying to hold his airplane in line.

It happened just when he thought he had control. Their speed was down; they needed just a mile or two more. The plane was holding, the tires finally biting into the snow. But they had gone farther than he planned. The ice below was no longer flat. It was rough and broken by pressure ridges.

He didn't see the hill until it was too late. The huge Galaxy hit it like a ramp and vaulted into the air. Holloway blasted power into the engines in a vain attempt to prolong the arc, hoping he could take the plane up and over the next ridge of broken ice and into a stall landing in the plain beyond.

"Jack, she's not gonna make it!" Holloway heard Washington grab the radio. "Mayday, Georgia Leader! Mayday—"

The pressure ridge hit the Galaxy's nose like a fist. The metal crumpled like aluminum foil. Both wings cracked and swung forward like the blades of a giant scissors, the engines spitting fire. The tail came up as the nose went down and crashed back down hard onto the ice. Holloway was thrown forward by the impact, and his head hit the steering yoke. He felt something warm sliding down his face under his flight helmet and he wanted to shout something to his copilot . . . and then he felt nothing at all.

The Galaxy came to a final stop. Snow fell over its once gleaming skin and began to cover it. Inside and out there was silence.

Seawolf

"Radio, what about the C-Five? What's happening up there?" MacKenzie demanded.

"They're down, but I can't raise them, Skipper. That last transmission is all we got."

"Sonar, have you got a fix on them?"

"Yes, sir. We heard the bang right through the ice."

MacKenzie turned to Justine, her rank as operations officer entitling her to be present in the conn. "You heard. They've crashed. They're not too far from here. Maybe a mile."

"We have to get them, Mac."

"We're going to try." He hit the intercom. "Jake, are repairs complete?"

"Aye, Skipper. Right as rain here," said Chief Engineer Jake Cardiff.

"Very well. Stand by. Navigator, take your coordinates from Sonar and plot a straight course to Georgia One."

"We've still got our Russian friend nearby, Mac," Lasovic reminded him.

"Can't be helped. Besides, he must have heard us evading the torpedo and the ice keel, and his sonar will pinpoint the crash anyway. For better or worse we're out in the open now."

Santiago looked up from his instrument table. "Course zero nine five, Skipper.

"Helm steer course zero nine five. All ahead flank. Joe, what kind of ice is over us?"

"Medium thick, Skipper." Santiago read from the upward-looking Fathometer. "Three to five meters. Thicker in some spots."

MacKenzie thought of the men up there in that storm. Brave men risking everything under impossible conditions. "Tom, break out the cold-weather gear."

Lockheed C-5 Galaxy

Holloway awoke to the pleasant sight of snowflakes falling. It looked like Christmas in his beloved New Hampshire. Gentle. Sweet. There was even the smell of a wood fire in the fireplace . . . the fireplace . . .

Consciousness came rushing back suddenly and he realized two things. The snow was drifting over him because there was no longer any cockpit windshield to prevent it, and the smell of burning was no dream. The plane was on fire.

Holloway tried to get out of his seat, but he couldn't move his arms or legs. He managed to turn his head to get a look at his copilot. Washington was unconscious, but Holloway thought he detected the shallow rise and fall of his friend's chest under his flight suit. Both of them were trapped under the control consoles that the crash had crushed down on them. He craned his neck back as far as he could. Charlie Woodson had been literally torn out of his seat and thrown across the cabin by the crash. It looked as if his neck was broken.

Holloway's nose crinkled. The smell of smoke was stronger now. The engines were burning, and the fire was getting closer. Well, it didn't much matter that poor Charlie had bought it in the crash. They were all going to die. Holloway couldn't move, and it didn't seem likely anyone was alive back there to put the fire out.

He thought about trying to rouse Frank, but for what? Neither of them could move the ton of metal console off them. And the fire would be here soon. Better he be unconscious when it came. Holloway settled back and tried to compose himself. The scene in front of him was eerily beautiful in its own way. The snow was an utter whiteness. With his wrecked cabin wrapped around him he had a front row seat.

He stared up into the storm. He was sorry his last mission had been a failure. He thought about the men in back. He'd tried to get them down safely, but a C-5 was never meant to land here. It made a weird kind of pilot sense that in the end it was the ground that had rejected him.

The smoke was closer now. Tendrils curled into the cabin. He forced himself to stare into the snow and remember the sights he'd seen during three decades in the air. Red backlit clouds in the dawn sky. The lights of desert cities coming up fast in the night. He felt the first vibrations right through his seat and idly wondered what had exploded. The plane was probably consumed by fire now. Just a matter of time before it hit the fuel tanks. Then he felt it again, like a jackhammer hitting him from underneath, and suddenly Jack Holloway knew that all the sights he had ever seen amounted to nothing beside the one that was now appearing before his eyes. If he ever witnessed the Second Coming it would surely be a minor occurrence compared to the vision of *Seawolf*'s mighty black sail crashing up through the ice in front of the C-5 and towering over him.

The sail continued to rise. Great chunks of ice fell away from *Seawolf*'s wetly gleaming hull. Men in thick parkas clambered out of the hatches as soon as the deck cleared the ice. Holloway saw them run around to the rear cargo hold. Outside, he heard someone climbing the cockpit ladder. A hooded face peered in.

"Hey, anyone in there? Can you hear me?"

"Here . . ." Holloway managed weakly. "My copilot . . ."

The man pulled his hood up and stared down, smiling. "You're alive. I had my doubts anyone would be. Jesus, what a mess. Captain Holloway, I'm Tom Lasovic, *Seawolf*'s XO. We'll have you and your copilot out of here in a jiffy. Anybody else back there?" Lasovic looked back into the cabin, and his face fell. "Your navigator . . . I'm sorry."

"What about the others?"

Lasovic turned to shout for more help then began to clear the debris himself. He shook his head in amazement. "I don't know how you did it, Captain. I'll lay odds this bird will never fly again, but apart from some busted arms and legs back there, everybody else made it okay. Including the equipment."

Holloway heard the whooshing sounds of fire-fighting equipment. He felt strength flowing back into him. Helluva thing.

Justine had a team on the fuselage cutting away the tail section with torches. She'd been inside. The robot sub and prefab buildings were all in good shape. She looked at the C-5 lying flat on its belly with its spine crushed. All things considered, they were lucky as hell. Reports were the pilot was okay. He deserved a medal for bringing this one in.

She stood in the snow waiting for the cutters to finish. Four of the SEALs and two of the loadmasters had broken limbs, so she split her party up to take them back to *Seawolf*. A C-130 would be sent for the wounded.

"Tail's coming loose! Everybody back!"

The tail section fell to the ice and rolled aside, revealing the cavernous hold. Crates were stacked high and Quonset hut sections were laid out on the floor. One of the loadmasters, a big man in a down parka, jumped down to the ice.

"You'd have to be Ms. Segurra. I'm Sergeant Winestski. I was told you're in charge of this operation."

"That's right, Sergeant. Let's get this stuff unloaded and the huts set up at the base camp site. I've about had it with this snow."

Winestski grinned. "Me, too, ma'am. How close are we to the site?"

"Two miles."

"Pleasant walk, ma'am," said the big man, taking a deep breath, "after that landing."

"I understand. Take the torch crew and I'll see if Mr. Lasovic still needs his men."

MacKenzie watched it all from *Seawolf*'s sail. It was unbelievable that the C-5 had made it. The plane looked as if Godzilla had stepped on it. But the injured men were already on board *Seawolf*, and Tom had radioed that the pilot and copilot were alive and he was bringing them in.

126

Justine reported that the equipment they needed was in good shape as well.

The unloading went as smoothly as it could in a snow-storm, and everything was soon packed on sleds. Justine moved everyone off toward the spot where *Red Dawn* lay under the ice, and MacKenzie had to pick up his binoculars to follow them. They looked like a line of ants weaving their way over the ice cap through the snow. He'd meet them at the campsite, where the real work would begin.

He looked at the C-5. It was nothing but scrap metal now. One man had died within her. "Mr. Randall, this is the captain. Rig topside for dive and submerge the ship."

Red Dawn had claimed her first casualties. MacKenzie wondered if it was a portent of things to come.

Chapter
Ten

The black limousine sprayed slush from under its wheels as it swept down Kalinin Prospect. It had been a miserable winter. The snow on either side of the road was piled as high as most people's heads. The car's markings showed it belonged to a member of the Supreme High Command, so it barely slowed at the Borovitsky Gate and passed unobstructed into the red brick courtyard of the Kremlin.

Admiral Nikolai Korodin, deputy minister of defense and commander in chief of the Soviet Naval Forces had the springy gait of a natural athlete and strong features with dark, intelligent eyes that could be easily imagined peering out to sea. Korodin got out of the car and took the metal tape canister from the seat beside him. The gray metal case was still cold and rimmed from the salty arctic air. Korodin was a thorough man, and he had viewed the tape more times than his first porno film, which an academy buddy had smuggled into their dorm one night. He had some answers. Not as many as he would have liked.

The walkway had been improperly cleared and snow squashed over the tops of his shoes. From *Red Dawn* to wet socks it had been a bad day. And now this meeting of the Wartime Defense Council. They wouldn't have called him out of the planning session at three in the morning for anything minor. Something big must be going on to convene the senior decision-making body for national security policy at this hour.

The council room was a large chamber left over from czarist times. A long polished mahogany conference table with high-backed chairs around it dominated. Plaster cherubs adorned the cornices and heavy green draperies hung over the tall windows. Of course, the general secretary's chair was empty. Korodin knew he was meeting with the International Monetary Fund's bankers in Paris, desperately seeking a solution to the country's financial problems. The meeting was chaired by Solkov, the minister of defense. He looked up when Korodin sat down and fixed him with his heavy-lidded eyes.

"Good evening, Comrade Admiral Korodin," he said. "We are pleased to see you."

Korodin felt a twinge of anxiety. Old habits died hard, and one learned from early childhood never to be singled out for special attention. But fears were unseemly in a senior official, so he joked, "You, too, Comrade Solkov. It's good to be called out in the middle of the night. Helps my wife to think I do this regularly."

The remark brought laughs from those seated, many of whom kept mistresses in the city. Nighttime meetings were far less frequent than most wives believed.

"The council is glad to be of service to you, Nikolai," Solkov said dryly. "You brought the tape? Good. You can brief us afterward." Solkov signaled to an aide, who put the tape in a machine and dimmed the lights.

"Wait till you see this. It's unbelievable," Korodin said.

Korodin watched their faces as the static cleared and images formed. There was the minister of defense, Solkov; his first deputy ministers of defense; then the deputy ministers like Korodin, commanders of the ground, rocket, aerospace, and air forces respectively; the chairmen of the KGB, Gosplan, and the CPSU; and the chief of the General Staff. They were hard, smart men, veteran professionals who had flourished in a system that rewarded only the most adept at personal survival, something like the American

Mafia. But they looked like children now, faces mirroring both the unreality of the scene and the undeniable beauty of it. The Arctic waters were remarkably clear and gave them a perfect view of *Red Dawn* encased in its tomb of ice. Flashing white numbers in the corner gave the time, date, and coordinates.

When the tape ended, Korodin completed his briefing. "I only have one question, Sergei," he said as he finished, directing his attention to Solkov. "The navy is capable of handling the situation. Our planning session is yielding possible solutions, and ships have already been dispatched. Why this meeting? Is there something I don't know?"

"There's something all right," said a voice to his left. Korodin looked over to the chairman of the KGB. "The Americans are making a rescue attempt."

"But they have no right," Korodin said angrily. "Warn them to stay away. That's our sub. Those are our people."

Abrikov, the chairman of the KGB, was a wiry, white-haired old man with immense energy, but he just stared at his gnarled hands and snorted. "You'll get no disagreement from me, Comrade Admiral. But I'm not the one to argue with."

Korodin looked around him. "What's going on?" He suspected the first deputies already knew. Their faces were deliberately blank. "All right, Sergei," he said to the minister of defense. "Tell me."

Solkov said tiredly, "I'm sorry, Nikolai, but we are not permitted to warn the Americans off. The general secretary is very clear on this point. He won't risk a breakup of the romance between our two countries. Remember, the cold war is over."

The last was said sarcastically. Korodin and everybody else at the table knew how the ultraconservative minister of defense felt about peace with the United States. He believed it was the beginning of the end for the Soviet empire. Of course, this put him at odds with the general secretary, who was wooing the West at every turn. Only Solkov's loyalists in the armed forces and his long and extensive knowledge of where the bodies were buried kept him at his post.

"This is a Soviet military ship of the line," insisted Korodin emphasizing every word. "The Americans have no salvage rights, no right to interfere at all."

"Nevertheless," said the KGB chairman, "our sources tell us they are moving men and material into position on the ice cap right now."

"Then if we can't threaten, sue," Korodin argued. "We've got a veritable army of lawyers. Have them file something at the Hague, for Christ's sake."

"The result would be the same, considering the time frame for such an endeavor," said Solkov. "The Americans hold the upper hand. If they raise *Red Dawn,* they'll be as offended as a reformed whore that we made any suggestion of impropriety. They'll return our rescued people with the whole world watching and even give us back the ship——"

"Minus the propulsion system and enough irinium to enable them to duplicate it in their own labs," finished Korodin. "The espionage coup of the decade."

"If it were our plan I would say it's brilliant," said Abrikov, the KGB chief. "You know, Comrades, it's a new age. Wars of weapons are over. They spent us all into the poorhouse. We're moving into the era of the intelligence war. Think about it. Why buy jet fighters when they'll only be obsolete in a few years? Think how many men can be suborned for the price of one jet plane. Twenty? Thirty? A hundred? And they will work for you for ten years, twenty years, maybe forever if they are very good and very careful. Maybe we can't afford ICBMs anymore, but we will always be able to afford men's greed. I guarantee it will never be in short supply."

"Do you have a rescue plan formulated, Nikolai?" Solkov asked.

"We were working furiously when you called me here. We got this tape only a few hours ago. I've already dispatched subs from Kola Bay and rerouted several more from the North Atlantic."

"How long will it take them to get there?"

"Forty-eight hours. Remember, we can't use surface ships. *Red Dawn* is under the ice cap, for God's sake. And air support's impossible with the weather that's moved in."

"True enough," said Abrikov. "We have reports an American C-Five crashed."

"When will you have a rescue plan?" asked Solkov.

"I hate to be pinned down. A thing like this . . . a hundred details . . ."

"We understand that."

"Then, say, proposals by morning, final decisions by noon, an additional twelve hours to move in whatever's necessary. Twenty-four hours. Our best estimate of *Red Dawn*'s air supply gives us a slight margin."

Solkov shook his head. "It will be too late. Wait," he said when Korodin held up a hand, "I'm not saying anyone can do better, but the Americans are already in place. They'll be making a first attempt in a few hours."

"We started mobilizing the minute we were alerted. It's not my fault the Americans found *Red Dawn* before Kalik did," Korodin said defensively.

"The captain's behavior in this matter merits further discussion," Solkov said grimly. "He's acted criminally."

"What about purely obstructive measures?" asked Abrikov. "Slow them down till we can get up there. We can say we are assisting."

"Can I drop bombs on them?" Korodin asked bluntly. "Or send in your KGB Spetznaz?"

Abrikov sighed. "Unfortunately that is not an option."

"Then that answers your question."

Solkov rose. "All right, Comrades. Thank you for your attendance. The meeting is over." The rest of those at the table got up to leave, but Solkov motioned to Korodin. "Nikolai, one moment, please."

Korodin remained sitting. So did Abrikov. That wasn't so much of a surprise. Solkov and the KGB chairman were old allies, both cut from the same conservative cloth.

Solkov waited till the others had left the room and the thick oaken door was shut behind them. "So, Nikolai, the children have all gone to bed. What do you think of all this?"

"I think it stinks," Korodin said honestly. "I'm a navy

man. I have been since I was fourteen. I'd rather blow *Red Dawn* to pieces than let the Americans get her."

"That's good, Nikolai. It saves us a good deal of trouble."

"How so?"

"Because that's precisely what we want you to do."

"I don't follow, Sergei."

"I will explain it. *Akula* is on station, right?"

"Yes."

"Do you still have faith in *Akula*'s commander?"

"Vassily Kalik?" Korodin frowned. "I did. But, like you, I'm deeply concerned about his disobeying orders and leaving *Red Dawn* to decoy away an American sub. On the other hand, it's always hard to second-guess a field commander. Certainly we did not want the Americans to witness the testing of the new drive. But his orders were clear. So I classify his actions as either command prerogative or a sign of more dangerous things to come. I am somewhat inclined to the former because until now Vassily Kalik has been the best we have. He is among the best ever, according to those who've served with him."

"Overly independent commanders need watching," Abrikov said.

"That's KGB thinking."

"I disagree," said Solkov. "Kalik's arrogance has made the situation much worse. If he had reported losing *Red Dawn* earlier, we'd have ships in place by now."

Korodin was tired. It was time to end the guessing games. "I don't understand where we're headed with this. *Akula* is a powerful weapon, but if the general secretary won't let us intervene—"

"Listen, Nikolai," said Abrikov. "The general secretary has ordered us not to engage the Americans directly. So we won't. Most of our analysts say the chances of raising *Red Dawn* are slim at best anyway. But the Americans are tenacious. They love crash programs and desperate adventures. It's their frontier mentality. They'll go to hell and back to rescue a lost child or a few whales trapped in the ice."

"In other words," said Solkov, "it's always possible the

Americans will succeed. We cannot allow them to take *Red Dawn* if they do."

Korodin's eyes narrowed. "Comrades, when I said I would blow *Red Dawn* to pieces, you knew I was speaking figuratively. We still don't know how many men are on board—Ligichev and his daughter, the crew . . ."

"No battle is won without casualties," Abrikov said flatly.

"Put it plainly. What do you want me to do?"

There could be no misunderstanding Solkov's words. He said, "Order Captain Kalik to destroy *Red Dawn* if the Americans manage to raise her."

"And what happens to the drive and the irinium?"

Abrikov shrugged. "We have Ligichev's notes and the rest of his team. They should be able to reconstruct his work."

"Kalik reports *Seawolf* is in the area. We'll have a fight on our hands."

"Unavoidable," said Solkov. "But I can't imagine too great a stink. After all, both sides know damn well what they're trying to do. How can the Americans complain we took the candy from them when they stole it in the first place? No, win or lose it's a limited action. It will go no further."

Korodin mulled it over. There was one more sticking point, the biggest of all. "What about the general secretary's orders?"

Solkov didn't answer directly. Instead he asked softly, "Nikolai, how do you think things are going? How do you feel about these times we live in?"

Korodin knew he was on dangerous ground. The atmosphere had subtly changed. They weren't talking about a military mission anymore, regardless of how important it was. They were talking about a coup. A man would be blind not to see it, not to know that if any two men in the country could put it together, these two could. The Red Army and the KGB—the tools of real power in Russia.

"I am not a Stalinist," Korodin said carefully.

"Nor are we," said Solkov. "But as a military man surely you would find a more conservative approach to governing appealing, no?"

"You are correct in one respect," Korodin responded. "I am a military man. Therefore I am content to leave politics to the politicians."

Abrikov laughed. "Well said. The apolitical military man gives us a most politic response, eh, Sergei?"

"Quite." Solkov nodded, still appraising Korodin. "Will you give the order, Comrade Admiral?"

"I will use every weapon at my command to prevent *Red Dawn* from falling into American hands. That you can count on, Comrade Minister."

"Very well, Nikolai. That is enough. For now. Good day, Comrade."

Chapter
Eleven

Red Dawn

Captain Galinin opened the valve in the conduit that issued from the torpedo tube hatch and sniffed for incoming air. He shook his head, "Nothing."

Pytor was disheartened. "I'm sorry, Comrades. I'm certain the fault is mine."

Ivanna patted his arm. "Don't be discouraged. I can use the tube to vent the engine exhaust for a few minutes. It'll help with the batteries. We'll try again."

"But not blindly," said Galinin firmly. "This time we clear two tunnels, one for a watcher. That way we can see to direct the torpedo."

Pytor grabbed his drill. "I'll begin work at once. Comrade Ligichev, I'll need help with the new circuits."

"Yes, all right," Ligichev said absently. It was evident he had something on his mind.

"If something's bothering you, Comrade Ligichev," observed Galinin, "this is no time to hold back."

"I'm not. It's just that I really couldn't be certain. Did anyone else feel a second explosion?"

"From one torpedo? Impossible," said Galinin flatly.

"But what about two torpedoes?" Ligichev said. "What about the possibility that *Akula* is out there?"

"And for some reason it fired a torpedo?"

Ivanna pounced on the idea. "Maybe it was a signal of some kind."

"We would have had some kind of communication long ago if *Akula* knew we were here," argued Galinin.

"I suppose so," Ligichev agreed, troubled. "But I was so sure I felt two explosions, just a minute or two apart."

Ivanna was suddenly worried. "I hate to say this, but if it *was* out there . . . well, the second explosion could have been *Akula* being destroyed."

Galinin faced Pytor. "Did you defuse the homing device in the warhead?"

Pytor was pale. "It never occurred to me. I just set the course. I never thought anything was out there to trigger a homing signal."

"In so thinking, you may have destroyed our only hope of rescue," Galinin said tightly.

"Comrade Captain, no one could have anticipated this," said Ivanna.

Ligichev spoke up at once. "I'm certain I am mistaken." But no one believed he was, especially Pytor.

The younger man drew himself up. "I'll begin work at once. This time . . . I promise—"

"We need more men, Comrade Captain," said Ligichev, "He can't dig both tunnels."

"I'll send them. How many hours of air left?"

"Less than a day."

Galinin faced them. His voice was hard. "Listen to me. There is no way to repair the radio and no way to raise a mast even if we could. We have one day to live, but we may not last even that long. Asphyxiation is what every man who serves on a sub fears most but never admits. It starts with a funny tightness in your chest. Then a pain in your gums. The men on the lower decks won't be able to catch their breath, and they'll know what's happening first. They'll come to the upper decks fast when the panic hits. And we've got a woman on board . . ." He deliberately left the thought incomplete. "You've never seen a man die of asphyxiation.

He'll claw at anything within reach for air, face distorted, neck bleeding from where his own fingers ripped through his skin—"

"Comrade Captain . . ." Ligichev put a hand on his arm to stop the images from coming. They all saw the ghosts in Galinin's eyes remembering other times and other places. Galinin refocused on them.

"My advice to all of you is to work quickly."

Polar Ice Cap

The two battered Quonset huts had gone up first. There were plenty of dents in the corrugated gray metal from the crash landing. They stood defiantly on the ice side by side about twenty feet apart with a canvas tarp stretching from roof to roof, creating an outdoor working area immediately dubbed "the carport." A radio tower was erected behind the buildings next to the generators, and a small American flag fluttered from the mast.

The camp was a tiny piece of civilization on the broad, uninviting ice plain, and everyone shared the feeling that one good gust could blow it all away. But despite its transitory nature the pressure ridges gave the camp a small degree of protection from the wind-driven snow and as far as the men who had flown in on the C-5 were concerned, anywhere you could hang your hat on this godforsaken iceberg was home by anyone's definition.

Inside the huts, propane heaters brought the temperature to a comfortable level. The usual amenities for such quarters were missing, too heavy and of too little use to transport here. Crates were stacked in the space where bunk beds should have been. The few nights the SEALs were expected to be here would be spent in sleeping bags on the floor. There was a microwave unit for sandwiches, coffee, and soup. The divers would need a continual supply of calories to overcome the Arctic chill. Most of the food would come from *Seawolf*'s galley.

They called the other building "the warehouse," and it housed the *Argo,* one of NOAA's robot subs. It looked like something out of a science fiction movie. Its bright yellow chassis was hung within a tubular framework. Movable television cameras were mounted on the bow and bracketed by banks of floodlights. Electrical motor–driven propellers in the stern swiveled to provide thrust in any direction. Although the *Argo* was squarish and squat in design with stubby overhead wings for stability, the submersible was quick and responsive and could hover in one place providing television pictures for as long as the operators required.

In the dorm, as the SEALs—the navy's experts on sea, air and land—called their building, everyone was gathered around a plywood sheet propped across a pair of sawhorses, which was serving as the operations table. MacKenzie, Lasovic, and Justine were studying the charts with Captain Ephraim W. Hansen, a clear-eyed, no nonsense veteran who had served three tours of duty in Vietnam; his assistant, Lieutenant Bernie Greene, a strapping young man from New York with an engaging grin and forearms the size of the scuba tanks he'd been hefting all day; and NOAA's Dr. Allen Rose, *Argo*'s operator.

"Everybody got a hot cup of something? Good. We all know one another by now," Justine began amiably. "A crash landing and a few hours in sub-zero weather will do wonders for relationships."

There were some snorts and dry laughs. She continued, "But we're through all that now, and we've got a mission to accomplish. Gentlemen, you've already met Captain Mac-Kenzie. Below the waterline it's his show."

MacKenzie pushed across the table a photograph of *Red Dawn* taken from the video periscope. "Look at it. It would be beautiful except that within a few hours it will be a tomb for the people on board. They're running out of air. Also, unless they can clear their engine exhaust valve they can't restore power for heating."

"What's the time factor?" asked Hansen.

"Our best guess is less than twenty-four hours."

"Going to be tight," Greene said.

"Not if we do it in stages," MacKenzie responded. "First we get them air and power. That'll buy us time for the next step."

Dr. Allen Rose, the *Argo*'s operator, studied the photograph. "What do you need from me exactly? Frozen subs aren't exactly NOAA's line."

"We need to study the submarine at close range," MacKenzie explained. "First, has she got a towing eye pad on her? Second, how far in is it and how much ice do we have to clear to get it free? Third, once we have the tow hook set, where do we plant the charges to blast her out of there?"

Justine was watching Dr. Rose, a balding man of slight build. "You're shivering, Doctor."

"I'm sorry, Ms. Segurra," he said, clutching his parka tighter, "but I was doing research work in Grand Bahama when I got the word I was coming here. That was less than twelve hours ago. So me and Ethel . . ."

"Ethel?"

Rose sniffed. "Her official name is RSV-One-twelve, USS *Argo*. I call her Ethel."

No one said anything. Hansen broke the silence, "I once knew a guy who gave his grenade launcher an engagement ring." He shrugged. "I've seen worse relationships."

Justine cleared her throat delicately. "So you and Ethel . . . ?"

"So it was ninety-five degrees when I got on your navy transport. It's twenty below out there. That's a drop of a hundred and fifteen degrees in half a day. You bet your sweet life I'm cold. And uncomfortable. But I'll do my job, thank you."

MacKenzie liked the game little man. He didn't call *Seawolf* by a pet name, but Justine's earlier remark about two wives wasn't far from the truth. If Rose wanted to personify his craft . . . "We'll get you out of the cold as soon as we can, Doctor. You and the *Argo* are up first."

"Good. Then maybe I can find a warm bed on your ship, Captain."

"I'll make the reservation personally."

"One problem, Captain." It was Lieutenant Greene. "Am

I reading your charts right? The ice cap over the sub is almost twenty feet thick?"

"That's correct."

Greene whistled. "It's going to take a big charge to blow a hole in ice that thick. We're not going to be able to get real close to the sub or we might just knock her out with the same shock wave that opens up the ice cover."

"How close can you get?"

Greene thought it over. "Maybe a hundred yards. Hundred and twenty to be on the safe side."

"Dr. Rose?"

"We can handle that. We're used to a lot deeper."

"It brings up another problem, though," said Hansen. "If me and my men have to go down in that water, well, a hundred-yard swim there and back plus whatever time we stay under the surface adds up to a lot of exposure. Even with the new dry suits."

MacKenzie had seen reports on the new suits and they were supposed to be excellent. Wet suits, which divers used in warmer waters, let in a thin film of water, which body heat turned into an insulating layer. Dry suits were coupled with helmets, special enclosed fins, and gloves, and they kept you completely dry. But Hansen was right. Nothing kept out the bitter cold in these waters for long. In fact, the water temperature was only twenty-eight degrees, lower than the freezing point because of the salinity.

"I'm hoping to cut down your exposure time," he said, "by using the DSRV to place the charges in the deeper sections of the ice keel."

Hansen nodded. "That'll help."

Justine was scanning her manifest. "Captain Hansen, who's going to handle the explosives?"

Greene spoke up. "Ma'am, me and shape charges are old friends. I'll give them to Captain MacKenzie. All he's gotta do is plant them."

Justine put down her clipboard. *"Phoenix* will be here in a few hours. That's it, gentlemen. Let's get some hot food, then dig us a fishing hole."

Naval Command Headquarters, USSR

Korodin kept going over the council meeting in his mind on the way back to his office. Such a small thing, one downed diesel sub. Yet so much rested on it. If not handled properly it could precipitate a power play by the defense minister and the KGB chief and make or break the general secretary. Everybody in power was jumpy these days, with the sweeping changes taking place and the Union so close to dissolution. Losing exclusive possession of irinium technology, and losing it in such a humiliating fashion, might be just the spark to ignite a powder keg of conservative hostility. You could read the feeling on everybody's face. Things might have been bad under the old leaders, but at least they were *strong* and bad.

Korodin entered his office and picked up his phone. "Where's Rudy?"

"He called five minutes ago, Comrade Minister," answered his secretary, "The meeting is over. He's on his way."

"Send him in as soon as he gets here."

Korodin's chief aide, Captain Rudolf Meledov, had run the planning session in his absence. Korodin was anxious for the results. He knew he was in a difficult position. Whatever the short-term cost to the country he genuinely believed that democracy was its only hope. Korodin was a student of military history, and no great military power ever survived without a correspondingly strong economic and political base. It took no genius to see that communism had crumbled. So he had supported the general secretary from the beginning along with his initiatives with the Americans. If it had been up to him personally he might have taken the long view and let *Red Dawn* go. But the long view might never materialize if the diesel sub precipitated a crisis that propelled the defense minister into power. On the other hand, there was risk to Korodin personally if he provoked a confrontation with the Americans. The general secretary could accuse him of disobeying policy. Solkov and Abrikov had boxed him in neatly. Like another sailor, the ancient Ulysses, Korodin was caught between Scylla and Charybdis.

The door opened and Rudy entered. "Good, you're back. What was so important you had to be called out at three in the morning?"

"Wait till you hear this. The Americans are planning a rescue attempt. They're after the drive and the irinium."

"Shit."

"It gets worse." Korodin told him about Solkov's orders. Meledov settled onto the office couch and looked grim. "That puts us in a very tough spot. What are we going to do?"

The "we" wasn't lost on Korodin. He appreciated it. "I don't know yet. Tell me what the group came up with."

"We're under incredible time pressure if we want to get them out of there alive. I don't need to remind you how much air they're using if they're running the engines, and they have to run them or they'll freeze to death. Americans or not, we only have about eighteen hours."

"Use that as a working figure. Go on."

"Nothing works in the time we have. A few of the options, like using jets to blast them out of there, won't work because we can't assume they can control the ship. It might be possible to send in a team of Spetznaz who could make air and power connections, assuming we can ferry in enough support matériel by air. But the weather is worse than ever and Abrikov himself would have to approve the special forces."

"Forget it. He's already ruled them out. He won't oppose the general secretary so openly."

"Then it comes down to one idea."

"Which is?"

"Send in the *Ural*."

Korodin sat up. "The icebreaker? It would take days to get it to the pole."

"Finally we get a break, Nikolai. Remember the ice problem we had at the refueling station on Zemlya Vilcheka?"

"By God, that's right. The *Ural* moved up there a month ago to clear out the northern channels. How close is she to *Red Dawn?*"

"Unless she runs into ice too thick to handle, twenty hours."

Korodin's face fell. "Too long."

"Not actually," said Meledov. Then, hesitantly: "Uh, you gave it sailing orders over four hours ago. I am willing to submit myself for disciplinary action for making such a presumption."

"Submit yourself for a medal, Rudy. Maybe there is a way out of this. *Ural*'s not a warship. The Americans won't dare fire on it or even get in its way. How do you figure to get *Red Dawn* out?"

"Drop tow cables over the side, use divers to attach them, and then blast it out. *Ural*'s got so much tonnage it can drag *Red Dawn* all the way back to Kola like a big fish."

"Excellent. *Ural*'s orders are confirmed. Radio *Akula* to stand by. Kalik is to take no offensive action. Make sure he understands that. In fact, have him stand by in case the *Ural* needs help."

"I'll see to it right away."

Korodin sat back in his chair. Sixteen hours for *Ural* to get to *Red Dawn*. That was the gap they had to close. The icebreaker was a strong ship, and her captain had more experience in the Arctic ice than most seals. He could do it. Things were beginning to look brighter. What was the expression the Americans used for a contest? He finally remembered.

Now it was a horse race.

Polar Ice Cap

MacKenzie surfaced *Seawolf* through the ice a short distance from the camp to provide easier access. He, Justine, and the recovery team held a last planning session over a meal of roast beef, boiled new potatoes, and fresh-baked bread; then everyone went back to the camp. Bernie Greene had been working with the shape charges, and they were all set to go. Shape charges delivered their explosive power in a single direction rather than in an outward sphere like conventional devices. Greene wanted to blow a hole in the ice with a clean, strong edge for getting *Argo* and the divers in and out. If the ice fractured it would land everything in the water and might splinter all the way back to the camp.

The SEALs split into two teams, one wheeling the drums of explosives from the storage building out to the drilling area, the other managing a bright yellow self-propelled drilling machine that up to a day ago had belonged to a well-drilling unit of the Army Corps of Engineers. The box on wheels had a cabin in front and segmented drill in back. Complete with its own generator, it could drill a six-inch-diameter hole to a depth of a hundred feet. MacKenzie and Justine followed it as it rolled over the ice on black tires. The snow had stopped falling and their breath blew feathery plumes in the cold, but their insulated parkas and coveralls kept them comfortable. Captain Hansen used a radio transmitter linked to *Seawolf* to calibrate the correct distance for the drilling, and a metal rod had been implanted in the spot. Using that as a center point, one of the SEALs used a steel tape to inscribe a twenty-foot-diameter circle in the ice.

Except for the older Hansen and Greene, the SEALs were all big, strong men in their mid- to late twenties with military crew cuts and easy grins. Bright and committed to their task, with a jock's love-the-pain attitude, they worked quickly and efficiently.

Captain Hansen started the generator up with a roar, and the drill operator moved the machine to the center of the circle. The marker rod was removed. Poised over the spot, the big drill bit into the ice. Shards sprayed as it dug in, and the machinery whined louder. It took only a minute or two for the drill to reach twenty feet and then retract.

Hansen directed the driver to maneuver the machine over the inscribed circle. The drill cut another hole in the ice. They continued to drill every two feet around the sixty-foot circumference.

MacKenzie was still concerned about the torpedo from *Red Dawn*. What was its purpose? Could it have been a deliberate attack on *Seawolf?* What was there to gain? And the enemy Boomer was still out there. Would it permit them to extricate *Red Dawn,* or would it attack? Sooner or later the Soviets would have to make a rescue attempt of their own. Time pressure was increasing. He wanted to get *Argo* launched as soon as possible.

"The way they're preparing the ice reminds me of wood shop," he said to Justine as another hole was drilled.

"Mac, I just had a horrible thought."

He was immediately on guard. "What?"

"I left so fast I forgot to ask our neighbor to water the plants. The ficus is going to lose all its leaves. Damn it."

He stared. "In the middle of all this you're worried about the ficus tree in our apartment?"

"Not directly . . . I mean, I was watching them drill and I thought about how at least Antarctica, at the South Pole, is a real continent, but here we're all just standing on a big sheet of ice in the middle of a huge ocean. There's no ground at all, so there are no trees, and that started me thinking about the ficus in the living room and, well . . . C'mon, you only worry about business? How would you feel if I forgot to tell the super about the leaky pipe in the hallway bathroom?"

"You forgot that? Justine, we're going to have a flood."

"I didn't forget it. It was just an example."

"Wait a minute. Did you tell him or didn't you?"

"I told him. Why are you getting so mad?"

MacKenzie sighed.

Bernie Greene called out, "Captain, Ms. Segurra, we're ready to plant the explosives."

Justine signaled him to go ahead. Each charge was lowered by a ten-foot line to the proper depth. Detonation was by wireless remote. Greene personally saw to each electrical connection. When the charges around the circumference were completed, he fixed the largest one in the center. Done, he walked over to MacKenzie and Justine.

"Here's what's going to happen," he explained. "The shape charges around the circumference are all built to explode 'flat,' as we say, like a knife's cutting motion instead of a blast in all directions. The charge in the center will blow vertically. So what we got is a series of simultaneous explosions that should sever the circle of ice and blow it right out of the hole."

"Six thousand cubic feet of ice weighs"—MacKenzie did a quick calculation—"almost a quarter of a million pounds. You used enough explosive?"

Greene grinned. "You ever see a building demolished? I can bring skyscrapers down with fifty pounds of this stuff. CX-Three-ninety-one, it's called. Put a little on your heel and stomp down and say hi to the moon as you pass by."

"I'm convinced," said Justine. "Fire when ready."

"Yes, ma'am." Greene trotted back.

MacKenzie looked at her. She shrugged. "I always wanted to say that."

They retreated to a safe distance. Greene yelled, "Fire in the hole!" Everyone took cover.

The blast was a muted *whump* and then a loud *wa-bang!* as the explosions threw ice into the air, pelting the aluminum roofs of the Quonset huts. Greene was the first one back to the blast area, and a satisfied smile crossed his face when he saw the results. MacKenzie walked up next to him and regarded yet another startling image possible only in this Arctic region: a perfect cylinder had been blown out of the ice. Cold gray ocean swirled down inside it and chunks of ice floated on top.

"One fishing hole," Greene said proudly.

"That's amazing," said MacKenzie.

"Practice makes perfect."

"Ever think of doing bank jobs?"

Greene laughed and gestured at the bleakness around them. "And give up the easy life?"

Hansen was already sending men for the robot sub. Dr. Rose, looking no happier with the freezing clime, emerged from the dorm.

"Ethel's ready to go. I set up the monitors inside."

"Can you put a VCR on line?" asked Justine.

"Already have one," Dr. Rose responded. "We'll record

everything Ethel sees." He looked to the fishing hole where the SEALs were erecting *Argo*'s launching scaffold, and he frowned. "Wait a minute. Those guys are about to mess up that scaffolding and then where will we be? Go ahead, I'll meet you inside."

Rose trotted over to where Hansen and his men were putting up a scaffold of metal tubes rising fifteen feet over the fishing hole to raise and lower the *Argo*. The tubular frame with twin winches on top bulging with a mile of wire looked like a spider perched over the ice. A power cable "tail" trailed back to the generator behind the warehouse.

The wind was rising and the temperature dropping. It was near twenty-five below. The simplest of jobs was maddeningly difficult in this climate. Threading a simple wing nut onto a bolt was tedious when you were wearing thick gloves. And pity the man who grew frustrated enough to bare-hand it. Metal this cold killed exposed skin on contact. Pulling off your face mask to see meant a frostbitten nose in under a minute. A slip or fall that immersed a foot in water would mean chunks of dead skin that would slough off with your socks.

The whole body rebelled at being in this environment too long. The SEALs working outside faced particular dangers. Strenuous exertion used up so much fluid under these conditions that blood actually got too thick to flow through veins and arteries, especially through the narrow capillaries in the extremities. Even inside heavy snow clothing the body began to retract its energies inward to protect the vital organs. The result—hypothermia from dehydration, frostbite from the inside out.

The SEALs rolled the *Argo* out of the warehouse and over to the fishing hole. The robot sub moved easily on a wheeled trailer, and Dr. Rose walked alongside it like an anxious parent guiding a child on his first bike ride without training wheels. At the edge of the fishing hole the SEALs attached guy lines to either side of the craft and fastened heavy wires from the power winches to bow and stern.

"Raise her up," Dr. Rose ordered. "Carefully, please."

The winches whined into life. A pair of SEALs took up the guy lines. The *Argo* slowly lifted off her trailer and would have swung out fast, but the SEALs kept her from moving too quickly. They centered the craft, then lowered it into the hole until it finally bobbed comfortably on the cold gray water. "All set, sir. We'll release on your order."

"Make sure that aft cable is secure and the clutch is on," Rose directed.

"We've checked it, sir. It's on tight."

"I'll radio when I'm set, Captain."

Dr. Rose rushed back to the dorm, and MacKenzie and Justine followed. The warmth inside was almost suffocating after the cold outside. Justine went to get coffee and MacKenzie went with Dr. Rose to examine *Argo*'s control setup. There was a thirteen-inch TV monitor with a VCR, a console with a series of gauges to display the *Argo*'s depth, pressure, speed, and course, and a control panel with an antenna extended.

"She's wireless," MacKenzie said in surprise. "I hadn't realized that."

Rose nodded, flicking on the switches. "The cable is only for emergencies, in case we have a malfunction and have to tow it back. You have the navigational information ready?"

"Steer course two nine zero magnetic. It's a direct line to the *Red Dawn*."

"Depth?"

"One hundred feet will take *Argo* under the ice keels."

Rose flicked on the monitor. It showed only a dull white. At first, MacKenzie didn't think the cameras were working, but suddenly he realized he was actually looking at the walls of the fishing hole from inside the shaft.

"Ready to descend," Rose said. He picked up a walkie-talkie and ordered Hansen to release the guy lines.

There was a sudden drop, and the color on the screen changed from the fishing hole's dull white to slate gray to faint blue as *Argo* dropped below the surface. MacKenzie was fascinated with the computer-controlled craft, which took in ballast and kept itself trim in much the same manner as any submarine. Its big floodlights illuminated a wide area and the electric motors propelled it at almost ten knots.

"On course two nine zero. Depth one hundred feet," Rose informed MacKenzie. "We'll be coming up on it soon."

Red Dawn

"**We're** down to ten hours of air. Roughly the same for heat, since Ivanna ran the engines briefly," Ligichev informed Galinin over a meal of beef and noodles. They were sitting in the officers' mess, both tired and dispirited from heavy work with little prospect of success.

To his credit, Galinin greeted the announcement with equanimity. "How is the rest going?"

"Petrov and his men have the second tube almost cleared." Ligichev took another bite. "I wish I had more faith in doing it like this a second time."

"Is there any other way?"

"I can't figure one. The air lies beyond the ice. To get to it we have to break through."

Galinin hesitated. "Comrade Ligichev, there is something I'd like to discuss, but it is of a very personal nature."

Ligichev shrugged. "Nothing is more personal than dying together. Feel free, Comrade Captain."

"I have been thinking. Maybe I am not as good a parent as you are, but I like to think I would protect my children as fiercely. If things come to an end there will be no discipline in this ship. Dying men will listen to nothing but their own panic. So I thought . . . your daughter . . ." He hesitated, then shrugged and pushed a triangular pouch across the table to Ligichev.

Ligichev opened it. Inside lay a small .25 caliber automatic pistol. He looked at Galinin wretchedly and shook his head. "No. I . . . I couldn't."

"You may have to."

Ligichev looked at the pistol for a long time, then took it with trembling hands and put it inside his coat.

Akula

In the officers' mess, Kalik read the orders from Naval Command and crumpled up the paper angrily. "The Americans are attempting to raise *Red Dawn*," he told Volkov. "And we are told to do nothing but wait on station for the *Ural* and the rest of the fleet to arrive."

"The icebreaker?"

"It's on its way. We've become superfluous. An unwanted appendage. No force is to be used."

"How can we just sit here and let the Americans proceed without making some attempt to slow them down?" asked Volkov. "I can't believe it."

"Read it for yourself."

"But they have already blasted a hole in the ice, and sonar reports the deployment of a robot sub."

"Naval Command knows that," said Kalik bitterly. "It appears not to matter."

"I'm shocked."

"Don't be. It's politics. That I'm sure of. Admiral Korodin supports the general secretary. Minister Solkov does not. On the general secretary's orders Korodin has tightened the rules of engagement to where even tagging the Americans with sonar is not permitted. Conflict with them is unthinkable. These are the butter days. Guns take a backseat."

"They've lost their guts. Just a few years ago we would have sent in the bombers before giving *Red Dawn* up." Volkov said angrily. "Perhaps we should communicate with Galinin, tell him help is on the way."

"The Americans are on the way. What else besides that would we have to tell him?"

"I cannot believe Korodin's lack of nerve."

Kalik grew pensive, his mood darkening. "There is another factor here, Viktor, one not good for me."

"What is it?"

"I made one serious mistake, just one in a long career, but it has brought my command capability into question by Naval Command."

No."

"Yes, I'm sure of it. I'm being punished for leaving *Red Dawn*, with worse yet to come, I'm sure." He held up a hand to stifle Volkov's protest. "Maybe it was the wrong decision. I don't know. What I mind is not being given a chance to correct it. If mine was the error let me erase it. Am I going to end my career like this?"

"Vassily, your record is unmatched."

"It was. But one mistake—"

The crackle of the intercom stopped him. "Comrade Captain, this is Sonar. We are picking up small high-speed motors."

"Torpedoes?"

"No, a single craft. The robot submersible, we think."

"Course?"

"Heading two nine zero."

"Acknowledged. I'm on my way."

"It's heading for *Red Dawn*," said Volkov, following Kalik back to the control room. "The Americans are further along in their plans than we thought."

Kalik walked into the control room and over to his radio officer. "Is the craft radio-controlled or wire-guided?"

The man was turning dials and listening into his headphones intently. "Radio-guided. I have a strong signal."

"Can we jam it?"

"Yes, but they will know the interference emanates from us."

"That can't be helped. Send it," Kalik ordered.

Volkov moved close and said in low tones that only Kalik could hear, "What about our orders? Command says no interference. This is gross insubordination, Vassily."

Kalik pulled away. "Radio Officer, you will note in your log that a radio malfunction occurred at this hour."

The radio officer looked confused, but only for a moment. "Of course, Comrade Captain. A malfunction."

Kalik turned back to his senior lieutenant, who still wore a worried look. "I've come to a decision, Viktor. There is only one way for me to redeem myself."

"It's dangerous, Vassily."

Kalik nodded. "Perhaps. But here's the truth of it. In the end, no one remembers the mistakes you made in a game you won."

Red Dawn

Pytor crawled into the second ice tunnel. Below him the first shaft had refrozen but had been evacuated again. He could see Ivanna lying on her stomach checking the thickness of the ice seal. They were both exhausted from work and cold, but more than ever he was determined to escape from their icy prison with the woman he had fallen in love with.

Pytor came from a good family. His father was a journalist for a newspaper, and his mother was a computer operator in a bank. He had one brother still in school. Pytor had known his share of girls back home and more in his travels with the navy, but he had never said "I love you" to any of them. That was a matter of pride. He was not like most of his brother officers who said it for any favors it would buy. Love, not sex, was what he was saving for marriage. He reminded himself that their circumstances could be clouding his judgment, but he was sure that what he felt for Ivanna was real. He was in love for the first time.

Below, Ivanna must have felt him looking down at her because she looked back up and smiled bravely. Then she made an "I'm finished" sign and squirmed back out of the tunnel.

Pytor kept digging. The ice in front of him was as clear as glass, and again he marveled at the sight of the ice cap above them and the ocean below. He forced himself to concentrate on his task. Keep working. Time was running out.

He cleared the second tunnel and shinnied back into the torpedo room. Galinin and Ligichev were waiting beside Ivanna, who was toweling off her clothing and wet hair.

"We are down to six hours," Galinin said. "When can we shoot?"

"The tunnels are ready, Comrade Captain. What about the controls?"

"Here." Ligichev handed him a metal box with an antenna and a toggle switch, which he pointed to. "The homing device is disconnected. You control it with this. It's wireless. Left, right, up, down. As soon as the torpedo travels the appropriate distance for the minimum motor turns, send it toward the surface. This is the motor cut off switch in case of an emergency."

"I understand." Pytor took the control box and placed it in the tunnel. His men were just completing the insertion of the second torpedo into the tube. The snorkel and coiled tubing were about to be loaded. Pytor noted the torpedo's number, CP 274. He patted it for luck. Ivanna leaned close to him and whispered, "Be careful, my love."

"I will be."

He grabbed the upper lip of the torpedo hatch and swung himself in. The sound of the tube door closing was a lonely one, like a cell door slamming shut. If the force of the torpedo leaving the first tunnel shattered the second, only one man would drown.

Pytor set himself up with the control in his lap. Left, right, up, down, he tested the switch. From below him he felt the grinding of the motors as the outer door was opened and then the shock of the compressed air ejecting the torpedo. Then CP 274 shot out from under him and plunged through the tunnel's ice seal into the water with the wire guide pulling the snorkel behind. The ice tunnel filled with water at once and although his tunnel shuddered and spider cracks appeared, it held. He strained to follow the torpedo in the dim blue-gray light and counted the seconds. When it was time, he pushed the switch and aimed the torpedo up toward the ice cap.

He was so intent on the flight of the torpedo that when he saw the glowing sea monster rise in front of him his only thought was that they must have awakened some hideous sea creature from the abyss and it was hovering there before his eyes. He fell back in fear till logic reasserted itself. Those weren't eyes, they were lights and camera lenses. It wasn't a monster at all. It was a miniature sub. Someone had found them!

Pytor made an instantaneous decision. A mother ship had to be close by, a ship come to take them off *Red Dawn*. The torpedo might damage their only hope of rescue. His hand stabbed at the cut-off switch and rammed it home. He peered into the ocean beyond and prayed the torpedo motor had not made the minimum turns necessary to arm the warhead. He waited, counting the seconds. There was no explosion. He let out his pent-up breath. Somewhere out there, torpedo CP 274 had lost power and was slowly tumbling down to the ocean depths, no danger to their rescuers.

Pytor let out a sigh of relief and, when he couldn't think of anything else to do, waved at the camera lens.

Polar Ice Cap

"Jesus, will you look at that," said MacKenzie, watching the monitor alongside Justine and Dr. Rose. He had just been assured by *Seawolf*'s sonar that the torpedo motor had stopped and the fish was no threat. "They tunneled right into the ice keel itself. Then they fired the torpedoes to blast a hole in the ice cap overhead to get the snorkel up into the air. Pretty clever."

"Would it have worked?"

"I don't know. It would've taken a very lucky break, but they're desperate."

"I wondered when he was going to see us," said Justine. "Must have been quite a shock."

Dr. Rose, watching the young sailor scurrying back out of the tunnel, said, "Where's he going?"

"To get his captain, probably," said MacKenzie.

Rose angled the craft. A young woman had crawled into the tunnel and was looking out, her face a study of relief and hope.

"I would guess that is Dr. Ivanna Ligichova, the chief scientist's daughter. Mac, something just occurred to me."

"The ficus will live?"

Justine gave him a withering look. "The captain is going to try to talk to us. Probably by writing."

"So?"

"So you read Russian?"

"Gotcha." MacKenzie picked up his walkie-talkie to call *Seawolf,* but Dr. Rose stopped him.

"Captain, I've been on a few oceanographic ventures with the Soviets. I can translate for you."

"Offer accepted, Doc."

Justine pointed to the screen. "Here comes someone."

"That's a Soviet captain," said MacKenzie as an older, bigger man pushed his way into the ice tunnel with some difficulty. As Justine predicted, he held a slate and some chalk. The slate was covered with Cyrillic writing. He held it up to the camera.

"He's asking who we are," said Dr. Rose.

"How do we talk back?" Justine asked.

"The only thing I can do is blink the lights."

"Wait. Turn to port side," said MacKenzie. "Let him see our markings."

Rose manipulated the controls and the view on the screen shifted to the blue-gray waters as *Argo* spun around. A few seconds later he turned the craft back. The captain's face appeared in the monitor again wearing a thoughtful expression. He wiped the slate clean with his sleeve, wrote something, then held it up for the camera to see.

AMERICANS?

"He speaks English," said Justine. "Great."

"Blink the lights, Doc," MacKenzie requested. "Let's establish some rules here. Once for yes, twice for no."

Rose reached out and flicked the toggle switch. The picture on the monitor faded when the lights dimmed. The man nodded, wiped the slate clean and wrote again.

5 HOURS OXYGEN, SITUATION URGENT

"Signal yes," MacKenzie directed.

17 DEAD, 14 WOUNDED, 15 ALIVE AND WELL

"Signal yes again."

NO RADIO, LOW POWER, BLOCKED EXHAUST, VALVES OUT

"No wonder they're so quiet. And he can't start his engines till he can dump the exhaust. Signal yes."

"How do we get air to them, Mac?" Justine asked.

"We'll get him to feed the snorkel out the torpedo tube into the ice tunnel. Then we'll use the DSRV's robot arm to take the snorkel to the surface."

"How do you tell him that?"

"My Morse code is a little rusty but I'm going to give it a shot. Doctor, may I?"

"This switch is for the lights, here."

MacKenzie thought for a moment, then began to flick the lights on and off in a series of dots and dashes. "Let's try something simple first."

He sent: "MacKenzie, captain *Seawolf.* Greetings."

The man on the screen nodded vigorously and wrote on the slate: CAPTAIN GALININ, *RED DAWN*, WELCOME.

MacKenzie smiled. "Okay, we understand each other." He began flicking the lights on and off again and sent: "Leave snorkel in tunnel. We will take to surface."

He had to send the message twice while they watched Galinin's expression slowly change from concentration to understanding. He nodded vigorously and a smile broke over his features. He turned his head and yelled something back into his ship. There was apparently some activity offscreen, and then someone handed up to him and he held out the business end of a snorkel with its air tube coiled behind it. He pointed upward.

"That's it," said MacKenzie. "Smart fellow. Catches on quick."

Dr. Rose was just reaching for the controls when the image on the screen flickered and began to break up. "Captain, something's wrong. I'm losing control. Some kind of interference. I can't hold her steady."

"What is it?"

"I can't tell. My signal . . . *Argo's* not responding."

MacKenzie grabbed his walkie-talkie. *"Seawolf,* Mac-Kenzie."

"Seawolf, aye."

"We're getting interference up here. Scan all channels."

"We're picking it up, Skipper. It's a jamming signal. Coming from the Russian Boomer. Sonar is reporting strong contact."

Rose's voice broke in, filled with concern. "Captain MacKenzie, I'm losing control. She's ramming the ice keel."

MacKenzie looked quickly to the screen. The *Argo* was out of control, surging up against the keel. The captain held up his hands in fear. One crack in that ice and not only would he drown but the whole sub would flood. "Bearing on that sub, Sonar. Quickly."

"Course zero nine five. Speed twenty knots. Depth one zero zero feet. But, sir, it's not a Boomer at all. We finally got enough to correlate the signature. It's the same ship that's been sneaking around off our coastline, Skipper. Our computers log it as the *Akula."*

So that was what had been dogging them all this time. *Akula,* the latest and most powerful attack sub in the Soviet fleet. MacKenzie's mind raced. The missile launch had been a fake, just a ploy to lure them out of the area. But after all the subterfuge, why come out of hiding now? The answer was simple. They knew where *Red Dawn* was and had begun a campaign to block the rescue attempt. Maybe *Akula* was planning a rescue of its own. But all the conjecture had to wait. He had to block the jamming before *Argo* was lost.

"Skipper, Navigation. I don't know if it helps, but at its present course and speed the sub's going to pass within three hundred yards due north of your position in . . . four minutes."

MacKenzie stopped short. Joe Santiago had given him an idea. It was a long shot, and the move was from another time and place, but it was certainly possible. "Sonar, active search. Keep it up," he ordered. "And watch your ears for loud noises."

"Skipper?"

"You heard me. Do it. Captain out."

Justine caught his arm. "Mac?"

"No time, Just. Doc, hold her steady. Do the best you can." He grabbed his parka and face mask and raced out of the building.

The intense cold hit him in the face, and the wind swirled around him as he ran. Hansen and Bernie Greene were working at the scaffolding, their hair and eyelashes caked with ice droplets. They looked up as MacKenzie raced over, correctly reading on his face that something was very wrong.

"Captain, what gives? We got tugs on this line like we hooked a shark."

"A Russian sub's jamming the control signal. Mr. Greene, are there more charges?"

"Plenty. Why?"

"Bring them and follow me." MacKenzie raced for the drilling machine, "C'mon, get this thing moving."

Hansen understood urgency when he heard it. He leaped into the cab, and the engine roared into life. MacKenzie jumped in beside him. "Three hundred yards due north." He pointed. "That way. I'll tell you when to stop."

The drill bumped and skewed over the ice. MacKenzie held on and looked back for Greene. The lieutenant had picked up a sack of explosives and was running after them. They hit a bump, and MacKenzie's head almost went through the roof. He checked his watch. Two minutes. He looked back to the dorm, made a mental measurement, and picked a spot ahead. Best estimate. No time for anything else.

"Stop here. Start drilling holes for the explosives to drop through. As many as you can in two minutes."

Hansen wasted no time. He ran around back and within seconds of MacKenzie's command he was drilling into the ice cap.

Greene ran up breathlessly. "What's up, Captain?"

"Those things are waterproof right?"

"Right."

"The Soviet sub jamming *Argo*'s signal is going to pass under this spot in less than a minute and a half—"

Greene grinned. "And you want to drop a few presents on him?"

MacKenzie clapped him on the shoulder. "You got it."

"Can do." Greene dropped to his knees and began pulling the charges out of his sack, talking as he worked. "I can't set these for pressure, like a depth charge, but I can set them for time. How deep is he?"

"One hundred feet. Say, fifteen seconds." MacKenzie checked his watch. "That means you have to drop them in one minute. No, forty-five seconds."

"Just let me get this in here." Greene set the detonator on the first charge and kept working.

"Forty seconds."

"One set. Working on two. Working . . . Two set. Working on three."

"Thirty seconds."

"Got three."

"Get them into the holes," MacKenzie ordered. He looked over. Hansen had bored three holes. "That's all we have time for. Move the drill." Hansen jumped back into the cab and complied, then waited for MacKenzie with the motor running.

MacKenzie looked at Greene. "Ten seconds."

"Go with the drill, Captain. I can handle this."

"I'm staying."

"C'mon, when was the last time you ran the hundred-yard dash in twelve flat? Get going."

"Be goddamn careful."

Greene winked, gathered the charges from the ice, and headed for the holes. "Count on it."

MacKenzie jumped on the drill, and Hansen tore out. They flew over the ice, and MacKenzie held on for dear life every time they hit a ridge. They stopped at a safe distance and waited, engine idling. MacKenzie leaped off, cupped his hands, and yelled, "Now!"

A hundred yards back, Greene dropped the charges down the holes in succession, then sprinted off at full speed. He ran across the ice like a broken-field runner, knees high and

160

pumping, his breath like a rocket trail in the freezing air, snow spraying from his feet.

MacKenzie was counting, "Three, two, one—"

Then there was a deep bass *whumppf* that he could feel through the soles of his boots, and the ice cap turned upside down.

Akula

Kalik's brow was furrowed as he stood over the sonar table and watched the display. "Active sonar? Why, what are they looking for?"

"No change in their position, Comrade Captain. *Seawolf* is still on the surface."

"I don't like this. It's almost as if he wants us to know he's there. And now this drilling, almost over our heads." Kalik's expression changed. "What is that?" he pointed to the screen."

"It looks like some ice debris falling toward us."

Kalik's mind and body reacted as one. He grabbed the intercom. "Emergency dive! Emergency dive! Six hundred meters. Viktor, take us down fast. Dive!"

The dive bell clanged frantically, and the angle of the ship increased rapidly. Kalik used the wall stanchions for handholds and plunged into the control room.

"Depth!" he roared.

"Fifty meters . . . sixty meters . . . seventy meters . . ."

"Everyone prepare for—"

The first blast rocked the ship. Steam pipes buckled and couplings strained. Kalik was thrown against a bulkhead and felt something inside him snap. He barely had time to feel the pain that roared up his shoulder. An unconscious crewman landed on top of him, pushing him onto the deck. The second blast merged with the third and pounded *Akula* as if some angry god had hurled it to the ground and stomped on it. Systems failed. The ocean poured in as seawater fittings ruptured and the main ballast tank skin was holed. They dived for the bottom.

Kalik fought the pain and pushed the crewman off of him. *Akula* was plummeting to the depths. Alarms were blaring, men screaming. Steam hissed from auxiliary lines that had split open. He crawled to the periscopes and climbed up to grab the dangling intercom.

"Engine room, all engines full astern. Full astern!"

The speaker was filled with static. "We have a steam leak in the reactor auxiliary steam system. We are trying to isolate it . . . trying—"

"I need power. Do not shut down the reactor. Full astern!"

"Trying . . ."

Kalik felt the lurch as the propellers bit. He looked at the depth gauge. They were slowing but not fast enough. Another ten minutes and they would pass below crush depth. He pulled the main ballast tank blow lever. The feeble blast told him the ballast tank was ruptured.

"Vassily . . ."

It was Viktor. He was lying in a pool of water unable to lift himself. Kalik reached down with his good arm and helped him up. Viktor turned white. His arm hung limp at his side. Kalik suspected the collarbone was shattered. He managed to get him propped up against the scopes.

"Vassily, too fast . . . Not enough power . . . to stop us . . . but look."

He was pointing to the screen. Kalik saw what he meant. There was a shelflike ledge protruding from a huge ice keel almost directly ahead of them. The keel itself had to go down half a mile or more. The ledge looked about sixty feet wide. It would be close, but it might be wide enough to save them. Kalik made his way forward. The helmsman was dead in his seat, hunched over the controls. Kalik tried to pull him out, but couldn't manage it with one arm.

"Viktor, help me."

Volkov held his arm to his side and climbed over the wreckage in the control room. Together, they pulled the dead man from his chair.

"Can you steer?" Kalik demanded.

Volkov dropped into the seat. "I can steer. You handle the planes."

Kalik slid into the seat next to him. "Engine room," he called on the intercom. "Starboard stop."

"Yes . . . Comrade."

"Right full rudder."

Volkov steered for the ridge. "We're going to hit hard."

Kalik gritted his teeth. "Just don't overshoot it." The pain in his arm made it hard to see. They were a projectile hurtling out of control. He had to cut their speed at just the right moment or they would go right over the edge and tumble straight down till the pressure crushed them.

"Engine Room. All stop. All engines emergency full astern."

He heard no reply, but he could feel the cessation of vibration that told him his command had gotten through. Now the emergency astern bell had both propellers biting into the icy sea.

"Now, Viktor. Hard right rudder. Use the wall to brake us."

Kalik held steady on the planes, forcing them down onto the ridge while Volkov steered them into the keel wall. They hit with a crunch and Kalik heard the hull popping and groaning.

"It's too short," Volkov yelled. "We're going over!"

"Hold us against the keel!" Kalik shouted. He rammed the control yoke forward and the bow dropped like a deadweight. It scored the ice ridge and slowed their speed. Sheer momentum pushed them toward the edge. Kalik held the planes down and Volkov forced them tighter into the wall. The hull screamed from abrasion against the ice. The edge of the ridge came rushing at them. For a moment it looked as if it could go either way, but with a final deep and troubled groan, *Akula* shuddered and came to a stop fifty feet from the abyss.

"All stop." The engines coasted to a halt. Kalik dropped the yoke and looked to Volkov, sagging wearily beside him. Pain contorted Kalik's features, but a slow, feral grin

163

crossed his face. He bashed his fist on the control yoke and said fiercely, "Not yet, eh, my old friend? Not goddamn yet!"

Volkov nodded tiredly, his face flushed and sweating. "No. Not yet."

The monitor showed their position. Perched on the shelf of ice over a mile of ocean, *Akula* was bent and broken, but she was not yet ready to die.

Chapter
Twelve

Benton Garver looked up from his desk, surprised to see Winestock standing in his doorway.

"May I come in?"

Garver eased back in his seat. "Sure. Want a progress report?"

"I've already got one." He looked at his watch. "They should be getting the DSRV ready to leave *Phoenix* in under an hour."

Garver laughed. "I forgot who I was talking to. What can I do for you?"

Winestock dropped a file on Garver's desk. Inside was a stack of eight-by-ten photographs. "Take a look."

Garver thumbed through them. "These are satellite recon photos."

"Yes, and they show a disturbing situation evolving."

Garver squinted to make out the detail. "Christ, a Russian icebreaker."

"Plowing toward *Red Dawn*. We figure the Soviets know where their sub is and they're sending the *Ural* to do something about rescuing her."

"Well, our exclusive was too good to last," said Garver. "And now that we know their sub in the area is really the *Akula,* we have to count on some kind of attack. To tell you the truth, I'm surprised they didn't send in their commandos or some kind of light, fast force to rough us up even before this."

"There are quite a few who want to. But the general secretary's got a leash on them. Look, screw all our bombers and subs. That's not what the top leadership is worried about. Practically speaking, there's only one thing that could really harm long-term Soviet-American normalization."

"And that is?"

"American public opinion. Twenty years ago, Ho Chi Minh understood the power of public opinion and won a war. More recently, China didn't, blew away a few hundred kids on TV, and that action may yet cost them their most-favored-nation status. In real terms that's several billion dollars a year. Ben, public opinion polls say eighty percent of the country now likes the Russians, up from twenty percent just a few years ago. Now, imagine the field day the media would have showing on the eleven o'clock news the bodies of American seamen killed by Soviet troops at the North Pole. Public opinion could easily shift again. With his entire economic bailout in the hands of Western bankers, the general secretary just can't risk the PR fallout from a hot little war with us at the North Pole."

"In some ways, it works just as much against us. We won't go to war over this, either. If their attack subs converge on *Red Dawn* before we can get her out, we'll have to back off, too, right?"

"Right. Timing is everything," Winestock said.

"How long will the general secretary's leash hold?"

"We don't know. Speed's still of the essence."

Garver studied the photos. "This breaker poses a problem. *Red Dawn* is a Soviet government ship. They could claim that the *Ural* has the legal right to raise it and order us off."

"If they make it in time. Can they?" Winestock asked.

"It's going to be close."

"What would you say to sending in one of our own icebreakers?"

"Why?" Garver said.

"Head them off at the pass, so to speak. Throw a block. Choose your own metaphor. Give MacKenzie more time."

Garver ran a hand over his lower face. "I'd like to oblige. But the sad fact is that we don't have an icebreaker in this man's navy."

"What? You're kidding."

"Wish I was. The last navy icebreaker was transferred to the coast guard over ten years ago. Some of the bigger oil companies may have one or two that they use for oil exploration, Humble Oil's *Manhattan* comes to mind, but it isn't under our control."

"I need something to run interference with the *Ural*. But it's got to look like we're still helping. C'mon, Ben. Nobody gets to be CNO without a good strong larcenous streak."

Garver grinned. "The *Ural's* a big ship. Bigger than anything we ever built, public or private. In fact, I know of only one icebreaker any bigger, and the Arctic's her stomping grounds. Hell, she was built for the ice cap. With any luck she might be in range."

"C'mon. Let's have it."

"I don't know if even you guys swing enough weight to manage this one. These folks are awfully touchy about sovereignty up there. That's why they built it."

"Ben, we've got weight you never dreamed of."

"I hope so. You speak good French?"

"I sound like I'm gargling." Winestock listened to Garver's idea, finally nodding in admiration. "Mind if I use your phone?"

"Be my guest. I just wish I could be there to see it. God, what a race it'll be."

"I'll send you pictures. Hello? This is Winestock. Patch me through to the White House."

Ottawa, Canada

The prime minister of Canada was an inveterate poker player, and Wednesday was poker night. Smoke hung in the air and chips clicked across the green felt table. It was an old friends' game filled with old friends' talk.

"Seven times," the PM said, shuffling the deck. He was a big man with long-fingered hands, and his skill with cards was legendary. "Seven times it takes to shuffle the deck completely." He winked. "I read it in the *New York Times.*"

"Seven times or seventy, we're still watching you," said the minister of finance archly.

The PM's administrative assistant yawned. "Deal, Peter. It's getting late."

The prime minister smiled. "An eternal truth of the game, George. The winner smiles, the loser says 'Deal.' " The other men at the table laughed, and the PM sent cards whizzing around the table.

"Remind me to vote for the opposition," said the AA.

The door to the study opened and the PM's secretary peeked in. "Excuse me, sir, there's a call for you."

"Tell whoever it is I'm in a meeting. An urgent nighttime national damn security meeting."

"Well, sir, I would . . . but it's the president of the United States."

"All the more reason," said the PM, eyes twinkling. "Wait. Forget that. I'll take it." He put his hand down. "Nobody touch the cards. Hello, Brendon. *Ça va, mon ami?* Good. . . . Well, you caught me right in the middle of a security conference." He listened, then laughed. "Of course the cards are being good to me. They're always good to me." He looked over the mouthpiece at his poker buddies. "Which one of you is CIA?" He listened again. "What's that, Brendon? A favor for a cut of the pot. What pot? . . . *Bien, j'écoute,* I'm listening."

The PM did listen, for a full five minutes. Then he did a thing his poker buddies had never seen before, and they went all the way back to his gold-prospecting days in the tundra. He hung up the phone, tossed his cards on the table, and said, "I fold." Then he was out the door yelling for someone to locate the defense minister.

The *Ural*

The *Ural* was a big, sharp-bowed 20,000-ton icebreaker with 30,000-horsepower engines that at the moment were propelling it through ice almost three feet thick at a constant speed of better than two knots. It plowed forward under a flat, dim Arctic sun like a giant ice-eating behemoth, making a steady booming noise as its prow crunched through the ice cap, leaving a long, winding, watery trail behind it.

On the bridge, *Ural*'s master, Captain Boris Ivanov, sat in the captain's chair and scanned the ice field ahead with binoculars. His ice specialist, Lieutenant Stephan Portnov, was next to him also watching the surface closely, alert for the slightest sign that the ice was thickening past the point at which *Ural* could penetrate it at constant speed and would have to start breaking through with stop-and-start procedures.

Some people said the Inuit Eskimos, who used the ice cap like a highway, had over a hundred words for ice and snow. It seemed to Ivanov that Portnov knew them all. Rumor even held that he'd spent time with the Inuits. The slightest change in the coloration or swell of the ice somehow sent signals to him. He almost seemed to sense the thickness of the ice ahead by some extrasensory means, and he often warned the captain of changing conditions long before they were visible to anyone else.

Ivanov saw that his junior officer was tiring. Portnov had been on station far too long and only the urgency of their orders, coming from Admiral Korodin himself, and the instruction to make all possible speed made Ivanov use him this way. He was worried about straining the man. One didn't bang on a Stradivarius, and certainly Portnov was as much a fine instrument.

"Over there, those striations. The ice is about to thicken," Portnov announced. "Right ten degrees rudder, Comrade Captain."

"Right ten degrees rudder," commanded Ivanov. "Maintain headway if you can." Sure enough, the thickness held and their forward progress continued unabated.

"What's the latest weather report?" Ivanov asked his navigator.

"The temperature is minus thirty-five degrees centigrade and falling, Comrade Captain. We're tracking an Arctic low that could produce a localized storm, and we've got heavy fog coming in."

Ivanov considered what he had just heard. Fog usually meant areas of open water. When water was exposed, the air overhead became saturated immediately because the water-vapor capacity of cold air was so low. It was less common in this area, but at the edges of the ice cap there was usually low, clinging fog most of the time.

"Conditions are deteriorating," he said to Portnov.

"Uh-huh, it smells like a storm. How long to our destination?"

"If conditions hold, we'll make *Red Dawn*'s position in three hours."

"I'll do my best, Comrade Captain."

"I'm certain of that, Stephan."

Ivanov started thinking about the submarine. He had rescued many subs stuck on the surface in grinding pack ice, but one stuck in ice *under* the surface? Never. Getting tow lines on it was going to be a bitch. He'd have to send down divers. He was just about to call a meeting of the division officers who would be involved when Portnov's shocked tone yanked him out of his thoughts.

"Comrade Captain, look! Off the port bow. What is it?"

Ivanov swung his glasses around. At first he thought it must be some trick of the northern atmosphere, that somehow a reflection of the *Ural* had been transposed out onto the ice fields, like a desert mirage. But as he gazed through his binoculars at the huge, dark shape approaching over the icy white horizon his heart sank.

"Unfortunately, Stephan, that is the biggest and most powerful icebreaker in the world. The *Polar Eight.*"

"What flag does it fly?" asked Portnov in awe.

"Canadian," Ivanov responded. "And if we have the same goal in mind there is plenty of reason to worry."

Ivanov had heard about the Canadians' *Polar 8* icebreaker, but he'd never actually seen it. It was 55,000 gross tons with 96,000 horsepower of brute strength. The "Polar" in its name meant it was capable of year-round service in the Arctic. The "8" meant the ship could defeat hard, level ice at least eight feet thick. Ivanov shook his head. Eight feet of ice and it could still maintain headway at a constant four knots. *Ural* could barely defeat ice half that thick, even when backing and ramming.

"My God, will you look at it?" said Portnov. "It's huge. At least twice our tonnage."

Ivanov's curse was heartfelt. "Now I know how a midget feels in a whorehouse. Radar, what's their speed?"

"Four knots, Comrade Captain."

"Even with your talent to guide us, Portnov, we can't go where they can," Ivanov said bleakly. "They'll reach *Red Dawn* well before we do."

"They're not omnipotent, Comrade Captain. If the ice gets thicker than eight feet they'll be just as stuck."

"True enough, but they're unlikely to run into anything that thick."

"Maybe, maybe not." Portnov turned to the navigator. "If we increase our speed to four knots, could we overtake them?"

The navigator bent over his chart table and ran rapid calculations. "At that speed we would reach *Red Dawn* before they do."

"Fine thought, Stephan. But we can't make four knots, not with this ice."

Portnov shook his head. "There's thin ice out there, Comrade Captain. We just can't find it from up here." He began pulling on his cold-weather gear and fur-lined parka.

"Stephan, where do you think you're going?"

"Down on the ice," said Portnov with equanimity.

"Look, there's fog ahead. That means open water. Probably thin ice all around it. Give me two men and a radio and I'll lead you right to it. We'll make that four knots."

"I won't have you wandering out on that ice in the fog. It's suicide."

"I've done it before. The ice cap and I are old friends. Tie us to the ship with long lines. Any trouble, you can pull us in."

"Soon you'll be saying if worse comes to worst, you'll pull the whole damn ship."

"I would gladly try. You know that."

Ivanov looked out to the horizon. Already the *Polar 8* had pulled ahead. "All deliberate speed," Korodin had ordered, and Portnov was a man to count on. Besides, damn it, the *Red Dawn* was a Russian ship!

Portnov was fully dressed, waiting expectantly. Ivanov came to a decision. "All right, Stephan." He clapped him on the shoulders proudly. "Go assemble your party at the bow ladder and we'll put you on the ice."

Chapter
Thirteen

Seawolf

MacKenzie got up from the ice and brushed himself off. The drill had been knocked over by the force of the explosion, and Hansen was thrown from behind the controls. He was just getting to his feet. Greene was still breathing hard from his run.

"That's powerful stuff, Lieutenant," MacKenzie said.

"I did tell you so."

"I suppose you did. Good run."

Greene grinned. "Motivation's the key."

The charges had blown a jagged hole the size of a school bus in the solid ice. Churning water and broken plates of ice ground together inside it.

"Mac, are you okay?"

He turned. It was Justine coming over the ice. "I'm fine. What happened to the *Argo?*"

"Dr. Rose has control again. He's completing the surveillance you asked for. He'll bring the tape over to *Seawolf.*"

"How is Captain Galinin?"

"I managed to communicate that we had a temporary malfunction," said Justine, "and that we'll start rescue operations as soon as the DSRV gets here."

"How'd you tell him that?"

"Mac, we used to use Morse code over the AGR-Nines we liberated from the guardsmen."

"That was a long time ago, Just."

She shrugged. "True, and I'm a little rusty. I either told him we'd be right back or asked him to shower with me."

"Either one would be a comfort, dear."

Hansen was standing at the edge of the hole. "Hey, Captain. Take a look at this."

MacKenzie joined him. Hansen pointed into the water. "Oil?"

MacKenzie bent over and dipped a finger in and held it to his nose. "Captain Hansen, tell Dr. Rose to bring up the *Argo*. I've got to get back to *Seawolf*."

"Sonar's picking up surface ships approaching, Mac," Tom Lasovic said as soon as MacKenzie and Justine entered the conn. "Breakers. Signatures identify them as the *Ural* and the *Polar Eight*."

"The big Canadian ship?"

"That's her. Heading right for us."

"They must be additional rescue missions. How soon till they get here?"

"Several hours. We've got time to get *Red Dawn* out, but it's going to be close. The *Ural*'s making faster headway than I would have figured. She's ahead of the *Polar Eight*."

MacKenzie figured time and distances. They'd have to work faster.

"What happened out there?" asked Lasovic.

"We almost lost the *Argo*." He explained how he'd stopped the jamming.

"That's got to be a first," Lasovic said. "Depth-charging a sub from dry land."

"Dry ice. What did sonar make of their condition?"

"We had a solid fix on *Akula* and you . . . we could hear the drilling loud and clear. Then contacts merged and the explosions went off. *Akula* went down like somebody opened the hatches. Really rocked them."

"Under power?"

"Their engines were working overtime to keep them

afloat. Plenty of internal damage. Pipes bursting. Certainly fatalities. We tracked them as far as we could, but we lost them. Too much ice and signal attenuation. They took the blast very close. It may have ruptured the outer ballast hull. We can't say for sure."

"I don't like it," MacKenzie said darkly. "It's like having a wounded animal in the area."

"This captain's smart," said Lasovic. "That trick with the missile launch was a beaut. I wouldn't count him out yet."

"No, I wouldn't either. That's the trouble," MacKenzie said sourly. "Tom, those charges were supposed to bounce him around a little and foul up his gear, not sink him. If he manages to save his ship, he'll be back. Count on it. I would."

"The rules of engagement are unclear here, Mac," said Justine. "You did exactly the right thing. He was interfering with a rescue mission."

"Save it for the troops, Just. He *knows* what we're after." MacKenzie looked worried. "This could develop into a shooting war."

"If it does we're vulnerable as hell up here, Mac," Lasovic pointed out.

"You're right, Tom. Rig for dive and then submerge the ship. Keep on constant alert status. Stay in defensive posture and make sure we've got running room. Let's stay hidden and quiet. Wounded animals do unpredictable things."

"Mac?" Justine began, but he brushed past her grimly. "Later, Just. I've got some things to think over. Take over, Tom. I'll be in my cabin."

He walked out. Tom Lasovic was concerned. It didn't take much to see that MacKenzie was upset. He started after him, but Justine caught him. "Let me, Tom. Okay?"

Lasovic nodded, "It might be better." He turned back to his command and Justine headed aft.

The Kremlin

KGB Chief Abrikov walked into Solkov's office and handed him a sheet of paper. "Read this."

"What is it?"

"Korodin's orders to Kalik. My people picked them up."

Solkov scanned the document. "But he's told Kalik to stand down, not to interfere. Christ, we want him to attack."

Abrikov took the paper back. "Korodin's sent in an icebreaker. He's clever. He avoids the military confrontation and so he remains loyal to the general secretary, but he can still say he obeyed your orders."

"This isn't what we want, Agi. The worst thing of all would be for the *Ural* to succeed. Without a military crisis with the Americans—"

"We have no cause to remove the general secretary. I know," Abrikov finished. "Don't worry. You're sending Kalik a new set of orders. I had them drawn up. It ought to provoke things. Here, take a look."

Solkov read them and smiled. "Much better. Kalik will like this. He'll like this very much."

USS *Phoenix*

Captain Phil Arlin looked at his TV screen and studied the image of *Red Dawn.* "If I didn't see it I wouldn't have believed it," he said to his XO, Pete Binz. "Have we got a fix on *Seawolf* yet?"

"We do. They're at five hundred feet. Captain MacKenzie would like you on board as soon as possible."

"Well, we didn't rendezvous with the plane that dropped *Avalon* by chute and ferry it the rest of the way here on our back at top speed just for show," said Arlin. "Make the craft ready and notify Lieutenant Johnson we'll be crossing over to *Seawolf* as soon as possible."

"Captain MacKenzie advises extreme caution. *Akula* is in the area and is considered hostile."

"Make continual ESM searches and keep our ears out. Stay close."

"Will do, Skipper."

Akula

Kalik walked his ship surveying the damage. His anger was white-hot in his mind. Three men dead. Twenty wounded. Enough system damage to send them limping home under ordinary circumstances. It was a bitter roll call.

He shifted his arm in the sling. It wasn't broken as he feared, just badly sprained. A day or two would see it back to normal use. Viktor hadn't been so lucky. His collarbone was broken, and the hasty rigging the med tech had been able to fix up for him probably meant the bone would have to be reset when they got back to base.

Kalik wanted revenge. He was the head of his ship, and what hurt *Akula* hurt him. The constraints of his orders plagued him like a nagging wife. The more he lost, the more he had to win.

The air was fetid inside the engine room. The chief engineer and his men were sweating over an array of broken gauges, installing new ones. The bandages on the chief engineer's head were stained with blood. Kalik brought his anger under control and put a lighter tone in his voice.

"Comrade Chief Engineer Melkon," he said loudly, "haven't I told you that driving the engines with your head will only dent the plates?"

The burly Melkon spun around angrily but relaxed into something of a smile when he saw who it was. "Pity the poor engineer who works for you, Comrade Captain. Next time when I tell you I need to stop the engines, let me stop them!"

"What, and make your job too easy? You must want the surface navy, my friend."

The men all laughed. "All this and insults, too," said Melkon feigning hurt.

Kalik felt the tension lessen. It was his way of telling them, I am still here. Trust in me. If I can laugh at all this, why should you be worried? "Tell me," he said to the engineer, "what is our condition?"

"For all the shaking up you gave us we are not in such bad shape. The steam leaks were mostly in the secondary system, no radiation has escaped, and we should be able to give you full power as soon as the reactor auxiliary pump is replaced."

"How long?"

"Say three hours."

Kalik felt his spirits rise. "Good. Very good."

He left feeling better than when he'd walked in. Without serious damage to the engines, and with the electronics in the control room now being replaced, *Akula* would soon be back to combat readiness. Even the rupture in the outer hull that had holed a ballast tank wouldn't be a real loss. Other tanks could make up the difference. Thank the ship designers for their double-hull design. Without it, *Akula* would be lying on the bottom.

Kalik walked back to the control room, talking to the crew and making sure his presence was felt at every station. Men didn't put their faith in machines, they put it in men. They put it in him.

Kalik felt weakened by the brush with destruction. Hands shook *after* an accident. Introspection started *after* you put down the smoking gun. He had been a combat captain for a long time, but he'd never come so close to losing his ship. He hated the weakness. It felt like . . . cowardice. He expunged it by replacing it with the anger lying so close to the surface. Damn his orders. Damn the *Ural*. Damn *Seawolf*. He wanted action. Revenge would cure him. He'd made too many mistakes—that fear worm bit him hard. Was he losing his capacity to command? He had to prove differently. *Seawolf* and its clever captain were becoming more than just adversaries. If he beat them, it would be proof his hunter's prowess remained intact, like bringing home a lion's skin or an eagle's feather. Through the hunt, he would be reborn.

Around him he felt *Akula* coming back to life, and with it, his strength was returning, too.

"Vassily?" It was Volkov, come to find him.

"Yes, what is it, Viktor?"

"We just received this."

Kalik scanned the order from the minister of defense. "You read it?"

"Yes, and I don't like it, Vassily," said Volkov, nursing his shoulder. "Since when do orders come from Solkov? Only some kind of power play would have made him go over Korodin's head. Korodin says hold, Solkov says attack. We could find ourselves in the middle of a very nasty situation. Vassily, we could be starting a war. Who do we listen to?"

But Kalik already knew which voice he would listen to. The one that spoke of the hunt. He even thought he heard drumbeats, till he realized it was his own heart, beating hard. The gods of war had given him authorization to act. He was ready. Three hours, the chief engineer had said. Three hours.

Three hours . . .

Seawolf

There was a knock on MacKenzie's cabin door. He looked up from his desk where he was half working, half staring into space, surprised to see Justine standing there.

"May I come in?"

"It's your cabin, too."

"Well, I didn't know who was in here, the captain or my husband."

MacKenzie laughed. "Who was it you wanted?"

"My husband."

MacKenzie pushed back from the desk. "Okay, he's listening."

Justine closed the door and perched on the bunk. "Talk to me, Mac. Something's bothering you."

"I'm fine."

"Nope. It has to do with what you said to Tom Lasovic, doesn't it?"

MacKenzie looked away. "I don't know if I can explain it to you," he said. "Maybe you have to be navy."

"Try."

"Justine, what I did was a crime. An unprovoked attack. And men died. I have to live with that."

"Mac, you've been in battle before."

"That's the point. It was battle. I had direct orders to engage the enemy, and we had certain knowledge there was a threat to the United States. Look, I know that my orders may result in loss of life. Every C.O. has to be prepared for that, but I almost sent a hundred men to the bottom with a cowboy stunt that may have results I can't even begin to predict."

Justine watched him struggling with inner demons for a while. "Mac, what's the difference between a soldier and a murderer?"

"Legal right," MacKenzie answered unhesitatingly.

"Wrong," said Justine. "Moral right."

"You're splitting hairs."

"No, I'm not. When we were down in that stinking jungle waiting to ambush Somoza's troops, you think we had a legal right? For Christ's sake, he was the legal president. But he was slime. That gave us the right."

"According to that, I'm still wrong. There's no slime on board that sub. Just men. Average read-the-sports-page men. The officers are professionals like me. The rest just want to do their service and get the hell home." His eyes held something she had never seen before. It took Justine a moment to realize it was self-doubt. "But some of them aren't going home because I made a mistake and murdered them."

"Which bothers you more, the murder or the mistake?"

MacKenzie reacted as if stung. "You know me better than that."

Justine regarded him steadily. "Maybe. When's the last time you made a mistake?"

"C'mon, Just. I make them all the time. Everybody does."

"When's the last time you made one that really counted?"

"What's your point here?"

"It's no stretch to forgive yourself because you forgot to buy oranges at the supermarket. Now, just a second, don't jump at me. I know we're dealing with something a lot more major. You're calling it murder. Okay, we'll deal with that in a minute. Mac, I know you better than anyone else does, and I can see you're also feeling bad about making a mistake in the first place, wondering if it's a reflection on you as a man and as a commander, and that's almost as hard for you to deal with as the nature of the mistake itself."

"That's pretty complicated."

"So are you. So is life."

MacKenzie shook his head ruefully. "A lot of what you say is true. I'm not sure how to deal with this. Do I just say 'too bad' and move on? It's like the captain who shot down that Iranian passenger plane by mistake. No matter how you cut it, lives were lost and I'm responsible."

"I understand that. I was responsible when I was seven."

"I know. I didn't mean—"

She ticked off points one at a time. "As for the mistake part, if you hadn't done something, we would have lost *Red Dawn* and everyone on board, as well as the *Argo*. The entire mission was in jeopardy. You had to act. As for the responsibility part, in my opinion the tragic consequences of your actions were unintended and, frankly, unforeseeable. The bottom line is you stopped the jamming. If it helps any, I'm in charge here and I say what you did was both effective and prudent, given the circumstances and the need for immediate action."

"I appreciate that. But that's what I have to decide now, isn't it?"

"Mac, let me help." She reached for him.

He held back. "We're different, you and I, in this, Just. Maybe you're more flexible. God knows you should be, given how you had to grow up. But I need the rules. The codes. You can do *this* under certain conditions, you *can't* do it under others. That's how I know. That's how I justify what I do. It's how I can take lives if I have to and still sleep at night."

"The rules are never enough. You're deeper than that. Even the captain part of you knows it."

"The man doesn't."

"Mac, I learned this in the jungle. The rules are only a temporary refuge. There always comes a time when you have to operate without them."

He sat down next to her tiredly. "I don't know."

Justine looked at him tenderly. He was in such pain. She wanted to say "You'll learn to live with it" because it was true, but she decided to spare him that particular sadness. Instead, she brushed his hair back and kissed him and drew him down to her because in the end a really good wife knew when words should end and comfort begin.

MacKenzie convened a conference in the crew's mess. Tom Lasovic watched him closely, still concerned. MacKenzie returned his gaze, unruffled. Whatever his personal feelings, the job came first. The look in his XO's eyes seemed to say that he knew it would.

The intercom crackled. "Captain, Randall here. *Avalon* is docking over the aft escape hatch."

"Send Captain Arlin and Lieutenant Johnson up as soon as they're on board."

"Aye, Skipper."

A few moments later a wiry black southern lieutenant in a blue nylon jumpsuit sauntered into the room beside *Phoenix*'s captain, Phil Arlin. He grinned when he saw MacKenzie and stuck his hand out. "How are you, Captain? Mighty nice to see you again."

"Hello, Luke," MacKenzie said with genuine affection. "Good to see you, too. Been too long since Gitmo."

Lieutenant Lucas Johnson—"Luke" to MacKenzie—had been his copilot once before, on the DSRV *Mystic* during a near fatal trip through the Cayman Trench. Luke was a fine pilot in his own right and an expert mechanic. Probably his most important skill was having the velvet touch of a surgeon with the DSRV's external hydraulic arm.

"You know they had to give me another ship after what you did to the first one, Captain. But wait till you see the new modifications. *Avalon*'s got real heavyweight punch now and a new arm with more attachments than a French vibrator. Say, any truth to the rumor you got married?"

MacKenzie felt Justine stir behind him. "Er, Luke, meet Justine Segurra, also Mrs. MacKenzie. Central Intelligence. She's in charge of this operation."

Luke looked sheepish. "Excuse me, ma'am. Pleased to meet you. I didn't mean—"

"Relax, Lieutenant. I know technical talk when I hear it. I'm delighted to hear the arm is so versatile."

"Yes, ma'am. That's it. Versatile."

There was muffled laughter from the others gathered in the mess to watch the videotape: Dr. Rose, Captain Hansen, Lieutenant Greene, and Joe Santiago.

Phil Arlin was an old family friend. He gave Justine an affectionate hug. "How's the toughest lady this side of the equator?"

"Fine, Phil. Was it a good trip up?"

"Piece of cake. Of course," he said dryly. "I didn't have the navy's newest sub to tool around in. Getting into trouble again, eh, Mac?"

MacKenzie shook hands warmly. "Welcome to *Seawolf*, Phil."

"Glad to be aboard, Mac. She's quite a boat."

"A champion. Everything we hoped for and more. We had a nasty situation a few hours ago, and she came through without mussing a hair."

"I'd like a look at the engagement tapes."

"As soon as we're done here."

"Gentlemen, time is pressing." Justine motioned them to take their seats. "Okay, Mac. It's your show. Dr. Rose, please do the honors."

The oceanographer put the tape into the VCR, and the

picture of *Red Dawn* encased inside the ice keel came onto the screen. MacKenzie explained what they were seeing as Captain Galinin went through his message writing and again when the picture jumbled as *Akula* jammed the signal.

"Keep in mind several objectives as you view the tape," MacKenzie instructed. "First, to locate their towing pad eye, if there is one. Second, to see how to clear it so we can plant the towing rig. Third, to map out the points on the keel where Luke and I in the DSRV and Captain Hansen's men in scuba gear will plant the charges to blow the sub out of the ice. All right, you can see Captain Galinin being reassured that we were back in control and coming for the snorkel soon. We're coming up on *Argo*'s first complete circuit."

The discussion was animated as the group formulated a plan of attack. Through *Argo*'s camera lens they could see that *Red Dawn* did indeed have a pad eye located forward of her sail. Luke Johnson assured them that *Avalon*'s drill-tipped arm could handle the distance through the ice to the pad eye, a little more than fifteen feet. "But it's got to be done fast or the hole will refreeze," he added.

"The ice charges are tricky," said Bernie Greene. "We'll plant them inside the keel and direct the force out and away from *Red Dawn*.

"But not too close to the sub or we'll rupture the hull," Hansen added.

"Mac, are you assuming that by 'valves out' Galinin means his main ballast tank vent valves are damaged and can't be opened?" asked Phil Arlin.

"I think so. To those of you unfamiliar with submarines, that means even when we blast *Red Dawn* free she won't be able to bring enough water into her ballast tanks to submerge under the ice so we can tow her out."

"What's the alternative?" Justine asked.

"We'll have to flood her sufficiently to take them down. The only way to do that is to drill into the main ballast tanks."

"That'll give them the weight," Arlin agreed. "By the way, Mac, my engineers think they have a good idea of how to do the towing."

"Shoot."

"We've never towed a sub this big underwater before, so we're on new ground, but we're going to have to use a fairly long line. They calculate at least eight hundred feet."

"Why so long?" asked Justine.

"*Red Dawn* has no power to stop herself," Arlin reminded her. "If we stop short, she'll ram right into *Phoenix*'s aft end and damage her propeller. Then you've got two disabled ships."

"Where did you attach the line?" MacKenzie asked.

"To the two main cleats on *Phoenix*'s main deck. They should be strong enough to take the strain. It's the cable we're worried about. There's got to be a bend in it of some kind so it doesn't taut up and pop when we put pressure on it. The engineers had a clever idea. They rigged up a metal ball that'll hang in the center of the tow line and hold it down. We run the tow line from the cleats back to the ball, then from the ball to *Red Dawn*."

MacKenzie saw the inventiveness of the arrangement. "It'll hang under the sub and pull against *Phoenix*'s belly so the pressure backs up against the cleats. You're right. It is clever."

"That's the way we see it, Mac," Arlin finished.

"Okay, that about wraps it up. Anything else?"

"We need to get back to the surface, Captain," said Hansen, "and we'd better take plenty of hot food. Once our men get into that water they're going to burn calories like they're going out of style."

"Our cooks will provide anything you need."

"I'm heading for the surface, too, Mac," said Justine, "The wounded are being airlifted out. Dr. Rose, you better get Ethel ready for pickup. You'll both go out if we can get a second plane down."

"I was wondering when anyone would remember us."

"Well, we did," Justine said, taking the finicky scientist by the arm. "You didn't think we'd leave you here, did you?"

MacKenzie hid a smile and glanced at his watch. "All right, we have our assignments. Luke, all set to go?"

"Avalon's powered up and ready, Captain."

"Okay. Let's give those folks some breathing room."

MacKenzie paused below the aft escape trunk for a word with Phil Arlin. They discussed Norfolk's latest intelligence estimate of the number of Soviet subs steaming for the area and the potential problems posed by the breakers overhead. Then Mac related recent events concerning *Akula* and *Seawolf* and finished with a description of dropping the charges to stop the jamming.

". . . So we lost him in the commotion, but unless I miss my guess he's out there somewhere. He's been hurt and battered, and he can't be happy we're about to pull *Red Dawn* out of there."

"I don't like this, Mac," Arlin said. *"Phoenix* is going to be too damn easy a target towing that Tango out of here. If *Red Dawn* goes down she'll take *Phoenix* right along with her."

"We'll be right on your tail, Phil. I just wanted you to know things could get sticky. It was my mistake; I don't want anyone else to pay for it. So be prepared."

"Justine and her people would have a fit if we lost *Red Dawn.*"

"It's your call, Phil. I'm just talking."

Arlin nodded. "Okay. Thanks for the warning."

MacKenzie climbed the ladder into the escape tube, followed by Arlin. They passed through the bell-shaped skirt that joined *Avalon* to *Seawolf.* When the skirt was pumped free of water, as it was now, outside pressure created a leakproof seal between the two craft. Arlin belted himself into the middle cabin, actually the second of three internal spheres that made up *Avalon.* Mac went forward.

Luke was already in the padded copilot's chair, and MacKenzie slid in beside him. *Avalon* was in most ways a duplicate of her sister ship, *Mystic.* The deep submergence rescue vehicle was a fifty-foot, thirty-seven-ton cigar-shaped craft with an inertial guidance system created for the Apollo spacecraft. She could move up and down, right and left, forward and back, and her hull was constructed of twenty-six layers of fiberglass, titanium, and steel, enabling her to dive more than a mile deep. *Avalon* could hold up to twenty-four men and off-load a downed submarine in four or five trips.

"Power on, Luke."

MacKenzie felt the craft come alive. His hands drifted over the controls. It brought back memories of fading air supplies and the search for his old sub, the *Aspen*. That hunt had almost ended in their death. He remembered how much he had wanted to come back from that trip. He had just met Justine and for the first time in his life had something to lose. Now, after two years of marriage, he was risking even more.

"You married, Luke?" he asked as they ran through the checklist.

"Five years. We have a three-year-old. Little boy named Jake."

"We're thinking about kids, too. Makes me wonder why we don't call it quits. Come home at five and watch the ball game. Hydraulics."

"Check." Luke looked at MacKenzie curiously. "You're thinking long thoughts, Mac. Problem?"

"Nope. Batteries."

"Fully charged. What, then?"

"Momentary lapse. Forget it."

Luke laid a sympathetic hand on his arm. "You got a right. We all do sometimes, y'hear?"

"I hear. Thanks. Ready?"

Luke grinned. "Lay on, Macduff."

Mac punched commands into the on-board computer. A smooth power curve flowed onto the screen. The rest of the board was green. He seized the radio mike dangling on a spiral cord between their padded seats.

"Seawolf, Avalon. Ready to disengage."

"Avalon, Seawolf. This is Lasovic. On your mark."

MacKenzie hit a switch on the panels surrounding them and pumped water into the bell housing matching external pressure and breaking the seal.

"Mark." Simultaneously he fed power to the electric

motors lifting *Avalon* off *Seawolf*'s deck, and Tom Lasovic dropped the sub a few feet.

Luke called out, "Separation."

"Good luck, *Avalon*. *Seawolf* out."

Mac took firm hold of the steering yoke and slid *Avalon* swiftly off into the icy waters heading for *Phoenix*. *Seawolf* would take the others to the surface and would come back to wait for *Avalon*'s return. It was eerily beautiful. There were crystal-clear waters around them, and the occasional polynyas above were clearly visible on *Avalon*'s TV screens and in her round forward viewports. MacKenzie felt a sense of personal freedom in the small craft, like flying a single-engine Cessna after a 747.

Luke tested the hydraulic arm. It was originally intended to remove any debris that might be covering a downed submarine's escape hatch. Ice digging was a brand-new application.

"Coffee?" asked Luke, reaching between the seats for a thermos.

"I forgot how prepared you are. Love some."

MacKenzie kept their depth constant. They were approaching *Phoenix*. He took a few sips of coffee and put the no-spill container in a holder.

"Coming up on *Phoenix*," Luke reported.

"*Avalon*, this is *Phoenix*. Ready to engage."

"*Phoenix*, *Avalon*. Hold her steady. Coming in over the aft trunk."

MacKenzie settled the DSRV onto *Phoenix* and blew the water out of the bell housing. The radio crackled. "*Avalon*, you are properly engaged."

Arlin called from the inner sphere, "Thanks for the lift, fellas. We'll be ready when you need us." Arlin opened the hatch and disappeared below, sealing it behind him.

"*Phoenix*, *Avalon*. Ready to disconnect." MacKenzie brought the DSRV up from *Phoenix*'s deck and sped off, this time toward the ice keel.

Red Dawn grew larger on their screens. "There," said MacKenzie. "See the snorkel in that lower tunnel? They must have dug it out again."

"I've got a fix on it," said Luke. "Come in on the port side. I can get a better angle."

"First the exhaust path. Once that's cleared they can run the engines and get some heat in there."

MacKenzie moved in and hovered just off the ice keel like a fish poised effortlessly in the water. Luke swung the arm's boxlike control panel down into his lap. He rotated the arm and began a slow chipping motion against the ice. It took less than half an hour to clear the exhaust path. Pieces of ice broke off and floated slowly away, a shower of icy diamonds scintillating in the light of *Avalon*'s powerful beams.

"You haven't lost your touch," MacKenzie observed.

"Nope. Just a little bit more . . ."

Luke cleared the last of the ice from the hull. They could see the first trapped bubbles rising from the unblocked valve.

"She's open. Good work, Luke."

MacKenzie lifted *Avalon* and moved back across the ice keel. *Red Dawn* slid by beneath them under the glistening ice, black and shimmery. The snorkel and air hose were coiled behind the ice seal in the lower tunnel. Mac hovered in close and Luke began chipping at the seal.

"Hey, look," Luke exclaimed. "Up there."

MacKenzie followed his finger and saw Captain Galinin watching them from the upper tunnel.

"We have an audience."

"That's good. Because I think it's . . . yep . . . show time!"

All at once the ice seal got too thin to withstand the water pressure and it crumbled. Seawater flooded the tunnel, pounding *Red Dawn*'s hull like a fist. Then the turbulence settled down and the snorkel floated calmly inside the watery chamber with a long length of air hose attached to it. Luke reached in and grabbed the snorkel head in the arm's pincers. MacKenzie backed *Avalon* out a bit. The snorkel came free of the keel with the air hose trailing behind it. Above them, Galinin still watched.

MacKenzie headed for the surface.

Galinin crawled back into the torpedo room. "They've taken the snorkel. We should have air going into the fan room in just a few minutes. The exhaust path is clear, too."

The mood on board changed from grim anticipation to jubilation. Men clapped one another on the back. Ligichev was already trying to figure out how to restore the drive. Ivanna threw herself into Pytor's arms. With power and a renewed air supply they could await the towing in relative comfort. It wouldn't be a Russian ship that rescued them, but survival was beyond politics. Sooner or later they would be returned home.

Everyone was happy but Galinin. Of all the things he had imagined, rescue by the Americans was not among them. It posed serious problems. *Red Dawn* was not an ordinary submarine on an ordinary mission. There were dire security considerations. He left the torpedo room and walked down the main corridor, ignoring the spontaneous celebrations that had broken out.

He was the only one on board with the combination to the wall safe in his cabin. It contained the usual code books and system schematics, but also the special orders he had been given before sailing. In order to open the safe if he were incapacitated or killed, a sub tender would have to be summoned to bring the safecracker it kept on board for just such emergencies.

Galinin opened the safe and spread the material on his desk, skimming over the usual nonsense—the standing orders, the protocols, and the ROEs. But as he read through the special orders he came upon a section that began simply, "In the event of capture . . ."

Halfway through it, he understood why he had been chosen to captain the *Red Dawn*.

Polar Ice Cap

Stephan got down on his hands and knees and scooped up the top layer of snow, sniffing it as he had seen his Inuit tutor do. Around his waist was a line trailing back to the *Ural*'s surging bow. The ship was now making a steady three knots just a few hundred yards behind him.

The icebreaker's passage was thunderous. Stephan could feel vibrations through the soles of his boots. He looked into the sky. The pale sun was barely discernible through the cloud cover. He sniffed the snow again. The water was near. He could smell the thin film of condensation on the surface layer.

"Comrade Lieutenant, which way?"

His two crewmen, Seamen Rolf and Pinkov, trudged alongside him. They were also guyed to the ship. Both looked colder and more miserable by the second. Rolf was a heavy man with curly hair, moist eyes, and full lips. Pinkov was short, squat, and barrel-chested with a nervous smile that showed missing front teeth.

Stephan took care not to laugh at their discomfort, but it was barely thirty degrees below zero. An Inuit would have his shirt off in this weather, thinking he was lucky to have such a warm winter.

"Tell the captain to steer left fifteen degrees rudder. The ice will be thinner and he can increase speed."

"Increase speed? I'm getting tired of running ahead of the ship now, Comrade Lieutenant," Pinkov said as Rolf called the ship on his portable radio. "What happens if they go faster?"

"I have an idea, Pinkov," Stephan said lightly. "Just remain where you are and when the ship passes it can pull you with it."

Not sure whether the often puzzling lieutenant was serious, Pinkov gave him a worried look and began coiling the lines.

"The captain acknowledges your signal, Comrade Lieutenant," Rolf said, slinging the radio back over his shoulder.

"Good. Let's move on."

They walked, a process of fits and starts that had Stephan on his hands and knees as often as on his feet. This far north, nature had different rules and he had come to know many of them during his time with the Inuit. It was a far cry from the warm, sunny beaches of the Crimea where he was born.

Most Soviet citizens would have considered themselves lucky to live in such a place. The Russian Riviera, it was often called. Party bigwigs and union officials vacationed there, hastily fleeing Moscow's bitter winter. The stores were usually pretty well stocked, and the restaurants had better than average food procured from a thriving black market catering to the tourist trade.

No wonder his parents told him he was foolish to want to leave. What was the point of seeing the world when they had so much right here? Besides, the world, especially the West, wasn't accessible to anyone but the *nomenklatura*. Did he see himself a big shot like that? Stephan didn't, and he soon realized the Party schools were not for him. He took the next best route. As soon as he was of age he joined the navy.

Chance brought him to the Inuit and to the ice. He was assigned to a vessel that routinely supplied an arctic weather research station. The captain of the vessel was a morose, sullen man who lived first to regale his crew with stories of his exploits during the Great Patriotic War and second to drink himself into unconsciousness every night.

One day the drinking started earlier than usual and resulted in his trapping the vessel in grinding pack ice. The hull was holed, and the crew had to take off over the ice or drown. Most died of exposure in the first few hours. The rest ran into a storm, and Stephan was separated from them in the blinding snow. When morning came he found himself alone on the ice cap, colder and more scared than he had ever been in his life. He dreamed of his childhood beaches, wishing he had never left them.

Wandering over the ice he lost all sense of time and place. He had no idea in what direction the research station lay, and his fading strength made reaching it unlikely even if he could find out. There were no signs here to read like in the woods. Everything looked the same, and the shifting snow obscured his tracks virtually as he made them. For all he knew he had been walking in circles.

When he ran out of food he knew he had just hours to live. He made peace with that knowledge. There was little choice, really. After one footstep or another or the next, whenever he finally ran out of strength, he would lie down and go to sleep and dream of the beaches and never wake up.

He came to an open lead in the ice. He could see fish swimming below. Faint with hunger, he fashioned a fishing line using cloth ripped from his uniform. His belt buckle became a hook. It was a desperate and creative act, but it didn't work. The fish were maddeningly close, and yet he couldn't catch a single one. Delirious, he got mad at the fish for not biting. Bad fish. Mean fish. They could help him live, but they weren't going to. He could actually see them swimming happily by. He got angrier and angrier, especially when he realized he couldn't move his legs anymore, so he hit the water and cursed the fish. He slapped at the ice cap and threw snow into the hole. At last, frustrated beyond endurance he grabbed for one fish that happened to swim near the surface and even managed to get hold of its slippery skin before he overbalanced and toppled into the numbing water.

The Inuit brave who was traveling over the ice to visit his wife's mother's home that day had been watching Stephan for the better part of an hour and enjoying his antics more even than the "I Love Lucy" reruns they played on the tavern TV at the outpost where he traded his furs for tools and medicines. In return for such pleasure he dragged Stephan from the water, stripped him naked, dried him, and wrapped him in furs from his sled. Then he began cutting ice blocks for an igloo, a temporary shelter the Inuit built on the ice while traveling.

Stephan awoke to find himself warm, dry, and naked, lying on a fur-covered pallet on the igloo floor. Rancid smoke from a fish oil heater lamp filled the ice shelter with light and warmth. The temperature was a pleasant twenty-five. The waiting Inuit squatted across from him chewing on a piece of raw fish. Unsure whether Stephan would live or die from exposure to the water he had elected to let the gods decide. Now that it seemed they had come to a favorable decision, he offered the stranger food and water, and by the end of the day Stephan had recovered some of his strength.

Stephan spoke no Inuit, and the Inuit spoke no Russian. To the brave, however, Stephan's tenacity and will to survive were as pleasing as the young man's clumsiness was amusing. He managed to communicate that he was planning to be here for a while to run a string of traps and that he would not throw Stephan out. Stephan thanked him, but for his own sake he wanted to be able to carry his own load. He wanted to learn how the Inuit survived on the ice cap. The Inuit seemed to find the humor in this roughly on a par with Lucy's learning to work on the chocolate candy assembly line, but he soon discovered Stephan was a fast learner and a dependable partner, and while Stephan mended, his skills slowly increased.

Stephan learned to fish and to work the sled dogs, to render oil for the lamp, and to retain his body heat at temperatures that once would have made him loath even to stick his head outside. He learned about trapping, and finally he began to learn about ice.

He learned that there were more colors in white than he had ever dreamed of, and he learned what each one meant. He learned to spot, from a quarter of a mile away, thin ice that could break under his feet, and he learned to smell unseen open water on the wind. By the time they broke camp to begin the long haul to the research station, which the Inuit knew of and had passed many times, Stephan probably knew as much about the ice cap as any eight-year-old Inuit, which meant he knew more than almost anybody else about it, anywhere.

The scientists in the research station were shocked to see him. A whole summer had passed since Stephan's ship went down. All hands had long ago been presumed dead. His tale was incredible, but here he was looking healthy and fit, and beside him was an Inuit who took one whiff of the inside of the research station and left for clean air with a simple wave good-bye. It only occurred to Stephan much later, when he was in the airplane winging his way back home, that he would probably never see the Inuit again.

"Comrade Lieutenant? Comrade Captain Ivanov radios he is making four knots," Rolf announced, so many ice droplets caked on his lashes and mustache that he looked like a coal-eyed snowman.

"What? Yes, sorry. Tell the captain to come right with ten degrees rudder. And you'd better keep moving or you'll get run over."

Pinkov groaned as Stephan picked up the pace. Keeping up with the lieutenant was hard work. Didn't the man get cold or tired?

Stephan moved on, remembering. The men of the high command weren't stupid. They realized what a find they had in him. They had tried to get him to lecture, but the academic world wasn't for him, so they sent him for officers' training and then to ice specialty school, where he ended up teaching the teachers. That was eighteen months ago. He had served on the *Ural* with Captain Ivanov ever since.

The time he spent with the Inuit had changed him. The ice cap was central to his life now in a way that no one understood except the Inuit he would never see again. This close to the ice in the cold clear air lit by a pale distant sun, his own captaincy assured one day, he was content.

"There, Pinkov, do you smell it? Open water. Close. Follow me."

Pinkov gathered the slack in the line, and Rolf grabbed the radio, and they followed the enigmatic lieutenant across the ice.

Polar 8

Captain Roland Maré of the Royal Canadian Navy looked at his radar operator and asked for the report again, unsure he'd heard it correctly.

"It's true, Captain. They're making four knots now."

"Impossible," said Maré. "Not in ice that thick, eh?"

"It's an odd course he's weaving," said Lieutenant Jean Renaud, *Polar 8*'s icemaster. He quit studying the radar screen and switched to high-powered binoculars. "First this way, then that. It's like he has eyes out there on the ice. He's catching up."

"Relax, Jean," said the bearded Maré. "One mistake and he'll wedge himself in for hours. I'm not worried."

Renaud wasn't so sure. The *Ural* was moving with a confidence he found unsettling, almost as if it saw obstacles before it got to them. He read the Fathometer report and studied the ice ahead of his own ship. It was holding at six feet, and the *Polar 8* was eating it up like croissants for breakfast.

The two behemoths of the Arctic continued to crash ahead, pitting their power and the knowledge of their icemasters against each other. A race was shaping up, and Renaud had his money solidly behind his ship, but he kept a close watch on the *Ural* as both icebreakers split the ice field and surged on.

Polar Ice Cap

Justine came inside, knowing they had been lucky. The storm had lifted enough to get the wounded on the first C-130 able to get in and out. No one knew how long it would take for a second plane to land. The dorm was a hubbub of activity. Dr. Rose was finishing packing the *Argo* for transport on the next plane. Bernie Greene was taking a party of SEALs to the fishing hole to wait for Mac to bring up the snorkel, and Captain Hansen was readying his men to go underwater to plant the explosives in the ice keel.

"Need any help, Doc?" Justine asked.

"Just get me on that plane. I want the sun. I want warm water. The closest I want to come to cold ever again is a frozen daiquiri."

Justine had to laugh at the man's steadfast aversion to the region. "Isn't there anything you like up here?"

"Frankly, no."

"Well, then, relax. You did a fine job with the *Argo*. We'll take it from here."

"Glad to help. Will you get those people down there out alive?"

"We're sure gonna try."

Then Rose said something unexpected. He said, "I hope so. I'll pray for you all."

Justine completed her report to Winestock in Washington over her satellite link radio and signed off. The news about the *Ural*'s increased speed and the fast-approaching Soviet subs wasn't good, but all indications were that they would be done before the ships got there. In the case of the *Ural*, there was still the *Polar 8* to head it off.

"Nice rig," commented Hansen. "Satellite direct?"

"Yes."

"They used this kind for the Iranian rescue mission. Unfortunately, it let the president second-guess his field commander."

"Sometimes reach out and touch can be a bad thing, hmm?"

Hansen laughed. "I suppose." He put out another dry suit from an open crate. "Not much interference up here."

"Nope." She smiled. "Straight down."

"Don't you mean straight up?"

"I meant to the U.S."

"Yeah. Right. Funny thinking of it that way."

"This whole region reorients you," she said. "All you hear about is the east and the west. Especially where I come from. You begin to think there's only one direction, *across* the globe. Then you come up here and realize that Russia and the United States are closer here than at any other point except near Alaska, and the two continents are separated only by an ocean full of ice and missile subs. We're south of them, really, not west. And they're north of us. So no wonder everybody's running under-ice maneuvers like they're going out of style. I suppose I've bought into Mac's concern about this region."

"He's a good commander, your husband. His men like him. Mine, too."

"Thanks. Me, too."

"Yeah, I can see that. I wouldn't mind my wife looking at me the way you look at him. What's the secret?"

"He makes me laugh."

"That's it?"

Justine smiled. "That's part of it. Most of all I guess I like his confidence and his intelligence. He's not scared of anything, I don't think. And the way he sees things. Mac's a tried and true optimist. Most people think the world is coming to an end. He sees diseases we've cured and political differences being resolved and a more just society evolving, things like that. He's completely unthreatened by my talent and success, and he honestly trusts in the basic dignity of every human. That's rare."

"And that makes you laugh?"

"No, that makes me respect him, because even though he believes what I consider to be naive malarkey, he is nobody's fool. And when I'm in one of my most serious and depressed moods and the accumulated weight of my life feels like God singled me out for special punishment and I barely have the energy to get out of bed, he comes bounding into the bedroom to tell me how neat it is that somebody just invented a way to put four billion phone calls in a wire the size of a piece of spaghetti, or that some song on the radio made him feel so good we should go out to brunch because it's Thursday, or that this really is the land of the free, or that he's double-jointed and can touch his thumb to his wrist or some such thing, and I laugh. Trust me, don't sell lightheartedness short."

Hansen couldn't help but smile.

"See? That's Mac. He's catchy."

"I think I'm envious."

Justine just smiled. "Me and Mac, we're a funny combination, but it works."

"Well, it's been nice talking to you, Mrs. MacKenzie. Thanks."

"Justine, okay?"

"Sure. Look, I've got to get some tanks from the warehouse. Be back."

Hansen left the dorm. Justine found Dr. Rose and had just started helping him get squared away when harsh words broke out across the room. She looked over to the SEALs, two of whom were shoving each other angrily. She sighed. Conflicts were inevitable under the stress of these conditions. The only thing unusual was that something hadn't happened before now.

"I don't give a shit why you did it!" yelled a SEAL named Ellis. "I told you I was gonna flatten you if it happened again and I'm gonna."

The other SEAL, Burke, glowered and hefted a weight belt like a ball and chain. "Try it, asshole."

Justine moved toward them. "Excuse me. That's enough. We're all tired. Put that down and let's forget it."

Ellis looked at her and started to say something, but he caught himself and got back under control. The one with the weight belt just couldn't. Justine had seen it before in the jungle, the product of fatigue and tension. "Excuse me, lady," Burke said nastily. "This doesn't concern you, so fuck off."

Justine let out a tired breath, stepped forward, and slapped him hard across the face. "I am your superior officer. Get hold of yourself. Put it down. Now."

It was the wrong move. The slap was the last straw, and Burke blew. Justine saw it in his eyes. They unfocused, and as the others yelled for him to stop it and shouted warnings to Justine, he leaped forward swinging the belt over his head, coming straight for her.

Later the SEALs would tell the story among themselves,

and no one would be quite sure which version was correct. One said he saw her foot hit the big man first in the groin, then in the chest, and then in the side of the head so fast it looked as if all three blows occurred simultaneously. Another said the kicks came later, that it was the forearm block that came first, when she let the weight belt wrap around her arm and shifted her weight like a dancer to flick it back at the man, taking him hard under the chin and snapping his head back like a hammer. Yet another said it was the sudden skip-spin move that really did the trick, taking her inside the man's reach to drive her elbow into his solar plexus, doubling him over and exposing the back of his neck to the quick sharp chop that sent him senseless to the floor.

In any event, five seconds later Justine, without a hair mussed, was standing over the unconscious SEAL. The rest of the men looked at one another in amazement and broke into applause.

"Jesus, did you see that?"

"Christ, where did you learn to move like that, Ms. Segurra?"

"Ma'am, that's the greatest thing I ever saw. He's gotta outweigh you by a hundred pounds and be taller by a foot."

"It was unfair, really. I started early," she said simply.

The SEALs roared with laughter. One named Jackson, whom she had seen managing the others, spoke up. "Please, ma'am. Burke didn't mean it. It's just the damn cold. It's got us all a little crazy. Captain Hansen, ma'am, well . . . I mean, it's up to y'all, but . . ."

Justine had led too many men into battle not to know when stress was the real enemy. These were disciplined men, and the offense wouldn't be repeated. She grinned mentally. Especially not now. "What say we get him off the floor and pump some coffee into him? Cold's got me jumpy, too, boys."

"Thanks, ma'am," said Jackson. "We won't forget it."

There was a collective grin of relief as they lifted Burke off the floor and dumped him on a cot. Justine felt sorry for him. He was in for quite a ribbing when he came to. She went back to work with Dr. Rose.

A few minutes later she saw the oceanographer look past her and blink a few times. "Ah, Justine . . . ?"

She looked up. SEALs with friendly smiles were standing there. Jackson was holding a flask.

"Ma'am, it's against regs, but to say thanks . . . well, would you care to join us?"

Justine was touched. "Gentlemen, my pleasure."

Akula

Volkov took the final damage-control reports from his division officers and went to find Kalik. He found him sitting alone in his cabin nursing a cup of coffee like a grudge.

"Repairs are complete, Comrade Captain. Engineering reports the new cooling pump is installed and they are able to produce maximum power. All our other systems are fully operational. We are ready to resume patrol."

"Where is the *Ural?*"

"Twenty miles from us. Sonar reports they are approaching at a steady rate of four knots, but they have been joined by a Canadian icebreaker, the *Polar Eight*. The computers verify the signature." Volkov paused, then plunged on. "The *Polar Eight* is twice as large as the *Ural*. Given the ice between us I can't say with any certainty that the *Ural* will get here first."

"I see. And the Americans? Is the DSRV still in the water?"

"They're working at the ice keel with the hydraulic arm. We can read the sounds plainly."

"My guess is they're taking the snorkel to the surface. That would be the logical move." Kalik pushed his cup away. "Sound battle stations."

"Battle stations? Why? Vassily, what are you planning to do?"

"Don't question me, Viktor."

"I'm only asking you. Have I lost that privilege?"

"I'm going to give the *Ural* time to get here."

"How? What do you intend to do?"

Kalik's face darkened. "Careful, Viktor."

"Vassily, I'm worried. We're in the middle of something. It's more than just *Red Dawn*. It stretches all the way back to the Kremlin. Solkov and Korodin are part of it. If we aren't careful we're going to get caught in the middle."

"I'm tired of politics," Kalik said forcefully. "I'm a submarine commander and I have a job to do. The Americans aren't going to steal *Red Dawn* from us."

"I beg you, Vassily. Think. There are larger issues here. You're going against Korodin's direct orders and siding with Solkov. It could start a coup. What if we gain *Red Dawn* only to lose everything else?"

"You're questioning my authority?"

Volkov took a deep breath. "Not your authority, Vassily. Your wisdom."

Kalik reacted as if he'd been slapped. "That's enough, Viktor. Now order battle stations and get to your post before I replace you for insubordination."

Kalik tested system after system and found *Akula* sound again despite the fresh welds on the pipes in the control room and the scars on bulkheads and consoles. He glanced at Volkov standing calmly in his place, as ready as the rest of the crew under battle conditions. There was no sign of discontent on his face. If nothing else, Viktor was a professional. No one would know of the words between them—or of the trust and faith that had been so badly damaged.

"Comrade Diving Officer, begin pumping variable ballast to sea and raise us off this shelf," Kalik ordered. "Helm, steer course one eight zero as soon as we're clear."

As *Akula* grew lighter, she shuddered and lifted clear of the ice shelf. "All ahead one-third." At this low speed he didn't need the reactor-cooling pump operating. *Akula* would be a silent shadow. They moved out into the cold waters. "Bring us to one hundred meters," he ordered.

"One hundred meters," echoed the diving officer a few moments later.

"Torpedo Room, what is the status of tubes one and two?"

"Both tubes are loaded and ready, Comrade Captain."

"Sonar, lock in the coordinates for the Americans' camp on the surface. Attack Center, match sonar bearings."

Kalik looked across the cabin. Volkov was watching him, his eyes hard and unyielding. Kalik continued to reel off commands under his senior lieutenant's stern gaze, feeling as if he were performing the ritual for Volkov alone. Look somewhere else! Kalik wanted to shout at those watchful eyes. Who are you to judge me and what I must now do?

"Attack Center. We have matched the coordinates, Comrade Captain. A firing solution is ready."

Kalik could almost hear Volkov in his mind. You don't know who's up there, he would complain. There could be civilians, maybe even women. This is not a military maneuver, it is . . . vengeance. It's murder.

Kalik stopped listening. "Fire tubes one and two."

Polar Ice Cap

When Captain Hansen returned he noted a subtle change in the dorm's atmosphere. He couldn't identify it exactly, but everyone seemed in better spirits. As long as the work was progressing he ceased to wonder about it. Besides, even goddamn Burke seemed downright contrite.

Justine was helping with the equipment. Twenty-eight-degree water left no room for error. It would paralyze a man's muscles before he knew what had hit him. Engrossed, she bolted up when her radio suddenly crackled into life.

"Base Camp, this is *Seawolf*. Base Camp. Emergency." It was Tom Lasovic.

"Base Camp, over."

"Justine, quick, Sonar's reading high-speed motors. It's *Akula*. There are torpedoes headed straight for you. Get out.

Get everybody out. Now. Don't wait. Fifty seconds is all you've got."

Justine turned. Hansen and his men had already heard and were grabbing supplies. "Forget all that," she yelled, "and get out. Now!"

Seawolf

"Release noisemakers," ordered Lasovic, hoping to draw the torpedoes away from the camp. Goddammit, they had come out of nowhere. They had to be from *Akula*.

"Noisemakers away. But it's a long shot, Mr. Lasovic. Awfully far."

"Sonar, keep tracking."

"Conn, Sonar. I can hear them. They're not going for the noisemakers, sir."

"Keep tracking," Lasovic said, clenching his hands helplessly.

Avalon

MacKenzie saw the fishing hole above them and relaxed a bit. "Get set, Luke, they should be waiting to take the snorkel."

But instead, Luke clutched his earphones tighter. "Captain, it's Mr. Lasovic. Incoming torpedoes! Navigation has them headed straight into the base camp. They're evacuating."

MacKenzie hit the controls and rammed the steering yoke all the way back to its stop. "Emergency deep. C'mon, Luke. Move!"

Luke hit the pump switches, and *Avalon* dropped like a rock. MacKenzie cut in the hydrophones. Sure enough there they were. Incoming high-cycle motors. *Akula* had come back to finish the war he had mistakenly started.

He had to draw the torpedoes away from the camp, had to give Justine and the others time to get out of there. Twin fish would blow the ice for a hundred yards in every direction. He heard *Seawolf*'s noisemakers going off in the distance, trying to decoy the fish away. They were useless, too far away. There was only one target that might turn the fish. He had only seconds.

"Luke, they've got only one chance topside, and that's if we decoy the torpedoes away. You understand? I'm making us the target. We're not too deep. You can get out the hatch."

"One hundred feet. Sonar tracking. Range one half mile and closing. Get stuffed, sir."

"I'm gonna kiss your ugly face if we get out of this. All right. We need to find a big ice keel, then draw them in and duck behind it right before they hit. Got it?"

"Quarter mile and closing. Fat chance. Sir."

"Sweet talker." MacKenzie scanned the screens. The keel had to be big enough to take the blast, near enough to get to in a hurry.

"Mac, over there . . . maybe?"

"I see it. Yeah, that's the one. Here we go."

Avalon sprinted for the keel, her propellers cavitating bubbles wildly in a wake behind her.

"One thousand feet. Five hundred feet . . . Oh, sweet Jesus, Mac, they hear us. They're changing course."

"Closing. Almost ready to run." MacKenzie held the ship steady, hovering in water as clear as air. He had to be certain, had to know the fish were coming straight in and could not change their course till it was too late. He ran the motors for noise, waiting. The big ice keel beside them beckoned like a shield. He longed to dive for it.

"C'mon, Mac! Three hundred feet!"

"One second more . . . It's going to be rough, Luke. Hold on tight."

"One hundred feet! Mac!"

"Now!" MacKenzie hit the power switch and put everything *Avalon* had into one urgent surge for the keel. The props bit hard into the water as he dived hard to starboard and *Avalon* jumped as if it had been kicked. On the screen he could see the ice sliding in between them and the torpedoes. MacKenzie pushed the motors as hard as they could spin.

The blast shattered the ice keel and turned the ocean into a maelstrom. Ice chunks the size of boulders blew away and tumbled past them into the deep. MacKenzie tried to dodge the flying debris, but the blast created horrific currents that bounced off the surface ice and drove *Avalon* into the explosion. Systems blew. Power failed. They were plunged into darkness, pummeled by icy debris. Luke's head slammed into a bulkhead, and he slumped over in his seat.

MacKenzie's last thought as they were swept away by the irresistible currents was that all of this was his fault. His mistakes had come back to haunt him. Then the aftershocks hit and he lost consciousness, so there was nothing to think of at all.

Polar Ice Cap

The explosions caught them as they ran. The ice cap buckled up from underneath as if a giant hand had punched it, and cracks appeared by the thousands. It sounded like a thousand panes of glass shattering as the ice split open. Water spurted through the fractures like geysers, forced up by the pressures below.

A chasm opened before Justine. She lost her balance and fell toward it, digging her fingers into the snow to keep herself from falling in. There was no purchase. A SEAL got hold of her and pulled her back. They scrambled to their feet and continued running for the hills that ringed the camp.

All around them the tiny valley the camp had been nestled in began to shatter. She heard a scream of pain and turned to see that Dr. Rose was caught behind them on a rising sheet of ice frantically trying to jump off. She started to turn back. One of the SEALs grabbed her. "You'll never make it!" Ellis shouted. She struggled to get free, but it was too late. The frail Dr. Rose slid helplessly down the ice into the freezing water and disappeared from sight. Justine felt tears of rage and frustration freeze on her cheeks. He had been right about the Arctic. In the end it had killed him.

Another SEAL tripped and slid headfirst into the icy churning waters before anyone could grab him. They ran. Hansen stopped for one of his men whom a chunk of ice had hit hard. He felt for a pulse. There was none. The ice behind him began to break up. Somebody shouted a warning. Hansen rolled aside and leaped to his feet as the ice cracked. Then he was running again with the rest.

The ice was breaking up, and the plane was no longer level or solid. Justine leaped across a chasm that had opened virtually beneath her feet. The ice on the other side reared up at the same time. She grabbed for the edge of the rift as it rose up, dropping the precious radio as she tried to lever her body over it. She rose into the air with the ice, hanging on for dear life. The strain in her arms was intolerable. She felt her fingers slipping, but hands encircled her wrists and she looked gratefully into Burke's face as he grabbed her from the other side. "Kick!" he shouted and she dug her feet in, scraping enough friction to bring her up and over the ice and into his arms. She stood for a moment dizzy and shaking.

"Thanks—" she began.

"No time. Run!"

She ran. On the other side of the basin Greene and his men bolted away from the fishing hole. Fissures were traveling along the ice just behind them. Hansen and the other SEALs yelled for them to run faster. They watched in horror as the very last man in Greene's party failed to outrace the widening fissures and was swallowed up. A second man and a third went in and were covered by ice.

The basin that the camp had lain in became an undulating maelstrom before collapsing back into a mass of huge grinding pressure ridges. Every trace of the Quonset huts had disappeared. Greene and his remaining men finally joined up with Justine, Hansen, and the rest of the SEALs, cursing the treachery of the ice beneath them.

As if in response the ice under them shifted and moved in warning. Fissures were still a danger. No one knew how far the fracturing might spread. They had to make distance, get out of the basin onto firmer footing.

It was almost forty below zero and the temperature was still dropping. Eerie dark fog lay over the distant ice. Thunderheads were moving in fast. They had no food or shelter.

They moved off, wondering how long it would be before they envied the dead.

Red Dawn

Galinin turned the air tube over and over again in his hands like a snake that had bitten him. "Nothing."

"What could have gone wrong? The Americans were right here," Ligichev said angrily, showing the first sign of temper Galinin had seen from the scientist. "To be this close . . . What could have gone wrong?"

"What indeed?" wondered Galinin. He was worried, too, but for a very different reason. They couldn't die like this. His orders were clear. Under no condition could he permit the Americans to plunder *Red Dawn,* and therefore he could not allow the ship to become an unprotected tomb. It was up to him. He had to hope the Americans did succeed in raising them so that he could send *Red Dawn* to the bottom. Scuttle the sub in two miles of ocean, that was the only grave deep enough to hide the professor's work. Nothing in this world could raise it then, and in the next . . . well, he'd know about that soon enough.

He watched Ligichev looking at his daughter. He so wanted life for her. Galinin was struck by the irony of it. The flow of oxygen would doom them just as surely as the lack of it.

Galinin had nourished the hope that *Akula* would return and somehow save him from what he had been ordered to do. But he realized now that he was to have no reprieve. It took a certain kind of man to scuttle his own ship and kill his crew. Galinin wondered at the dubious distinction of having been chosen as one who could do it. But the more he thought about it the more he came to understand. It wasn't his lack of family ties or a character flaw. On the contrary, it was his ability to see this sacrifice as no different from charging into an enemy machine gun or diving onto a grenade to protect his fellow soldiers. Wasn't the ultimate act of heroism to give one's life unflinchingly? For a moment he felt a kinship with the kamikaze who screamed the name of the emperor while diving his tiny airplane into an aircraft carrier. For a moment he felt . . . divine.

Galinin understood. If life was war, death would be the peace he had always been denied.

Chapter
Fourteen

Winestock summed it up. "We've definitely got a situation up there, Mr. President. It's up to you to decide how far we go with it."

Brendon Connors didn't like being woken up in the middle of the night with bad news. And padding around the Oval Office in pajamas, robe, and slippers made him feel less like the second-term president of the United States than some character out of "Father Knows Best." "How did this happen, Arthur? You told me the operation was cut and dried."

Winestock looked pained. "It's Solkov, sir."

"The defense minister? What's he got to do with this?"

"We believe he's making a run at the chairmanship. With Abrikov's backing. They've been damn smart. The general secretary is in a bind. The army isn't in love with him in the first place, and they've set him up to look like a weak sister if he lets the U.S. take Soviet technology without a fight. It was Solkov and Abrikov who took the muzzle off the *Akula*. We have reliable information they went right over Korodin's head after he called in the *Ural*."

"This will not do, Arthur. That bastard Solkov hates us."

"He's a relic. Just like Abrikov. The last of the cold

warriors. It'll be a cold day in hell before you get a START treaty out of them."

Connors fixed Winestock with a gaze that had stared down political opponents and TV cameras for forty years. "But better for you. What would happen to the Agency in a peaceful world?"

"Sir, the day the last spy retires will be the happiest day of my life."

It was said with simple sincerity, and Connors felt he had heard the truth. "Go on, then. Paint me a scenario."

Winestock ticked off points on his fingers. "The attack by *Akula* has led to the loss of American lives and the destruction of American property. The Soviets could probably make the same claim."

"We could withdraw. We don't need irinium that badly."

"That's arguable. What was our edge worth when we had transistors and they didn't, or integrated circuits or computer chips? It's as big as that."

"What's the alternative, bring in the big guns?"

Winestock sighed. "Ten years ago, even a *year* ago, that would have been the answer. But now?" He shrugged. "I think we have to keep this strictly local. Win or lose. Right now there's a pretty good balance of forces. If MacKenzie can pull it off and we come out on top, okay. We take the irinium and return the sub, but at least the general secretary has put up a fight. If we lose, the general secretary looks just fine to the conservative hard-liners and politics stays pretty much on track. We'll keep trying to get the irinium some other way."

"What about our people up there?"

"Unfortunately, they're on their own, sir. With *Akula* gunning for them. But if we bring in one more warship the general secretary won't be able to stop Solkov from bringing in two, and then we'll have to bring in three and the fighters, and then we're back on the same goddamn merry-go-round that got us here in the first place."

"I don't like this. I know MacKenzie."

"And you'll like it even less if the press finds out you've abandoned him. They'll fry your hide. Sir. But are you willing to risk starting a bigger conflict that might screw up our relations with the Soviets? At this point?"

"No," Connors said firmly. "I'm not willing to risk that. All right, if you're sure this is the way."

Winestock shrugged. "Sure? I haven't been really sure of anything since grade school. No crystal ball, sir. Just a best guess. We can't let Solkov come to power."

"What will MacKenzie's orders be?"

"Raise the *Red Dawn*. Any way he can. Engage and destroy *Akula* if he has to."

"Very well. The general secretary's still in Paris?"

"We can reach him at the embassy."

Connors looked out at the lights of the city. "It looks as if they're on their own up there," he said finally, reaching for the phone.

Moscow

KGB Chief Abrikov swept past Solkov's bank of aides and into his office. Solkov was at his desk, not working, just staring out the window.

"What is so important I had to rush over here?" Abrikov demanded. "I have enough cryptic messages from my spies, Sergei. I don't need any more."

Solkov spun around in his chair and pointed to a small *korobka* on his desk, the kind children kept chess sets in for transport back and forth from school clubs. "This just arrived. Look inside. Damn it, Agi, I told you we were underestimating him."

Abrikov took the little box and turned it over in his hands. Under closer scrutiny it was no ordinary *korobka*. It was constructed of many different woods all laced together in an intricate pattern as subtle as the grain itself. He opened it. There were only five pieces inside, a black king and a white one, a black knight and a white knight . . . and a red crystal pawn. It took a moment for the significance to sink in, and then he smiled in understanding. The old fox might be way the hell out on a limb with his reforms, and he had certainly shaken the country and maybe even the whole damn world to the roots, but he had lost none of his subtlety. It was a trait Abrikov admired above all others, but of course the general secretary knew that, too.

"It's a message," he said to Solkov.

"What does it mean?"

Abrikov smiled. "It's quite simple, really, Sergei. He's setting terms and conditions. He's telling us he knows all about *Red Dawn*. That's the red pawn. By choosing a pawn he's letting us know *he* knows it isn't the real prize of the game. The knights are the submarines *Akula* and *Seawolf*. By this he lets us know he is aware that we and not Korodin are controlling Kalik. Finally, he sends the kings, the ultimate prize. We are one king and he is the other, or more accurately, he knows we're after him. There are no other pieces because the conflict is to be limited to what is already in place." Abrikov said admiringly, "You've got to admit Sergei, the man has style."

"How can his knight be an American submarine?"

"Think of it philosophically, Agi. In the final analysis what are warships but physical manifestations of government ideology? If *Seawolf* wins the day, we lose the irinium technology but we continue to move closer to the Americans —becoming weaker, you and I would say, but that's the issue. The general secretary can always say he sent in the subs and Korodin sent in the *Ural* and it was too bad we lost, but he'll wave some new grain treaty and ask who really wants to risk another cold war with the Americans. On the other hand, if by unleashing Captain Kalik we enable *Akula* to win the day, we will have clearly outmaneuvered the general secretary, the proof of which will be that we retain sole possession of the irinium and force the Americans to back down. This will demonstrate that *our* policies are the stronger."

"And if not?"

"To complete the metaphor, we are mated and must

resign." A truly ingenious way to send his message, Abrikov thought. Worthy of a grand master.

Solkov thought it over. "So it all rests on what happens up at the pole?"

The chess pieces were smooth in Abrikov's gnarled hands. "It always has, Sergei," he said softly. "It always has."

Chapter
Fifteen

Seawolf

Sonar, report," Lasovic demanded. "Can you get a fix on *Avalon?*"

The explosion had knocked loose tons of debris, complicating the sonar search, "Sorry, sir. Still no contact. There's so much stuff flying around out there it's impossible to read anything with all the echoes."

"Communications, anything from the SEALs or Mrs. MacKenzie?"

"Nothing, sir."

Lasovic was worried. *Phoenix* told the same story. Both subs had followed Mac's attempt to decoy the torpedoes away from the base camp. Did he maneuver his craft away at the last second? Even if he did, he was practically on top of the explosion. Lasovic's concern gave way to anger. He had no way of telling if MacKenzie was alive or if Justine and the others had gotten out before the torpedoes hit.

He surfaced and tried a radar sweep, but the ice was too irregular with too many pressure ridges for him to spot anything. Justine and the SEALs could have been a hundred yards away and he probably wouldn't have seen them. An air search wasn't feasible. Jets flew too fast and couldn't get low enough under the cloud cover. The only plane that made sense for this kind of search was the C-130. Although the one transporting the wounded could not return, thankfully another was already on the way to pick up Dr. Rose and his equipment. But the weather still hadn't let up and its ability to land in this storm was doubtful.

For the moment, all of that had to be put aside. Lasovic had to make the most difficult decisions of his career. There was no way of knowing if Mac had succeeded in restoring air to *Red Dawn* before the torpedoes hit. Given the timing, he'd guess probably not. He had to assume the DSRV was damaged, maybe even sunk. That put the decision in his hands alone. With Phil Arlin's help, he could try to rescue the Russians, but that would leave *Phoenix* and *Seawolf* vulnerable to *Akula*'s attack. Or he could go after *Akula* and possibly be sentencing *Red Dawn*'s crew to death by asphyxiation. Often over the years he'd seen Mac face difficult choices. He had always been secretly relieved that the ultimate responsibility wasn't his. Until now.

Mac had borne the responsibility when he attacked *Akula,* and now he carried the burden of having mistakenly taken lives, or so he felt—undeservedly, Lasovic thought, but what man of good conscience suffered the death of others lightly? It was only in the movies that anyone pulled the trigger without remorse. In the real world you carried on your conscience every mishap, every accident, every mistake that cost from a finger to a life. You could only lay off so much on being a naval officer. The rest you lived with, because under the uniform was just an ordinary man.

He made his decision. "Take her down, Mr. Randall. Five zero zero feet." He called his division officers together in the wardroom and held a meeting. Word spread fast. The division officers returned to their posts and told the junior officers, the junior officers told the chiefs, and the chiefs told the men: it was time for all the training, all the endless repetition of tasks day after day, to be put to the test. They would hunt *Akula* while *Phoenix* conducted a search for Mac and the base camp survivors. It had become a shooting war.

In the conn, Lasovic's hand swept out and hit the alarm.

"Attention, this is the captain speaking. Man battle stations. We are under enemy attack. Our base camp has sustained damage from Soviet torpedoes. The DSRV *Avalon* is missing and presumed lost."

The alarm blared throughout the ship. Men went to their stations poised and ready for action. In a way the ship was in its most alive state now, every system manned and ready, all extensions of the mind and will of the captain—his eyes and ears, his arms and legs, his fists. The attack center was aglow with computer tracks on its screens. Sonar was monitoring to the farthest extent of its range, and every passive sensor in *Seawolf*'s hull was turned to the max.

"Torpedo Room, load tubes one, two, three, and four with MK-forty-eight torpedoes. Fire Control, merge your data with Sonar's," Lasovic ordered.

"Fire Control, aye."

"Mr. Randall, make your depth three zero zero feet."

"Three zero zero feet, aye."

Lasovic hit the intercom. "Maneuvering, secure main coolant pumps. Keep her quiet as she'll run, Mr. Cardiff."

"Maneuvering, aye. Ready to answer all bells, Mr. Lasovic."

"We are at ordered depth," reported Randall. "But, uh, sir?"

Lasovic knew what Randall was about to ask. No one thought more of MacKenzie than the young officer. "If the captain's still out there, we'll find him. Make no mistake about it, Mr. Randall."

"Yes, sir. Thanks."

Lasovic knew Randall spoke for everybody in the room. Lasovic wished he felt as confident as he'd sounded.

"Conn, Torpedo Room. All tubes loaded and ready."

"Very well," Lasovic acknowledged. "Helm, all ahead one-third. Maneuvering, make turns for five knots. Sonar, if a seal so much as burps I want to know about it."

"Sonar, aye. We're tracking them, too."

Lasovic nodded. They were ready.

Seawolf began her prowl through the cold waters, as silent as a shadow.

"Take us up, Viktor," Kalik commanded, "and hold us under the ice." The maze of ice keels and stalactites jutting down from the ice cap would safely hide *Akula* from the American subs.

Kalik ignored the sober and somewhat disapproving look on his senior lieutenant's face, a look that had nothing to do with the pain in his broken collarbone. Kalik himself felt ecstatic in spite of the pain in his own arm. Both torpedoes had deviated when they picked up the DSRV motor noise. After the explosion, the motor noise was gone. He had gotten two birds with one shot. He felt loose and relieved, like finally reaching climax after too much foreplay.

Now the battle began in earnest. *Seawolf* would come for him; he was sure of it. All the tactics and all the under-ice maneuvers would be put to the test, with each side trying for an advantage that would lead to a strong contact and a clean shot. Kalik felt his adrenaline rise. He touched the cold cleanliness of the stainless-steel periscope housing. Maybe it had been a premonition when he told Viktor he wished he could test *Akula* against *Seawolf.*

Kalik looked at Volkov across the control room. He was still reserved, still totally professional, but Kalik knew he was watching him closely. This would be Viktor's last cruise, he decided. There was room for only one captain on a sub, and he couldn't have his orders or his intentions second-guessed. Something inside him warned about silencing opposing voices. Was he failing to heed Volkov's good advice just to fight some private war of his own? Nonsense, he decided, the man had ceased to be loyal, had failed to understand the strength of Kalik's desire to walk away from this affair with honor.

Seawolf and *Akula.* Soon they were going to get the chance to prove who was the better captain, which was the better ship.

Polar Ice Cap

Justine, Hansen, Greene, and six SEALs including Jackson, Burke, and Ellis, made it over the basin's craggy ice ridge and stumbled onto the frozen terrain beyond. Heavy snow was falling steadily, driven by the bitter wind. Exhausted from the run, they huddled together.

"We won't last two hours out here," said Justine, her breath a smoking plume. "And I lost the radio."

"Go easy on yourself, ma'am," Burke said. "You couldn't hold on to the ice and the radio, too."

"Thanks for that," said Justine. "But we'll die out here if we can't let *Seawolf* know where we are." The white plains of ice and snow surrounded them. The sun was invisible in the overcast sky, and the snow swirled around them like a mad matador's cape. Already their faces were caked with frost. "I'd count on Tom calling for air support, but with this storm . . ."

Hansen shook his head. "They'll never see us."

Bernie Greene cursed forlornly. "God, I wish I could've taken the explosives, but there was no time."

"We've got to do something. We're dying as we stand here," Justine said, frustrated. "Maybe we can lower something into the water and make some noise. Hope *Seawolf*'s sonar hears it. And Mac . . . Oh, my God, Mac! He was in the DSRV. Those torpedoes—"

"Easy, ma'am," said Greene. "Smart fella, your husband. He was probably nowhere near."

"There's nothing you can do right now in any event," Hansen said. "We have to worry about ourselves."

Hansen was right. Standing there, stamping her feet to keep warm and shivering at an increasing rate, Justine fought for control. Priorities. She had to get them to some kind of shelter. *So lock up everything you feel in a tight box inside you and come back to it when there's time, when it's safe.* She searched for the music in her head, not what she had played so long ago at border crossings so her father and brothers could ambush the guards, but the music that was hers alone, her refuge. Where were the clean soaring notes of spirit that came through her fingers the times she was happy, the times with Mac? *Have faith.* In the end that's what it came down to.

"Mr. Jackson, some of that brandy, please."

"Yes, ma'am. Sir?"

"Fine idea. Ladies first," said Hansen. "Warm the metal or it will tear your lips off," he advised.

Think, Justine exhorted herself, taking a sip of the brandy. Its fire coursed down her throat and exploded in her gut. "There's nothing we can use for shelter, no fuel or wood to burn, nowhere we can walk to . . . walk to . . . Wait a minute!" The realization hit her as sharp as a slap. "The icebreakers!"

Hansen jumped on it. "There are ships? Near here?"

Justine's excitement drew everyone tighter. "Tom Lasovic told Mac that two icebreakers are heading for the *Red Dawn.* One is Russian. The other is Canadian. *Polar* something. They've got to be close by now. Very close. Within a few miles."

"Which way were they heading?"

"South southeast, right for *Red Dawn.*"

"That way." Greene pointed, squinting into the wind. "Maybe we can intercept them."

"No maybes about it. What other choice do we have?" said Hansen.

Justine shivered violently. A few miles. God, what would it be like to walk a few miles in this wind and cold? She steeled her mind to it. "We move or we die. We can't count on *Seawolf* finding us."

Hansen nodded. "Let's go."

She moved off into the snow. Within a few hundred yards she realized her mind was finding it hard to accept what her body knew at once—that in this environment even the simplest actions were close to impossible. A trot of two or three miles wouldn't have winded her on a normal day in a normal climate. Here her feet felt like lead after a hundred feet. She trudged on, the men following in a ragged line. Their clothing was so crusted with ice they almost merged with the snowfall. Hansen, then Burke, then Ellis and Jackson, the rest of the SEALs, and then the frozen-faced Greene like an icy shepherd pushing them all on.

A ragged line. A singsong rhyme filled her head: "There was a crooked man, and he went a crooked mile. . . ." She forced herself to concentrate. One foot after the other. One foot after the other. She trudged up a sharp rise hoping to see the black shapes of ships crunching through the ice. There was nothing but snow cutting visibility even further. She slid down the other side of the slippery slope. The wind bit her face, and her eyes hurt from the ice on her lashes. One foot after the other. Keep moving. Somewhere ahead there were warm ships with steaming galleys all filled with heat and food and life. One foot after the other. Keep moving. One foot after the other. One foot after the other. The snow built up on her shoulders like epaulets. One foot after the other . . . One foot after the other.

Red Dawn

"I'm going into the tunnel," said Pytor with a determined look.

Sadly Ivanna shook her head against his naked chest. "It's no use, my love. If anyone were still out there we would have known it by now."

They were lying in the bunk in her father's cabin, naked under the coarse woolen blankets. Elsewhere in the ship the remaining crewmen were still waiting, refusing to admit what Ivanna knew in her heart—that rescue was a dream from which they had woken too soon. So she had brought Pytor here to share the only happiness remaining to them, the comfort of each other.

"But those explosions—we felt them," Pytor insisted.

"So the Americans were blown up or blew themselves up. Or blew up somebody else. Whatever. What does it matter? No one is there, Pytor. No one!" She moved his hand to her breast, pressing his palm against her nipple urgently. It hardened into a turgid point. They had little time for all the things that lovers try when they are new, so she was bold with him, hungry for his mouth and hands and organ. She was like a child with a new toy, and she wanted to play with it for hours, examining every crease and fold, tasting, licking, probing. It was fascinating, so big and hard in her hand and yet so soft, like velvet-covered steel. She wanted it everywhere. And when he grew tired she took him in her mouth and coaxed him till he was hard again and could love her once more. She reached for him.

"Please, Isha," he groaned, using her pet name tenderly. "No man can do what you ask. It will ki—" He stopped. His eyes rested lovingly on her face, and his hands trailed down her body to her moist thighs. "All right, my love, once more. . . ."

Pytor waited until she was asleep, then put on his clothes and slipped out of the cabin. He passed the captain huddled over coffee with Ivanna's father, no doubt planning some new way to save them. His lips tightened bitterly. It was always the old ones who got them into trouble. Now it was up to the young ones to get them out.

The second torpedo tube was still clear of ice. He opened the hatch and crawled in. It was still breathtaking being on the inside of the aquarium looking out, but what he hoped to see wasn't there. There was no ship to carry the snorkel to the surface. The air tube left the sub and trailed off into the sea beyond where he could see it. He was about to give up hope when something flashed in the distance. He couldn't be certain at first. It was far away under the ice cap and he couldn't see it well. He almost had to turn his head and look sideways to be sure he had seen anything at all. Then he saw it once again, a burst of light like the flash from an electric lamp. He hurried back inside.

Galinin put down the field glasses and crawled back inside the torpedo room. Pytor, Ivanna, and Ligichev were waiting expectantly.

"You were right," he said. "There is something out there. I think it's the American DSRV. It looks inoperative. The flashing is one of her navigation lights."

"If they're out there, why don't they come back?"

"I don't think they can," said Galinin. "They're just hanging there, wedged up under the ice. Maybe the explosions we felt damaged her."

"The craft had to come from somewhere," said Ligichev. "What about the mother ship?"

"I have no answers," Galinin said tersely. "If you want to go ask them, feel free."

Tempers were too frayed for such a remark. "If it hadn't been for your stupidity we wouldn't be in trouble in the first place," Ligichev said hotly. They faced each other like aging boxers and might actually have come to blows but a voice stopped them.

"I'll go, Comrade Captain."

"What?"

Pytor said it again. "What you said. To ask the Americans. I'll go."

Galinin and Ligichev looked at the young chief engineer and then at each other. The absurdity of his offer drained their anger. "What are you talking about?" demanded Galinin.

"We have scuba gear on board. I request permission to swim to the American ship."

"Pytor, no!" Ivanna said.

"If it is disabled, maybe I can help. I don't know. But we must try something."

"Pytor, you can't. Father, don't let him."

Galinin cut her off. "Do you know what you're saying? We don't have arctic diving equipment. You'd last ten minutes in that water, maybe less."

Pytor nodded. "I know that. But I ask you this, Comrades. How much longer will we last if I don't go?"

Pytor stood stark naked in front of them, trying to retain his dignity by staring fixedly ahead. Every square inch of skin including his face was covered with dark gray grease from the main shaft. On top of the grease Ivanna was wrapping elastic bandages from the infirmary.

"I feel like a mummy," Pytor muttered.

"Quiet. Let her work," admonished Ligichev. "A couple of layers of grease and elastic under the wet suit will stop the cold from penetrating so fast. It could save your life."

Michman Rostov came into the room. "Comrade Captain, the escape hatch is cleared of ice. The scuba tanks are ready."

"Very good. Wait there for us." He turned to Pytor. "You understand now, you'll have to go up the escape hatch and break the ice seal yourself. The water pressure is going to be hell. And you've got to get back quickly or the ice will refreeze and you won't be able to get into the ship."

"Listen to him," Ivanna told him, still wrapping intently.

"I was."

"You weren't."

"How do you know what I was listening to?" he demanded.

"I know."

"But . . . all right. I will be back before the tunnel refreezes, Comrade Captain."

"Good."

Ivanna sniffed, knotting an end to finish. "I don't want to argue."

Pytor softened. "Me neither. Let's forget it, okay?"

"Okay."

Ligichev wanted to cry.

Pytor donned the wet suit. Galinin applied an epoxy cement to the seams between wrist and gloves and between boots and leggings. The neoprene bubbled as it melted together. "As good a seal as we're going to get. Let's go."

Pytor padded aft to the escape hatch. His tank, regulator, hood, mask, and fins were waiting. Galinin drew a weight belt around him. Rostov and several crewmen had hot coffee and blankets ready to warm him when he got back. Optimists, thought Pytor dryly.

"Ten minutes, fifteen at the most," Ligichev warned. "Remember."

Pytor kissed Ivanna and climbed up the ladder into the escape tube. He closed the hatch behind him. Rostov had left the hull hatch open, and Pytor climbed the iron rungs out onto the hull. They had cleared a good space. The ice was like a dome overhead. He had to remember to protect his head when the waters crashed in.

He hit the purge valve on his regulator and heard the reassuring burst of air. He made sure the air hose was draped properly over his shoulder and put the rubber mouthpiece between his lips. He bit down and drew in a few breaths, tasting the metallic dryness of compressed air. He carried only a single tank. He couldn't stay in the water long enough to need a second.

He hefted the ice pick and swung it hard against the ice. Once. Twice. Drops of water formed and slid down the crystal-faceted sheet, then became a stream. Suddenly the ice imploded, shattering toward him as if hit from the other side. Seawater burst in like an icy hammer, hitting him full in the face and throwing him down against the hull. He tried to swim out of the chamber but the water pressure was too great. He held his hands over his face as the water pounded him. He was twisted backwards. The water roared in, pushing, pulling. His neck was crushed back against the tank valve. His vision blurred and for a moment he feared he would black out, but just as suddenly the water pressure subsided. The ice chamber was filled with seawater, and he was floating in it. He slowed his anxious breathing. Steady, now. Each breath brought the sound of the valve releasing air into his lungs, each exhalation sent bubbles traveling up past his ears. He reached into the indents in his face mask, clamped his nostrils shut and blew hard to equalize the pressure in his ears. They cleared and the pain in his head subsided. He kicked out, and his flippers pushed satisfyingly hard against the water. He shot out of the ice keel into the open sea.

There was no way to describe the cold. His head felt as if

someone had put it in a vise. His heart was pounding. Every muscle had a protest of its own to make, and all of them wanted to lock into immobility. He forced himself to swim, kicking hard, wriggling his torso for warmth. One arm was pressed against his side, the other pointing forward like a spear.

He hovered for a moment in the glassy sea to clear his face mask. A glance at his diving watch told him two minutes had elapsed. One-fifth of his precious time. He swam for the American ship. The gray, torpedo-shaped craft was lodged under the ice, as Galinin had said. As he got closer he saw that the DSRV didn't appear to be damaged, but there was no sign of activity.

He located the forward observation window and pressed his face mask against it. There were two men inside. Naval officers, judging by the insignia. Both were slumped over in their seats, unconscious, but he could see the slow rise and fall of their backs. They were still breathing.

He swam around, looking for a way in. The ship was listing slightly. He found a hatch that was unobstructed. He tried it. It was locked. Probably had to be released from inside. There was no time to figure it out. Five minutes had elapsed. He had only half his time left to make something happen.

He swam another circuit around the ship. It told him only that the propellers were undamaged and there were no holes in the hull. He swam back to the observation window. He tried pounding on the thick glass with his gloved fist. It made only a dull thud. He slipped a lead weight out of his belt. It fit nicely into his hand. He had to swing it in short strokes because of the water pressure. *Crack, crack, crack.* Neither man stirred inside. He hit the glass again. He had to awaken them. Still no response. He was getting colder now, feeling it deep down in his muscles right through the layers of grease and bandage. He had little time left. He wanted to shout with frustration. *Red Dawn* was going to die unless these men woke up. Ivanna was going to die. His arm felt like lead, and his head was swimming. He was beginning not to care if he broke the window. A blast of cold water in the face would wake the bastards up! He had nothing left to lose. He checked his watch. It was past the time he should have gone back. The escape tunnel would be iced over. There was no way in. It didn't matter. His strength was fading. His head felt as if a black bag were descending onto it, so he wedged his other arm into a handhold on the hull and hit the glass again and again. *Crack, crack . . . crack . . . crack . . .*

Polar Ice Cap

Stephan felt it through the ice. Deep vibrations. Strong enough to be an explosion. But how far? Close, his senses told him. Maybe a mile or two. In the direction of *Red Dawn*.

When the fog that enclosed him cleared, he could see *Polar 8* through wispy vapors about a mile to starboard. It was almost abreast of the *Ural*. Stephan had stolen every inch of speed he could from the ice, but the bigger ship's power was unmatchable.

Stephan moved across the ice like a wraith. New crewmen struggled to keep up. Rolf and Pinkov had been rotated back to the ship to eat and warm themselves. Stephan remained outside. It would have been too easy for the ship to run into thick ice without his lead. It was dead of winter cold, and the snowstorm was fouling their instruments and making it harder and harder to see.

Stephan plunged on. He ate as he walked, as an Inuit would. A thermos of hot coffee was more than enough to keep up his internal temperature. There was open water somewhere, but where? If he found a good patch, the *Ural* could surge past the *Polar 8*. He had thought they would get to it long before now.

Stephan had seen bad weather on the ice cap before, but nothing compared to this. Ice rime covered every mast on the *Ural,* and the radar housing had stopped turning. The instrument was probably fouled. Icicles hung from every porthole and hatchway in jagged edging. The *Ural* looked like an ice-encrusted ghost ship dredged up from the deep. Only the constant rumble of its bow crashing through the ice was proof that somewhere human hands were still in control.

He saw the *Polar 8* again, closer. Its heavy bow crunched ice far too thick for any other ship. They were making a run for it, pulling out the stops to get ahead and reach *Red Dawn* first. Stephan didn't know much about the laws of salvage, but he understood that getting there first was important. He lifted his binoculars and scanned the ice ahead. "Left five degrees rudder," he reported over the radio. Thin ice lay in that direction. This course would bring the *Ural* even closer to the *Polar 8*, but that couldn't be helped.

Polar 8

Out on the foredeck, Icemaster Renaud lifted his binoculars and peered through the snow, searching for the *Ural*. The air cleared for a moment, and he saw that the two behemoths were virtually neck and neck, huge dark shapes charging side by side through a frozen land like a hunting party. He shook his head. For *Ural* to keep pace with the *Polar 8* was a remarkable feat, one Renaud would have sworn was impossible any day before this.

How were they doing it? Conditions couldn't have been worse. Their radars had to be as fouled as the *Polar 8*'s were. Both ships were sailing half blind in the blizzard. Celestial navigation was a joke. The satellite relays were quirky. Crewmen with ice picks had been sent up to clear the frozen antennas and had come back frostbitten in a matter of minutes.

Inside, Captain Maré was pushing the ship to the maximum. Renaud knew he was determined to reach the sub before the Russians did. Renaud was feeling the strain of keeping them moving through the ice. His shoulders ached from hunching over his instruments, and his eyes felt as if his binoculars had been permanently screwed into them. It was the icemaster's responsibility to steer the ship away from ice that could stop or entrap them. Often in the past few hours the ice had thickened past eight feet, almost to ten, but they had enough momentum to move through it. Each time Renaud held his breath. If they lost so much as half a knot of speed they'd lose their headway and be forced to back and ram. That would almost assuredly give the race to the *Ural*. Maré was taking a dangerous course heading directly for *Red Dawn* through this ice. Renaud would normally have advised against it but *Ural*'s speed forced their hand.

Five miles to their destination. Renaud climbed the frozen stairs to the bridge deck. He was freezing. He clutched his hood around his head to lock out the cold, but also to block out the sound. Out here the cacophony was awesome, like the crashing of Titans. The constant crunch was amplified because this close to each other the ships created a kind of echo chamber. Renaud shivered. Sound this loud and piercing unnerved you in a primordial way. Fear of it was marked deep down in the genes so that ancient man knew instinctively to run from the heavy charge of woolly mammoths. Renaud heard distant thunder rolling across the ice, heaven's angry response to the din. He couldn't tell which was louder or scared him more.

Suddenly the dark silhouette of the *Ural* appeared through the swirling mists. The two ships were almost side by side, dark frozen shapes prowling the land of ice. Then the weather rolled back in and the *Ural* was gone.

Only the great crashing sound remained.

"Conn, Sonar. Still nothing, Skipper."

"Keep looking, Sonar."

"Sonar, aye."

Arlin tried not to let his concern show. Repeated searches of the area had failed to turn up any sign of the DSRV. There was more than a mile of ocean below them. It could be anywhere. Finding a needle in a haystack was easy compared to locating a tiny craft whose systems were apparently silent, hopefully not because they had been destroyed.

He had already surfaced twice to look for the base camp survivors and had even gone up onto the sail himself. The blizzard was madness. The cold was instantaneously cruel, and the snow obscured everything. Sound carried a few feet at best. Within minutes *Phoenix*'s black sail had been transformed by the snow into just another white hill. He wasn't sure it could be seen unless you knew it was there. Reluctantly he had taken *Phoenix* down again and continued the search for the DSRV.

All the while he kept one eye out for *Akula*. Tom Lasovic was running a tricky search pattern, staying as silent as he could, and in *Seawolf*'s case that was amazingly silent, hoping to draw her out. Arlin hoped the Russian captain would make a mistake and show them his face. Paying him back for the attack that might have cost them both two dear friends, one on the surface and the other under it, would be welcome business for both Lasovic and himself. But so far they had no sign of *Akula* either.

"Conn, Navigation. Polynyas ahead."

"Very well," Arlin acknowledged. Time to try once more. "Prepare to surface the ship."

Avalon

Somebody wanted something somewhere, but it was too far away to matter so MacKenzie drifted along without worry in a black dreamy sleep.

Crack.

It was irritating being woken from a sound sleep and MacKenzie wanted to tell somebody so. Later. He wanted to go back to sleep.

Crack, crack . . . crack!

What was that noise? He tried to turn over to locate the source of the annoyance but something restrained him. He pulled at it. A seat harness? That was enough to bring him back. *Avalon!* The memory of the explosion pushed him up with a start. The control panels of the DSRV were all around him. The mike dangled freely on its tangled cord.

"Luke, wake up. Luke?"

He nudged Luke's shoulder to rouse him. He was rewarded with a muffled groan. The blood was congealed on his copilot's forehead. Had they been unconscious that long?

Luke woke. "Ooh, my aching head. What happened?"

"Torpedoes, remember? *Akula* attacked the base camp."

Crack!

"What the hell?" Luke exclaimed.

MacKenzie looked around and found himself staring right into the face mask of a scuba diver through the observation port. Thick grease covered his exposed skin and his eyes were pleading, almost frantic. It was a sadly compelling sight. A whole world was summed up in those eyes.

"Luke . . ." Mac pointed.

"What's he doing out there? Jesus, he's not even in a dry suit. He's got to be freezing."

"That's Russian gear," said MacKenzie as the diver gave a final crack with the weight, then pointed anxiously toward *Red Dawn.* He looked relieved but deadly tired. MacKenzie understood. "We lost the snorkel. They saw us floating and sent him out here."

"It's a one-way mission."

"Not if we can help it."

"Right." Luke tested the controls. "We've still got power. No radio for a while, though. That blast shorted a bunch of electronics."

"See what you can do. The explosion was awfully close to the base camp. I want to check on Justine and the others."

Luke hit a series of switches. Lights came on. Power curves flowed onto the screens. "Still got some juice in the batteries. We should be able to move."

"How's the steering?"

"A little rough, but manageable," Luke reported. "Mac, look."

It was the diver. His eyes were closed and he was floating limply. His arm wedged into a handhold kept him from drifting off. MacKenzie stared respectfully. In the glare of *Avalon*'s lights the look on the diver's face was one of contentment. His mission was complete. He had swum into hell to waken the dead and save his ship. He'd just used up too much of himself.

"Brave son of a bitch," Luke said sadly. "Too weak to make it back. He's dying out there."

MacKenzie shook his head. "Not yet. Is the arm working?"

Luke tested the joystick and secondary controls. "Operational."

"Take us down a few feet. Not too far or we'll damage his ears. He may not be able to clear them."

Luke hit the pumps and *Avalon* sank six feet taking the diver along with it. It was enough to give them clearance under the ice. MacKenzie grabbed the throttle and fed power to the motors. They sped toward *Red Dawn,* leaving a trail of bubbles. "By the way, I've decided not to have you court-martialed for telling me to stuff it earlier."

Luke grinned. "You are good to me, sir."

"No more than you deserve. Seriously, thanks for not ditching."

"And miss this? Riding with you is always an experience."

Ahead, the submarine's snorkel tube led out of the ice keel. MacKenzie steered for it. "By the way, how come I get sirred now?"

"You didn't kill us. I respect that." Luke smiled. "Okay, there's the air tube. Could have been damaged. You want to follow it down?"

"No." MacKenzie pointed to the diver. "He can't take a big pressure change. Grab the hose and we'll reel it in on the surface. How's the radio?"

"Still out." Luke lowered the hydraulic arm controls into his lap and took hold of the joystick. He snared the air hose on the first try. "Okay, take her up."

MacKenzie brought *Avalon's* nose around and headed for the surface. He kept one eye on the stream of bubbles from the diver's regulator, careful not to rise too fast and risk giving the man the bends. The bubbles were reassuring. The man was still alive. But the cold was killing him by degrees. They had to find an open lead. The ice here was too thick for *Avalon* to break through.

MacKenzie moved cautiously under the ice cap, looking for an open lead to surface through. He wasn't worried about the radio being out. *Seawolf* was nearby and sure to hear *Avalon's* motors. Tom would head right for them. In fact, he was sure by now that Tom would be telling a relieved Justine that he was just fine.

Akula

"We have a contact, Comrade Captain. Small motors. Just under the ice. It's the DSRV."

"It can't be," Kalik said gruffly. "Recheck the signature."

"The computers verify it, Comrade Captain."

Kalik went into the sonar room. "I want you to play back the tape for me of when the torpedoes hit." He put on a pair of headphones.

The technician ran the tape, listening on his own headphones. Kalik wasn't a trained sonar technician, but he could follow most of the sounds. He heard the high-cycle noises of the torpedoes and alongside them the DSRV's electric motors. He looked at the visual display. The contacts moved closer until they were almost one, but suddenly —and he might not have seen it if he hadn't been looking for it—right near the end they moved out of alignment. The sound changed subtly, too.

"There." Kalik pointed. "Could something have happened right there?"

"Let me isolate it," the technician replied. He moved dials slightly, increasing the gain on the frame Kalik had chosen. "I can't say for sure, Comrade Captain, but . . ." He hesitated.

"This is not a test, Comrade. Give me your best guess."

"If I read things correctly, I think the DSRV might have sprinted away at top speed in the last seconds. You see there? A hard dive to starboard. And that echo? Possibly an ice keel."

Kalik cursed under his breath. It was suddenly clear to him. The waiting, the dive to starboard at full power to put the ice keel in between the DSRV and the torpedoes—he knew damn well who was driving her. Those moves were the habits of *Seawolf*'s captain. Twice he'd performed that dive maneuver, first to avoid the ice chunk and now to avoid the torpedoes. How many lives did the man have? Kalik's respect for him increased tenfold. What an adversary. Twin torpedoes coming at his surface camp and he uses his own ship to decoy them into an ice keel. God, the man had industrial-size balls! The blast might have knocked him out of commission for a while, but he was back now. All well and good, Kalik decided. He was going hunting.

"What happened, Comrade Captain?" Volkov asked when he returned to the control room.

Kalik explained quickly. "We may be able to get him now. Sonar, what is the DSRV's course and speed?"

"It's hard to track him. We're getting interference. He's very close to the ice."

"Other contacts?"

"None on *Seawolf. Phoenix* has surfaced."

Kalik decided the prize was worth the risk. Without its captain, *Seawolf* would be half the ship. "Use active sonar. I want a clean fix on him. Torpedo Room, report on the status of tubes one and two."

"Tubes one and two loaded and ready to fire, Comrade Captain."

"Attack Center, lock in to sonar for target acquisition."

"We are locked in, Comrade Captain."

Bursts of sound shot out from *Akula*, probing for the DSRV. Active sonar was more accurate than passive sonar. Once the sound pulse hit, there was no avoiding the echo that bounced back to *Akula* to give her computers an accurate fire position.

Volkov took up his position. He could do nothing but follow his commander and wonder what the final price of Kalik's private war would be.

Avalon

The first ping struck them, echoing inside the cabin with a screech that raised hackles like nails on a blackboard.

"That's active sonar," warned MacKenzie. *"Akula's* come back for more. If he gets a good fix on us . . ." MacKenzie applied power to the motors and steered them behind an ice keel. The sound faded. "I don't think he could have gotten a fix off a single burst."

"Hurts my ears," Luke complained.

"I know. The favorite game of sub captains is to sneak up on an enemy sub and rake him with an active sonar ping. It's our way of saying that under other conditions it could've been a torpedo. Keeps everybody honest."

Another loud ping raked the cabin. Luke covered his ears.

MacKenzie dodged, quickly driving *Avalon* between ice ridges to lose the pursuing sub. "Our motors are the problem," he explained. "They were never meant for quiet. Sonar can hear them for miles in these waters. We could shut down and hide, but then Tom won't be able to find us, to say nothing of how long our diver will last. He can't take much more of this."

"Neither can the air hose. We're gonna run out of length soon," Luke said, but suddenly his voice became excited, "Mac, look. Over there. See it?"

It looked as if someone had painted a lightning bolt on the underside of the ice. "A lead. Big enough to surface."

"Could be miles to another one. What do we do?"

MacKenzie was determined not to lose the diver, and *Red Dawn* was surely close to suffocation. "We risk it. Grab your suntan lotion. We're going up."

"Yes, sir! Blowing ballast."

MacKenzie brought them up as quickly as he could. "Use the arm. Don't let him slip off."

They broke through the surface. Avalon bobbed on the frigid water, and Luke deftly used the arm to hold the diver, but he couldn't lift him out of the water. "His arm's wedged too tight. I'm going out."

MacKenzie sighed. "I wish you could, but I can't use that arm at all. Stay here and hold us steady."

Luke didn't bother to conceal his better-you-than-me grin. MacKenzie pried himself out of his chair and slid back into Avalon's third compartment. There were coveralls and blankets in a storage locker. He wrapped a blanket around himself and another over his head and zipped his jacket over them. More blankets served as hand coverings. It was the only protection he was going to get. He cycled the hatch open. It gave with a hard push. A stream of icy water poured in, making MacKenzie shudder and curse. Just as he was about to push himself out, he heard another sonar ping. It was faint, on the low edges of the signal.

"Mac?"

"I heard it. It will take them some time to work out their attack. Power up and be ready to move as soon as I get him back in."

Outside, the blizzard was ferocious and MacKenzie almost lost his balance on the curved deck. The water was a cold metallic gray lapping at the hull. He made his way forward to the hydraulic arm, wrapping the blanket around his face to protect it. God, it was cold. He freed the vinyl air hose and pulled it out of the water with blanket-covered hands. It was like wrapping a coil of ice around his arm, but finally the snorkel broke the surface. He made sure it was cleared and left it bobbing freely.

He crawled over to the diver. The man was frozen stiff. MacKenzie gently pried his arm out of the rung and dragged him onto Avalon's swaying deck. The seawater drenched his blankets, and his skin was so cold it burned. He managed to release the catch on the scuba tank harness with stiff fingers, losing skin in the process, and slid the straps off the diver's shoulders. The tank tumbled into the water. He peeled off the man's face mask and tossed it aside. The diver's skin was colder than anything human MacKenzie had ever touched except a dead man.

The sodden blankets were useless now. The cold water stole his body warmth faster than the air. He ditched them and got his hands under the man's limp arms. He pulled him to the open hatch. Luke was there waiting. MacKenzie lowered the diver into his waiting arms and followed, slamming the hatch shut and ripping off his wet clothing.

Ping . . . ping . . .

"They've been coming closer together," Luke said. He used a knife to cut the wet suit off the diver. There was ice in the bandages underneath. Luke slit the elastic open carefully. The diver never stirred.

MacKenzie pulled on a pair of coveralls from the locker. His lean frame was shivering spasmodically. "Can you handle this alone?" he asked, toweling himself vigorously. "We've got to run for it."

"Go. Get us out of here."

Ping . . . ping . . . ping . . .

MacKenzie slid into the pilot's chair and flicked switches, taking on ballast. He shoved the control yoke all the way to its stop, diving hard. He hadn't wanted to tell Luke, but they'd taken too long. *Akula* had a solid fix on them. The torpedoes would be arriving long before they could outrun them.

Akula

Kalik knew he had the shot, but a sudden thought stilled the command to fire. Why had the American captain remained in one place for so long?

"Attack Center, Comrade Captain. We have computed the range to target. We are ready to fire on your command."

Kalik hesitated. Was it a ruse? Why stand still in an unprotected DSRV? Was the American baiting him to fire? He had been suckered by this captain once before when he thought he had the upper hand. It wasn't going to happen a second time. He went over it again. What could he be up to?

"Comrade Captain?"

Kalik looked up, annoyed. "What is it, Viktor?"

"The solution is changing as we both move. Should we recompute it?"

Kalik wanted a reason to condemn Volkov, but so far Volkov hadn't given him one. He could see only support on his senior lieutenant's face. Kalik decided he was being an old lady. "No. Prepare to fire." The American captain had gotten under his skin. It was not his nature to second-guess himself. "Torpedo Room . . ."

Ping . . .

"No, it can't be!" Kalik covered his ears and looked around furiously as the speaker overhead crackled with Sonar's worried voice. "Comrade Captain, we are being raked with enemy active sonar. They have a position fix on us."

Ping . . .

Seawolf! It had to be *Seawolf.* Any second now her torpedoes would be on their way in, following the active sonar signal right to them. He had waited too long. While he was ranging the DSRV, *Seawolf* had traced his active sonar and ranged him. Could he shoot before he had to take evasive action? But suddenly a sound with a different pitch filled the control room.

Ping, ping . . . ping, ping . . .

"Sonar, what is that?" he demanded.

"Comrade Captain, a second submarine has a position fix on us. It's the *Phoenix.* We're caught between them."

Damn them to hell. Kalik wanted to attack with every fiber in his body.

"Comrade Captain, *Phoenix* is closing."

But now was not the time.

"Cancel the attack. Slow all propulsion. Take us down to three hundred meters." He stalked out of the control room.

Seawolf

Akula is backing off, Mr. Lasovic. Going silent. We're losing them. . . . That's it. Last contact, range three miles, course zero three zero, speed ten knots. They may be diving. They've gone passive. We can't hear them anymore."

"Do we still have a fix on *Avalon?*"

"Clear as a bell, sir." Sonarman Bendel read out her course and speed.

"Plot an intercept course, Mr. Santiago. All ahead two-thirds."

"Aye, Mr. Lasovic."

Lasovic allowed himself to ease up a little. It had been close. The only reason *Akula* would have gone active was to attack. *Seawolf's* run at them had prevented it—by seconds, he guessed. It said something that *Akula's* captain would risk exposing himself just for a shot at the DSRV, almost as if he knew Mac was on board. But that was impossible. Another thought came darkly. How was he going to tell Mac about Justine?

"Any word from the air surveillance?"

"The C-One-thirty pilot reports conditions are terrible. He'll stay up and look as long as he can. And, Mr. Lasovic, the icebreakers are within five miles of us. Very close together. They must be running almost side by side."

"Very well. Mr. Randall, steady on course. Chief, prepare to take on the DSRV."

Avalon

"How is he, Luke?" MacKenzie asked from the pilot's chair.

"Can't tell yet. Body temperature's way down. I've got him wrapped up best as I can. By the way, how come we're not dead yet?"

"Honestly, I don't know. He's had more than enough time to make his shot. I don't hear anything on the hydrophones, unless—"

Ping.

"Oh, no." Luke grabbed his ears. "We spoke too soon."

MacKenzie turned with a start, but a grin of relief crossed his features. "Not this time. Take a look portside."

Seawolf's long, sleek shape swam into view. Tom Lasovic was blinking his running lights in greeting. "Now, that's a beautiful sight," said Luke. "Goddamn beautiful."

"I'm heading in. Do the best you can for him; then I need you up here."

Red Dawn

The crew was jubilant. Fresh air flowed in through the snorkel tube and was drawn into the fan room and pumped throughout the submarine. Stale odors broke apart as the cold, sweet air rushed in. Galinin saw that the final connections were completed and then led Ligichev and Ivanna back into the officers' mess. Hot coffee was waiting.

Ivanna let herself be led. She was subdued, her face drawn and tight. "It's been too long," she said to her father. "He's not coming back."

Ligichev steered her into a seat. "I'm sorry, my dear," he said sadly.

Galinin said, "It was a heroic feat. He saved us all. He deserves a medal."

"Screw your medal," Ivanna said bitterly. But what did it matter now? Her head sagged into her arms on the table. "Maybe his family will want it. Do as you please."

"Yes, all right," said Galinin. "Comrade Ligichev?"

"Yes?" The scientist looked away from his daughter. Galinin looked like a man with something on his mind.

"Comrade, I am sure preparations to tow us will be under way shortly. I do not know how the Americans will treat us. The future is unclear to me. I just wanted to say . . . to say . . ."

Ligichev saw him look for words and fail to find the right ones. In light of Pytor's sacrifice he wanted to be kind. "Please . . . I think I know how you feel, Comrade Captain. It has been a difficult voyage. We are lucky to have survived." He held out his hand. "We'll forget the past. We've all kept our promises as best we could."

Galinin took his hand. "Promises. Yes, in the end we must always keep those. Thank you for understanding, Comrade."

Galinin left. Ligichev stood there, thinking. Galinin seemed . . . grave. Ligichev didn't know how to put it any other way. Perhaps he was disturbed by the loss of Pytor. But still, it was the nature of human beings to be selfish, and their rescue was a great relief. If anything, Galinin looked as if his burden was now heavier.

Ligichev sat down next to his daughter waiting for the inevitable. She was a fine girl, strong and bright, but she had lost her love. When the tears finally came he held her and murmured the things fathers say to their daughters when life and men have hurt them. But even as he held her he couldn't help wondering about the captain.

Why, at the last, when he shook hands, did it feel so much as if he was saying good-bye?

Chapter
Sixteen

Seawolf

MacKenzie took the news hard. Lasovic saw it in the way his shoulders sagged and the sudden terrible pain in his eyes. He had come back with his friend to his cabin, waiting till they were alone to tell him. When he did, it was as if the life went out of MacKenzie.

"Christ, Tom, I thought we pulled the torpedo far enough away. The whole base camp's gone?"

"We surfaced. There's nothing left."

"I never thought this could happen, me back and her gone."

"We'll find her, Mac. Maybe they doubled back."

"I was outside for five minutes and I almost froze. She's been on the ice for over two hours now." MacKenzie's voice came close to breaking, "I tried, Tom. I thought we'd blocked the blast—"

"You can't blame yourself. Justine's a pro. She's probably working out a way to contact us now. The C-One-thirty is still up there looking. We'll find her, Mac. Believe me."

"I wish I knew how. One mistake leads to another. I can't help feeling I'm to blame."

"You're not."

MacKenzie stood and grabbed his jacket. Lasovic had

never seen him so drawn and tired. "I'm going to take us up for one more look."

MacKenzie stood on the sail and peered into the blinding storm. It was impossible to see anything. The winds were gale force. The temperature was seventy below zero. It was futile to send a search party out in this weather. They'd soon be lost, too. Was there anything he could do to find his wife? A bitter voice inside told him there wasn't.

For the first time in his career MacKenzie hated his responsibilities. He felt chained to his sub, to his command. He wanted to head out onto the ice and find Justine. But he couldn't, any more than he could risk any operation for one single crew member. The navy had known the risk when it sent Justine up here. Personal considerations were to be put aside. She was the senior operative in charge of this mission, but like everyone else she was expendable. Except to him . . .

Spent, he climbed down the sail ladder and secured the hatch. The snow on his parka melted at once in the warmth of the conn and dripped to the deck. There was nothing more he could do. He gave the command reluctantly. "Prepare to dive."

"Straight board, sir," announced the chief.

MacKenzie knew his next order could be a sentence of death for his wife. He had no choice. "Take her down, Tom."

There was a knock at the cabin door. MacKenzie composed himself. He was surprised to see Diving Officer Randall enter.

"Welcome back, Skipper. We were worried about you."

"I appreciate that, Mr. Randall. How's the diver coming along?"

"We made a tub in the infirmary from some empty crates and lined it with trash bags. Warm water and Cook's coffee did the trick. He came to. Medics say he'll lose some fingers and toes and lots of skin, but he'll make it."

"That's good to hear. What's the preliminary report?"

"The Russian translator is debriefing him now. It seems the situation on *Red Dawn* is just about what we figured. Some kind of new drive unit failed and caused the problems. Limited battery power. No way to repair communications. He came out to take a stab at getting the snorkel to the surface."

"He's a brave boy. Who's in charge over there?"

"The same Captain Galinin you saw in the ice tunnel and a scientist named Ligichev." Randall colored a little. "From the way the diver talks about Ligichev's daughter, I think they're in love. Asked me if we could get a message to her that he's okay."

"As soon as conditions permit. What's *Avalon*'s status?"

"Lieutenant Johnson reports repairs are complete. Chief Feeney replaced all the electronics. You've got full communications and control."

"Inform Lieutenant Johnson we'll be leaving for *Red Dawn* as soon as he completes the checklist."

"Right away. But, uh . . . Skipper?" Randall hesitated.

"Something on your mind, Mr. Randall?"

"Yes, sir. May I speak freely?"

"Of course." MacKenzie had a personal affection for the young man. In spite of his youth and inexperience Randall had real character, the kind you could depend on. In a pinch he'd be right at your side.

"It's about your wife, sir. Everybody knows . . . I mean, we all heard . . . Well, I'm real sorry. But I was thinking . . ."

"Go ahead, Mr. Randall. I have to believe she's okay up there. I just wish I knew where."

"Well, that's what I wanted to talk to you about. I figured . . . I mean, if it were me and I was lost on the ice, where would I go?"

"There's nowhere to go," MacKenzie said bleakly.

"But, Skipper, there is somewhere and I'll bet your wife would figure it out, too. What about the icebreakers? They're up there and coming this way. I know your wife knows about them 'cause I heard Mr. Lasovic tell you their position and she was standing right there next to you. But you've probably got all this figured out already, huh?"

MacKenzie was open-mouthed. "I sure didn't, Mr. Randall. I don't know how I could have missed it." He grabbed the hope with both hands. "I forgot all about the breakers. It makes perfect sense. They're only a few miles out and closing fast. If she couldn't find us she'd head straight for them. Sure." MacKenzie flicked open the intercom and spoke to Lasovic in the conn, quickly explaining Randall's theory. "Tom, radio the C-One-thirty to cover the transit line, and tell the *Polar Eight* to keep a sharp lookout for survivors." He hesitated. What he was about to do violated procedure and would probably alert the Soviet sub captain to how devastating his attack had been, but in this case he was going to make an exception. He would allow himself that much. "And, Tom, send out an SOS on an open channel to look for the survivors as well. Request *Ural's* humanitarian assistance."

"Akula will hear it, Mac."

"I am aware of that."

If there was any further hesitation in Lasovic's voice it didn't come over the speaker. "Roger. Right away, Mac," said the XO.

MacKenzie looked at his junior officer. "Mr. Randall, I . . ." He stopped, because he could not cross the line a captain was obligated not to cross. But Randall seemed to know that.

"I'm glad I could help, Skipper."

MacKenzie felt his heart lighten. He had made mistakes, serious ones, but maybe they wouldn't cost him his wife. And maybe he could still pull a successful mission out of all this. He drew strength from the hope. "Back to the conn, Mr. Randall. We have a lot of work left to do."

"Yes, sir."

"And, Mr. Randall?"

"Sir?"

"Thank you."

Polar 8

"Sir?" The radio officer handed Captain Maré a sheet of paper from his message pad. "This just in. From the USS *Seawolf.*"

Renaud looked over from his vantage point on the bridge, interested. "That's the American sub we're here to assist, isn't it?"

Maré nodded. "That's her. Hmm . . . seems they've lost some of their people on the surface. It is likely they're headed for us. They want us to keep a lookout for them." He turned back to the radio officer. "Send: Message received and understood. *Polar Eight* has a sharp eye out."

"Lot of good that's going to do." Renaud snorted. "Between the fog and the snowfall we're down to zero visibility. We could run over them and never spot the bodies."

"Let's try not to, shall we?" Maré said with equanimity. "Rather a bad tone to set for international relations, I should think. Do what you can, eh?"

"Yes, sir," said Renaud. He looked into the swirling gray mist beyond the bridge windows. If anything, conditions were growing worse. Only the *Ural* seemed not to notice. She was still keeping up with them, still making an almost impossible four knots under treacherous conditions. Renaud shook his head. Now they were supposed to find some lost souls wandering out on the ice cap in the middle of the worst storm in Renaud's memory.

He swore under his breath, "Good goddamn luck."

Phoenix

Phil Arlin listened to MacKenzie's plan over the radio and shook his head skeptically. "I don't know, Mac. It's a hell of a risk. If we breach her pressure hull, *Red Dawn* will drop like a stone when she comes out of the ice."

MacKenzie and Luke were on their way to *Phoenix* to pick up the tow hook. The captain was speaking by radio from

Avalon. His voice came over the conn speaker. "That Russian breaker is too close to wait. If it gets a towline on *Red Dawn* before we do, we'll have a right-of-salvage question arising."

"But blowing it out of the ice. Are you that good a shot?" Arlin asked, only half kidding.

"You'd better hope so," Mac said. "But I'm going to stack the deck in my favor. I'll plant taggers from the DSRV."

A tagger was a torpedo that penetrated a ship's hull and sent out a homing signal to other torpedoes. It made destruction a certainty even if the ship took evasive action.

"How much of a charge in the fish?"

"Ten percent. We take *Red Dawn* out of the ice with two shots."

"That's not going to get the ice off her hull."

"We'll drill it off as best we can and blow the rest with shape charges," MacKenzie said. *"Seawolf* has a few in the armory. We've got to drill into her ballast tanks to flood them anyway, remember? And it's a good way to test out the swimmer delivery vehicles."

Arlin thought it over. "Who was it said, 'Better a bad plan than no plan at all'?"

"Wish I knew. But he must've been familiar with the Arctic. We're running out of time, Phil."

Arlin sighed. "I know. How close are you?"

"Coming up on you now. I see the tow hook on the cleats."

There was a silence for a few moments; then MacKenzie's voice came through. "Luke's got it. We're paying out the line now."

"Mac, is there any word on Justine and the SEALs?"

There was what Arlin would have called a pregnant silence, but his friend's voice came back firm and under control. "We think they're heading for the breakers. Have to wait and hope."

"My prayers are with them, Mac."

Arlin heard MacKenzie take a deep breath. "Okay. The towline is secured to *Avalon. Phoenix,* we're heading for *Red Dawn.* Follow us in."

Polar Ice Cap

Justine looked up through ice-crusted eyes and cursed the storm. It howled back, swirling around her like something alive and bent on her destruction. It had become a personal thing, the conflict between her and the storm. Saving the men struggling along behind her was no longer her main goal. The mission to raise *Red Dawn* was forgotten. Even personal survival had ceased to matter inasmuch as it meant preserving her life. Survival had meaning only if it meant beating the storm.

She trudged up to the summit of another ice ridge and looked through the snow and the mist, searching for the icebreakers. They had walked at least two miles. They couldn't take much more. Where the hell were the ships? A body's core temperature could go only so low and then the machine began to slow until it finally stopped, like a sensitive mechanism someone poured molasses into. The blood got too thick to flow. The mind got too fuzzy to command. The inner flame flickered and went out and then you just . . . stopped.

She had heard it was peaceful to die in the snow. You just lay down and went to sleep, drifted away. Well, it wasn't true. The cold wasn't a friend; it was a lying thief. It stole from you bit by bit till you had nothing left to fight with. Cold was a monster that sucked you dry in stages. Better to die in a blazing fire, she thought, better to go in one last moment of all-consuming energy than to die by degrees, your body succumbing an inch at a time.

Valor. That was another illusion. There was nothing valorous about fighting the cold. Putting one foot in front of the other, that was what you did. All her life she had fought enemies with guns and knives and even bare hands. How could she fight the cold with those? All her training had left her with nothing but putting one foot in front of the other and shuffling on.

The wind drove the icy flakes at them in swirling staccato

bursts. Her lips bled from friction against the face mask till the cold froze them, too. She cried when she realized she would no longer be pretty if she survived this. Would Mac still love her? Patches of her face had no feeling. She was sure big chunks of flesh were frostbitten and dead. She pictured taking off the mask and her face peeling away with it. That made her want to start screaming, but she knew if she started she might not stop.

She forced herself to concentrate. One foot in front of the other. One foot in front of the other. She turned back to count the remaining men. Four left. Burke was gone, Hansen, too, lost somewhere in this howling madness. She could do nothing. Except put one foot in front of the other. One foot in front of the other . . .

Her arms and legs were encrusted in rime. She shuffled forward like a crystalline robot. She no longer felt her feet. Her fingers were lifeless, maybe forever. She thought about playing the piano. Once she'd been a concert artist. Her father had taught her, along with her brothers, Sebastion and Miguel. Everyone said she had the most talent, but it wasn't true. What she had was tenacity. She'd met enough of the truly talented, the divinely gifted, to know. They all had something she didn't—a direct connection to God, it seemed, a link to the wellspring that defied measurement. They had talent. She had tenacity. She practiced hour after hour, forcing the keys to obey her fingers, making the notes dance as they must. It was like that here. Others might be stronger. No one was more tenacious.

She was so cold. Her mind forced her complaints out of her head. Just put one foot in front of the other. Concentrate. One foot in front of the other. Follow me. Keep putting one foot in front of the other . . .

She had once read about a famous long-distance runner. How did he find the strength, he was asked, to finish a marathon? How could he sustain his drive and energy for that long? He had told them something Justine finally understood, here, freezing to death on the ice cap at the top of the world. There was no finish line. Winning was an illusion. You just kept putting one foot in front of the other . . . one foot in front of the other . . . one foot in front of the other . . .

She kept on putting one foot in front of the other . . . and trudged on.

Avalon

MacKenzie piloted the DSRV toward the frozen sub. "Coming up on position," he said to Luke.

"I'm ready," he responded.

MacKenzie moved *Avalon* in slowly. Phil Arlin had been right. What they were preparing to do was risky. Blasting *Red Dawn* out of the ice keel was a shortcut, and he had learned that under the ice cap was no place for shortcuts. But with the breakers almost on their doorstep and the time and manpower that *Akula* had cost them, there were too few options.

"Keep her as steady as you can, Mac. Slight forward pressure."

MacKenzie pressed forward on the steering yoke till *Avalon* was almost nudging the ice keel. A drill bit had been added to the arm since the last time MacKenzie had seen Luke use it when they were trapped by a rock slide in the Cayman Trench. The drill nipped and nibbled into the ice, and chunk after chunk fell away. It was tedious work, but Luke had a master's touch. Yard-thick shards drifted past the observation windows like jewels split from a mammoth crystal.

MacKenzie felt fatigue working on him, draining his last reserves. How long had it been since any of them had slept. Two days? Three? It seemed like a lifetime since they had picked up the signals from what they thought was a Soviet Boomer. The other captain was clever, no doubt about it. That fake missile launch was one for the books. He wondered how close *Akula* was. Their sonar crew would be listening to the DSRV's motor noise, probably ranging them as they worked. He searched the waters around him. *Phoenix* was a few hundred yards from them, waiting. The water was so clear the big black craft looked suspended in midair. Beyond *Phoenix* the sea faded into unseeable depths. That was where *Seawolf* was, on patrol, and *Akula,* ready to pounce.

"Up a little," Luke murmured, retracting the drill. Mac-Kenzie feathered the controls.

"There. Hold it." The tow eye was visible now. Luke extended the arm and the drill bored into the ice again.

While Luke worked, MacKenzie had time to think things over. There had been precious little opportunity to do that before now. He'd come to respect the *Akula's* captain as a powerful and cunning adversary. Regardless of sides they were both members of the small, elite fraternity of men who drove submarines for a living. In some ways, they were brothers; both had come to this bitter continent and both had kept their ships operating despite what man and nature had thrown at them. MacKenzie knew he had made mistakes. The truth was that both of them had. After all, *Akula's* captain had been unable to protect *Red Dawn.*

"I've got the forward ballast tanks uncovered."

"Drill into them. Small holes to vent the air slowly. If they can get the pumps working they may be able to surface under their own power."

"Why can't we just leave the ice on her?"

MacKenzie smiled. "Ice floats. Unless she's heavy enough to submerge under the keels we'll never tow her out of here. With the ice around her she'd just have a larger displacement and be even more buoyant."

Luke's face registered understanding. He went back to clearing the ice away. MacKenzie lapsed into silence. He was trying to keep a lid on his personal pain, but his normal control mechanisms were strained. In just a few days fatigue had penetrated his very bones. Responsibilities were more burdensome, the losses greater. He felt his years heavily.

With an odd, fey certainty that could only have come from his Scottish ancestors, MacKenzie knew deep down that the other captain was feeling these things, too. He wondered if the ice cap itself had done this to them, changed them both irrevocably as if just by being here a man could be robbed of spirit the way the cold robbed him of warmth. Could anyone come here and remain unaffected? He thought not. It was sad that he and the other captain would never get the chance to talk to each other, but as soon as MacKenzie placed *Red Dawn* in tow he would seal both of their fates. *Akula's* captain could not let the Americans escape with the prize. In the end, *Seawolf* and *Akula* would have to hunt each other down.

"Almost got the first one, Mac."

It went on, Luke steadily clearing the ice from the tanks, drilling holes to allow water to seep in. Finally Luke attacked the ice covering the tow eye. It sheared off in big platelets.

MacKenzie picked up the radio mike. *"Phoenix, Avalon.* We're about ready to attach the tow hook. Stand by."

"Phoenix on station, standing by."

Red Dawn was embedded in the ice at such an angle the tow eye was almost out of the hydraulic arm's reach. A foot or two more and they couldn't have gotten to it. Luke cleared the last chunks of ice from the hull and stopped drilling. The tow eye was accessible. Seawater flooded the cavity, washing ice off the deck and the forward hatch. Deftly, Luke uncoupled the tow hook from where it was secured to *Avalon's* own hull and maneuvered it toward the tow eye on *Red Dawn's* bow.

"Give me some slack. Yep, that's it . . ."

MacKenzie kept *Avalon* in close. They were less than five feet from the ice keel. It was a tricky moment. Once it was attached to *Red Dawn, Phoenix* lost every advantage an attack sub possessed. It couldn't run or dive, and the sound of the sub in tow as it trailed through the water would pinpoint the two ships for the enemy's sonar like a cow bell. He didn't envy Arlin's tactical position.

With a final snap of the joystick, Luke attached the two hook to *Red Dawn.* "There." He powered down and released a deep pent-up breath. "What Luke has joined together let no Russian put asunder." He smiled wryly. "Don't mind me, sir. I always get emotional at weddings."

MacKenzie picked up the mike. *"Phoenix, Avalon.* You have *Red Dawn* in tow. Repeat. You have *Red Dawn* in tow."

"Avalon, Phoenix. Message acknowledged. This from the captain: Shoot straight, seevooplay."

MacKenzie gave a dry laugh. "You heard the man, Luke. Let's plant the taggers." He reversed the engines and backed *Avalon* away from the ice keel. *Seawolf* had joined them and was hugging the ice for sonar concealment. A personal need surfaced, one he could not ignore.

"Seawolf, this is MacKenzie. How close are those breakers?"

"Lasovic here, Skipper. Less than a mile from us. No word yet."

"Keep me posted."

"Aye, Skipper. We will."

Luke spoke with a friend's concern. "She'll make it."

MacKenzie shrugged, powerless.

"You know," Luke said, pointing at the ice keel, eager to change the subject, "this close, the ice around *Red Dawn* looks like it's got fault lines running through it. You see? Like an uncut stone. I think we could split most of it off if we place the charges right."

"Think you have the spots?"

"A couple I'd like to try."

MacKenzie gave him the go-ahead. Luke picked up the controls and bent to the task. He was right. The ice around *Red Dawn* had frozen in chunks rather than in one solid floe. Pieces the size of small icebergs broke off as he drilled. "I should've been a diamond cutter," he said, admiring his work. A good deal of the ice on the sub had fallen away, but she was still frozen solidly into the keel. "That's as much as I can get. Ready for act two."

"Right," MacKenzie picked up the radio mike. *"Seawolf, Avalon.* What's the status of the SDVs?"

"SDVs ready to launch, Skipper."

"Launch SDVs."

Seawolf was one of the few submarines specially modified to carry swimmer delivery vehicles, or SDVs—two-man minisubs built for naval commando units. They were still experimental and their capabilities had not yet been demonstrated, but because of the loss of the SEALs MacKenzie had pressed them into service. They were being run by his own specially trained crewmen.

"SDVs away," Lasovic reported.

MacKenzie angled *Avalon* to get a look. It was quite a sight. Five dark green, torpedo-shaped crafts with Plexiglas bubbles over tiny cockpits slid out of *Seawolf*'s special hatches into the sea, propelled by electric motors. It looked as if a school of pilot fish had left the body of a great shark.

"The invasion of the teeny tiny subs," said Luke.

"Teeny tiny bombs is more like it," MacKenzie observed, referring to the shape charges that were attached to each SDV's front grapple. The grapple was a clever multi-hook apparatus that let the SDV attach a limpet mine to the hull of a surface ship or sub before fading back to the mother ship. MacKenzie picked up the radio and called the pilot of the first SDV.

"Avalon to Jolly Green One. Prepare to place the first charge. Can you see where our hydraulic arm is pointing?"

"Jolly Green One over. We can see it, Skipper."

"Deliver the charge right into that drill hole. Everybody else remain in position."

They must look like a collection of weird insects come to feed on the ice keel, MacKenzie thought as the first SDV moved in alongside *Avalon*. The pilot adeptly maneuvered the shape charge into the hole Luke had drilled. Within seconds, the water froze around it locking it into place.

"Well done, Jolly Green One. Head home."

"Roger, *Avalon*." The tiny craft dropped down and sped for *Seawolf*.

"Prepare to place the second charge, Jolly Green Two."

Carefully, the SDVs continued planting the shape charges

in the fault lines with Luke using *Avalon*'s hydraulic arm to point the way.

"That's going to have to do it on this level," MacKenzie said as the second and third SDV returned to the ship. He scanned the keel overhead and pointed. "Look, up there, about twenty feet above the sail. See it?"

"A waist where the keel narrows? Yeah."

"First tagger goes there."

"Roger." Luke took the controls for the hydraulic arm again, and MacKenzie brought *Avalon* up the ice keel like an elevator. *Seawolf*'s torpedomen had removed the tagger homing mechanisms from two torpedoes and placed them in waterproof casings. They would call the torpedoes in with unerring accuracy. Luke bored a hole in the ice, and the fourth SDV placed its mechanism inside the keel. They repeated the procedure on a section of keel underneath *Red Dawn* with a second tagger from the fifth and final SDV.

"*Seawolf, Avalon*. Mission accomplished. All SDVs homeward bound. How do the taggers sound, Tom?"

"Loud and clear, Skipper. Fire Control says it's a lock. The special fish are loaded in tubes one and three. We're ready to fire on your order."

"I'm going to keep *Avalon* out here for better vantage."

"Roger. Fire control says you should move off at least five hundred yards."

"Affirmative."

MacKenzie looked out the observation port. It was a scene no Naval Academy textbook could ever have predicted and one that would remain in his memory as long as he lived. Hovering in the crystal-clear waters half a mile away was *Phoenix*, its towline trailing back to *Red Dawn*, still encased in the ice keel. Less than a mile away, at the apex of the triangle, *Seawolf* had come to all stop to fire her torpedoes, and now she, too, was motionless in the water with the tiny SDVs gathered around her. For a brief moment *Seawolf, Phoenix, Red Dawn,* and *Avalon* were all suspended in space and time.

The speaker crackled. "This is *Phoenix*. We are prepared to tow."

A moment later Lasovic's voice came over loud and clear. "This is *Seawolf*. SDVs secure. We are ready to fire."

In *Avalon's* cabin Luke locked the arm's controls and said, " 'They also serve who only stand and wait.' "

MacKenzie drew *Avalon* back out of harm's way. It had no business amid the giants who were about to explode the sea.

Red Dawn

Ligichev came to the engine room. Ivanna was working hard on the propulsion system—an emotional palliative, he figured. "Have you heard? The Americans have engaged the tow hook. Galinin saw them from the ice tunnel. We'll be out of here soon," he said.

"Forgive me if I don't jump up and down."

Ligichev put an arm around her. "I understand. But please try to forget him. You know, you are not so different from most. All of us are hurt the first time we fall in love."

"Not this way. Please, Father, I know you mean well, but there's nothing to say. Let me get back to work."

"Forget the work. He sacrificed himself to save you, you know. He wanted you to go on."

She stared at a wrench in her hands. "I know that. It makes the pain worse. How can anyone else compare? My life is over."

Ligichev's smile was tender and wise. "I know you think that, but it isn't true."

"You can't know how I feel."

"Ah, but I do. I was young once, even though you don't believe it."

"Father, I didn't mean—"

He touched her face gently, "Shhh, I understand. I felt the same way about my parents. When you get older, you'll be just as surprised as I was—and as they were—to find you inhabit an old decaying shell, because inside you still feel as you always did. Sixty? My God, no one feels sixty *inside.*" He stopped. His pontificating was only making the tears come again.

"I'll never get over Pytor," she said morosely.

"Listen to me for a moment. A long time ago I was in my final term at the institute and it was spring and I met and fell in love with a beautiful raven-haired girl at a party given by a friend. She was everything I ever wanted. She seemed happy, too. We soon spent all of our time together. We talked about the future we would have. When we slept together it was the first time for both of us. I swear to this day I can still remember that night with a clarity that staggers me." He reddened a little telling her this, but pressed on. "Summer came and we had to part, but a few weeks later I finished my thesis and managed to persuade a friend to borrow his father's car and drive me to the camp where she was training. She was a singer. A model, too."

"Really?" Ivanna had grown interested. She and her father had always had a healthy respect for each other, but now as she watched him absorbed in his memories, eyes shining, she realized how much more deeply she had come to know him these past days. As a person. And a friend. "This girl must have really been something," she said admiringly.

Ligichev blew out a short breath. "My dear, she had legs that went on for days."

Ivanna snorted with pleasure. "Tell me more, scoundrel."

"Well, my friend and I took so long to reach the camp that Shara and I had barely ten minutes together before my friend and I had to turn back. The car broke down, the muddy roads . . . Well, I don't have to tell you the rest."

Ivanna nodded, eyes bright, swept into his narrative. "Of course not. It must have been beautiful, Father. Ten minutes was all there was, but you declared that your love would last a lifetime."

Ligichev shook his head. "Sadly, no."

"No?"

"No. Ten minutes was all it took for me to learn that she

had found someone else. I was crushed. A letter from her reached me later. She said how sorry she was and how it had taken such a long time for this new love to bloom. What rubbish. It took about four days!"

Ligichev's expression was so hapless that Ivanna laughed out loud. "You're an old fool, telling me stories to make me feel better, as if I were a frightened child."

"All parents are old fools. Do you feel any better?"

Wiping the tears from her eyes, she looked at him lovingly. "No, but I love you anyway. Now go away and let me hurt by myself. I have a lot of work to do if I'm to dismantle the drive before the Americans board us."

"Right, I forgot. I'm glad to see Captain Galinin is thinking."

"Nonsense. Galinin is sulking around the ship like a man at his own funeral. He didn't give the order. I did. I mean, I just assumed he would, so I started to dismantle it on my own."

"Galinin hasn't given orders to secure the ship? It's standard procedure. The drive is top secret."

"Not a word."

Ligichev thought that over. "Keep working. I'll be back."

Polar Ice Cap

Stephan had never seen a storm like this one. The winds blasted across the ice in sudden vicious bursts, gusting to over 120 kilometers an hour. The crewmen alongside him had been knocked down so many times they had to be sent back to the ship. Stephan advised the captain to send no others, to send him ski poles instead.

He bent low against the wind, using the Inuit way of pathfinding, following the *sastrugi,* the long wavelike ridges in the ice formed by the prevailing winds. Without the *sastrugi* he would have been walking blind in the whited out world, for there was no other way to pinpoint direction. Behind him the breakers continued their steady crash through the ice. He could no longer see the ships because of the storm; he could only hear their violent progress. They were dangerously close to each other. Less than a mile separated them now.

Stephan was exhausted from being on the ice so long. The temperature was seventy degrees below zero and the wind-driven ice crystals were like razor blades. He held on, keeping his internal flame at a steady, even glow, as an Inuit would. The ordeal would be over soon. The race was nearing its end. The *Red Dawn* was within a few kilometers, and Captain Ivanov had told him over the radio that he had communicated with their submarine *Akula* and was already preparing the divers to go down and attach the ship's big tow lines to the downed submarine. As cold as he was on the surface Stephan didn't envy the divers. He had a healthy fear of open water on the ice cap. A dunking could freeze a man to death in seconds.

He tucked the ski poles under his arm and took up the slack in the line back to the ship. He wondered if his ears would ever recover from the noise of the breakers running side by side. The ringing was so loud that when a strange sound suddenly nipped at his aural awareness he doubted he had heard it. But there it was again. He stopped gathering the line and stood with his ears into the wind. He pushed his parka hood back briefly and cupped his gloved hands to his ears. Straining, this time he heard it clearly: the unmistakable howling of a pack of white Arctic wolves.

He had run into wolves before. Resources were so limited in this land that a single pack might roam an area thousands of square kilometers, their pup-filled dens hidden from other predators somewhere in the tractless wastes. Nature had built into Arctic creatures a ferocity found nowhere else, because nowhere else were conditions so harsh and sources of nourishment so scarce. Once, with the Inuit, Stephan had seen Arctic wolves kill and gut a polar bear. It was a grisly spectacle, the wolves darting in to bite and claw, the fiercest clamping its teeth into the bear's hindquarters and spinning around with the bear on the ice like a furry moon and planet. Despite their ferocity, Stephan had no animosity toward the wolves. Like everything else in the Arctic they had to fight to survive. The wolves' philosophy was simple expediency: anything they saw was food.

What were the wolves stalking that was making them howl like that? Could something else be out here? He peered into the storm, but eyes were useless here. He heard the howls again and felt danger deep in his bowels. He walked ahead quickly to gain distance from the ships behind him. He was following a river of thin ice, but it was leading closer and closer to the *Polar 8*. He had no choice but to steer the *Ural* closer. He radioed Captain Ivanov and expressed his concerns. Ivanov told him the all-speed order had not been rescinded and to steer them where he had to. Ivanov also informed him of an unusual American request for assistance in locating members of their party lost on the ice cap.

"Do what you can," Ivanov said, his tone indicating he was fully aware of how little that would be in such a storm.

Stephan made the immediate connection between the lost people and the wolves. Worried, he signed off, digging the sharp tips of his ski poles into the ice for traction and moving ahead as rapidly as the storm permitted. Things were coming together in an unpleasant way in his mind, but he couldn't just leave the ship and wander off in search of the people. In weather like this even he risked getting lost. His choices dwindled. The wolves would be closing. With lives on the line, he decided to try something he had seen the Inuit do one night long ago outside their igloo.

They had been traveling the ice for three days, and Stephan had the unpleasant feeling they were lost. The two didn't have many words between them, but a shrug was a shrug in any language. After another day of fruitless travel they built an igloo and settled in for the night. At least Stephan thought they'd settled in. He woke a few hours later to find the Inuit was gone. He panicked, thinking he was alone, and rushed outside. There was the Inuit sitting cross-legged on the ice, his face as blank and lifeless as a mask.

Stephan thought at first he had frozen to death, but saw that he was breathing. He sat down beside him. After a while life returned to the Inuit's eyes along with a renewed— Stephan could only call it awareness. He pointed confidently and made the sign for home. Stephan asked as best he could what the Inuit had done to discover this.

The Inuit put his hands on Stephan's chest, slowed Stephan's breathing and bade him stare into the vaulted night sky overhead. He pointed to a star. Stephan fixed his gaze on it. The Inuit began to chant softly. Over and over. Stephan had seen men meditate before and figured this was just another form of it, so he allowed his mind to drift. When he'd picked up enough of the chant to mimic it phonetically he joined the man on the ice chanting to a night sky ablaze with stars.

One of the things the ice taught you was man's capacity to fool himself. You could see anything in the ice if you needed it badly enough, or got cold enough. You could see your long-lost brother coming at you over green hills. You could see your first love. Stephan would never know if what he saw that night was real or a product of his exhaustion or created by an impressionable mind, but for one brief period of timeless time he left his body to become a light racing over the ice, a bodiless wraith who knew all the colors of the cold. From high above he could see himself and the Inuit sitting alongside the igloo below him as he danced on the wind. He had no boundaries. He was swept up into the color castle of the sky where he knew all things in one blindingly clear moment of comprehension.

It went on for the entire night. Afterward, like a dream, he was never able to explain it fully or even recall the complete imagery of it. It ended when it was morning and he woke to the sun and found the Inuit already packed and ready to move on. Stephan didn't speak for two days, staggered beyond words by the wonder of the experience.

He'd never reached for that dream state again. He always thought that he didn't want to be disappointed if he couldn't reach it. More truthfully, his intuition told him that, like the first act of love, it would never be quite the same again. But the scales had tipped here. There were people involved, lost people, and he had no other way to find them. He remembered how alone and frightened he'd felt when his ship went down, how close he had come to freezing to death. His Inuit training had taught him to look for balance in all things. Was there some basic cosmic reckoning occurring here? Did he owe the ice cap a life in return for once sparing his?

Stephan sat down cross-legged on the ice and stilled his breathing. Then he began to chant the Inuit song he had never quite forgotten, there on the ice amid the violent swirling winds of the worst storm he had ever seen with icebreakers crushing the terrain behind him.

After a while the noise lessened. So did the wind. For a moment the forces surrounding him seemed balanced in a kind of stasis. He was a part of the storm now and his perceptions traveled outward. He saw things his conscious mind did not fully understand, sensed things that would not be translatable upon awakening, but soon he knew in a deeper place, without knowing how he knew, that the people were lost out there . . . and the wolves were indeed hunting them.

Red Dawn

Ligichev found Galinin in the forward section of the sub inspecting the ballast tank valves. "Comrade Captain, can I speak to you?"

Galinin turned. He was holding a wrench and looked preoccupied. "What is it, Comrade Chief Scientist?"

Ligichev faced the bigger man squarely. "You're planning something. I want to know what it is."

"I don't know what you're talking about."

"Don't play the fool with me, Comrade. Every man on board this ship should be earnestly engaged in stripping it of classified matériel. If nothing else, certainly the drive should be broken down and prepared for disposal. Instead, what's left of the crew are feasting as if they haven't a care in the world, and you give no orders at all."

"So?"

"So I am a logical man. It is a curse sometimes, but one I bear happily. You always follow orders. You followed them so precisely you wrecked the drive. Your lack of such secrecy directives can mean only one thing."

"Which is?"

"There is no need for any additional orders because you are planning to scuttle the ship yourself to prevent the Americans from boarding her and taking the drive and the irinium."

"I have no intention of committing suicide. Go away." He bent back to the valves.

Ligichev took a deep breath. "I warn you. My daughter's life is at stake. I won't permit it."

Galinin turned back. His face was a mask of abnormal calm. It suddenly occurred to Ligichev that he was dealing with a dangerously unknowable quantity, a man who cared nothing for his own life, a fanatic.

"It is over, Comrade Chief Scientist, the whole affair of *Red Dawn*. I have orders to protect the irinium technology at all costs. This is the only way I can protect it. Maybe I wouldn't tell this to the others. They have no real capacity to understand. But you, you have a brilliant mind. Surely you can see there is no other way."

"You must see reason," Ligichev begged. "A few years, that's all you'll really be gaining. Soon someone else will discover irinium. That's the history of science. A few years, Captain. It's not worth the sacrifice. It's not worth the life of my daughter."

"Is your daughter's life worth more than Pytor's?" Galinin's eyes were bright. "There's an example. Did you see how willingly he sacrificed himself for his country? Should your daughter do less? And as for you and me, what do we have left, really, a few years at most at our age? Is having them worth betraying your country?"

"No one's country could ask this of him."

"You are a fool if you believe that," said Galinin. "A professional soldier has to face this sacrifice every day of his working life."

"I warn you again. I will stop you unless you promise me you won't try to scuttle the ship."

"You're threatening me?" Galinin laughed, a harsh, ugly bark. "Look at you. I could break you in half with one hand. Go away. Spend your last few hours with your daughter. Leave me to do what I must." Galinin bent back to the valves.

Ligichev said slowly and distinctly, "I have never knowingly hurt another man in my life, but I will if you don't get away from those valves."

Galinin turned fiercely, enraged. But he stopped short. In Ligichev's steady hand was the .25 automatic the captain had given him what seemed like ages ago. "So . . . it seems no good deed goes unpunished, eh? You threaten me with my own gun."

"I'm done with words," Ligichev said. "Get away from the valves. I'm going to lock you up in the trash room. Move."

Galinin didn't budge. Ligichev cocked the pistol's trigger. It was a loud sound in the small room.

"You don't have the balls," Galinin said softly. He took a step forward. "Fire that in here and pierce the hull and you'll do my work for me."

"Stop, I warn you!" Ligichev said, falling back.

"That's a mistake," said Galinin. In one swift movement he darted to one side and lashed out with his foot, kicking Ligichev hard in the knee. Ligichev shouted in pain, vainly trying to aim, but Galinin was just too fast. He moved in and chopped down viciously on Ligichev's wrist with the edge of his hand. The gun dropped from the scientist's nerveless fingers to the deck with a loud clatter. Galinin swept it aside with his foot.

"You see?" Galinin said calmly. He wasn't even breathing hard. "Act. Never threaten. Threatening is a mistake. You should have pulled the trigger without hesitation."

"Yes, I see that," Ligichev said despondently, nursing his

damaged wrist. His advantage over the burly captain was gone. He could never hope to best him in a fight. "What will you do now?"

"Simple," said Galinin. "I'm going to kill you. I can't have you alerting the crew, now, can I?"

Ligichev's eyes darted to the gun lying on the deck a few feet away. It might as well have been on the moon.

Galinin saw his glance and shook his head. "You can't get to it and I don't need it. Too loud." He advanced, hands clenched like a strangler's, eyes bright. "I will be gentle."

Ligichev knew he was going to die. In a final act of desperation he swung his fist at Galinin's head, but Galinin just caught it in his big palm and squeezed. Pain tore down Ligichev's arm and his legs buckled. Blackness swam in his eyes. He felt a hand touch his throat. . . .

The explosion shook the room like a blow from a giant hammer. Both men were thrown around. *Red Dawn*'s entire mass shifted suddenly and tossed them to the deck. Ligichev threw his arms over his head to protect himself as the force threw him into a console. Galinin was trying to get to his feet, but a second explosion picked him up and slammed him against the bulkhead wall. His eyes rolled up in his head from the force of the impact.

Dimly Ligichev understood what was happening as *Red Dawn* came free of the ice keel with a loud cracking sound that filled the ship. It had to be the Americans. Far away down the corridors he heard cheering, but he had no time to appreciate their rescue. Galinin was up and coming at him. Ligichev dived for the gun and came up with it. His hands were shaking and his wrist was on fire, but he wrapped both hands around the stock and pointed it at Galinin.

"Stop. Don't make me—"

Galinin leaped at him, his face an animal mask of fury. He landed on Ligichev, pummeling him with a big meaty fist as they grappled for the gun.

Blam! The shot was louder than anything Ligichev had ever heard. *Blam!* He felt a wrenching pain tear at his shoulder. His arm went numb, and the gun slid out of his hand. It was over. He had no more strength. The weight of

Galinin's body lay heavily on him. It was growing harder to breathe. He prepared himself to die.

Galinin's head rose before him like a ghost bobbing over the horizon. Ligichev's vision was swimming from the pain. "See?" Galinin said fiercely, his eyes waxen, blood streaming down his face. "Another mistake. Never threaten . . . never."

Ligichev closed his eyes and felt the world spin away.

Chapter
Seventeen

Avalon

Whooowheee! Will you look at that!" Luke shouted excitedly.

"*Red Dawn* is clear of the ice keel," MacKenzie radioed. He had to keep both hands on the steering yoke to control *Avalon* in the turbulence the twin explosions had created. There were angry scars on *Red Dawn*'s hull from the shape charges, but she looked intact and most of the ice had been blasted off her. She was floating at a slight downward angle, slowly drifting lower as her ballast tanks filled. Soon she'd be submerged deep enough to tow her under the ice cap's projections. The air hose had been severed by the blast, but it had served its purpose. *Red Dawn* had enough air to get out from under the ice cap.

MacKenzie had to admit it was a major show. He and Luke had watched the torpedoes spin through the icy waters and hit with unerring accuracy. Combined with the shape charges going off, the explosions had sent ice meteors spinning out in all directions. Crystal fragments still filled the sea, slowly drifting. It was as if they were in a snow-filled water bubble.

"Good shooting, Tom," he radioed when the water finally cleared. "*Red Dawn*'s in the open. Her tanks are filling slow and steady. We're returning to *Seawolf.*"

MacKenzie dropped, and skimmed along the eight hundred feet of steel cable stretching from *Red Dawn's* tow eye to the twin cleats on *Phoenix's* main deck. The line had bowed in the center from the weight of the steel ball, exactly as the engineers had hoped, and the tow line looped down under the boat. Most of the strain would be taken up by *Phoenix's* hull. It was another one for the record books. No submarine of this size had ever been towed underwater in such a fashion before.

"Phoenix, can you read me?"

"Arlin here, Mac. How's it look?"

"I just completed the inspection. Looks letter-perfect. You've got a good bow in the line, Phil. Prepare to get under way."

"Roger, *Avalon."*

In a way he was sorry that the spectacle of *Red Dawn* encased in its icy prison was over. They would never see anything quite like it again. It also meant that the most dangerous part of the mission was about to occur. It was one thing to raise the *Red Dawn,* another to get her out of here intact. He thought about Justine. There was no word yet from the breakers. But faith was an act of will. He willed himself to believe.

MacKenzie sped back to *Seawolf,* and within minutes he could see the crosshair-in-circle target over the aft escape trunk illuminated by *Avalon's* lights. He settled them down slowly. The crafts mated with a solid thunk. Luke pumped water out of the bell housing. MacKenzie shook his hand gratefully. "What can I say? You did a great job. As always."

Luke grinned. "Can't think of anyone I'd rather be made into a malted with in a DSRV than you, Cap. It's always interesting with you on board."

"Hightail it back. We've got a Russian captain out there who knows how vulnerable *Phoenix* is with *Red Dawn* in tow. It's going to get tricky from here on in."

"If anybody can get us all out of here in one piece my money's on you, Cap." Luke clapped him on the shoulder. "Good luck, Mac."

"To us all, Luke. See you home." Mac slid out of his seat

and went back into the aft section. With a final pat on *Avalon*'s hull, he cycled open the hatches, dropped through the skirt, and climbed down into *Seawolf.*

Akula

In the officers' mess, Kalik was still smarting from having to pull back from attacking the DSRV. He picked up his mug of coffee and warmed his hands. It was always so damn cold in here. The engineer insisted the ship's temperature was the same as it always was, but he had refused to believe it till he checked the readings himself. They were right, but rather than look like an idiot he had set the engineer to replacing all the gauges. He grimaced. He wasn't usually so petty or capricious. Things other captains had said about working under the ice cap filtered through his mind, how it fouled your natural rhythms and sapped your strength until you were edgy and out of sorts. Was it like that on *Seawolf,* too? Were they as tired? Had the cat-and-mouse game they were playing worn down the other captain, too?

Kalik was worried about himself—the problems with Viktor, the petty pique over the gauges. Worse, he was starting to second-guess himself. His doubts had caused him to miss the opportunity to fire on the unprotected DSRV. He had asked too many questions, overanalyzed the situation. The truth was he was afraid to be outmaneuvered again and he'd been too cautious. He promised himself that wouldn't happen the next time they faced each other. And they would, soon. It took no genius to know that if he let the Americans escape with *Red Dawn* he would finish his career in disgrace. He might even face a court-martial and prison. He wasn't about to let that happen. Destroying the Americans' land base hadn't done the trick, and the *Ural* hadn't arrived in time. He had one choice left. It was a daring move, but if he succeeded he would erase all his past errors in a single blinding moment of glory. Defeat *Seawolf,* then destroy *Phoenix* and steal *Red Dawn*. He had no doubt that dispatching *Phoenix* would be simple enough. With *Red Dawn* in tow, *Phoenix* was ridiculously vulnerable. His only worry was *Seawolf*. Since the beginning, *Seawolf* and her captain had beaten him at every turn.

He knew how the Americans were faring and had permitted them to continue without interference. Sonar had informed him when the DSRV planted the towing hook, and the sounds of the steel line scraping along *Phoenix's* hull gave him a pretty good idea of how they had rigged it. Communications had picked up the SOS for the survivors on the surface. He had hoped that *Seawolf* might break off from its mission to search for them, but the series of explosions that followed could only mean that they had forsaken the survivors to blast *Red Dawn* free of the ice. By now *Phoenix* would be ready to tow.

The contest between him and the American captain had grown keenly personal. Defeating *Seawolf* would be proof that his prowess remained intact, that his judgment was still strong. The power play in the Kremlin had nothing to do with it.

"Comrade Captain?"

Kalik came out of his reverie. "What is it, Viktor?"

"I feel I must talk to you, Vassily."

Kalik looked into Volkov's face. It was just as tired as his own. It gave him pause. He shouldn't forget he wasn't the only one under strain. His feelings eased. If he looked at things honestly he had to admit that Volkov had done nothing to undermine him, nothing to deserve being treated so coldly.

"You still have my ear, Viktor," he said and motioned for him to sit.

"You've been making plans?"

"Yes. Have you come to challenge them?" Kalik caught himself. What is wrong with me, he wondered, that I cannot control my own tongue?

"Just the opposite, Vassily. I . . ." Viktor let out a deep breath. "I wanted you to know that you can count on my full support. I am still your senior lieutenant. Still your . . . friend. I've always been a good ear for you, Vassily. I would like to continue that function. If you wish it, of course."

Kalik understood in that moment that his own career was over. No matter what the outcome was, he had lost something essential on the ice cap. Half-remembered fragments of Eliot's "Prufrock" slid across his mind like signposts leading him down the road to understanding. . . . *do I have the strength to force the moment to its crisis?* He had to face it, the thing that had wormed its way into his belly and stolen his strength. . . . *I have seen the eternal Footman hold my coat, and snicker, and in short, I was afraid* . . . For the first time in his career, Kalik realized he was afraid. The ice had robbed him. He could never again cross the gangway to his waiting ship and not know that fear lay buried deep within him. He was like a high-wire aerialist: one moment of fear had changed him forever; he could never again walk the wire with the same confidence. Kalik wondered if he could find the strength for the last engagement. Volkov was still watching him carefully, still trying for some . . . bridge. Kalik didn't want to make it tougher on him. He pushed a mug across the table and poured some coffee. "I am going to attack *Seawolf,* Viktor."

Volkov took the mug and nodded. "I assumed so."

Kalik went on, "Once *Seawolf* is out of the way I will be forced to destroy *Phoenix.*"

Volkov accepted it impassively. "Sadly I've had to come to the same conclusion."

"It's the only way I can avoid sinking *Red Dawn,* a ship manned by our own countrymen. Once *Phoenix* is destroyed we will pick up the towline and make straight for Kola Base and be done with this infernal region."

Volkov accepted that, too. He reached out for the deeper understanding they had shared in the past. "Vassily, I—"

"Spare yourself," Kalik said, pouring another cup of coffee. "I can't say that I truly understand what it is that happens to a man up here, but we began this mission with a job to do, and no matter how badly I have fouled things up I intend to see it done. I am grateful for your help, Viktor. I always have been."

Volkov stood, relieved. "You have it, Comrade Captain. In full measure."

Kalik put a hand on his shoulder. "Then come take your place beside me in the control room. It's time to write the final chapter of this thing." He reached out and hit the alarm on the intercom panel.

Volkov felt energy course through their physical connection. They were one again. A partnership with an adversary to best. A mission to complete.

He followed Kalik forward as the sounds of the battle-stations alarm rang stridently throughout the ship.

Seawolf

A quick, hot shower while Tom Lasovic assembled the division officers in the wardroom loosened MacKenzie's muscles and cleared his mind. He changed into a clean uniform and arrived as Joe Santiago was unrolling the newly completed charts MacKenzie had requested earlier.

"Spread them out on the table, Joe," he directed. "Everybody gather around."

Seawolf's navigator spread out a hydrographic map of the immediate area. "These," Santiago explained, "were slaved directly from the upward-looking Fathometer and fed into our computer to print the data in chart form. The result is an accurate representation of the ice cap above and the waters around us. *Red Dawn*'s ice keel is the center point, here."

"This is our sphere of engagement," MacKenzie said. The chart depicted the sea for ten miles around them, along with every keel, stalactite, and pressure ridge. "First we've got to get *Phoenix* and *Red Dawn* safely out of this sphere. Once they move beyond *Akula*'s range they'll make for the marginal ice fields. There's enough noise there to cover them. They'll have clear sailing till they can rendezvous with a surface escort group. Unfortunately we have several problems." MacKenzie looked around at his officers grimly. "I can assure you that as soon as we try to tow *Red Dawn* out of here *Akula* is going to attack."

Tom Lasovic scratched his head, thinking aloud. "We're at a real disadvantage in the noise category, Skipper. No way I can see to muffle *Phoenix* with *Red Dawn* in tow. That tow cable is already swishing through the water in the wake from *Phoenix*'s props. Under speed they're going to sound like an express train."

"Sonar's going to be ineffective," said Jim Kurstan. "With that much noise in the neighborhood, we won't be able to get a reliable fix on *Akula*."

"At least he's got the same problem," Santiago said.

"Not in the same way," said Kurstan. "He can move quietly and get a series of positions to triangulate. Or he can sit still while we move in tandem with *Phoenix*. If he does a quick leapfrog we could be heading right into his sights and not know it till he fires."

"What do we figure *Phoenix*'s max speed is with *Red Dawn* in tow?" MacKenzie asked.

Chief Engineer Jake Cardiff answered. "Ten knots, maximum . . . and that's pushing it to the limit, Mac."

"Ten knots means a thousand yards every three minutes. Hmm . . ." MacKenzie lapsed into private inner computations. "Let me think a minute."

Lasovic had seen MacKenzie in this hyperaware state before. He was a brilliant tactician, and if there was a way to get *Red Dawn* out of here Mac would probably find it. He watched thoughts play on his friend's face as he ran down possibilities, rejecting one after another. He seemed to come to a tentative conclusion, scanned the chart, then nodded more definitely. "Joe, does that big ice keel really extend as far down and across as the chart says?"

"I checked that keel when it first showed up. Even had Sonar take a ping or two at it. It's a giant, almost seven hundred feet deep and two hundred wide. Say five nautical miles from our present position."

"We heard some bergy bits breaking off, Skipper. It's big all right."

"How thick is the ice over the keel?"

Santiago showed him on the chart. "There's a fair-sized pressure ridge over it. Twenty feet of ice minimum."

MacKenzie calculated out loud. "Okay. Ten thousand yards to the keel. At a thousand yards every three minutes it'll take *Phoenix* half an hour to reach it. That's the time we've got to cover them. Once they move beyond that keel, it will block *Akula*'s sonar and *Phoenix* can tow *Red Dawn* safely the rest of the way to the zone."

"Won't *Akula* follow?" wondered Kurstan.

"Not if he can't acquire a contact, and he won't be able to with what I have in mind," MacKenzie said firmly.

"We're all ears, Skipper," said Lasovic.

"Gentlemen, we are going to take a lesson from the ice cap." MacKenzie's smile was grim. "I don't know about all of you, but I'm damn tired of being predictable. Here's what I've got in mind. . . . "

MacKenzie strode into the conn as the battle-station alarm sounded through the ship. "All right, look alert, everybody." Crewmen settled stiff-backed into their chairs or stood waiting attentively at their instrument consoles, ready, waiting, days of fatigue banished by the alarm. With Tom Lasovic standing beside him, MacKenzie flipped the 1MC switch on the intercom to address the entire ship.

"This is the captain speaking. As you all know by now, we've completed attaching the towline between *Phoenix* and *Red Dawn,* which is now free of the ice. We are preparing to escort both ships out of this area and back home. However, the Soviet submarine *Akula* is in the vicinity and knows of our intentions. I expect the *Akula* to attack. This is no drill. I repeat: I expect the *Akula* to attack us. But with God's help and a few tricks of our own thrown in, we are going to take the day. Be prepared for several high-speed maneuvers and a lot of shaking up. You have approximately ten minutes to secure everything possible. One personal aside. No captain

275

could ask for a finer ship or a better crew. Behave as warriors. Captain out."

MacKenzie stepped off the periscope platform and handed Lasovic a written order. "Tom, transmit this to the *Polar Eight* along with the ice keel's coordinates."

Lasovic read it and looked up, bewildered. "Mac, are you sure? This is going to reduce the survivors' chances by half."

"If there were any other way, Tom, I'd do it. But there isn't. Send it."

"Aye, Skipper."

MacKenzie hit the intercom. "Maneuvering, Conn.

"Cardiff here, Skipper."

"Jake, I'm going to need everything you can muster down there to keep on top of *Akula*. She's faster than we are."

"In a pig's eye, Captain MacKenzie!"

Mac grinned. "Well, just keep that power plant on the line and watch the big power and pressure transient. We may come to all stop on a moment's notice. Prepare to answer all bells. I'll want all ahead flank in"—he checked his watch—"six minutes."

"Maneuvering, aye. Whatever you need we'll deliver, Captain."

"Communications, this is the captain. Inform *Phoenix* we will be moving out in six minutes. I want constant secure communications with Captain Arlin. Use the ultralow-frequency pulse. At no time are you to turn the ULF carrier off. Keep that line open. Understood?"

"Aye, Skipper. Open line at all times. Informing *Phoenix* now."

"Sonar, Conn. Prepare to go active. Max power. Three six zero degrees."

"Conn, Sonar. All set, Skipper. We'll give them a major headache."

MacKenzie felt the familiar sensation of the ship energizing around him, his body replaced by infinitely subtle machines run by men to the terms of his own will. At moments like this the corporate entity that was *Seawolf* became one and truly inseparable from him. He wondered idly if one day sub captains would be linked directly to their boats by some contrivance that let them control the ships' movements by thought alone. Now, that would be something to command.

One by one departments reported their readiness. It was no small thing to take men into battle. Torpedoes were loaded, engines primed, machines fine-tuned to the maximum. This was what all the training was about, why you spent time learning tasks over and over again till you could do them in your sleep—or in the violent commotion of combat.

"I've got to hand it to you. This is going to be one for the books," said Lasovic.

"Let's just hope it's one *Akula* doesn't expect," replied MacKenzie. "Do what you don't usually do, Tom. That's what being up here taught me. That's how we're going to beat him. For thirty minutes."

Akula

Kalik took his ship deep and silent. Drifting slowly, he was waiting for *Phoenix* to move out. With their noise to obscure his movements he would move in, get a fix on *Seawolf*, and attack in the middle zone.

"Sonar, Control Room. Report your contacts."

"Comrade Captain, *Phoenix* and *Red Dawn* are still in the same positions relative to each other. Minimum rotations. *Seawolf* is cruising one half mile behind, course two seven zero, speed five knots."

"They're heading west." Kalik began to see how he would attack. He'd bring *Akula* far enough along course two seven zero to wait for *Seawolf* to pass, then turn in behind and shoot. "Comrade Navigator, assume *Seawolf* will proceed along course track two seven zero. In five minutes I want to be in a position about half a mile ahead of where she is now so that she will cross our bow and we can pull in behind her. Plot us a course and speed. Understood?"

"Yes, Comrade Captain."

It was textbook-perfect. He'd drift *Akula* down their route and let *Seawolf* and *Phoenix*, towing *Red Dawn*, run right past him. Subs tracked least well when their adversaries were behind them because their sonar was deafened by their own propeller noise. With both American ships ahead of him he'd have ample time to acquire the contacts and compute an attack. A classic maneuver. They'd never hear *Akula* through all the prop noise until his torpedoes were sliding right up their behinds. And what he liked best was that it was a page from the American captain's own book: wait silently for the enemy and let him sail right into the trap. Across the control room Volkov heard the orders and nodded slowly. He saw what Kalik was planning and approved. They were a team again, conflicts forgotten, intent on only one thing—defeating the enemy.

Soon. Very soon. Kalik felt it in his bones. He settled in to wait.

Polar 8

Captain Maré read the communication from *Seawolf* and shook his head. "Renaud, you think you've seen everything in this business, but this one has to be unique." He passed it over to the ice specialist.

"Hmm. They have the Soviet sub in tow. Well, that's good. To be honest, I always thought this was a fool's business." Then Renaud read the rest. *"Mon Dieu, est-ce qu'il fou?"*

"I wondered when you were going to get to that part," said Maré "Is he crazy ordering us to break through a twenty-foot pressure ridge?" The captain's mouth twisted sardonically. "Of course he's crazy."

"Do we comply?" Renaud asked.

Maré sighed. "We have been told to offer every assistance to the Americans." He passed the slip of paper to the navigator. "Can we make these coordinates, Claude?"

The navigator bent over his chart table and worked for a

few moments. "We can make the ridge. It's about five hundred yards ahead of us. The problem is the *Ural*. If she's still on course she's between us and the keel."

Maré raised an eyebrow. "Renaud?"

"Don't tell me," Renaud muttered, looking darkly out the frost-encrusted bridge windows. He didn't want to go out into that storm again. Wind-blasted ice crystals rattled against the glass. Icicles hung two feet down on the glass. He reached for his parka with a bitter snort. "Get the coffee ready."

He opened the bridge door and stepped out on deck. Clothing wasn't made that could keep out cold like this. He went to the railing and peered over toward the *Ural*. It was still there, he could hear it. But how close? And was it ahead of them or behind them? The big overhead lamps illuminated funnel-shaped bursts of snow, but the light couldn't reach across to the other icebreaker. Ice was caking up on Renaud's face. His lungs were on fire.

The noise roared on without interruption, but he still couldn't see the other ship through the storm. He searched for a light, anything to see where the other ship was. His eyes hurt. He wanted to go back in. But they couldn't risk crossing *Ural*'s bow unless they were sure of its position.

His patience paid off. The storm let up for a moment as if catching its breath. For a few seconds snow drifted serenely down devoid of the wind to propel it. Renaud could make out the lines of *Ural*'s superstructure. She was still perilously close. His instincts as an ice specialist told him they were probably following the same river of thin ice. He decided *Ural* was sufficiently behind *Polar 8*. As long as their relative speeds remained constant they could cross *Ural*'s bow without incident. All, he thought bitterly as he made for the warmth of the bridge, to comply with the crazy request of a crazier American captain.

He shot a last look toward the *Ural*, hidden once again as the storm renewed its fury, and ducked inside. Break through a twenty-foot pressure ridge? What the hell was the American thinking, anyway?

Polar Ice Cap

Stephan radioed Captain Ivanov to increase his speed back to four knots. He had located another river of thin ice. They could pick up some of the distance they'd lost while he was in the trance.

He slid the guy line off his waist and let it drop in the snow. Moving off onto the ice alone Stephan keenly felt the absence of the umbilicus. He was cut off again. He sought the Inuit harmony with the ice cap. The ice could be conquered if one understood it. The snow swirled around him. He let it blow, trying to become one with the storm. Don't fight it. No one beat such violence. Blend. Merge. Therein lay the strength to go on. Flow *through* . . .

He bent low, seeking the small space of calmer air at ground level and followed the *sastrugi* again. He could hear the sounds of the wolf pack every time the wind faded. There were at least three wolves, maybe four. They would be circling their prey now, waiting to strike, stalking closer and closer till they pounced in a well-coordinated attack.

He stopped for a moment. The noise from the breakers was louder. He tried to see the ships, but the snow obscured them. He squatted and put his hands on the ice to feel the vibrations. They were stronger. His brow furrowed under his hood. Could the ships be moving closer? They were both sailing virtually blind. It was possible they might be on a collision course and wouldn't see each other till it was too late. He radioed Ivanov and was told they would keep the sharpest lookout possible. Stephan wavered, almost turning back. He had to make up his mind quickly. Duty to his ship warred with responsibility for the poor lost souls out there in the storm.

All his life as a Soviet citizen he had been taught that the collective was everything, the individual meaningless. His teachers would surely have told him that his duty was to his ship. Let these others die. He waited in the storm for guidance. He was Inuit enough to leave it up to the ice cap. It was so cold he felt as if he were standing in a vacuum, in space. His ski poles barely scratched the glass-hard surface of the ice under its snowy cover.

He could hear the wolves more frequently now. He wondered when the storm would lose its power. Weather up here was a sudden thing. Storms could sweep in in a matter of minutes, blast the ice cap for hours or days, and then sweep off again just as quickly, blown by winds that had no surface features to arrest them.

He waited. The noise of the icebreakers surrounded him. A snowflake entered his mouth drawn in on a ragged breath. It dissolved on his tongue with wet sweetness. Such a small thing, an individual snowflake, each one similar yet uniquely different from all others.

Like lives.

He began to understand that the ice cap had made its decision.

Seawolf

Seawolf's conn was hushed, the crew ready. Sonar was at its highest state of alert. The technicians in the attack center were inputting data steadily into the computers. Helmsman and planesman were poised and ready to respond. The chief studied his board and nodded with satisfaction. Everything read straight and green.

MacKenzie checked his watch again. Three minutes. Time for one last duty. "Mr. Randall, come with me. Mr. Santiago, take his post. Tom, take the conn."

MacKenzie walked into the forward passageway and Randall followed. The rest of the crew was intent on its tasks. For a brief moment they were alone. "Sir, is something wrong?"

"Just the opposite," MacKenzie said. "Mr. Randall, you're a fine officer. I just want to take advantage of an opportunity for your continued education. So listen closely because I believe you are going to captain your own ship someday, and when that time comes you will need this to draw upon. No one can tell you all of it, but if you're going to command, this much you should know." He spoke intently, leaning close so that his words fell to Randall alone.

"In three minutes we are going into battle. It's going to get hot and heavy pretty quickly. First lesson. Remember, there's no way to be one hundred percent sure of things. You can't be completely certain what your adversary is planning or how he'll react. It's all a bet, an educated guess based on things you've observed—the other captain's psychology, his habits, the strengths of your ship. Understand? No matter how certain you think I am or how I look, I'm just betting on the odds as I see them. Follow?"

"I think so, sir."

"All right. My first bet is that *Akula*'s captain is counting on us to continue behaving like an American sub and that he's going to ignore his training and act like one, too."

"Sir?"

"Logic and psychology. Up till now we've both stayed as quiet as circumstances permitted, to mask our positions. Tactical advantage came from our knowing where *Akula* was and his not knowing where we were, and vice versa. Out on maneuvers, Russian captains often like to let *you* know *they* know you're there. Our side is content with knowing *we* know they're there. See the difference? He expects us to be silent. But with *Red Dawn* in tow *Phoenix* is too exposed. We're in a situation where we can't go silent to any great degree. So if I do things as my training suggests and try to sneak out of here we're going to be at a marked disadvantage from the start.

"Second, *Akula*'s captain has gotten burned twice now with flashy tactics. They lost him *Red Dawn* and *Avalon* and almost cost him his ship. He's got to be feeling conservative. I'm betting he's out there right now, keeping quiet as hell and drifting slowly into position to intercept our course and deliver a broadside of torpedoes as soon as we try to move out of here as quietly as he expects."

"But what else can we do?" Randall asked. "We're boxed in. We can't leave *Phoenix* and *Red Dawn,* and we can't make them any quieter or more mobile."

"You ever study judo?"

"Sir?"

"There's a lesson I learned from watching my wife throw much bigger guys around the gym. As soon as a man grabs her, she takes him where he wants to go faster than he wants to go there. That's how we're going to beat *Akula.*"

Randall's face mirrored his confusion. "I don't follow, sir."

"For almost an hour now I've been showing him our route out of here, giving him every indication we're going to run straight for the marginal ice zone on course two seven zero. He wants us bad, I'm sure of that. How would you feel watching the Soviet navy grab one of our ships right out from under your nose? So I think he'll take the bait and wait for us to run, then close on our tails as we pass. He'll think he's going to get a clean shot. And he might, too. We'll be blind back there for a while, so there's a risk, but if we can't go silent we've got to keep him engaged. Right away. He's got to have his hands filled with us for the full thirty minutes *Phoenix* needs to reach the ice keel."

"How does that stop *Phoenix's* noise? He can still locate her."

A slow, feral smile crossed MacKenzie's features, the look of a warrior. "We'll give him more than he bargained for there, too, eh? We're going to fill the ocean with so much noise that even *Phoenix's* sound will be covered. It's going to be a little hairy, but that's where my second bet comes in. I'm betting on *Seawolf* herself. Our conformal acoustic sonars are the best in the world, and the new fiber optic sensors give us additional range. When the time comes, I'm betting we'll be able to hear him before he can hear us. So . . . time's short. We'd better get back. And if you're wondering, yes, someone once gave me this kind of talk. It helped a lot later on. I hope it helps you someday. Questions?"

"Only one. Who was it, sir? I mean, who was your captain?"

"A tough old bird named Ben Garver."

"Admiral Garver? The CNO?"

"The same."

Randall gazed at him respectfully. MacKenzie hoped he saw past the veneer to the real truth, that captains were just normal men who learned to come to terms with a long list of uncertainties so they could do their jobs. Someday Randall would have to do the same.

"Thanks for the talk, Skipper. I just don't think I'll ever be as good as you."

MacKenzie smiled. "That's just what I used to think about Ben Garver."

Randall thought that over. "I'll try to remember that."

MacKenzie looked at his watch. "Okay, time to see if my bets pay off. Ready?"

"My money's on you, sir."

MacKenzie clapped him on the back. "All right, back to your station."

Watching Randall return to his position MacKenzie decided he'd given the young man enough food for thought. He came back to the problems at hand. It was time for action. "The captain has the conn. Sonar, how deep are *Phoenix* and *Red Dawn?*"

"Eight hundred feet, Captain."

"Mr. Santiago, I want to be informed of their time and distance to the ice keel. Every three minutes, every thousand yards."

"Three minutes and thousand yards, aye."

"Communications, inform *Phoenix* she is to proceed. Come up to ten knots, course two seven zero. Helm, steer two seven zero as well. We'll stay in the middle zone. Mr. Randall, make your depth five zero zero feet."

"Five zero zero, aye."

The conn responded smartly to MacKenzie's orders. There was one thing he hadn't told Randall—the number of times you crossed your fingers and prayed for a little dumb luck to protect your ship and see you through. They could use some for the next half hour.

"*Phoenix* is under way, Captain. Speed coming to ten knots. *Red Dawn* is fully in tow and moving with her."

"Very well. All ahead one-third. Keep us close."

MacKenzie knew they were still a long way from home.

Red Dawn

Ligichev awoke sprawled on the deck. His shoulder was on fire, and he wondered why he wasn't dead. Where was Galinin? He had to find the captain before he scuttled the ship.

He tried to lever himself off the deck but he lost his balance and fell. It was a minute before he could muster enough strength to try again. There was blood on the deck. A lot of it. His shirt was sodden, but he hadn't bled enough to create that pool. Was it Galinin's?

He tried to remember if Galinin had been wounded, too. All he could summon was the image of Galinin's face rising before him just before he lost consciousness. The captain *was* bleeding. He used the bulkhead to push himself up and staggered out.

The rest of the crewmen were in the mess eating and playing cards. They had no duties. They were just waiting for whatever came next. Ligichev remembered speaking to some of them days before, and he remembered the big man's name, the one with a snake and dagger tattoo on his thick forearm. "You! You're Seaman Boslik, correct?" He spotted another he remembered. "And you, Michman Rostov."

The michman looked up from his hand. "I'm Rostov."

"And you're bleeding," said Boslik, spotting the blood on Ligichev's shirt. "What happened?"

"The captain shot me. He is trying to scuttle the ship to prevent the Americans from taking the drive when they board us. We must stop him. Help me."

Boslik hesitated and looked to his mates. They made no

move to go. "Comrade Chief Scientist, why would the captain do such a thing? We have just been rescued."

"The rescue signed our death warrant," Ligichev insisted. "Captain Galinin is under orders not to let the Americans get my invention. I tell you he is planning to scuttle us to prevent it."

The men grumbled uncomfortably. Ligichev heard the word "mutiny." He looked at their faces. They were conscripts, most just marking time till they could get out of the service. Ligichev wondered how he could expect men who were really no more than uneducated laborers to go against their captain, the symbol of Soviet authority. But he had to try.

"What's wrong with you all? Are you such sheep you'll let him kill you without a fight? Think for yourselves for once. You once said I could depend on you. Now I'm asking. Get up. Find Galinin and restrain him. At least put him under guard so he can't move against the ship. Your lives depend on it."

Rostov was unconvinced. "And what if the captain says you're the one who needs locking up?"

"Then lock us both up," Ligichev said, exasperated, "and decide for yourselves who's doing the right thing, but for God's sake, hurry. We haven't the time to debate it."

Boslik eyed him closely. He turned to the others. "It isn't much to talk to the crew, but it's a damn sight more than any of those other official bastards ever did. If what he says is true—"

Rostov was almost as big as Boslik when he stood up. "And if it isn't? Things may be changing, but *perestroika* hasn't come to Siberia. I have no desire to bring it there."

Boslik stepped close to the other man. "You think we have it so much better?" He turned back to Ligichev. "Comrade Chief Scientist, are you *ordering* us to help you?"

Ligichev saw the out and grabbed it. "Of course. As a Party member and the chief scientist on this mission I am ordering you to restrain the captain. The responsibility is mine alone. Your protests are registered."

Boslik turned to the others. "I'm not dying in this crummy place."

Hesitantly Rostov nodded. The others rose to follow.

Ligichev clapped them gratefully on the arms. "Be careful. He's armed."

Ivanna was working in the engine room. A good part of the drive's guts lay on the deck, and multicolored wire harnesses spilled from the main unit as if a giant scavenger bird had yanked them out with a sharp beak. She had been forced to close the drive scoop manually, which had been enough of a bitch, but it was taking longest to remove the irinium plates. Each one was a small oblong about the size of a pack of cigarettes, and they were all wired into the electrical system. There were sixty plates in all. All but a few lay stacked on the deck now beside the collection of assorted bins and buckets she'd needed to bail the seawater out of the channel lest it touch the irinium and cause another heat flash. Cursing the awkward quarters one more time she reached in with an adjustable wrench to free the remaining bars and slipped them one by one into the pockets of her coveralls. It was annoying work, but it made sure no one would get home and report she hadn't done her best to keep everything out of American hands.

She was wondering how to dispose of them when Galinin entered. He was holding a cloth to the side of his head. He looked feverishly aroused.

"Comrade Captain, my father was coming to see you. Did he find you?"

"He found me." His gaze shifted to the stack of irinium bars and he shook his head in wonder. "It's remarkable, don't you think, that a pile of gold the same size would be worthless by comparison."

"I suppose it all depends on time and place." Ivanna wiped insulation off her hands. This man was trouble. She could feel tension coming off him in waves. Where was her father? "A few hundred years ago a pile of salt was worth more than anything," she said.

"Time and place," repeated Galinin. "Yes, that's the

key." He leaned over the drive unit and poked around inside it. "You're a strong girl to be able to close the intake scoop manually. It's this pressure wheel here, isn't it?"

"Don't fool with that. What are you doing?"

Galinin interposed his bulk between Ivanna and the drive. "Go find your father. He needs you. I'll finish here." He pushed her aside roughly. The cloth came away from his head, revealing a bloody gash.

"You're bleeding. What happened?"

"Nothing that concerns you."

Galinin outweighed Ivanna by at least a hundred pounds, but she knocked his hands away. "You're up to something. Father was right about you. Where is he?"

"Right now he is lying in a pool of his own blood. He tried to kill me. With this." The .25 automatic appeared in Galinin's hand, small in his meaty fist. "You should have gone when I told you to. Now stay where you are and don't move."

Ivanna looked from the gun to Galinin's eyes. They were too bright and shiny, like a light just before it burned out. She said quietly, "If you hurt my father I'll kill you."

Galinin smiled admiringly. "You are a haughty bitch, but you've got more guts than most men I know. I admire that. But I have no choice." He pointed to the irinium. "Even if you take all of those bars and dump them into the sea it wouldn't be enough. How many traces are left? One tiny microscopic smear would let the Americans duplicate the formula. And what about the drive itself? How can you dispose of that? My orders are clear. I must prevent these things from falling into American hands. And there's no way other than this." He stepped over the buckets and reached for the scoop valve.

"Get away from there!"

"I'm sorry. The end will not be pleasant. But"— something in his eyes changed, softening—"I have come to respect you, Comrade Ligichova, so I will give you this much. If you prefer I will kill you quickly."

He leveled the gun at her. Ivanna understood that in his own warped way Galinin was offering her something he felt

288

was valuable—a quick death instead of the horror of drowning when he flooded the ship. She squared herself.

"I hate the water. I have no wish to drown. I will accept your offer, Comrade Captain. Gratefully."

The gleam of admiration grew on Galinin's face. "As you wish." He stood back from the drive and pointed the gun at her heart.

Akula

"Control Room, Sonar. They are under way, Comrade Captain. *Phoenix*'s towing speed is ten knots."

"Course?"

"Still on two seven zero. Depth eight hundred feet."

"What is *Seawolf* doing?"

"Trailing at the same speed four hundred meters behind them. They are remaining very quiet, Comrade Captain. We are picking up only the faintest readings."

Kalik gripped the stanchion tightly, controlling his excitement. *Seawolf* was moving right into his trap. In a few moments the Americans would sail past him without even suspecting he had moved onto their flank. Then he would pull in behind them to fire.

"Continue to track them, Sonar."

The navigator looked up from his instrument console. "*Phoenix* and *Red Dawn* are passing us. Comrade Captain, you may begin your turn to starboard . . . now."

"Helm, bring us to course two seven zero. Use minimum rudder for a slow turn. Speed ten knots," Kalik ordered. "Torpedo Room, stand ready to fire." At this speed the reactor relied on natural flow to dissipate its heat, eliminating the need for cooling pumps and their associated noise. The rest of their sound was masked by the commotion of *Red Dawn*'s progress and *Seawolf*'s prop noise.

Akula slowly moved into position behind the three submarines, as silently and deadly as the predator shark it was named for.

MacKenzie stood on the deck in the conn and waited. It was going to be close, but he had to give his adversary enough enticement to commit himself. If he held *Seawolf* any farther back he might alert the Soviet captain to what he was planning. Wait, he thought, sending the thought out like a mental command to his adversary. Wait and savor the moment. This is what you've been hoping for. We're sitting ducks. Don't shoot yet. Wait just a little while longer. Then I'll be ready.

"Nine thousand yards to the ice keel. Twenty-seven minutes to go," Santiago called out.

Every second counted. Every second was five and a half yards closer to the keel, every minute three hundred and thirty. He had to cut it just right. Too little time and he risked alerting *Akula* to what he planned. Too much and *Akula*'s torpedoes might catch them before he had a chance to put his plan into effect.

He stepped into the sonar room. Bear Bendel had his headphones on. His hands were making minute adjustments at the controls. The dreamy look on his face told MacKenzie his senses were extended as far out as *Seawolf*'s sonars would allow. Jim Kurstan stood alongside him watching the visual display intently.

"Skipper."

"Jim, I need a contact. I have to be sure."

"Bear thought he had one just a few seconds ago, but we lost her. She's incredibly quiet, and the towing is kicking up a racket."

"What do the fiber optics read?"

Seawolf's sensors were a long way from simple sound-gathering microphones. Under an outer coating of anechoic tiles to dampen and absorb enemy sonars, *Seawolf*'s entire hull was studded with sheets of a special piezoelectric plastic, which generated electrical impulses in response to acoustic pressure, impulses that went directly to sonar's computers to be read and deciphered. Even more sensitive were *Seawolf's* new fiber-optic sensors. The sensing fibers carried beams of laser light, and when sound waves hit them they induced tiny shifts in the phase of the light that was detected by an interferometer and translated by sonar's computers.

"The F.O.'s are where we've had the most luck. Bear says he can hear a light bulb go on with them. We'll get him, Skipper."

"We're running out of time."

"Yes, sir. We'll keep at it."

MacKenzie returned to the conn. Santiago called out, "Eight thousand yards to keel. Twenty-four minutes remaining."

Where was *Akula?* Had he guessed wrong? Maybe he had been too obvious in presenting his unprotected stern to his adversary. Maybe *Akula* had gone into the shallow zone and was hiding behind a keel. Above two hundred feet, temperature gradients reflected submarine noise upward, preventing it from traveling any great distance. Could he be hiding up there right now? Alternate plans began to form in his mind. Within seconds he was going to have to make up his mind about whether to stay on this course or break away. It had to be now.

"Emergency stop. Maneuvering, all stop. Ultraquiet."

Abruptly *Seawolf's* prop ceased its spin and grew silent. It was an old Russian tactic, stopping suddenly to see if anyone was on your tail hidden by your own prop noise. In the sudden quiet, sonar had access to a full 360 degrees without any prop noise to block their tail.

"Conn, Sonar. Contact bearing zero nine zero. Contact identified as *Akula*. She's five hundred yards astern, Skipper. Speed ten knots. Right smack dab in the middle zone. Depth five hundred feet. Slowing rapidly."

MacKenzie felt relief sweep through him. He had been right after all. He caught Randall's admiring look. He would never know how close his captain had come to second-guessing himself and breaking off. "Well done, Sonar. Go active. Max power. Continuous ping."

"Sonar, aye," In the sonar room Jim Kurstan flicked the sonar onto active and turned the gain up to maximum. Sound beams at the height of their decibel range shot out from *Seawolf*. Bear Bendel pulled off his headphones before his eardrums burst. He pitied *Akula*'s sonarman. The ice cap magnified the screeching sounds like an echo chamber, making them amplify and reverberate. At max power *Seawolf*'s active sonar would render the enemy sonar almost useless.

"Communications, inform *Phoenix* we are commencing our run. Advise her to switch to course two one zero and good luck."

"Communications, aye."

If *Akula* was slowing she was getting ready to fire. "Helm, on my order we will execute a one-hundred-eighty-degree high-speed turn to starboard. Mr. Randall, maximum cavitation, I want a big knuckle for *Akula*'s sonar. Steer to course zero nine zero."

"Sir, but that's a collision course with—"

"Steer zero nine zero, Mr. Randall," MacKenzie repeated sharply. "Maneuvering, prepare to answer all bells. Flank speed in five seconds."

"Maneuvering, aye. We're ready for you, Captain."

"Torpedo Room. Status of all tubes."

"Tubes one through four loaded with MK-forty-eight torpedoes."

"Flood all tubes amidship and open outer doors."

"Flood all tubes and open doors, aye."

The intercom overhead crackled again. "Conn, Sonar. Contact's still slowing. Speed four knots. Some hull popping. Tubes flooding. She's getting ready to fire all right, Skipper."

"Fire Control, keep tracking *Akula* and be sure you have a constant firing solution. Bear in mind we will be turning to starboard and coming around straight at him. I intend to shoot the first units from tubes one and three."

"Fire Control, aye. Tubes one and three. Plotting solution."

"Phoenix is seven thousand yards from the keel. Twenty-one minutes remaining," Santiago called out.

MacKenzie felt his heart racing from the adrenaline. He'd given *Phoenix* nine minutes and a 3000-yard head start. They were heading right for the big keel. It was up to him to keep *Akula* off her track for the next twenty-one minutes.

"Maneuvering, this is it. All ahead flank. Helm, commence high-speed turn to starboard, hard right rudder to new course zero nine zero. Swing her as fast as she'll turn."

The helmsman jammed the steering yoke right to its stop. "Hard right rudder, aye. Answers ahead all flank."

"Fire control, firing point procedures."

"Fire control, aye."

Seawolf burst forward at top speed, turning as fast as her mighty engines could push her. Pivoting around through a full 180 degrees, she turned back on her pursuer. All over *Seawolf* men grabbed handholds to fight the pull of the tight turn. MacKenzie needed both hands on the railing to hold himself steady as *Seawolf* came around.

"Passing zero eight zero," Randall announced. "Steady on new course zero nine zero."

"Contact dead ahead. Range four hundred yards and closing."

"Very well. Sonar, maintain max power. Continuous ping."

"Sonar, aye."

"Maintain present depth, Mr. Randall," MacKenzie ordered. *Akula* was at four hundred feet. Where would she go with *Seawolf* coming right at her? Probably dive deep to avoid collision and give herself room to escape their torpedoes.

"Torpedo Room, enable torpedoes for the deep zone. Unit one for seven hundred feet. Unit three for one thousand."

"Conn, Sonar. We're hitting them, Skipper. Full contact at max power."

"Keep it up, Sonar."

MacKenzie pictured *Akula*'s control room. Things ought to be pretty hairy in there right about now.

Akula

Kalik and all of the others in the control room had covered their ears in pain when *Seawolf*'s sonar first began raking them. He was furious. One minute he had a perfect shot straight into a slow and unsuspecting *Seawolf*'s tail, and the next the sea was exploding with noise and he had lost his contact. How could the American have known *Akula* was behind him? "Sonar, what is their new course?" he demanded.

"Comrade Captain, we are still having trouble hearing with this noise. It is a nightmare. The sonar operator is bleeding from the ears."

"Get another operator, damn it. What were they doing?"

"They were coming around hard at top speed."

Coming around? They were coming right back at him! *Seawolf*'s captain was using a tactic Kalik himself had used many times on Americans, suddenly doubling back on your own course to see if anyone was following you. The enemy had to get out of your way or risk collision. It was a double bind, for as soon as they moved, if your sonar was quick, you could hear them. *Seawolf* must have acquired the contact and was now roaring back on him while Kalik was blinded by the noise from his sonars and the high-speed maneuvering—and all the while *Phoenix* was slipping farther out of the area with *Red Dawn* in tow. But he had to deal with *Seawolf* first.

"Comrade Captain, we may have a very faint contact bearing two nine five. It is uncertain, but—"

Kalik jumped at it. "Weapons Center, prepare to fire on Sonar's contact. Helm, as soon as the torpedo is released, steer hard left rudder. We'll shoot, then move at maximum speed up into the shallow zone. Let this clever captain come at us. We'll fire on his track and escape right over him."

"Comrade Captain, Weapons Center reporting a lock on target."

"Set torpedoes for five hundred feet," Kalik said confidently. "Flood tubes one and three and open outer doors."

"Ready to fire, Comrade Captain."

"Fire tubes one and three."

"Torpedoes away."

"Full rise on both planes. Take us up into the shallow zone."

Seawolf

Betting his adversary would avoid the collision by diving deep, Mac set his torpedoes to enable—to become active—four and six hundred feet below *Akula*'s last position. "Fire Control. Firing point procedures."

"Ship ready. Weapon ready. Tubes ready. Solution ready."

"Match sonar bearings and shoot."

"Set. Stand by. Fire tube one!"

"Set. Stand by. Fire tube three!"

MacKenzie waited. Sonar tracked the shoot. If *Akula* went deep they had her.

"Conn, Sonar. Our torpedoes running hot and straight. Wait . . . Captain, two additional high-cycle motors! Torpedoes from *Akula* on course two nine five. They're headed for the knuckle. No danger."

MacKenzie nodded. *Akula* had fired on the only contact he had given them, a batch of bubbles. Now it was time to see if his own shots ran true.

"Akula sweeping active. God, somebody must have steel ears. Both fish converging on your knuckle . . . trailing off . . . lost contact."

MacKenzie wasted no time in self-congratulations. A

burst of bubbles from his propeller to fool enemy sonar wasn't going to confuse this captain for very long. He had to engage him again, had to keep him too busy to go after *Phoenix.*

"What about our fish, Sonar?"

"No explosions . . . trailing off . . . Lost them both, Captain. No contact."

"Where did *Akula* go?"

"We can't be certain, sir. Bear thinks they might have gone up into the shallow zone. We got some bow noise. They could be turning."

Santiago looked up from his charts. *"Phoenix* is more than halfway to the ice keel, Skipper. Three thousand yards left. Nine minutes remaining."

Polar Ice Cap

Justine would never think of hell as hot again. It was cold, like this, and ghostly white from top to bottom without respite. She looked behind her. Only Greene, Jackson, Burke, and one other SEAL named Pollard were left. They shambled after her like mummies wrapped in tattered cloth. She could barely see their faces through the ice crust, but mottled blotches of dead skin told the story. The end was near.

It was beginning not to matter. She had no more strength. I'm sorry, Mac, she said to herself. There was only so much you could do. She thought of all the others who were gone now, especially Captain Hansen, brave men just frozen shapes on the ice cap now. Ashes to ashes . . . to ice.

And now the wolves. She had been hearing them for a while now and had occasionally seen them circling, moving steadily closer, their howls merging with the crying of the wind. There was nothing she could do but keep moving and hope the wolves found other prey. But every time a howl penetrated the storm, Justine felt a hot liquid fear in her that no reasoning could quell.

She was so deeply engrossed in pushing herself onward that the noise of the icebreakers penetrated her consciousness slowly and it took a while for her to realize that the crashing noise she was hearing came from the other side of the big pressure ridge right in their path. So close. She would have shouted with triumph if she'd had the strength. But she couldn't. Fate was too cruel. They had made it through the storm only to face what her tired mind thought were statues, until pink tongues suddenly slavered slickly over dark gums, and fear clutched her anew.

The wolves had come. They were staring steadily from an ice shelf jutting out of the pressure ridge. She stood as still as she could, swaying on her feet from exhaustion. The fierce red eyes fixed hungrily on her. People were wrong, she decided. There is no limit to fear.

Greene, Jackson, Burke, and Pollard came up behind her, puzzled she had stopped. "What?" they mumbled. For too long now her moving feet had been their only guide.

"Ships . . . on the other side." Her voice was a harsh wheeze. She tried to make her frozen lips work. "Wolves . . . there."

Jackson sank to his haunches, shaking his head weakly. Greene said nothing. It was too much. The wolves eyed them without moving. Wind rustled their thick white fur. Clumps of snow stuck to them. They had time and they knew it. Why hurry for dead men?

"Stay together," Justine whispered, her throat a dry fiery thing. "They'll go for stragglers. We need something to fight with, anything . . . weapons."

The first wolf got up and moved sleekly to one side, shaking its furry head. Suddenly its lips twisted back in a snarl. It sank lower, growling in a low, menacing tone.

She felt a snap as Greene broke something off her back. "Here," he said, handing her an icicle at least a foot long. It had a dagger-sharp point. He shrugged. "There's nothing else."

He broke another off Jackson's back. Pollard and Burke swayed alongside her, not knowing what to do next. The sound of the breakers was a low and steady crashing.

"You hear that?" Justine said bitterly. "They're just over this ridge. So close. We would have made it."

The second wolf slid to one side watchfully. Its mouth held hot yellow teeth.

"Maybe . . . make a run for it," said Jackson.

Greene shook his head. "They'll be all over us. Last stand. Here."

"So close," Jackson whispered weakly. "Jesus, behind us—"

Justine turned. Two more wolves were stalking them twenty yards away. They were caught in between. She hefted the icicle, feeling its weight in her hand. She tried to summon the battle rage one last time. One last time. Where was her strength? They had come so close, had almost beaten the ice cap. She cursed the wolves, hissing at their unblinking, measuring gazes. "You come to *me!*"

She felt Greene's back press up against hers. "That's the spirit, ma'am." His eyes were dark shadows in deep wells. "But like the Indians say, it's a good day to die, eh?"

Jackson, Burke, and Pollard backed up to them. Strength fading, they all stood together like some ancient phalanx, back to back, ice knives glistening in the diffused white light of the storm, waiting for the wolves to charge.

C-130

Pilot Mick Halperin had been fighting the storm for hours to stay over the area. He had never seen weather like this. "I'm going down," he said, bringing his plane lower.

"We can't take much more pounding," pronounced his tired copilot, Bob Polansky.

"I know," Mick agreed, taking a long pull of hot coffee. It was the only thing propping up his worn-out eyes. "Maybe this time we'll see something. I didn't stay up here this long to go back empty-handed."

"Anybody else would've been back in the barn a long time ago." Polansky squinted out the cockpit window as the plane dropped through the snow. He watched the wings. There was enough ice on them to start a skating rink. "We're getting serious ice buildup, Mick."

"Wind's shifting. May be able to see better now."

"Last call, Mick," Polansky said. He shifted around for a better view as Mick brought the plane down even lower. It was true. With the shift in wind, visibility was better. "Look, there are the breakers!"

"I see 'em. Okay, that's where they're supposed to be headed. Look for the people. They've gotta be real close by now."

Polansky grabbed a pair of binoculars hanging overhead. Mick dived low over the ice cap. To Polansky's anxious eyes he almost skimmed the surface. "Jesus, watch it, Mick."

The C-130 swooped low over the ice. Polansky fought the g-force and fixed his binoculars on the ice cap. "Hey! I think I see something. Mick, you hear me? Somebody's out there!"

Seawolf

"Skipper, two thousand yards. Six minutes remaining."

"Very well. Helm, right full rudder. Steer course one eight zero. Swing her fast. Maintain your depth, Mr. Randall."

Sonar was still pumping out a racket, and Seawolf's high-speed maneuvers dumped even more sound into the sea. With the ice cap bouncing it all around, it was still too noisy out there for either ship to hear anything clearly. Six minutes left. His adversary was not without his own tricks. He had outmaneuvered Seawolf by going up into the shallow zone to escape the torpedoes. MacKenzie would remember that.

"Navigation, your best estimate of Akula's last depth, course, and speed."

"Somewhere around fifty meters, heading west at around twenty knots."

MacKenzie frowned. *Akula* heading west was too likely to pick up *Phoenix*. "Sonar, report your contacts."

"Sonar reports no contacts, Skipper."

"Conn, Communications. C-One-thirty overhead reports spotting people on the ice."

Concentrating on *Akula,* MacKenzie almost missed it. It registered a half second later and he pounced on it. "Communications, this is the captain. Repeat that."

"C-One-thirty pilot reports seeing people out on the ice less than a mile from the breakers. That's good news, sir."

There was no way to know if it was Justine, but MacKenzie felt hope burn away his fatigue. If any of them had survived the ice cap, Justine would be among them. He uttered a silent prayer. God, let her make it to the breakers. He had to get through this first. But if Justine was safe . . .

"Helm, shift your rudder and steady on course two seven zero. All ahead flank. Make our depth three zero zero feet, Mr. Randall."

"Conn, Sonar. Possible contact bearing one eight zero, speed ten knots, range three thousand yards. Very faint. In the middle zone, Skipper."

MacKenzie saw he'd guessed wrong about the depth again. "Torpedo Room, enable torpedoes in tubes two and four for middle zone. Two five zero feet."

"Resetting torpedoes for middle zone, aye."

"Helm, continue left with hard left rudder to course one eight zero. Head right for him. Sonar, keep raking him max power."

"Sonar, aye."

Seawolf turned onto *Akula's* track and accelerated to top speed. MacKenzie had no intention of stopping. The trick in playing chicken was never to give your adversary the slightest idea that you would get out of the way first, that you would ever stop. He had to believe in his deepest soul that you were just one damn minute crazier than he was.

"Conn, Sonar. He hears us, Skipper. He's running. Hard left turn back up into the shallow zone. New course one three five. Contacts! Mines, Skipper. They've released mines."

"Emergency deep. Shift your rudder. Countermeasures, release noisemakers."

"Countermeasures, aye. Noisemakers away."

Seawolf dived hard. Seconds passed grimly. "Popping all over the sea, Skipper," Sonar reported. "Mines are armed, and are all mooring at three hundred meters. There goes one. And another."

MacKenzie grinned happily. More sound, just what they needed to hide *Phoenix*. Just a little while longer. *Phoenix* was almost to the keel. On the other side, Phil Arlin would have its natural properties to protect him, and the marginal ice zone was just hours away. "All ahead two-thirds."

"All contacts accounted for. We're clear, sir."

"Very well. Mr. Santiago, he's moving hard on course one three five. Plot us an intercept course to engage him again."

Santiago worked feverishly for a few seconds. "Steer to course zero seven zero."

MacKenzie gave the order, "All ahead flank. Bring us back up to four zero zero feet. That should take us above the mines. Let's stay on her. *Phoenix* isn't out of danger yet."

Akula

"Explosions, Comrade Captain. No merge."

Kalik cursed under his breath. He couldn't get away from the American, and nothing he did seemed to stop him. He moved to where Volkov was studying the undersea charts along with the navigator and looked them over closely. Where might *Phoenix* be heading?

"We've got to get ahead of him, Viktor. Too much more of this and *Phoenix* will escape with *Red Dawn*. We must think like he does." He let his eyes wander over the tracings. Sound. Sound was the key. How else could his adversary plan to make sound work for him? "You know, Viktor, I think the American captain knows he cannot keep up this racket forever. He's running at high speed with his own sonars at maximum power, making it hard for him to see.

He faces a high risk of running right into a mine or an ice keel or failing to hear us and taking a torpedo. So he plans this noise for a limited time. But until what? Now look at this. Here."

"Big ice keels. Several hundred feet down. And this one, here, almost to a thousand. They would make a very good wall for sound. Is that what you're thinking?"

Kalik nodded. "If I were in his shoes I might be kicking up all this fuss to put big keels like these in between *Phoenix* and us. Once they're on the other side we would lose their sound completely."

"We would have to be very lucky to hear them at this range," agreed Volkov.

"So he'll come at us again to keep up the noise," Kalik said, drumming his fingers against the chart. "You can be sure of that. Any time now."

His words seemed prophetic. Sonar's anxious voice rang out, "Contact, Comrade Captain. *Seawolf* is coming fast on an intercept course. High-cycle motors. Torpedoes fired!"

Kalik came to a decision. "We're faster than she is, and we can dive deeper. We'll outrun them. Emergency deep. Take us down to our maximum depth. Level off at seven hundred meters. Helm, prepare to reverse course to two seven zero as soon as we lose our pursuers." He grabbed the periscope housing as *Akula* dived hard and fast.

"Contact's fading, Comrade Captain."

Kalik nodded. "Viktor, I think we'll find *Phoenix* and *Red Dawn* heading for those keels. Helm, bring your rudder to left full and steady on course two seven zero. All ahead full."

Polar 8

A worried Renaud slid back onto the bridge and shook the snow off his parka. "Captain, they're coming up fast. I think they must be back to making four knots."

Polar 8 was still on course attempting to cross *Ural's* projected track. Maré picked up the bridge phone. "I'll be damned if I'm going to let her cut us off." His practiced eye took in the distances. "Engine Room, this is the captain. I want every bit of steam we've got. Every last bit. Navigation, how close are we to that keel?"

"Less than three hundred yards, Captain."

"How thick is the ice ahead of us, Mr. Renaud?"

Renaud was glued to the big bridge window with his binoculars. "Looks thick. At least ten feet."

"Increase our speed to six knots," Maré ordered. "The engines can take it."

"We're going to hit that keel awfully hard," Renaud warned. "We might split the ice cap in this area.

"No ship half our size is going to run us off course."

Renaud felt a powerful surge under his feet. Fresh black smoke poured out of *Polar 8*'s stacks. The engine room gang was pushing her hard in response to Maré's orders. Even through the thick snow he could pick out the pressure ridge on the ice ahead. A hill of big tumbled blocks of ice rose almost fifteen feet high, the result of two big ice plates grinding together hard enough to protrude above the ice cap.

It was going to be close. Like Maré, Renaud felt his pride and his competitive spirit rising within him. He wasn't about to turn back now either.

"We can make it, Captain," Renaud said gamely. "If the ice holds, we'll make it."

Polar Ice Cap

Justine crouched low, ice knife ready. There was something deep and primordially terrifying about facing a hungry animal. She'd known two-hundred-pound guerrillas who wouldn't balk at facing armed men of equal size but who would cower at the charge of a forty-pound dog. She forced herself to stay calm. She was fast and she'd been using a knife since she was twelve. Forget the fear. Focus.

The wolf crept toward her, a sleek shape in the falling

snow. She shifted her weight to the balls of her feet. She felt clumsy in the heavy boots. Behind her she heard a rush of feet and felt emptiness where Pollard had been. She heard growling and screams . . . and willed herself not to hear. There was only *her* wolf. *Her* wolf stood between her and the pressure ridge and the safety of the icebreakers on the other side.

Her wolf sprang. She leaped to one side, slashing up with the point of the icicle, trying for its exposed underside. The point hit home, but the wolf sailed past. The wound wasn't deep enough. She rolled across the ice and struggled to her feet to meet the next charge.

She wiped a sleeve across her eyes to clear them of snow. Half blinded, she failed to spot the flying mass of fur until it was too late. It landed on her chest and knocked her down. Sharp teeth closed on her arm. Only the thick clothing saved her, blunting the wolf's bite. Every instinct screamed for her to push the slavering wild beast away as it clawed at her, but she realized that if she let it free it would just attack her again. Instead, she wrapped her arms around it and hugged it to her with all her strength, plunging the icicle deep into its side. The wolf clawed at her legs and bit wildly, but she held on to it and drove the icicle in again and again.

Blood stained the snow red, the only color on an all-white canvas, and the wolf went slack in her arms. Weakly, she let it drop to the red-splattered snow. Adrenaline pumped her up past the pain and fatigue. Twenty feet away, she saw that Greene and Jackson had killed a second wolf. Blood ebbed from lacerations on Greene's face and neck, but his powerful arms were locked around the beast's neck. Justine realized he had probably broken its neck.

Burke hadn't been so skilled or so lucky. He was a lifeless bundle on the ice that the remaining pair of wolves tore at. His body jerked like a rag doll as their teeth rent his clothing to get at the warm flesh. Justine looked away, sickened.

Greene, Jackson, and Pollard stumbled into a run. Greene pulled at her. "He's past all caring. Come on. Over the ridge."

Justine ran. The pressure ridge was at least fifteen feet

high. She tried to vault up to the shelf the wolves had been on, but it was too high. Greene went down on one knee. "Up on my leg. Quick."

She put a foot onto his bent leg and climbed. It was almost enough. Her fingers reached over the lip of the shelf, but suddenly there wasn't any support under her and she tumbled back into space with the frightening sounds of snarling wolves all around her.

Greene was down, and one of the wolves had sunk its teeth into his leg. He writhed in agony, beating at it in vain. Others had pounced on Pollard and Jackson. A wolf leaped at Justine, but she darted aside, pushing off the ice and righting herself. She found her balance, stepped in, and kicked the wolf on Greene as hard as she could. She heard the gratifying sound of broken ribs. The animal yelped and released Greene, but the move had given the remaining wolf time to charge. It landed on her back with all its weight, and she went down hard. The wolf tore at her with teeth and claws, a berserk fury she could not dislodge. She got her hands over her face and tried to roll away, but it was no use. It clung to her, biting deeply. She felt its teeth tear into her skin through the parka. She managed to get a hand in its fur and execute a throw. It spun across the ice, paws skidding, but she had done no real damage. It stalked back toward her, muzzle low, teeth bloody, snarling.

Justine knew she was going to die. She didn't have the strength even to lift herself off the ice. The snow felt good on her hot forehead. She was glad it was snowing hard. It would cover her like a blanket. She felt the sticky wetness of her own blood soak her skin. The icicle was long gone. She put her hands up in a last futile gesture of defiance as the wolf charged . . .

The man flowed across her vision like a wraith. His movements had the flawless grace of a dancer, and he executed his strike as perfectly as anything she had ever seen. From out of nowhere the man seemed to *flow* under the wolf as it leaped, and he thrust the razor-sharp steel point of his ski pole straight up. It caught the wolf in its vulnerable belly in midair. The yelp of pain ended almost as it began, and only a lifeless mass of red and white fur landed on Justine. She pushed it off her, looking dazedly around in the snow for the man who had saved her life.

It took a second for her to realize that he was wearing the arctic gear of a Soviet naval officer, but that wasn't what entranced her. The man had already sent the wolves on Pollard and Jackson fleeing and was moving toward Greene with a speed and grace on the ice she wouldn't have believed possible. He seemed to drift over to where the battered and bloody SEAL was fighting to keep the wolf's teeth and claws from his face. They were wrestling furiously, and Greene was almost at his end.

The Russian slid in like a bullfighter and drove his ski pole down once, sharply. The wolf arched his back as if hit by a cattle prod and rolled off Greene. It bit at the air, snarling at the Russian. Not so much faster, but more smoothly than anyone she had seen on ice, the Russian flashed in and struck it sharply on the hindquarters with his ski pole a second time. The wolf yelped in pain and backed up, still growling but less sure this time. Justine finally understood what the Russian was up to. He didn't want to kill it. He wanted it to give up! He hefted the ski pole again threateningly and the wolf scampered off. The Russian seemed satisfied.

Greene was torn and bleeding, in shock. He couldn't get to his feet. Jackson wasn't in much better shape, and Pollard's face was a mask of frozen blood. The Russian hefted Greene over his shoulder in a fireman's carry. He looked to Justine, searched for words, and seemed to find them. He pointed to the ridge. "Dees way. *Da?* Dees way."

"Who are you?"

"Stephan. . . . Speak only little English," he added shyly.

She pointed to herself. "Justine. And thank you."

But Stephan was pointing at the ridge again.

"You bet your life," she said. The world was reeling around her. She had to wait for the waves of blackness to pass. She was light-headed from fatigue and loss of blood.

She and Jackson helped Stephan heft the semiconscious Greene and the depleted Pollard up onto the shelf on the pressure ridge. Then Stephan helped her and Jackson up. She lay there panting while Stephan climbed up the ice wall after them.

It was evident Greene could go no farther. Justine looked to Stephan. He took a deep breath and hefted Greene over his shoulders again. Pollard and Jackson got to their feet weakly. Justine was fading fast, but she got a hand over the top of the pressure ridge, found traction, and scampered over. The rest followed.

The sound hit her like a physical thing. She was so totally unprepared for the sight of the huge icebreaker towering high above her, steaming right toward the ridge, that she almost fell backwards. It flew the Canadian flag, and *Polar 8* was stenciled on its prow. Stephan reached out to steady her. He peered into the snow surveying the situation, and she could tell he didn't like what he saw. But how could he see anything in this blinding snow? She tried to follow his gaze. There was too much snow. Suddenly a big gust of wind shifted the heavy snowfall, and she was able to see the reason for his concern. A second, smaller icebreaker with Soviet markings was steaming up on the big Canadian ship that had apparently crossed the Russian's bow.

Unable to see the *Polar 8* through the snow, the Russian icebreaker was on a collision course.

Stephan was already sliding down the ridge as the snow closed in again. *Polar 8's* sound this close was enough to make Justine physically sick as its sharp prow cut through the ice toward them. She could feel the intense vibrations through her boots. They had to get out of the way. She ran with Pollard and Jackson as fast as she could after Stephan, not knowing or caring where he was leading, desperate to get away from the ridge before the icebreaker crashed into it.

On it came, devouring the ice. She couldn't believe the Russian ship didn't see the *Polar 8* ahead or, worse, that perhaps it did and wouldn't stop. They would surely collide. There was no room. Justine knew no icebreaker in the world could break through a ridge like the one she had just crossed.

Ahead of her Stephan pulled a radio from his parka, extending the antenna as he ran. The *Ural* was still back far enough for him to prevent the crash if he notified it in time. They almost made it, but the ice betrayed them.

The Canadian icebreaker rammed the pressure ridge at full speed. Pummeled by the huge ship and the vibrations of both icebreakers, the ice shifted and buckled. A spiderweb of cracks spread out from the ridge. An open lead appeared just ahead of Stephan, and he didn't see it till it was too late. Overbalanced by Greene's weight on his shoulders he fell hard. The radio slid into the open chasm and was lost to sight. Stephan sprawled forward sliding toward the hole.

Stephan heroically thrust his charge from him. Greene slid out on the ice away from the lead. Justine dived for Stephan and managed to grab his parka. She dug her feet in and held on with all her strength, stopping his fatal slide toward the icy gray water just as his legs dangled over the edge of the ice sheet.

She might have been able to pull him out if the ice hadn't continued to shift, but under the force of the breakers a new pressure ridge was building beside the old one, and a huge plate of ice shifted and climbed over the open lead trapping Stephan's legs under it. She saw his face go white and heard the awful sound of bones breaking. For a moment she thought she had lost him altogether, but the plate rose momentarily, releasing the limp and broken body.

Justine dug in and pulled with everything she had. Pollard and Jackson were trapped on the other side of the open lead, too far away to help. Stephan had saved their lives and had almost given his own to save Greene a second time. She wasn't about to let him slide into the icy waters. She managed to pull him a few feet out of the lead. She held on. Her fingers cramped and she had no more to give, but she held on. It wasn't enough. She was losing him. He slipped toward the emptiness. . . .

Another set of hands took hold. It was Greene. Pale-faced and sweating he had managed to crawl back to help her haul the battered Stephan out of the way. Together they yanked him out of the crevice seconds before the ice plate came crashing down and snuffed the open lead out of existence.

Greene collapsed beside her, done in. Justine knew he had nothing left to give.

Stephan was almost delirious with pain. His broken legs were bent at a sickening, unnatural angle but he managed to raise a hand and point toward the *Ural.* "My ship . . . tell them. . . . You . . . you go . . . up line." He tore a naval insignia from his parka and pressed it into her hands. His eyes were imploring. *"Pazhalsta*—please—climb."

Justine hoped she understood him. Some kind of lifeline must be trailing from the ship. Would she have the strength to climb it? Pollard and Jackson arrived at her side. "Take care of them," she ordered. "I'll be back."

She took off over the ice. She owed the Russian too much to let his ship founder without trying to save it. The thick snow obscured the icebreaker, barely a quarter of a mile away, but as she got close, she could make it out well enough. It was half the size of the Canadian ship and still coming on fast. In a flash of understanding she realized several things. Of course, they must have been depending on Stephan out on the ice to lead them, and for reasons she might never know he had chosen to leave his post and help her and the others. Judging from the track in the ice the larger ship had changed course only a few hundred yards back. Without a danger signal from Stephan the Russian ship was plowing on unaware of the *Polar 8* ahead.

Justine knew she was running on nerve alone because her body was exhausted. Tenacity. One foot in front of the other. Too many lives were at stake to quit now. The noise was a steady thing that pounded at her. This close to the Russian ship it sounded like the legions of hell were screaming.

She saw the line. It hung from the bow of the ship and trailed onto the ice. She squinted up to the main deck. It was at least a sixty-foot climb, and it would take her out over open water when the rope swung back against the ship. If she fell, she would die. Plain and simple.

She wrapped the rope around her leg and started to climb. It was a nightmare. She pulled herself up one arm's length at a time, releasing the rope around her legs and grabbing it again with her legs to help her tired arms support her. Snow caked on her face, and she had no hands to wipe it off. Once more. Halfway. Keep going. Once more . . .

When she was about thirty feet up, her weight swung the rope toward the hull and slammed her against it. The metal hit her shoulder like a sledgehammer. It took her breath away. She lost her grip. She slid down, frantically trying to arrest her fall, biting the rope with her teeth, anything to stop her slide. She finally stopped herself and spun slowly in midair.

She climbed again. She heard voices. She ignored them. Once more. Release your legs, pull up, grab hold. There was nothing else but moving up one pull at a time. She pulled with all her strength. She felt the hull slide by with increasing speed without realizing what it meant. She pulled again . . . and tumbled over the bow railing onto the main deck, drawn up and over by six astonished Russian seamen.

A man with captain's stripes, wearing a thick parka, elbowed his way through the crowd. A well of blackness was fast engulfing her. "Do you speak English?" she managed.

The captain stared, open-mouthed. "*Da.* Yes, I do."

Justine smiled. "Good. Your Stephan and some of my men are badly hurt on the ice. Over there," she pointed. "And you are about to crash into the Canadian icebreaker dead ahead of you."

She was about to suggest he stop his ship right away, but that seemed redundant. Besides, the warm blackness was too thick now to shut out. She closed her eyes and dropped down into it gladly, and from a long distance away she heard the yells of men and loud alarms ringing out.

Akula

"We're approaching the ice keel, Comrade Captain," reported the navigator.

"Take us up to two hundred meters. Twenty-degree up

angle." Kalik stepped into the sonar room and leaned over his operator. "Have you located *Phoenix?* I'm certain they are in this area."

The sonarman held his headphones pressed tightly against his ears. "The noise is less here. . . ." He listened and turned up the gain. Suddenly his face changed. "We have a faint contact, Comrade Captain. It could be *Phoenix* and *Red Dawn*. It is bearing . . . Comrade Captain!" He tore his headphones off in pain, and his hands went to his head. "My God! What is that?"

The sonar technician grabbed the headphones and held them near his own ear. A wicked screech like electronic feedback emanated from them. His face registered confusion for a few seconds. Then he looked at Kalik and shook his head sadly. "There is an icebreaker directly overhead. This is their propeller noise. I believe they rammed the pressure ridge over the keel and are churning their propellers continually. It is unlikely they can break through or that they really plan to. Their purpose is to make more noise. And between the ice breaking and the propellers . . . I'm sorry, Comrade Captain. It creates more sound than we can sift through. We could not isolate *Phoenix* in this racket if it were right alongside us."

Kalik heard the news and knew that once more he was one step behind the American captain. Under cover of the breaker's noise, *Phoenix* and *Red Dawn* would sail past the ice keel undetected. The distance they would gain on him made it virtually impossible for Kalik to pick up her trail again.

It added a new chapter to the combat as an old one ended. Red Dawn was gone. But there was still a price to pay, and he vowed to himself that the clever American captain would pay it. *Red Dawn* had divided his attention too long. Now there was nothing but the two of them in their warships under the ice cap, and that was what Kalik knew best.

He walked back into the control room and called Volkov to him. "We have lost *Red Dawn*, Viktor. There is too much noise. We can't track her, and I have little hope of picking her up again before she makes the marginal ice zone."

Volkov took the news stoically. "Then it's time we headed home."

"No. Not empty-handed," Kalik said fiercely.

"Vassily," Volkov said softly, "the day is not ours."

"The day is not over. Comrade Navigator, return us to the other side of the keel. And take us deep. Viktor, do you still stand with me?"

Volkov met his gaze. "As always, Comrade Captain."

"Then let us finish what we started out to do."

Chapter
Eighteen

Conn, Sonar. *Polar 8* is banging away at the pressure ridge and making enough noise to mask the entire area. Sounds like Times Square on New Year's Eve out there. No word of our people yet, Skipper."

"Very well. Signal them to keep those props churning. Steer course two seven zero. Let's stay nearby. Just in case."

"Aye, Skipper."

MacKenzie walked over to the navigation table. *Phoenix* should be well past the keels. He studied the chart as they all waited tensely for Phil Arlin's signal.

"Ten thousand yards. Thirty minutes," Santiago announced jubilantly. "They should be on the other side, Skipper."

MacKenzie wasn't relaxing yet, not until he heard from *Phoenix*. The Russian captain might guess about the keels and pursue—and anybody could get lucky. Until *Phoenix* reported they were safely out of the area, nothing was a certainty. Additionally, his concern about the survivors on the ice weighed heavily on him. The pilot of the C-130 had reported he'd lost track of them in the storm. He was still circling, looking for them, hoping to land if he spotted them. MacKenzie had no way of knowing why the survivors hadn't made it to the *Polar 8* yet. He just had to force himself to trust that they would, and that Justine would be among them. Anything else diverted his attention from the battle at hand.

"Conn, Communications. This from *Phoenix*. 'All clear. Proceeding to MI zone with caboose intact. Many thanks. Arlin.' Congratulations, Skipper."

There were cheers in the conn, and MacKenzie grinned with relief. They had done it. *Red Dawn* and *Phoenix* were well on their way.

"Communications, tell *Polar 8* to give it fifteen more minutes and then break off. Repeat our request for immediate notification if they pick up any of our party. Send our thanks."

Tom Lasovic came over. "Nice work, Mac."

"Thanks, Tom." MacKenzie fought the lassitude relief brought, resisted the need to let his guard down now that the first part of their mission was over. It had been a harrowing thirty minutes. He looked at his XO and said with a certainty that surprised him. "But that was only round one. I'm as sure of it as I am that the sun will rise tomorrow. *Akula* will be back."

"Let her come," said Lasovic. "At least *Red Dawn* is safe."

Red Dawn

Galinin leveled the gun at Ivanna, in his own warped way having offered her a token of his repect—a quick death instead of the horror of drowning when he scuttled the ship.

Desperate to dissuade him, Ivanna faced the bloody captain and tried to reach a part of him that would balk at following suicidal orders. "What about Captain Kalik? How do you know he isn't coming to our rescue?"

Galinin shook his head sadly. "It has been over an hour since the towing began. If he were going to attack *Phoenix* he would have done so by now. I'm sorry. I cannot count on any reprieve from *Akula.*"

Ivanna's shoulders sagged. A few hours more and they would have been out from under this godforsaken ice cap. After all they had been through, including Pytor's sacrifice, safety was so near. It was too cruel. "I don't want to die," she said, glancing toward the open hatch.

"Forget about running," Galinin commanded, moving quickly between her and the open door. He had to take his eyes off her for a split second to avoid the water buckets, but he was as agile as a big cat and the gun never wavered from her even as he stepped over them. "No one wants to die." He shrugged. "It can't be helped." He cocked the hammer and leveled the sights on her heart.

Ivanna timed it perfectly. The bar of irinium she had palmed out of her coveralls in the brief moment he had taken his eyes off her spun out of her hand in a perfect arc and landed in the bucket of seawater by Galinin's legs. She dived for cover just as he fired. The blast of heat and toxic fumes rose up like a sorcerer's column of flame and engulfed him. The shot went wild. He dropped the gun and clutched his face, blinded by the steam that scored his flesh. He staggered back and fell into the bulkhead.

Ivanna saw her father leading crewmen down the corridor. "Quick, in here! Father, help!"

The gun slid under one of the diesel engines. Ivanna dropped to the deck and reached desperately for it. It was too far under to reach. Galinin was still clutching his face in agony. She rammed her shoulder against the oily engine reaching as far as she could. Her fingers touched the gun. She hooked one into the trigger guard and it came free. She pulled it to her, looking for Galinin.

He hit her like a football tackle, driving the breath from her body. They tumbled out the hatchway. She got her arms around the hatch's wheel lock, trying to stop her fall into the corridor beyond, but the steel hatch just swung shut behind them. She tried to fire. It was no use. Galinin's big hand encircled her wrists and he plucked the weapon from her hand. He grabbed her by the hair and yanked her to her feet.

"Stop or she dies!" he yelled at the approaching men, shoving the gun into her side harshly. Ivanna winced in

315

pain. Galinin's eyes were bloodshot orbs in a burned and bleeding face.

The crewmen stopped short, milling behind Ligichev. "Let her go," Ligichev said quietly. "There are too many of us to stop."

"If you move I will shoot her."

Ligichev sighed. "Remember I told you about logic? What choice do you offer us? Either way she dies."

"Time, that's what I offer." Galinin looked at him intently. "Can you be the one to sign her death warrant? You are stronger than I thought, Comrade Chief Scientist. But are you that strong?" He reached behind him and tried to turn the wheel lock. The crewmen surged forward.

"Wait," commanded Ligichev.

The wheel would not turn. "Blast you, I forgot about the electric lock." A sudden wicked smile crossed Galinin's features. "But it was you who gave me the combination, remember?" He pressed the keypad.

"I warn you, Galinin . . ."

Whatever Ligichev was about to say was interrupted as Seaman Boslik broke through the crowd of men and leaped for his captain. "I am not going to die! Follow me!"

"No, wait!" shouted Ligichev, but it was too late. Galinin spun and fired, hitting the big seaman in midleap. Boslik fell to the deck with a heavy thud and a hole in his chest. Ligichev dropped to his side and felt for a pulse. He shook his head sadly. "I don't understand you. What kind of captain murders his own crew?"

"In this case, a patriot." Galinin kept the gun leveled at them as he held Ivanna tightly. "Now, are there any more heroes?"

The crewmen backed up uncertainly. Boslik's body lay on the deck between them and Galinin, mute proof of rash action. A scant five yards separated them, but no one dared to cross it. Galinin stepped back and reached for the keypad a second time. Still holding Ivanna, he punched in the combination that would open the engine room hatch and let him put an end to *Red Dawn*.

Akula

"Comrade Captain, the icebreaker is no longer churning its propellers. Sonar is operating normally again."

"Scan the area for contacts," ordered Kalik.

Phoenix and *Red Dawn* were long gone. Kalik had returned *Akula* to the other side of the keel.

"No contacts, Comrade Captain."

It was just the two of them now. *Seawolf's* captain had surely lost *Akula* in all that noise, just as he had lost *Seawolf*. Now each was trying to pick up the other's trail to maneuver for a clean shot. Where would the American captain go? What was his next plan? The man was cunning and resourceful, a better opponent than anyone Kalik had ever faced. But he had to make a mistake sooner or later.

"Viktor, what was the American's last course?"

"One eight zero. He made his attack run straight at us and fired two torpedoes."

"Come here, Viktor." Kalik walked over to the navigator's charts and traced his finger along course one eight zero. "This is how he came at us. He fired . . . here. If he acted as he usually does he made a hard turn to starboard," Kalik's finger traced the route as he spoke. "That would take him right back to two seven zero to follow *Phoenix* past the keel. Yes, very neat. Even with the breakers putting out all that sound, he wanted to be close in case we found them. Say he held that heading for six minutes or so. Then, when *Phoenix* is out of danger, he turns back to look for us"—his finger stabbed out—"most likely just past the keels in this area here. Comrade Navigator, plot us an intercept course."

"What are you planning, Vassily?"

Kalik explained as the navigator bent to the task. "In all this time the only flaw I have seen in this captain's performance is that signature turn to starboard. He is a genius at thinking into the future, and every time we have come up against him we have failed because he was one step ahead of us. This time we must not allow him time to plan. He mustn't be able to think his way out of the situation. We have to push him hard long enough to make a mistake, just as he did to us with *Phoenix* and *Red Dawn*."

"You want to force him to react the wrong way?"

"That's the key word. React. If he does so incorrectly we will hit him with everything we've got and finish him once and for all." Kalik turned forward. "What is our depth?"

"Seven hundred meters, Comrade Captain."

"Viktor, I think the American went deep, around three hundred and fifty meters, after his last run. But we are already deeper than that and at this low speed we are a hole in the ocean. He can't hear us. So if he's turning back on course zero nine zero searching . . . Comrade Navigator?"

"New heading, Comrade Captain, steer course zero three five. Intercept in three minutes."

"Good. Viktor, we are going to come up under him at flank speed and deliver our torpedoes right into his belly before he knows what hit him. Helm, hard left rudder, steady course zero three five. All ahead flank. Maneuvering, increase speed slowly to flank. Do not cavitate. Acknowledge that."

"Increase speed slowly to flank. No cavitation."

"How do we hear him?" Volkov asked. "We'll be deaf again at that speed."

"I don't need to hear him," Kalik said grimly. "He's there, Viktor. I know it."

The radio officer turned from his console. "Comrade Captain? The *Ural* reports picking up survivors."

"They must be from the base camp, Vassily."

"Good. Tell *Ural* to render all aid. We are not murderers." He hit the intercom. "Torpedo Room, status on all tubes."

"All tubes flooded. We are ready to fire, Comrade Captain."

"Arm torpedoes." Kalik held the thought like a prayer. "He's going to go down deep. Every time he goes deep."

"He's clever. Maybe he is just setting us up."

Kalik ran a hand over his tired face. The American's

patterns. Were they unconscious or a deliberate ruse? If he held to his pattern one more time he would make a hard turn to starboard and dive emergency deep under attack. Kalik knew there were other possibilities, but he had to stop second-guessing himself. He came to a decision. "Set all torpedoes to enable at maximum depth. Open outer doors."

"Outer doors opening."

"Answering all ahead flank," reported the helm.

"Very well."

Akula was at top speed now, racing up from the depths of the icy sea to where Kalik reasoned *Seawolf* would be. Even this fast, without propeller cavitation she was still ultra-quiet and her new reactor used natural-flow cooling, even at this speed, for short periods, so her pumps were shut down as well. As silent and deadly as the shark it was named for *Akula* roared up under the dangling legs of its prey, jaws open and hungry.

"Attack Center, fire all tubes on course track zero three five."

"Torpedoes away."

Four torpedoes leaped from the *Akula*'s tubes and raced for where Kalik prayed *Seawolf* would be. He tapped his fingers on the scope housing impatiently. "Come on. Come on. . . ." *Seawolf* would be picking up the incoming torpedoes any second now and would have to maneuver hard. Then they would betray their position. He had bet everything on this shot. Where the hell were they?

"Comrade Captain, contact bearing one eight zero, range seven hundred meters, depth three hundred. Sudden fast turn count. High-speed maneuvers. It's *Seawolf*. And they're running!"

Kalik pounded his fist on the scope with unsuppressed excitement. "We've got them, Viktor. Helm, right ten degrees rudder. Maintain speed."

"Conn, Sonar. Contacts, Skipper! Four torpedoes in the water bearing two one five! Coming from port to starboard. Range two thousand yards. Their homing sonar is activated."

MacKenzie knew instantly that *Akula* had found him first. He reacted immediately. "Release noisemakers. Hard right rudder. All ahead flank cavitate."

His adversary must have gone very deep and somehow picked up their course track. Where were *Akula*'s torpedoes going to enable? The upper stratum was a poor choice because the ice cap itself confused torpedo sonar. Besides, there were vulnerable breakers up there, one of them Russian. He'd probably try to keep the attack lower than two hundred feet. On the other hand, *Akula* had to be way down deep to sneak up on them like that, well below two thousand feet, an easy depth for the deep-diving sub. That set the upper and lower limits. No captain as competent as this one would risk running into his own torpedoes. MacKenzie figured the fish would be armed to explode between two hundred and, say, sixteen hundred feet. To escape them he either had to go very deep with *Akula* or very shallow with the breakers. He hesitated. His instinct told him to go shallow, but drawing fire toward the surface ships was too dangerous.

"Mr. Randall. Emergency deep. Twenty degrees down bubble. Call out our depth. All ahead flank. Let's get ahead of those fish."

"All ahead flank, aye. Diving hard. One thousand feet. One thousand fifty . . ."

"Conn, Sonar. Two of the torpedoes pursued the noisemakers, Captain. Fading . . . No contact. We lost 'em, Skipper. The other two are right on our tail."

MacKenzie was diving deep to bring *Seawolf* down below the torpedoes' enabling depth, but he needed time to get down there. Maybe he could slow them up. "Sonar, go active. Max power."

"Sonar, aye." Beams of immense acoustic power burst

from *Seawolf* to confuse the torpedoes' tracking sonar. "They're confused, searching . . . searching . . . It's not working, Skipper. They've picked us up again."

"Shift your rudder. Swing her around as fast as she'll turn."

"We have cavitation," Randall reported.

"Sonar, Conn. Are they buying it?"

"Stopping, scanning . . . damn! No, sir. They ran right through the knuckle turbulence. Still coming at us."

"Depth twelve hundred feet. Twelve hundred fifty . . ."

Seawolf's hull groaned and popped from the pressure. The tension in the conn was so thick it was tangible. MacKenzie felt the men's fear as they fought to stay in control—no easy task with death homing in on the sub. "Easy, now," he soothed. "Stay calm. Remember your training. We'll get through this."

"Conn, Sonar. Torpedoes converging . . . thirty seconds to impact."

"Depth twelve hundred feet, Skipper. Twelve hundred fifty . . ."

Seawolf was diving with all its power, but the torpedoes were still gaining. MacKenzie wondered if he could have figured this all wrong. Had the Russian captain outguessed him in the end?

"Twenty seconds to impact."

"Fourteen hundred feet, Skipper."

A small seawater pipe burst from the pressure, spraying icy salt water around the compartment. Men clambered up, only to fall back from the force of the stream. Tom Lasovic managed to reach the main hull valve and force it shut. "Flooding secured, Skipper."

Men gripped their instrument consoles with sweating palms and held their breath. MacKenzie knew he had only seconds left.

"Skipper, they're still coming," said Lasovic. "Try a hard pivot."

"Right. We're going to have to duck and dodge. Helm, on my order, full rise on the bow planes. Pivot her up as fast as she'll go." He grabbed the emergency main ballast tank lever, a gray steel T in the overhead. "Maneuvering, prepare for back emergency. Watch the pressure transient."

"Maneuvering, aye. Don't worry, Skipper. She can handle it."

"Ten seconds to contact. Nine . . . eight . . . seven . . . six . . ."

MacKenzie yanked down the emergency main ballast tank lever for two seconds. Water shot out of the main ballast tanks as fast as the vent holes allowed. It would stop *Seawolf*'s mad plunge. "Maneuvering, back emergency. Full rise on the bow planes. Chief, keep her bow up. Vent main ballast tanks."

"Slowing . . ." yelled Lasovic.

Seawolf came as close as a 9,000-ton object could to a sudden and complete stop. The whine of tortured main engines could be heard throughout the ship, and the hull's popping and groaning rose to a steady thunder. 'All stop!"

"Here it comes. Four . . . three . . . two . . . one. No contact! Captain, the first torpedo shot right by us. It's trailing off . . . turning the wrong way . . . searching."

"Countermeasures, release noisemakers."

"Noisemakers away."

Lasovic looked over to MacKenzie. "Almost to sixteen hundred feet."

"Keep an eye on that first fish." MacKenzie ordered. The torpedo could turn around and come right back at them.

"Conn, explosion. First torpedo detonated. Must have hit a keel, Captain. Second torpedo incoming! Ten seconds."

"Very well." It wasn't over yet. "Emergency deep. All ahead flank."

"Depth fifteen hundred fifty feet," called Randall.

"Conn, Sonar. Here it comes. Six . . . five . . . four . . ."

"Depth sixteen hundred feet."

"We should be below their enabling range, Tom. Helm, we will conduct the same maneuver. Everybody get set—" MacKenzie never completed the command. Even as *Seawolf* dived below what he had figured was its enabling depth the second torpedo struck. Another second or two and it might have missed them like the first, but instead it hit high on the sail, and the explosion rocked the sub as if a tidal wave had shoved it with irresistible force. In the conn, men were thrown out of their chairs and sent reeling into bulkheads. Pipes burst and a steam leak flooded the engineering compartment. Lights dimmed. MacKenzie was knocked off his feet and crashed into an instrument console. His vision darkened. He fought to stay conscious as water poured in from the ruptured sail piping above them.

"Damage control!" MacKenzie yelled. Freezing water rushed over him as he struggled for a handhold and pulled himself to his feet. *Seawolf* was listing badly. "Get back to your positions. Mr. Randall, what's our depth? Mr. Randall!"

"Depth . . . almost there . . ." Randall was climbing into the helmsman's chair. The crewman who should have occupied it was lying on the deck up to his chest in the icy water. Jagged white bone protruded through the sleeve of his torn uniform blouse. MacKenzie sloshed through the flood and helped the white-faced crewman to his feet.

"My arm, Captain." He moaned, teeth chattering from shock and the cold.

"Easy, son. We'll get you help as soon as we can. Help this man out of here. Mr. Randall, depth! Right now."

"Eighteen hundred feet. Ten degree down bubble," Randall said, wiping the water from his face. He was pale and shaking and MacKenzie suddenly saw the reason. Blood stained his torn uniform from a deep gash on his shoulder. "I'm sorry, Mr. Randall. I didn't realize . . ."

Randall followed his gaze. "It's okay, sir. I have the helm."

MacKenzie turned quickly. "Chief of the Watch, emergency blow main ballast." The ship vibrated and responded, indicating most of the main ballast tanks were basically intact. He barked orders. "Secure the blow. All ahead one-third. Vent main ballast tanks to maintain control. Bring us up to three zero zero feet. Chief, do your best to keep her trim. See if you can cure this list." He sloshed back to his station and punched the intercom. The water was still cascading down from above. "Maneuvering, report status. Jake, what's going on back there?"

"I think we're okay, Skipper. Slight steam leak in the auxiliary steam system, but the reactor plant is secure. No damage to main shaft. We're holding out all right. We'll have power when you need it."

"Keep her quiet. Let's not advertise the fact that we can maneuver just yet. Let her drift."

MacKenzie looked around the conn. Brave men reacted to the situation with professionalism that bespoke the best training in the world. The chief and his men carried the wounded helmsman and radio officer out. The second-class radio technician, a boy barely twenty-one, scampered into the radio officer's seat to take over the radio console and began to test it. Randall ripped off his shirt and wadded it over his wound, never releasing his hold on the steering yoke.

"Joe, are you all right?" MacKenzie asked.

Joe Santiago was soaking wet and bleeding from a head wound, but his eyes were clear. "Managing, Skipper." He gave MacKenzie a tentative thumbs-up and bent back to his charts to reestablish their position.

Seawater was still pouring in from the damaged sail piping overhead. It appeared to be controllable, but the compartment was filling fast. The icy brine was up to their shins now. Electronic systems began to short out, and acrid smoke from burning insulation filled the air. Lasovic was up the sail ladder. MacKenzie yelled to him, "Tom, where's that water coming from? What have we got left up there?"

Lasovic had to shout over the noise of the water cascading down. "Two of the mast grease lines that penetrated the hull and the antenna fittings are all blown to hell, Mac. That's where the water's coming in. The upper hatch got blasted right off its hinges. The lower hatch seems to be holding."

"Get it sealed up as best you can. We'll lose the electronics if this flooding continues."

Lasovic grunted and stuck his head and shoulders back under the waterfall to wrestle the hull valves with a heavy crowbar. The muscles of his back bunched with exertion even as he winced from the shocking cold. MacKenzie couldn't imagine what it must be like standing under that flood of ice-cold water trying to plug those leaks with only the hundred-pound lower steel hatch cover holding out the briny deep. But Lasovic never stopped working.

"Captain." It was Randall. "Reporting some difficulty with trim. That blast must have damaged one of the main ballast tanks. We can't take on enough ballast to fully straighten her out. But we are at three zero zero feet and holding."

"Do the best you can, Mr. Randall. All stop. Hover at three zero zero feet."

"Captain, all communications except the underwater telephone are out, sir," the radio technician reported.

MacKenzie acknowledged that. It came as no surprise. Losing the masts meant losing not only communications but both periscopes as well.

"Attack Center, do we have damage reports? Where's Mr. Talmadge?"

One of the other technicians replied. "Mr. Talmadge was knocked out by the blast, sir. I can run things, but I'm not qualified for command."

"Good work, young man. Give me your report."

"The main tubes appear to be undamaged, but all our computers are out. It'll have to be a pretty straight pattern, Skipper. We can't compute anything fancy. But we can shoot if we have to."

"All right, son. Stay in place till I can relieve you." MacKenzie wiped the water off his face. Damn good thing it hadn't been a direct hit on their keel. It would have ripped them in half. Although the damage to the sail was serious, *Seawolf* wasn't crippled. He suddenly realized the sound of water had stopped. He looked up to see a drenched and frozen Lasovic climbing down.

"That's it, Mac. She won't hold forever, but the hatch is back in place for now."

"Fine, Tom. Get some coffee and put on some warm clothes. Then get back here. Chief, keep those main drain pumps working overtime."

"Aye, Skipper."

MacKenzie took stock. They were down, but they weren't out. He had maneuvering and he had limited weapons. Now he needed time to repair the rest of his ship. But with Sonar's next words he knew it was too late for that. Far too late.

"Conn, Sonar. Contact bearing one zero zero. Range one thousand yards. It's *Akula*, Skipper. She's closing fast."

Akula

"Contacts merging . . . We hit her, Comrade Captain! Explosion. One torpedo. Sounds of air escaping and metal breaking. They are slowing."

The men in the control room roared their approval. Volkov threw his arms around Kalik's shoulders and pounded him. "You did it, Vassily! They are down."

Kalik felt fierce exhilaration spread through him. "I told you we wouldn't go home empty-handed. The day is finally ours, Viktor."

"My God, what will Command say when we tell them we sank the newest and best American submarine? This engagement will be talked about for years."

Kalik laughed. "Let's hope so. Then maybe they will want us around and not shoot us for losing *Red Dawn*. Sonar, what is *Seawolf*'s position now?"

"They are drifting, no propulsion. Slowly rising from three hundred meters. Range twelve hundred meters. We hear sound from their drain pumps only."

"They are probably listing badly," Volkov observed. "Sitting ducks."

Kalik felt no glee in what he was about to do. The American was an adversary to be respected, not torn apart with a second salvo of torpedoes. He had never before faced the challenges the American captain had given him. It had been close to the end, the outcome always in doubt. This captain was a warrior. Kalik felt sure they would have liked each other under other circumstances. What a pity to destroy such a brilliant adversary. But *Red Dawn* had sealed both their fates. He either brought back the American's head or sacrificed his own.

"Helm, bring us up to three five zero meters. Weapons Center, match your bearings with Sonar and prepare to fire a second salvo. Full pattern." Kalik steeled himself. There was no other choice. They might be brothers, but only one of them could leave the ice cap alive.

"Prepare to fire."

Seawolf

"Conn, Sonar. They're coming, Skipper. *Akula* is running fast on course two seven zero, range fifteen hundred yards, depth one thousand feet, speed twenty knots."

MacKenzie was thinking hard, picturing the area of engagement in his mind. It was just possible he could pull this out. But there was no room for error and it was now or never. "Navigation, how close are we to that big ice keel we used to hide *Phoenix?*"

Santiago had a cloth pressed to his head to stanch the flow of blood. "Close, Skipper. About five hundred yards behind us. Our drift is taking us back toward it."

"How deep does it go?"

"More than seven hundred feet."

Lasovic had returned in fresh clothing. "What do you have in mind, Mac?"

"When we played Russian roulette before, he surprised me. I never figured he'd go up into the shallow zone. And he did it twice. Maybe we can make him do it again."

"Why?"

"Sorry, Tom. There's no time. You're just going to have to back me."

"Whatever you say, Mac."

"Take charge of Fire Control. Manually flood tubes two and three. Stand by for a simple straight shot."

"Aye, Skipper."

"Conn, Sonar. Range one thousand yards and closing. He's flooding his tubes."

"Keep tracking, Sonar." MacKenzie moved behind Randall. "Now listen to me. We're going to start up, but slowly, like we're barely managing. Nothing sudden. Blow some bubbles, then hold, then go up again. Make it jerky. But keep that ice keel behind us as we rise. Got it?"

"Okay, Skipper. Coming up slow."

"Keep me apprised of our depth."

"Yes, sir. Depth is now two nine zero feet."

"Torpedo Room. Status of tubes two and three."

"Tubes loaded and ready to fire MK-forty-eight torpedoes."

"Open outer doors on tubes two and three. Tom, compute a basic, simple, straight-running shot. Firing point procedures."

"Fire Control, aye."

"Conn, Sonar. Range five hundred yards."

MacKenzie felt himself swept up. *Akula* was approaching fast, thinking *Seawolf* was a sitting duck. The trouble was, if his trick didn't work, *Seawolf* would be. But he needed to keep looking helpless. Any defensive move at all right now would alert *Akula*'s captain and make him break off his attack—and that was the one thing MacKenzie needed him not to do.

"Keep coming," he whispered. "Keep coming."

"Captain, ship ready, solution ready, torpedo room ready."

Akula drew closer, coming straight at them.

"Depth, Mr. Randall."

"Two hundred feet, Captain."

"Conn, Sonar. Range four hundred yards. *Akula*'s opening outer doors. He's getting ready to fire, Skipper. Not much more room."

"Steady," MacKenzie ordered. "Everyone. Not yet. Not

just yet . . ." *Seawolf* rose slowly. MacKenzie could almost feel the presence of the ice keel looming behind them.

"Conn, Sonar. Three hundred yards. *Akula's* come up to a depth of six hundred feet. She's slowing to fire, Captain."

This was it. As good as it was going to get. "Okay, Tom. For all the marbles. Match sonar bearings and shoot tubes two and three."

"Set. Stand by. Fire! Tube-two unit away. Set. Stand by. Fire! Tube-three unit away."

"Go," MacKenzie said fiercely, willing the torpedoes in. "Go!"

Akula

"Comrade Captain, torpedoes in the water! Range two hundred yards. They are not yet active."

Kalik stopped dead in his tracks. He heard but did not believe. "So the American was playing dead. Is there no end to his tricks? Quickly, up and over them. At this range the torpedoes won't even be armed yet." He strode to the helm. "Emergency. Blow all ballast. Take us up, Viktor. Twenty-degree up angle. Engine Room, all ahead flank speed."

Akula shot forward in a burst of speed, rising steadily upward. "Sonar, report!"

"We are rising over the torpedoes, Comrade Captain."

"Depth!"

"We are at five hundred feet, Comrade Captain."

"Sonar, where are those torpedoes?" Kalik demanded.

"They are passing under us. . . . Torpedoes are still passing . . . passing . . . gone. Right by us, Comrade . . . Comrade Captain! Dead ahead. An ice keel is dead ahead! We are going to hit it!"

For a split second Kalik froze. He had forgotten all about the devilishly deep ice keel that *Phoenix* had vanished under. "Hard rudder to port. Engines full astern. Viktor, turn as fast as—"

It was too late. With a sickening crunch *Akula* drove bow

first into the ice keel as she tried to turn aside. Kalik was thrown to the deck. Crewmen were knocked from their chairs by the force of the collision. Consoles were ripped from their fittings and swung in deadly arcs across the control room. Electric fires burst out. Volkov was driven into the steering yoke, crushing his chest. He slid to the deck blinded by pain and unable to move.

Akula's outer hull crumpled like tinfoil. The torpedo tubes, all located forward, were virtually welded to the collapsed metal of the superstructure, rendering the entire attack system inoperable. The forward ballast tanks burst like balloons under the pressure. The bow planes sheared off and tumbled into the abyss below. Bent and broken, *Akula* slid off the keel and hung dead in the water.

Emergency lighting went on in the control room. Kalik picked himself up and helped his men who could not stand alone. He looked around for Volkov, saw him, and rushed over. A bloody froth was on his lips. Tears filled Kalik's eyes, blinding him. "My old friend. I am so sorry."

"Nothing . . ." Volkov hissed. Bloody bubbles burst as he spoke. "Nothing to be . . . ashamed of. He was just . . . better. . . ." Then Volkov was gone.

Kalik lowered the limp head. He could barely manage to stand and pick up the intercom. "Compartments report damage," he said weakly.

He listened. They were badly damaged but not in danger of sinking. He took stoically the report that the torpedo tubes were all inoperable. No one could shoot through five feet of crumpled metal. The weapons would sit in their tubes, still fixed upon his adversary, never to be fired.

"Comrade Captain. We have some sonar capability. It is my duty to report that the Americans are making a final attack run. Thirty seconds."

"Yes, thank you. I understand." Kalik looked over to the helm. "Good-bye, Viktor," he said softly. He picked up the mike and flicked the intercom to the all-ship channel. The rest of the men in the control room were looking at him. His voice caught on the first attempt to speak. He fought for control and found it.

"This is the captain speaking. We do not have much time left. I want to commend you all on your valor and courage. Our enemy is a valorous and courageous man. I am sorry to report that it seems the day is his. . . ." Kalik stopped. Valor and courage. That was the key.

Suddenly he knew what he had to do.

Seawolf

"They're not moving, Skipper. Another trick?"

MacKenzie scratched his chin. "I don't think so. They hit hard enough to be disabled. I don't see where we have a choice though. Continue the attack run. We have to sink her."

"Uh, sir?" It was the radio technician who had taken over when his officer was hurt.

"Yes, Mr. . . . ?"

"Cavelli, sir. Edward Cavelli, radio technician second class."

"What is it, Mr. Cavelli?"

"I'm picking up something funny on the underwater phone. I . . . I think it's *Akula,* sir."

"What's he up to now?" Lasovic wondered from his position in the attack center.

"Put it on the speaker and get a translator in here, Mr. Cavelli. ASAP."

"I can translate, sir."

"All right, Mr. Cavelli. Go ahead."

The speaker crackled into life with a blast of sound. MacKenzie had heard enough Russian to identify it but no more. "What's he saying, Mr. Cavelli?"

"If I got it all, sir, I'm pretty sure he's saying his torpedo tubes are all inoperable and he wishes to surrender. He wants you to break off the attack. He . . . he says he gives his word, sir."

"That and a buck fifteen will get you on the subway,

Mac," said Lasovic caustically. "He'd have sunk us without remorse. He tried to twice."

MacKenzie ran a hand through his hair tiredly. "I don't know, Tom. You could hear the crunch of their bow all the way to Cleveland. All his tubes are forward. He could be telling the truth."

Lasovic's face was cold. "We have sustained wounded, Captain."

"Conn, Sonar. Attack position in ten seconds."

Lasovic turned back to the console. "Ship ready, solution ready, torpedo room ready. Mac?"

MacKenzie said nothing.

"Conn, Sonar. Target bearing two nine zero. He's dead in the water, Skipper. Making no move to get out of our way."

Seawolf shot ahead. MacKenzie could have fired the torpedoes with a word—and sent *Akula* to a watery grave. What was stopping him?

"Captain, ship ready, solution ready, torpedo room ready. Do I have the order to fire?" Lasovic asked.

MacKenzie felt *Seawolf*'s power as they raced toward the seemingly defenseless ship. Once before he had made a mistake and killed men almost needlessly. The weight of that tore at him. But he had his ship to protect, and *Akula* had fired upon them. Was this a trick? Or did his adversary, pleading for the lives of his men, deserve a more basic human value—trust?

"Mac? We are ready to fire. Closing on target."

And what about the young men under his own command in *Seawolf?* What would he tell them? Could he really explain that he was risking his ship to gamble on the very oldest of a captain's perogatives—his own intuition? Could he risk it all on that?

"Captain, he's just repeating the message over and over. He's asking for permission to surface."

"The breakers have made a minor lake up there, Skipper," Santiago reported. "There's room for both ships if you want it."

MacKenzie looked at Tom Lasovic. Prudent. Wise. He would protect his ship at all costs. Every bit of MacKenzie's training told him to do the same. Lasovic's hand was poised over the torpedo release. MacKenzie took a deep breath. Maybe compassion was the most important lesson of all.

"Cancel the attack. Secure from battle stations. Tom, keep your weapons pointed but do not fire." He took a deep breath. "Mr. Cavelli, tell our friend if he so much as turns his bow to us we will blast him into rubble . . . and tell him he has permission to surface. Mr. Randall, prepare to surface."

Red Dawn

Boslik's body lay on the deck between Ligichev and Galinin. The crewmen held back. Galinin was still holding the gun. Shifting the weapon, one arm around Ivanna, he reached for the keypad a second time and punched in the combination that Ligichev himself had entrusted to him so many days ago. A lifetime ago. But it would all end soon.

"Again I ask you to relent," said Ligichev. "You can't stop all of us."

Galinin punched in the last numbers. The LED on the keypad changed from red to green. "I can do what I have to. Stand back." Galinin hit the Open button . . .

"Ivanna, drop!" commanded Ligichev.

And the intruder-protection device implanted in the bulkhead shot out a spray of bright yellow powder right into Galinin's face, covering him like flour. It blinded him and settled into his lungs. Ivanna dropped from his hold as the resulting coughing fit doubled him over.

The gun fell from his hands as he swiped at his eyes and nose to rid them of the offending powder. Ivanna kicked it to her father. He picked it up and turned it on the hapless Galinin, who was panting and wheezing, trying to breathe through the irritating dust. Rostov and the others rushed in and pinned his arms tightly.

"Confine the captain in his cabin," Ligichev ordered. "Ivanna, are you all right?"

"Fine, Father. But your arm . . ."

"Eminently fixable." He hugged her tightly. "You're a brave girl. Like your mother."

"And you're a tricky old fox. How did you know that first day not to trust him with the lock's secret?"

Ligichev smiled. "Prudence, daughter, in all things."

Galinin sagged in the crew's hands. The light had gone out of his eyes, but he summoned a last vestige of interest in his own downfall. He looked to Ligichev before the crew led him away. "I know I remembered the correct combination. When did you change it to trigger the alarm?"

"I didn't."

"But the powder?"

"I told you the correct combination the first day in the engine room. What I didn't tell you is that the lock was also equipped with an intruder alarm and that the Open and Close buttons are reversed. Anyone trying to gain unauthorized entry, even if he stole the combination, wouldn't know he had to press the Close button to open the door and vice versa. The powder is quite irritating but perfectly harmless. It's only there to mark anyone trying to get in. Even if no one saw him, the yellow stain would reveal the attempt."

"What will you do with me?"

"Do with you? Why, nothing." Ligichev's face was drawn and tired, but compassion showed through. "I suppose you were acting heroically in your own way. But you're the navy's problem now. We all just want to go home."

Polar Ice Cap

It was a sight to match all the others over the past three days. *Akula* surfaced first on the temporary lake created by the breakers' path, her once-sleek prow breaking through the icy waters and revealing its damage before settling back onto the surface. Then *Seawolf* broke through the surface, its powerful shape and damaged sail coming up less than fifty yards away. Soviet and Canadian seamen from both breakers crowded on deck to gaze at the two disabled men-of-war.

MacKenzie and Tom Lasovic climbed out the forward hatch onto *Seawolf*'s deck and looked at the damaged sail. "We were lucky, Tom. A few feet lower and we wouldn't be here."

MacKenzie looked around. It had stopped snowing, and the clear, cold air felt good in his lungs even at these temperatures. It was a heady feeling to have survived it all. To have won.

"Mac, look."

Across the choppy gray water *Akula*'s captain was standing on his sail bridge. It was a rare moment, two adversaries face to face for the first time. There were no words, not even a common language, but as they looked at each other, each one knew what the other had been through. Across the gulf they could see it in each other's eyes. For a brief moment they shared a respect between enemies, an admiration for skill and tenacity and, perhaps most important, the memory of a desperate appeal to higher values that in the end had saved lives instead of taking them.

Across the water *Akula*'s captain saluted. MacKenzie returned it crisply.

" 'Our conflict is not likely to end as soon as every good man would wish,' " Mackenzie quoted softly, watching the other man disappear back down into his ship. Already the Soviet breaker was moving in to provide escort.

"Mac, he's back up and pointing? What does he want?"

MacKenzie looked back to *Akula*. The captain had come up for a brief moment and pointed to the *Ural*. Was he smiling? MacKenzie couldn't see for sure before he vanished a second time. It didn't matter. When he looked back in the direction the captain had pointed he saw a sight that almost overcame him. A Russian launch was coming around the *Ural*'s stern carrying passengers, one of whom he could have identified at twice the distance.

"Tom . . . look. It's Justine!" For a second he had to turn away.

"I told you she was a pro," Lasovic said, grinning from

ear to ear. "I can't wait to hear this story." He stooped to shout down into the ship, "Get some men up here, Chief, and call the doctor. We have passengers to pick up. On the double."

On the deck, MacKenzie waited for his wife to come home.

Epilogue

Holy Loch, Scotland

Peter MacKenzie brought the man with him onto the deck of *Red Dawn*. The sub was floating in a concrete sub pen and was moored to the dock. After the engagement with *Akula*, catching up to the slow-moving *Phoenix* had been a simple matter. *Seawolf* had shepherded both submarines until they met the surface escort. They had all arrived in Scotland together three days after leaving the ice cap.

Intelligence teams had already been on board to remove the crew. They would be returned to the Soviet Union within a few days. Other teams were uncovering the secrets of the drive.

"Go ahead. I'll follow," MacKenzie said, climbing down after him into *Red Dawn*.

They walked through the control room. It still smelled of fire damage and close-packed bodies with too little fresh air. Bowls of food still stood half eaten on the tables in the crew's mess. "Wait here," said MacKenzie. "Please."

The man sat down wearily on a bench. He was still not healed from his ordeal.

MacKenzie walked aft. A lone figure was waiting in the engine room.

Ivanna Ligichova looked up, startled, when he approached. "Oh, I didn't think anyone was left on board. My father was the last to leave. Who are you?"

337

"Captain Peter MacKenzie, U.S. Navy. The *Seawolf* is my ship."

"Ah, our rescuer." She held out her hand. "I'm grateful to you for all you did. So is my father."

"Where is he?"

"He had to be taken to the hospital. Gunshot wound."

That spoke volumes, but MacKenzie let it pass. "My wife said . . . Well, I'm not very good at this cloak-and-dagger stuff, but I guess I'm supposed to say the word 'invictus' to you. Does that mean anything?"

Ivanna smiled. "It means she would have been here if she could, but I should trust you as I would her. Very well. Here, this is what all the fuss was about."

She dropped a block of irinium into MacKenzie's hand. "Just don't get it wet."

"Is that what happened here?"

"That, and a few other things."

MacKenzie turned the block over in his hands. "So you're the reason we knew what was on *Red Dawn?*"

"Yes. My father is a patriot of the world. He knew irinium should not belong to any one country. But always the supply was too well monitored and he was too closely watched. We all were." She shrugged.

MacKenzie nodded. "I'm supposed to remind you of our offer of asylum."

Ivanna smiled. "Thank you, but it isn't necessary now. Things are changing in my country. My father and I want to go back to strengthen those changes. Someday we will meet in the open, as friends should."

MacKenzie thought back to *Akula*'s captain. "Maybe we will at that." He slipped the bar of irinium into his pocket. "One last thing. It was impossible to tell you sooner, but we were able to save a diver off your ship. Brave boy. Without him none of us might be here. It was the cold that got him. My wife thought—"

Ivanna's face flooded with surprise and happiness. "Pytor? Can you really mean it? Pytor is alive?"

"We got him to the surface in a DSRV. I guess he'll tell you the rest himself."

"Oh, my God, he's here?"

"In the mess. Take your time. There's a car on the dock to take you to the others."

"But look what I look like, how can I?

MacKenzie smiled. "We're all a little worse for wear. Knowing the young man, I don't think it will matter. Good-bye, Ivanna Ligichova, and good luck."

He watched Ivanna run down the corridor like a schoolgirl.

Some things changed, some things never did.

MacKenzie walked back with a spring in his step.

★TOP★ GUNS

AMERICA'S FIGHTER ACES TELL THEIR STORIES

Joe Foss and Matthew Brennan

They were the high-flying heroes who fought our wars, inspired the country, and left a proud legacy. Now America's greatest living fighter aces tell their personal stories—many for the first time—in this extraordinary record of aerial combat from World War I through Vietnam.

Joe Foss and Matthew Brennan bring together twenty-seven fighter pilots to create this astonishing volume of oral history. You are there, in the major theaters of four wars in the cockpit, on life-or-death missions— seeing the enemy and the battle through the aces' eyes.

**COMING IN HARDCOVER
FROM POCKET BOOKS IN JUNE, 1991**

POCKET
B O O K S